THE
CANDIDATE
CORONER

THE CANDIDATE CORONER

BOOK THREE
OF THE
FENWAY STEVENSON MYSTERIES

PAUL AUSTIN ARDOIN

ISBN: 978-1-949082-07-4

First Edition: March 2019

For information please visit:
www.paulaustinardoin.com

Cover design by Ziad Ezzat of Feral Creative Colony
www.feralcreativecolony.com

Author photo by Monica Toohey-Krause of Studio KYK
www.studiokyk.com

Edited by Max Christian Hansen

10 9 8 7 6 5 4 3 2 1

TABLE OF CONTENTS

PART I

THURSDAY

CHAPTER ONE

THE SKY THREATENED RAIN AS FENWAY STEVENSON WALKED through the gate into the Hanford Women's Prison. She had an appointment to see the woman who had tried to kill her.

She carried her purse over her left shoulder, and her right hand held the envelope she had received the previous day. She put both in the plastic basket, walked through the metal detector, collected her things, and joined a line of people in front of a stark white counter staffed by two bored-looking guards.

While she waited, she opened the envelope, pulled out the letter, and read it again.

Dear Miss Stevenson,

I've had a lot of time to think, and now I know I was wrong. You didn't help cover up the death of my husband.

I need to apologize. I shouldn't have threatened you with the gun. I knew it was wrong when I did it, but I thought it was the only way I'd get to the truth. But now I've got proof you're not going to rubber-stamp everything your father wants.

I'm writing to apologize, but I'd also like your help. You must think I have a lot of nerve, asking you for help after threatening you. You don't owe me anything, and I won't be able to repay you. Instead, I appeal to your sense of justice.

My husband didn't get justice when he died in that hallway in the refinery. And I may be able to help get him the justice he deserves.

Please meet with me in person. I'm at the Hanford Women's Prison. I can talk more then.

Sincerely,
Lana Cassidy

Fenway wondered if it had been a good idea to reschedule that afternoon's campaign speech at the downtown association to drive all the way out here.

When she got to the counter, Fenway handed the guard her paperwork, her county identification card on top.

The guard saw her identification and the bored look in his eyes disappeared. "Fenway Stevenson? You're the county coroner, right?"

Fenway nodded.

He flipped through her papers. "You here to interview Ms. Cassidy?"

"Yes," Fenway said. "She has information pertaining to a cold case."

The guard narrowed his eyes. "Didn't Ms. Cassidy try to kill you a few months ago?"

"That's correct."

"Isn't that what she's in here for?"

Fenway held up the letter. "Looks like she's remorseful for her past actions. And wants to help."

The guard nodded. "All right. We'll bring her out to room four." He cleared his throat. "You have any trouble with her, you push the red button next to the table and a guard will be in immediately." He pointed at a corridor behind Fenway.

She nodded and turned to walk down the corridor, brightly but soullessly lit with fluorescents, before she opened the last door on the left.

The room was bare except for a metal table and two straight-backed chairs. Two windows along the back wall looked out into another hallway. Fenway put her purse down on a chair and paced around the small room.

After a few minutes, the door on the other side opened, and a different guard brought in the prisoner. The last time Fenway had seen Lana Cassidy, she had vibrant blonde hair; now it was a mottled light brown with streaks of gray. Lana sat down at her side of the table.

"Do you want me to stay in the room?" the guard said.

Fenway shook her head. "We need to talk privately."

The guard looked at Fenway, perhaps measuring her up. She then looked over at Lana, who avoided eye contact.

"Okay," the guard said. "You call me with that red panic button if you need anything."

"Thanks," Fenway said. "I'm sure we'll be fine."

Lana looked up and nodded. The guard left the room and closed the door behind her, taking up a station outside the window.

"Okay," said Fenway, moving her purse to the floor and sitting across the table from Lana. "I got your letter. I requested a meeting with you, like you asked?"

Lana pressed her lips together, her eyes shut tight, as if readying herself for battle. Then she opened them and took a deep breath. "Miss Stevenson—first, thank you for meeting me. I know you didn't have to."

Fenway noticed Lana didn't call her *Miss Ferris*; it was a welcome change from the first time they had met. "How can I help?" She hoped she was able to mask the curiosity on her face.

"You know my husband was killed in that refinery accident last year."

"Yes. You said Carl didn't get the justice he deserved."

Lana nodded. "Some things about the accident don't add up."

Fenway paused, leaned forward, and put her hands palms down on the table. "We've caught the man who killed your husband. Robert Stotsky authorized the venting of the poisonous gas into that hallway. Maybe he wasn't charged for it, but he's serving two consecutive twenty-year terms for the *other* murders. He'll be ninety-two when he gets out."

Lana looked down and sighed. "I know—I know he's one of the people responsible."

"You're saying there are more?"

"Yes. Carl had stumbled onto something—along with Lewis Fairweather. Stotsky pulled the trigger, but he wasn't the one behind it."

"Behind what?"

"That's the problem. I know something else is going on. It's *still* going on."

Fenway nodded. "What do you think it is?"

Lana lowered her voice. "I think it's something big. I think it has to do with oil."

Fenway grimaced. "Ferris Energy *is* an oil company, Lana. Lots of things they do have to do with oil."

"Let me start at the beginning," Lana said. "Carl worked on the team that coordinated the available space at the Estancia port. Space in the holding tanks, space at the docks, everything." She leaned forward. "About six months before the accident, Ferris Energy took two of their large holding tanks offline. They said it was a maintenance issue, but Carl saw a big oil tanker—not one he ever saw before, and not one on any of the manifests—dock at Ferris Energy, right in front of the tanks that were supposed to be offline. It was late at night. When Carl told me, I thought he suspected that something was going on. Something illegal." Lana took a breath.

Fenway tapped the table. "I'm not sure it means much. Oil tankers come and go, don't they? It could have been there for lots of different reasons."

Lana shrugged. "Carl never told me about any tankers showing up unannounced before. Anyway, two weeks before he was killed, he stayed late again, just as late as he had the first night he saw the tanker. And when he came home, he told me he saw another tanker. Then he was real quiet. I don't think he ever got to sleep that night."

Fenway pressed her lips together. "And then the ventilation accident happened."

Lana nodded. "And Carl and Lewis were both dead."

"This isn't much to go on," Fenway said.

"I know," Lana said. "But I think you can be trusted to follow where it leads." She looked hard at Fenway. "You're not afraid to take on your father. You're the only person in this county who isn't." She leaned back. "Maybe your dad didn't have anything to do with it. But it was *someone* high up at Ferris Energy."

Fenway thought for a moment.

Lana swallowed hard and leaned forward. "My husband's death is still an open case, right?"

Fenway nodded.

"Maybe you could look into it a little. Dig around. Like you did for the mayor's murder. Like you did for the former coroner's murder. If you find something—I mean, you don't want anyone else to end up dead, right?"

Fenway set her jaw. "What if I find out my father's innocent? How are you going to feel then? Will you come after me?"

Lana winced and looked down. "I deserved that. But I've changed. I'm not angry with you anymore." She leaned back, dropped her chin, and wiped her eyes. "You're kind of my last hope, anyway."

Fenway closed her eyes and shook her head. "I can't promise anything, Lana. It's a week before the election, I'm up to my eyeballs in the campaign, and the office is still shorthanded."

"Even if you did an hour of research, it would help," Lana whispered.

"I can't promise anything," Fenway repeated, standing up and putting her purse over her shoulder. "But I'll see what I can do." She walked over to the window and rapped her knuckles against the glass. The guard opened the door. "We're done," Fenway said.

"Thank you for seeing me," Lana said.

Fenway nodded, then turned, strode across the room and left through the door she came in.

***

Fenway thought hard about Carl Cassidy on her way home from Hanford. Lana had a point: Stotsky probably didn't act on his own. He may have made the final decision—pulled the metaphorical trigger, as Lana said—but he wasn't behind the *reason* those two men died in that hallway.

Her phone rang, and the display on her dash read *Nathaniel Ferris*. She pressed the answer button on her steering wheel to pick it up.

"Hi, Dad."

"Hi, Fenway. Just wanted to see if your campaign events were finished in time for you to make our session this afternoon."

"Oh." Fenway hesitated. "I had to reschedule my afternoon event, actually."

"Reschedule? What for?"

"I had to go see a—a witness. I got on the road about fifteen minutes ago. I'm coming up on the Windkettle exit."

"You're all the way out in Windkettle? You sure you're going to make it?"

"You're still making it, right?"

Ferris sighed. "Right."

A month earlier, she and her father hadn't spoken for weeks. He had still rented the campaign headquarters, and his money bought the lawn signs and the radio ads and the billboard on Ocean Highway. But everything was communicated through email or text, or indirectly through Millicent Tate, after she was officially hired as Fenway's campaign manager.

Then, in the early morning hours after her birthday celebration with Rachel, Dez, and McVie, Fenway awoke, in a cold sweat, from a hauntingly vivid dream of performing an autopsy on her father. She saw the images every time she closed her eyes to try to get back to sleep. She had called her father the next morning and told him they needed to see a family therapist. Insisted on it, in fact.

At first, it was uncomfortable and odd. Fenway thought Dr. Jacob Tassajera was fine—not great, not even better than average, but fine. She would have preferred a female therapist, since she knew she'd have to talk about a lot of issues in her past—especially the incident with her Russian Lit professor. But she also knew her father would prefer opening up to a man, especially someone like Dr. Tassajera, who was into golf and scotch. Fenway was wary, saying little of consequence the first two sessions. She kept reminding herself he was getting paid to help them have a decent father-daughter relationship. And Ferris had canceled the previous week's session because of a business trip.

"I'll see you at Dr. Tassajera's," Fenway said.

"Hang on, Fenway. I'm paying for your campaign, and Millicent Tate doesn't come cheap. I know you don't like campaigning, but you just can't blow off events like this."

"I'm not blowing them off."

"I think you are."

Fenway frowned. "You canceled our session last week. Did you blow it off, too?"

Ferris paused. "No. Don't be silly."

"Really? Because you didn't have a very good excuse. Dr. Tassajera is the only reason we're talking to each other without screaming. And it doesn't seem like you want to go."

"Of *course* I want to—" Ferris started. Then he hesitated and sighed. "No. Dr. Tassajera said you and I need to be honest with each other, so I'll say it. Of course I don't want to go. Definitely not every week. I never thought I'd have to go to therapy for anything. I want rights to an oil field, I negotiate for it. I want to buy another company, I go in with a plan. It's not about what I did ten years ago, or about the other company's feelings." He paused. "So it pisses me off that I've got to talk about all the shit we've gone through to get to this point."

Fenway didn't say anything. This was the most she'd heard her father talk about his feelings in a long time. Maybe ever. Although she didn't like that her father compared his relationship with her to an acquisition target.

She cleared her throat. "But you will be there, right?"

"Yes," Ferris said immediately. "Yes. I will be there."

"Good, because for a minute it sounded like you were going to flake again."

"I didn't *flake* last week. It was an important meeting. Give me some credit—I'm trying the honesty thing. I don't want to go. But I'm going to go because it's important to you."

"It's not important to me that you go to this, Dad. It's important for us. You and I need to fix our relationship, and these therapy sessions are how we're going to do it."

"I promise I'll be there," Ferris said.

Then her mother's face appeared in Fenway's head, and she felt a lump in her throat. "Okay," she said. "I'm going into the hills now. See you at Dr. Tassajera's." It wasn't true—the Cuesta grade wasn't for another ten miles up the highway—but she didn't want her father to hear the weakness in her voice. He was all she had left of her family now.

"All right. Bye."

Fenway hung up. She took a couple of deep breaths, and got ahold of herself. She turned the radio on, hearing the last notes of A Tribe Called Quest's *Check the Rhime*, and the traffic report came on. There was a jackknifed big rig on the Cuesta grade. Fenway groaned.

A few minutes later, traffic slowed to a crawl, and Fenway had to get on the shoulder to go past the accident. It delayed Fenway so much she didn't think she had time to stop at her apartment to change. But if she drove straight there, she'd likely have a few minutes to spare.

The imposing yet strangely elegant smokestacks from the Ferris Energy refinery came into view as she crested the hill. She looked to her right: the highway was meeting the ocean for the first time in fifty miles, and, not for the first time, Fenway saw a secluded beach on the other side of the highway. She wondered if she had ever been to that beach, but she didn't think so.

The closer she got to the Broadway exit, the stronger she felt the pull of a change of clothes and comfortable shoes. But she gritted her teeth as the exit passed, and she pulled off the freeway onto Vicente Boulevard instead, driving two blocks and turning into an office complex.

She pulled into a parking space in front of a sign that said *Vicente Professional Park*, looked at the clock on the dash, and sighed. She was twenty minutes early.

CHAPTER TWO

SHE DIDN'T SEE HER FATHER'S BLACK MERCEDES S500, SO SHE PUT on some Branford Marsalis, reclined her seat and closed her eyes. Listening to the *Trio Jeepy* album always made her feel rebellious: a full album with only saxophone, upright bass, and drums—no chordal instruments at all, no piano, no guitar. And yet, Fenway thought it was one of his most accessible albums—breaking all the rules, yet more satisfying than anything else he recorded.

Halfway through *Three Little Words*, the S500 pulled into the lot. Nathaniel Ferris got out of the back, closed the door and clapped the top of the car as if it were a cab, and the car drove off. Ferris walked over to the Accord and Fenway rolled down her window.

Her father had a quizzical look on his face. "This isn't Coltrane, is it?"

"Branford Marsalis."

Ferris shook his head. "That new stuff never appealed to me."

"This was recorded before I was born, Dad."

Ferris screwed up his mouth. "Great, make me feel old before we go talk to the shrink. One more knot for him to untangle."

Fenway sighed and rolled up the window. She turned the engine off and opened the door.

They started to walk across the parking lot. "What? Come on, that was supposed to be funny. You lost your sense of humor?"

"It's been a long day."

"You canceled your campaign events."

"Just for the afternoon, Dad. I was following up on a lead." She sighed. "Don't worry, I went to the Chamber of Commerce meeting before I left for Hanford."

Ferris paused. "Hanford? What's out in Hanford besides a bunch of cows?"

"The women's prison."

"The women's prison?"

Fenway nodded as the stepped up onto the sidewalk and stopped in front of the door marked *Suite 34B—Dr. Jacob Tassajera.* "You ready, Dad?"

He nodded, and Fenway opened the door.

The waiting room was eggshell white and spartan. Four wooden chairs, in sets of two with an end table in between them, were against two of the walls. There was a small ficus tree in a pot in one corner and a tiny, fake-looking succulent in a mauve-and-orange ceramic pot on one of the end tables. Another door was at the back of the waiting room, closed.

Fenway took a seat on one of the chairs next to the door, and set her purse on the end table in front of the succulent.

Ferris, taking a seat in the chair on the other side of the end table, cleared his throat. "What were you at the women's prison for? You said you were talking to a witness? Trying to get a jailhouse informant?"

"Jeez, and people say *I* watch too much TV. No, Dad. I had to talk to the woman who tried to shoot me a few months ago."

Ferris paused. "The widow of the guy who died at the refinery?"

Fenway nodded. "The good news is, she's not trying to kill me anymore. Doesn't think I was trying to cover up her husband's murder for you."

"Her husband's *murder*?"

Fenway nodded again. "Yes, Dad."

"Why did you talk to her? We settled with the families a few weeks ago. It was a generous settlement."

"I don't think Lana Cassidy thinks of it as settled."

"We're paying her son's tuition at Nidever. We paid off the house. Paid out two years' of the husband's salary. She should be happy."

"Doesn't bring her husband back, though."

Ferris bristled. "So what does that mean? Does it mean you're reopening the case?"

Fenway shrugged. "We never closed it. We think Stotsky turned the ventilation valve, but we can't prove it."

"You never closed the case?"

"I mean, we ruled out suicide so the families could get their insurance money." Then Fenway clamped her mouth shut. There was so much more she wanted to say, but she knew it would be unproductive, and being so close to the start of a session, it wasn't a good idea.

"Are you telling me you're restarting the investigation?"

"I haven't decided yet," Fenway said. She regretted bringing this up with him. It was unprofessional, but the doctor's office had lowered her guard. "I'm sorry. I shouldn't have mentioned it."

Ferris frowned, folding his arms. "Don't think I won't call my lawyers. That investigation should have concluded *months* ago."

Fenway leaned her head back and closed her eyes. "Just forget I said anything, Dad."

Ferris set his jaw, raising his voice. "You can't say you're investigating my company for murder and then tell me to forget about it."

"I didn't—"

"Do you have any idea of the pressure I'm under with the board of directors?"

"What do you mean?" Fenway asked.

"Cynthia Schimmelhorn is what I mean," Ferris said distastefully. "She got up at the board of directors meeting two weeks ago and all but asked for a vote of no confidence for me as the CEO."

Fenway was surprised—she thought he had a tight rein on the board of directors. But Cynthia, a former CFO of a local bank, had been appointed to the board as its first—and so far only—female member, and hadn't liked the boys' club feel of the company. With two high-profile murderers so close to Ferris over the last year, it was perhaps natural to question Ferris's judgement—but Fenway was shocked the board was actually performing its oversight duties.

"What did you do?"

"I went over the numbers. Profits are up. Costs are under control. Money talks—and it talks a lot louder than Cynthia Schimmelhorn." He coughed. "And don't think I didn't notice that this is essentially a cold case. You canceled your afternoon campaign events to go talk to a woman in jail about a year-old death? Where did you think she was going?"

"She wrote me a letter. She gave me an opening. I didn't think it could wait."

"You mean you didn't *want* to wait, and you especially didn't want to speak at the downtown association this afternoon."

Fenway was aghast. "You know my campaign schedule?"

"Better than you do, apparently." Ferris sniffed. "I like to see where my money is going."

Just then, the door opened, and Dr. Jacob Tassajera stuck his head out of his office. "Mr. Ferris? Ms. Stevenson?" His voice was a gentle baritone.

"Seems we have a lot to talk about today," Ferris said, getting up.

"I must apologize," Dr. Tassajera said. "I'm sorry to keep you waiting, but I'm afraid I have an emergency with another patient."

"An emergency?" Ferris's face fell. "Are you telling me you're canceling?"

"Postponing. Would you come in here so we can reschedule?"

"Sure," Fenway said.

Ferris frowned and went into the office ahead of Fenway.

The office had a desk off to one side of the room with a laptop, a small task chair, and a golf bag in the corner behind it. In the center of the room, two overstuffed brown leather armchairs were at a forty-five-degree angle next to each other with a small table in the middle. The table held a Kleenex box and a twin of the succulent in the waiting room. A wooden chair, with a muted green-and-blue floral upholstered seat, sat squarely in front of the two armchairs. Fenway looked at the comfortable armchairs with a little sadness; her back hurt from the drive and from the hard chair at the Hanford prison.

Dr. Tassajera walked over to his desk and consulted the large calendar on his desk blotter. "How does Monday look?"

"The day before the election?" Fenway asked. "I can't commit to anything then."

"Over the weekend, then."

"I can only do Sunday," Ferris said, a bit testily.

"I don't normally see patients on Sundays."

"I guess we'll have to schedule something in a couple of weeks, then," Ferris replied.

Dr. Tassajera rubbed his chin, thinking. "Sunday won't be a problem. What time?"

Ferris flinched, and Fenway smiled; Tassajera had called his bluff. "Uh, late morning, I guess."

"Perfect," Fenway said. "I've got a breakfast, but nothing else until a speech at a senior center after lunch."

"If you don't cancel those, too," Ferris mumbled.

Dr. Tassajera nodded. "Eleven o'clock?"

Ferris reluctantly agreed, and Fenway put the appointment in her phone.

"Until Sunday, then." Dr. Tassajera nodded, and they both walked out through the waiting room and stood on the sidewalk. The door closed with a click behind them.

They stood in an uncomfortable silence.

Ferris looked at Fenway. "Are we okay?"

Fenway looked back at him. "We're getting better, I guess."

Tracing his foot back and forth on the ground, Ferris looked like he was debating with himself. Finally he spoke. "Are you up for dinner? Charlotte is out with the girls tonight, and we haven't been to Maxime's in a while."

The thought of a four-course fancy dinner, complete with wine flights and waiters tripping over themselves to impress Ferris, made Fenway nauseated. She shook her head. "I'm going to eat something quick and head over to the campaign office. We're doing a phonebank tonight."

Ferris pulled his phone out and sent a text. "You cancelled the downtown association, but you're still phonebanking? Come on, Fenway. You've got to prioritize. Your campaign staff and volunteers are going to make calls for you whether you're there or not. The downtown association has real clout with the voters. They need face time with you."

"I'll remember that for next time, Dad." She went over to him and kissed his cheek. "Sorry about the board of directors."

Ferris grunted. "I'll see you later. Sunday at eleven, I guess, if not before."

"Right. Millicent will be thrilled to break up our day of campaigning with a visit to a shrink."

Ferris smiled as his phone dinged. He glanced down at the screen.

"Is your car here?"

"Roderick's a few minutes away."

"Want to walk me to my car?"

"Sure."

The walk across the parking lot was silent; Fenway couldn't stop thinking of how angry her father was about her restarting the investigation into the refinery accident.

Fenway said goodbye, leaving Ferris standing a few feet away from her Accord, waiting for Roderick to show up in the Mercedes.

She drove out of the lot into the early evening, the sun behind the horizon, throwing fingers of pink and lavender stretching through the high, wispy white clouds scattered recklessly across the sky. Fenway looked up through her sunroof, marveling at the rapidly darkening colors.

She didn't stop for food on the drive to the campaign office. Her stomach was still in knots from the meetings with both Lana in Hanford and her father at the therapist's office. As she pulled into the crowded parking lot and got out of her Accord, the conversations replayed in her head.

She opened the front door and was met with a wall of sound. Dozens of people were in the office—until the summer, the space had been rented to a failing department store. A hundred conversations were going on at once, and people were hanging up with smiles. A Latino teenager near the front, wearing a headset, stood up and high-fived the woman next to him. "Ten more yard signs!" he exclaimed. "She wants to pass them out at her book club tomorrow!"

Then he noticed Fenway. "Oh—Miss Stevenson!" He stood up straight. "Everyone—our candidate is here." He started to applaud, and it lightly scattered throughout the room, but most people were on the phone.

"Never mind, Rory," Fenway said. "Those ten yard signs mean more than applause right now."

"We've got a competition to see how many yard signs we can get out to the people on our lists. First prize is a five-hundred-dollar gift card."

"You're winning, I take it."

He flashed Fenway a smile. "It's not even close. You here to see Millicent? Let me take you back." He extricated himself from his headset.

"Your parents okay with you being here on a school night?"

"I'm getting extra credit in AP Government. And we've got a teacher in-service day tomorrow." He motioned for her to follow him.

As Fenway walked between the long rows of desks to the office in the back of the large space, she marveled at how good Nathaniel Ferris was at finding competent people to work for him. Perhaps they weren't always the most ethical, but they were highly competent.

Millicent Tate was no exception; she was fiercely intelligent and a bundle of energy. Fenway often saw emails sent by Millicent well after midnight. After Dr. Richard Ivanovich—an ear, nose, and throat specialist Barry Klein played golf with—announced his candidacy for county coroner, Nathaniel Ferris had engaged her services. She was young—almost as young as Fenway. Based in Sacramento, she'd made a name for herself getting a Republican elected to the House in a deep-blue district in the Bay Area, a race the RNC hadn't even had on their radar. And two years later, she flipped a red rural district to blue with an equally improbable Democratic candidate. She was used to working on congressional campaigns, but after Ferris promised her a hefty paycheck, all expenses paid, and a personal introduction to both California senators, she had dropped everything to run Fenway's campaign.

A large man sat at a desk in front of Millicent Tate's office. He had piercing brown eyes and skin so dark it was almost blue. He was in a well-tailored light gray suit and an expensive-looking white dress shirt with no tie. His massive shoulders and barrel chest seemed too enormous for both the desk and the task chair, but with the grace of a ballerina, he leafed through a stack of papers with his meaty left hand and typed quickly on the computer keyboard with the other.

"Evening, Miss Stevenson," he said without looking up from his work, his voice a deep, dramatic baritone. "Miss Tate wasn't expecting you for another forty-five minutes."

"My afternoon appointment was postponed."

"Serves you right for canceling on the downtown association."

"Oh, Marquise, not you too? I already got an earful of it from my father."

Marquise chuckled. "You better prepare yourself for another earful from Miss Tate. She's been running interference."

Fenway sighed. "Can I go in?"

Marquise nodded.

Fenway nodded at Rory. "Thanks, Rory. Keep up the good work."

"I will. That gift card is as good as mine."

Fenway walked into Millicent Tate's office. Behind the desk sat a white woman with small but quick eyes behind black cat-eye framed glasses. Her black hair was pulled back, and she held the phone receiver up to her ear with one hand and held the index finger of her other hand up in front of Fenway.

"Of course, Mr. Williams. Look—would you rather support a candidate who just tells you what you want to hear, or do you want someone who actually *works* to keep crime down? You've seen the statistics. You know she's effective." Millicent Tate paused, listening. "I remind her that she needs the support of communities like yours every day, Mr. Williams, but she seems to prioritize her *job* over making speeches." She nodded, listening. "I can certainly let her know. No, no, I know your group is busy. I appreciate the time."

Millicent Tate hung up.

"Sorry," Fenway said.

"It's a good thing your dad is paying me so well," Millicent snapped. "I've been on the phone with every member of the downtown association since you canceled."

"You can reschedule, though, right?"

"No, of course I can't. That was their last meeting before the election."

"Oh." Fenway paused. "You think I've lost them?"

"I don't think so," Millicent said. "A few of them think your investigation is more important than their meeting. It might have actually helped. But a couple of them are angry that you blew them off."

"I didn't—"

Millicent held up her hand. "Their words, not mine. Anyway, what's done is done. Let's get out there and rally the troops."

"Rory seems to be doing a good job."

"Over four hundred lawn signs since three-thirty. He's gotten more signs out there than everyone else put together. I'd hire him on my next campaign if he weren't going to college."

When Millicent and Fenway walked out with Millicent to the floor, everyone ended their calls quickly. Fenway delivered the short but rousing speech that Millicent's team had written. People cheered, people clapped, then people got back to work.

"Can I help make calls to the downtown association?"

Millicent shook her head. "Let's not make it worse."

"I'd make it worse?"

"If your story doesn't match the one I told them? Yeah, that'd make it worse."

They talked strategy for a while and went over the next day's schedule—the morning was surprisingly light, with nothing until a luncheon with the teachers' union. Fenway left the campaign office for home.

She drove to her apartment on autopilot, and found herself in her parking space with scarcely a memory of driving there. It wasn't yet eight o'clock, but she seriously contemplated going to bed. The discussion with Lana, the conversation with her father, and the speech to her staff and volunteers had taken a lot out of her.

Walking up the stairs required an almost Herculean effort, raising her foot to go up each step an exercise in willpower. She entered the apartment, cold from the chilly October day, and couldn't even bring herself to walk over to the refrigerator.

Maybe, Fenway told herself, *I'll feel better after I lie down for a while.*

She went to her room and lay down on top of the comforter, throwing her purse on the floor next to the bed, and fell asleep almost immediately.

At some point she pulled the covers down and threw her clothes off and slept in her underwear in the cold sheets with the warm blankets over her and the pillows bunched up all around her head. A little later she heard rain against her window.

She had a dream about her mother, who was chasing her around their house in Seattle, Fenway laughing, sunlight streaming through the windows covered with white, translucent curtains, and then as she rounded the corner to come back into the kitchen, pots and pans started banging together, and the noise got louder—and Fenway woke up, disoriented and feeling almost hung over. It took her a moment to figure out she was in her own bed in her own apartment, and her mother wasn't chasing her, and her phone was ringing.

She dug the phone out of her purse and saw it was five-fifteen in the morning. Sheriff McVie was calling.

"Craig?" she croaked.

"Morning, Fenway," he said. "We'll need you to come out here as soon as you can. A jogger found a dead body by the refinery."

PART II

FRIDAY

CHAPTER THREE

—◆—

AFTER THE STORM THE NIGHT BEFORE, THE BREEZE BLEW FRIGID off the ocean. Fenway hadn't seen a colder morning since moving to Estancia six months before, although she was still acclimated to the Seattle weather. The smell of the overnight rain made her feel more at home.

In fact, Fenway had stood in front of the mirror that morning, debating with herself about putting on a sweater or just a long-sleeved blouse. The sweater proved to be the right decision; the early morning mist put a damp chill on everything, settling in around the refinery's chain-link fence, obscuring both the smoke-stacks in one direction and the walking trail to the pedestrian underpass beneath Ocean Highway in the other. The temperature gauge on the dashboard in her Accord read 42°F, a cool morning even by Seattle standards. She would have used the word "brisk" before she moved back to Estancia.

Fenway didn't have a problem getting onto the service road next to the refinery's fence, but there wasn't a good way to get her car down to the pedestrian walkway running under the freeway. Three metal poles locked into place at the top of the asphalt trail that connected the service road to the walk-way leading to the secluded beach on the other side of the highway.

She parked on the edge of the service road, next to the sheriff's cruiser, and walked the last quarter of a mile. She had thought about putting on dressy flats, but the walk made her glad she had elected to wear her running shoes.

She crested the incline of the path and the medical examiner's van came into view. To the left of the van, Sheriff McVie stood next to Melissa de la Garza, one of the crime scene technicians. Both of them wore winter hats and parkas.

She walked up next to them. "Thanks for leaving the poles down for me."

Melissa smiled. "Hey, Fenway. Yeah, we had to lock them back up. Can't have the riff-raff driving down here."

McVie held a cup of coffee close to his face, the steam rising off the hot liquid.

"I feel underdressed," Fenway said. "I must have missed the memo about the Antarctic expedition gear."

"Very funny," McVie said.

Fenway smirked. "Man, I hope forty-two degrees doesn't ever feel like a frozen tundra wasteland to me."

"Yeah, well, it's the next best thing to a drawer at the morgue," Melissa said, gesturing to the body, under a mass of threadbare woolen blankets and several layers of clothing. Melissa handed Fenway two blue nitrile gloves. "Hey, only a few more days till the election. You ready?"

"Not according to my campaign manager."

"You're not worried about Dr. Klein's lackey, are you?" Melissa bent down over the body and started pulling back the blankets. "You've got a sixty-point lead."

Fenway shrugged and turned her attention to the dead man on the ground.

The body was supine, the face angled crazily off to the side, the open eyes staring at the upper corner of the pedestrian walkway, a neat bullet hole in the middle of his forehead. The dead man was white and had five or six days' worth of scraggly beard; he was perhaps in his late forties or early fifties.

"Not a lot of blood pooled underneath the head," Fenway said.

"Nope." Melissa pulled back the blankets near the dead man's feet. "Those look like drag marks." She pointed to two faint parallel lines in the concrete running to the beach side of the underpass.

"Good thing the body is protected from the elements," said Fenway. "If it had been out in the rain last night, we'd have a lot less evidence to work with."

"It looks like the body was dragged in here, the rain's probably washed the murder scene clean by now."

Fenway nodded. "Unless we get lucky."

Melissa pulled down the blankets below the dead man's shoulders, revealing more of his clothing. The sweater and long-sleeve oxford shirt underneath were a little bit dirty; the sweater had a smear of dirt or grease across the stomach. The man's blue jeans were dark, also dirty, but from a day or two of dirt, not months of it. He wore no shoes or socks.

Fenway looked at McVie. "This guy doesn't look homeless," Fenway said.

"From the old blankets he does," replied McVie defensively. "And he's barefoot."

"You have a time of death?" Fenway asked Melissa.

"Not a specific time," Melissa replied. "Liver temp is ambient, so he's been here awhile. With outside temp and lividity, I'd say he's been here between six and ten hours."

Fenway looked at the clock on her phone. "Between ten last night and two this morning. Gotcha." She squinted at the clothes on the dead body. "Melissa, doesn't this strike you as a little odd?"

"What? The clothes? Yeah."

"They seem too nice for a homeless guy, right?"

"Well, maybe not too nice—the shelters sometimes get some quality stuff donated. But definitely too clean. I mean, it's dirty, but it's one day worth of dirty. Not 'I haven't showered in two months' dirty."

"Right. That's what I was thinking too."

Melissa bent down. "And the clothes *are* nice. They're not cheap, for sure, and they're not ten years out of style, either."

"Do you think this guy was killed and made to look like a homeless guy, or did he look like this when he was killed?"

"Tough to say," said Melissa. "He certainly hasn't shaved in a while. I can see how the sheriff would get that impression at first glance." She glanced at Fenway's sweater and thin trousers that stopped a few inches above her ankle. "Aren't you cold?"

"I'm from Seattle," Fenway quipped. "If McVie hadn't called me, I'd be lounging by the pool."

Melissa shivered at the thought.

McVie took two steps closer and bent down. "Okay if I open his mouth?"

"I've already taken pictures," Melissa said.

He hesitated a moment, used both hands to gently open the dead man's mouth, then peered inside. "Look at this."

Melissa bent down and peered into the man's mouth. Fenway crouched and looked over Melissa's shoulder, although she couldn't see much.

"Oh," Melissa said. "Good dental work."

"Clean teeth, too," McVie said. "Yeah, you're right. This guy wasn't homeless. Or if he's homeless, he hasn't been for more than a few days."

Fenway shook her head. "I don't think he's homeless, not even for a couple of days. This looks to me like someone who's on vacation, not someone who's living on the streets."

"We should look into missing person reports," McVie said. "At least while we're waiting for the fingerprints to come back from the lab."

"You survey the area yet?" Fenway asked.

"Not completely," Melissa said. "I stopped when the sheriff got here."

"Any ID?"

Melissa shook her head. "No wallet, no ID, no money, no keys."

Fenway looked around. "Think his wallet's around here? Maybe a robbery gone wrong?"

McVie pointed to the drag marks. "Those aren't consistent with a robbery."

"Who found him?"

"A man coming off graveyard shift at the refinery." McVie stood back up.

"Did he stick around to talk to us?" Fenway asked.

"He stuck around for the officer," McVie said. "Callahan got here just before five-thirty. He took the statement from the guy. He radioed in—I told him he could send him on his way. Didn't see the point of keeping him too much longer."

"You don't think the refinery worker would have taken the wallet and keys, do you?"

"I can ask Callahan. That would be a pretty brazen move, though."

Fenway nodded, and then thought a moment. "Hang on— you said the guy worked at the refinery?" Fenway stood up too. "What was he doing *here*? This is a half-mile away."

"Jogging," McVie said. "The guy likes to go for a run on the beach when he gets off work."

"Oh, right," Fenway said. "You said it was a jogger on the phone."

"Lucky he ran this way," Melissa said. "We wouldn't have found him for a few more hours, at least. This isn't a heavily trafficked area."

"So *this* guy wasn't homeless," said Fenway, "but maybe we should see if anyone who *is* homeless saw anything. This seems like a good place to hang out if you're homeless. Good shelter, stays nice and cool in the summer, not a lot of people around to bug you."

"No," McVie said. "No one to bug you, but no one close by to help out or get resources. No services for the homeless, no place to panhandle, no restaurants who throw out food—not even a vending machine. You've got to walk for five miles towards Estancia before you even hit a fast-food place. And the homeless shelter is ten miles away."

"All right," Melissa said, looking out past where the drag marks went into the beach. "Let's divvy up scouting the area." She looked back over her shoulder. "I'm going to north side of the underpass."

"With you in a minute," Fenway called.

McVie stepped closer. "Listen, Fenway," he said in a low voice. "I know it's been weird the last couple of months with our campaigns. But we can still have dinner together."

"And I told you, Craig," Fenway whispered back, "Millicent said we shouldn't go on a date until after the election. It looks bad enough you're going through a divorce right now. Gene told you the same thing, as I recall."

"Millicent and Gene were hired to manage our campaigns, not our social lives," McVie said. "You've got a huge lead in the polls, and I'm ahead too."

"That last poll was two weeks old. More and more people are starting to be aware you and Amy aren't living together anymore, and people will start to wonder if your eye has been wandering."

"Well, it was *her* wandering eye, not mine."

"First of all," Fenway hissed, "you know as well as anyone it's the *perception* that matters, not the reality. And secondly, if people think *she* was the cheater, that might be worse. You look like you can't keep your woman in line."

"*What* did you just say?"

"*I'm* not saying that. I'm saying there are some voters who will think it."

"I seriously can't believe that came out of your mouth."

"If you can't believe that, imagine what I think the voters will say if you start dating a black girl half your age before the ink is dry on your separation papers."

McVie shot Fenway a look. "You are *not* half my age."

"No," Fenway said. "I'm twenty-nine and you're forty-three, and that is barely—and I mean *barely*—on the right side of the Creepy Equation."

"The Creepy Equation?"

"Oh, come on, Craig. I know you've heard of the Creepy Equation."

Craig looked puzzled.

"Melissa," Fenway called, "you've heard of the Creepy Equation, right?"

"Like with dating?" Melissa said, shining her light where the bricks in the wall met the concrete.

"Right."

"Sure. Half your age, plus seven. Younger than that, and it's creepy."

Fenway shot a look of triumph at McVie.

"You thinking about dating a younger man, Fenway? Some sexy college boy getting cougar vibes from you?"

"Shut up, Melissa," Fenway said, but she was smiling.

"I'll shut up when you start helping me scan the area for evidence," Melissa said.

Fenway looked at McVie out of the corner of her eye and started to walk toward the beach side of the pedestrian underpass. She passed the passenger door of the medical examiner's van and saw movement inside and almost jumped out of her skin.

"Holy shit!"

Melissa laughed and covered her mouth.

Officer Donald Huke rolled down the window. "Good morning, Miss Stevenson," he said. "I'm sorry, I didn't mean to startle you."

"What the hell are you doing in the medical examiner's van, Don—Officer Huke?"

Officer Huke was quiet, his face screwed up almost painfully and his ears getting red.

Fenway turned her head and looked at Melissa, who smirked and shrugged.

"Never mind, Officer Huke, don't answer that."

He looked relieved.

"Well, since you're here," Fenway said, "you don't mind securing the crime scene while we look for the decedent's possessions, do you?"

"No, ma'am—I mean, no, Miss Stevenson." He opened the door of the van and hopped out, all business.

Melissa and Fenway and McVie spent the next twenty minutes combing the scrubby bushes and the sandy areas around the edges of the underpass. They didn't find anything, and the three of them all found themselves at the edge of the beach.

"Should we search the beach too?" Fenway asked.

"We probably should at least do a visual search," said Melissa. "But if the killer wanted evidence to disappear, a good throw into the ocean might do it."

"Maybe fortune will smile upon us today." Fenway looked toward the cliffs and shaded her eyes. "What's up that way?"

"A couple of beachfront hotels," McVie said. "A little rundown now, but they're okay. Not like the Cactus Lake Motel or anything. We don't get many calls out this way."

"How far down does the beach go?"

"This area isn't too big—maybe five hundred yards. Then there's an outcropping and a bridge you can walk across to another beach. There are a couple of rock formations beyond that, right where Ocean Highway takes a sharp turn up the ridge."

Fenway nodded. She remembered driving down the ridge the day before, seeing the smokestacks of her father's refinery and looking out over that very beach. She sighed.

McVie gazed across the water. "If we need to search the beach, we might as well start."

"I've got a metal detector," Melissa said. She started walking back toward the van.

Fenway followed her. "All right, Melissa, you said no wallet or keys."

"Correct," Melissa said, lifting up the police tape Officer Huke had put up. "Whoever killed him left a pretty nice watch on his wrist, though. A Longines. Not top of the line, but someone paid at least five or six hundred bucks for it."

"Hmm," Fenway said. "That's inconsistent with a robbery, too." Fenway veered off to walk toward the corpse. She crouched next to it as Melissa came up behind her. "I think someone *want-ed* to make us think he was homeless, but did a pretty poor job of it."

"Maybe a last-ditch effort to cover something up? Maybe it wasn't premeditated?"

"Maybe."

Melissa shrugged. "I don't know either."

Fenway took out her phone, leaned over, and took a picture of the dead man's face, trying to keep as much of the hole in his forehead out of the frame as possible. "I think we might have luck if we check those beachfront motels up there. Maybe he went to get ice and ran into the killer."

Melissa nodded. "I was starting to think maybe it's a rich guy off his meds or something."

Fenway looked at the picture on her phone. She zoomed in, right on his nose. Then she turned back to the body and activated the flashlight on her phone, shining the light into his nostrils. "Or maybe he was self-medicating." She motioned at Melissa to come closer. "Does this look like cocaine residue to you?"

Melissa bent down. "Hmm. Could be."

"I can't see much in his nostrils, but maybe you can see if there's any tissue damage, or nasal septum perforation, anything symptomatic of cocaine abuse."

"We'll do a tox screen."

"Yeah, but those tests take a while to come back. If we can confirm he was using with any tissue damage you find, maybe it'll point us in the right direction. This could have been a drug deal gone wrong."

"Maybe." Melissa stood back up. "Did you call Dez or Mark yet?"

"No," Fenway said, pushing herself to her feet and following Melissa to the van. "Both of them caught cases over the weekend. The overdose at drug house down on twenty-second, and the hunter found shot in the state park. I wanted my sergeants to have at least a little bit of a break."

Melissa opened the back of the van and climbed inside. "I thought for sure you'd relish the chance to get back at Dez for calling you back from Seattle."

Fenway shook her head. "Ha. Maybe next time. I've got this one; we don't need all hands on deck."

Melissa nodded, pulling the metal detector out of a case as McVie walked up to them.

Fenway acknowledged McVie with a slight nod of her head. "Want to go take a walk with me?"

"Take a walk with you?"

"Fenway thinks those beachfront hotels might be a good place to start," Melissa said.

"Like our victim might have been a guest at one of them?" asked McVie.

"Yep," replied Fenway. "And Melissa and I found what might be cocaine residue below his nose."

McVie nodded. "How does that tie into the hotels?"

"I don't know yet. But I think it makes sense to go over there."

"Sure, let's go see if he checked in at any of those places. I'll take a snapshot of his face, see if anyone recognizes him."

"Already done," Fenway said, showing him the picture.

"Gotcha. Good job keeping the bullet hole off-camera."

"I like to make sure I don't gross out the witnesses," Fenway said, then turned to Melissa. "Can you and Officer Huke comb the beach?"

"Anything to get out of the grunt work, huh, Fenway?" Melissa smiled. "Yeah, we should be fine. I got word Kav should be meeting me here in about ten or fifteen minutes. We'll take a scrub of the beach, maybe for a half-mile or so."

"I can get Callahan back here too," McVie said.

"Maybe that's not such a bad idea," Melissa admitted. "It's a lot of ground to cover."

Fenway and McVie started walking toward the main road.

The hill was steep, and Fenway was trying to rush. She was several steps ahead of the sheriff, and he was getting winded. "Jeez, where's the fire? Hold up."

Fenway stopped on the side of the path, avoiding a muddy puddle. "I'm not trying to hurry."

McVie raised his eyebrows. "You know, part of the reason you said you weren't going to date me until after the election is to avoid the awkwardness. I'd say this is still pretty damn awkward."

"Well, we've waited this long. What's another week?"

"Sure," McVie said, catching up to her. "One more week."

"You worried about Klein?"

McVie shrugged. "You worried about Ivanovich?"

Fenway shook her head, and they kept walking. "I don't know. I mean, ever since I passed the nursing boards in September, I guess I haven't been worried about it." She looked at McVie. "Also, I guess it helps I'm so ahead in the polls."

"And no one knows who Richard Ivanovich is."

Fenway nodded. "I'm not even sure he wants to do it. I think Barry Klein talked him into it."

"Yeah. Well, we all know Dr. Klein will fight everything your dad wants tooth and nail, just because your dad wants it."

Fenway paused for a moment. "Hey, Craig, did something happen between my father and Dr. Klein before I got here? Like, did Charlotte used to be Klein's girlfriend or something?"

"Who knows?" McVie asked, although it sounded more like a statement. "Klein is so contrary. It's like he's afraid a meteor will fall on him if he shows an ounce of humanity."

Fenway was quiet. She thought back to her nursing classes and the overview of oppositional defiance disorder, and wondered if Dr. Klein had it but was undiagnosed.

"So," McVie said, "which motel do you want to start with?"

"The closest one," Fenway said. "And we might as well start with the front desk."

"You think he stayed there?"

"Only one way to find out," Fenway said.

They got to the main road and turned left, toward the motels. The breeze had picked up, and the hint of rain in the air was blowing away. The gentle wind felt refreshing against Fenway's face, although she thought it was probably playing hell with her hair. She looked at Craig, in his winter coat, shivering.

"So," McVie said, "maybe we should try to figure out where we want to go on our first date Wednesday night. You know, the day after the election."

Fenway looked out of the corner of her eye at McVie. Her functional khaki trousers weren't exactly flattering; her running shoes wouldn't win any fashion awards either. And yet here McVie was asking her out—again. She knew she was intelligent and sometimes even fun to be around. Given her history with men—or maybe it was something internal—she was surprised to be asked out when she wasn't dressed up. She wondered if she needed to change her attitude about herself and then briefly wondered how much Dr. Tassajera would charge to fix her. "Wednesday, huh?"

"Yeah."

Fenway laughed. "Maybe you should drop out now if you're thinking about dating me instead of paying attention to the voting public."

McVie smiled. "Maybe *you* should. You're the one who always says you're not cut out for politics."

Fenway elbowed McVie playfully. "That's why I'm so good at it."

McVie smiled. "So I was thinking maybe we could go to Maxime's."

Fenway rolled her eyes. "There's more to good food than fancy napkins and a sommelier who knows you by name."

"If that's supposed to be a segue into you suggesting the *taquería* on Third Street, forget it. I want to take you someplace a little nicer."

"Just don't take me to Maxime's. That's the place my father goes when he has something to celebrate." She paused. "Unless you want me thinking about my father on our first date."

"No," McVie said, "that's quite all right."

"I like Argentine food."

"What, the new steak house on Broadway?"

"Oh, Craig!" Fenway batted her eyelashes. "The new Argentine steak house! That's just where I wanted to go—how did you know? You're so *thoughtful!*" She put her hands out, miming the delicate raising of the sides of her invisible long skirt, and curtsied.

McVie tried to look annoyed, but the corners of his mouth and eyes betrayed his amusement. "Okay, Fenway, got it."

They reached the black wrought-iron fence bounding the grounds of the first hotel. The garden behind the fence, lovely from a distance, up close showed weeds and random bald patches of rock and gravel. After the fence ended, the circular driveway, made of multicolored bricks, provided a sweeping contour for the eye to follow, but it, too, showed signs of disrepair. Several missing bricks marred the smooth lines, with some spots more visible than others. In one area to the left of the entrance, two large swaths of missing brick had been cemented over. The dull, bumpy gray was an eyesore in the once-grand driveway.

"This looks like it used to be quite a nice place," Fenway said.

"About fifteen years ago, it was," McVie said. "Then the owner died. It was purchased out of the estate by a couple of new owners, but they didn't do maintenance on the place, and it's only gotten older and shabbier."

"It's a shame. This looks like it could have been a movie set."

McVie walked up to the hotel entrance. Fenway had halfway expected a grandiose door, perhaps made of a high-quality wood, carved into a decadent shape. Or maybe a metal door of some unusual material—titanium, or something that emulated modernity or wealth. Instead, it was a utilitarian entry door, glass from top to bottom, with a metal bar on either side at doorknob level. It made Fenway sad.

McVie pulled the door open and Fenway walked into the large lobby. The tiled floor was about twenty years out of date, but clean. She noticed some of the tiles were cracked or chipped, the walls had a pit or two in them, and other places had been damaged and fixed competently but cheaply.

The long registration desk at the front was dark mahogany, and in much better condition than the rest of the lobby. It looked like it had been handled with care and precision.

There was a thin Latina woman at the desk, typing on the computer, wearing an outdated business suit. "Good morning," she said, not looking up. "Welcome to the Belvedere Terrace Resort." She struck the last key on her keyboard with finality and raised her head. Her eyes widened when she saw McVie's black police uniform. "Oh—officer—how can I be of assistance?" And her smile came next, plastered on. Fenway hoped she didn't look that pained when she was faking a smile around her father.

"Good morning," McVie said. "Sheriff Craig McVie, ma'am."

"Sheriff. Sorry, I didn't realize who you were." .

"That's quite all right." Fenway looked at McVie's face and thought she could detect either annoyance or disappointment. If people didn't recognize McVie on sight, it wasn't a good sign for his mayoral campaign.

The woman cleared her throat. "I'm Lydia Hernandez. My family owns the Belvedere Terrace."

McVie nodded. "I was wondering if you'd be willing to help us identify somebody."

Fenway brought up the photo of the dead man on her phone.

"Certainly," Ms. Hernandez said, although her voice was a bit unsure.

"Now," said McVie, "I have to warn you, the picture is of a dead man. We found him down under the overpass by the beach, about half a mile back. But this is the closest building around, and we thought you or one of your guests or co-workers might have seen him."

The color drained out of Ms. Hernandez's face, but she nodded. "Of course. I'll do anything I can to help."

McVie took the phone from Fenway and glanced at the screen before showing it to Ms. Hernandez.

She gasped.

"Recognize him?"

"Yes," she said. "That's Mr. Potemkin."

"I'm sorry—you said 'Mr. Potemkin'?"

"Yes."

"Does he come around here often?"

Ms. Hernandez nodded. "He's kind of a regular. He and his wife have visited us on several occasions."

"Oh—he's a guest?"

"He is." Fenway saw Ms. Hernandez set her jaw and cross her arms. She was ready to protect the dignity of her guests—and the reputation of her hotel.

McVie must have seen this in Ms. Hernandez's body language too, because he became even more relaxed in his demeanor. "Is there any way you could show us his room?"

Ms. Hernandez uncrossed her arms. "I'll call up there and see if Mrs. Potemkin is in the room. I certainly don't want to burst in on her if she's showering or sleeping."

"No, no, of course," McVie said.

He took a step back from the desk and stood next to Fenway. "So—this wife. I wonder why it is no one's heard from *her* about her missing husband."

"Maybe they had a fight and he stormed out, and she doesn't expect him back. Or maybe she hasn't woken up yet and doesn't even know he's gone."

"Or maybe she took out a big-ass life insurance policy and took a walk on the beach with him and wanted to make it look like a robbery gone wrong."

"You are such a pessimist," Fenway said.

"She's not answering," Ms. Hernandez said. She made no move to do anything else.

"Maybe we could go to their room," McVie suggested.

"I don't want to disturb them. They've paid through Sunday."

Fenway took a step forward. "I apologize for the inconvenience, Ms. Hernandez, but with Mr. Potemkin found dead, I'm frankly a little worried about the safety of his wife. If she's in the room, then at least I will know her dead body isn't going to wash up on the beach later today."

Ms. Hernandez got a horrified look on her face. "Oh my," she said, covering her mouth. "I didn't think of that."

She rummaged behind the counter and dug out a plastic card key. "Okay," she said. "Their room is in the back set of cottages. One of our private villas."

Fenway doubted the cottages looked anything like *villas*, but she followed the woman out of the lobby and through a wide hallway toward the back of the property.

They exited through a set of white French doors onto a red brick patio. Like the front driveway, the patio, once glorious, now hovered on the edge of disrepair. A couple of chunks had been taken out of the bricks. The patio ended at a set of five steps leading up to a pool area. The pool was enclosed by another black wrought iron fence. As they got closer, Fenway saw the pool had been drained.

Ms. Hernandez saw Fenway's eyes go to the empty swimming hole. "It's off season," she said. "We drain the pool at the beginning of October."

Fenway nodded.

"The villas are past the garden terrace behind the pool," Ms. Hernandez said. "It's only a little farther now."

The walk got more overgrown. Fenway felt a pang of pity for Ms. Hernandez. There was too much work here to keep it looking good. She didn't see a staff big enough to stay on top of all the required upkeep—especially as the hotel fell further from grace and the daily room rates kept dropping.

The villa was at the end of the walk, and was designed, like the main building, to replicate Tudor-era architecture. On a small cottage like this, though, the design elements looked silly. The overgrown vegetation around the villa hid the most egregious architectural mistakes from view.

Ms. Hernandez knocked loudly. "Mrs. Potemkin?" she called out. "I'm sorry to bother you, but it's important. Mrs.

Potemkin?" She stopped and listened, and hearing nothing, knocked harder.

McVie let her knock a few more times. Fenway took the phone out of her purse and looked at the time.

"I don't think she's in," Ms. Hernandez said.

"Maybe you can try your master key," McVie suggested.

"She might have the deadbolt turned," Ms. Hernandez muttered to herself, but held the cardkey up to the reader. The lock flashed green and clicked. She turned the handle and swung the door open.

CHAPTER FOUR

"MRS. POTEMKIN?" MS. HERNANDEZ CALLED OUT. "I'M SO SORRY
to bother you, but the police are here."

McVie took a step into the room, hand on his holster. "Mrs.
Potemkin, this is Sheriff Craig McVie. Are you here?"

Silence greeted them; not even the hum of a fan or an air conditioning unit.

McVie looked around, took another step in, calling for Mrs.
Potemkin a few more times. He turned to his right and disappeared from view.

Fenway realized she was holding her breath.

"All clear," McVie called from inside the villa.

Fenway walked in, followed by Ms. Hernandez. "Please don't
touch anything," Fenway said. "I still don't know if we need to
process this room yet."

"Process the room?"

"For fingerprints, fibers, hair, that kind of thing."

"Oh." The wheels in Ms. Hernandez's head turned and she
realized what Fenway was implying.

The room was large and comfortable, even if the décor was

outdated. The colors of the furniture and the wallpaper—this hotel still had wallpaper—were muted earth tones and lots of gray-green. Art deco-style illustrations of tropical themes in the same hues hung on the wall.

The frames of the chairs, bed, and furniture were plastic made to look like bamboo. The bed was unmade and the sheets and bedspread on one side were pulled onto the floor. A gray suitcase lay open on a luggage rack next to the dresser.

"She's not here?" Fenway called to McVie, snapping on a pair of blue nitrile gloves.

"No," McVie said, stepping back into the main bedroom. "Looks like this stuff all belongs to a man. No women's toiletries at all in the bathroom. Got an extra pair of those?"

Fenway dug in her purse and handed over another set of gloves. He nodded his thanks and she took a look in the suitcase. "All men's clothes in here," she said. They looked through the dresser and the closet; men's clothes, mostly in the same style—and, Fenway thought, the same price range—as the clothes on the corpse.

Fenway walked into the bathroom, pulling a couple of evidence bags out of her purse. McVie was right; there was toothpaste and a toothbrush and a razor and shaving cream on the bathroom counter, but no sign of any women's toiletries. The vanity drawers were empty. She looked in the shower; the drain had several long blonde hairs around it.

"We should get Melissa over here," Fenway said. "Process some of this stuff."

"The lab is backed up for DNA analysis for three weeks," said McVie.

"If we can figure out who Mrs. Potemkin is in three weeks, that's better than nothing," Fenway said.

"*Who* Mrs. Potemkin is?"

"I'm almost positive it's a made-up name."

"I'm sorry?" Ms. Hernandez asked. "A made-up name? I don't think so."

"Did you take a credit card from Mr. Potemkin?" Fenway asked.

"No," Ms. Hernandez said. "He always paid cash."

"Not even for a deposit or anything?"

"Two-hundred-dollar deposit. After their third or fourth visit, I stopped asking for the deposit."

"So you never saw their identification or credit cards."

Ms. Hernandez stopped and thought. "No, I don't suppose I did."

"Did you ever catch either of their first names?"

"Let me think." Ms. Hernandez rubbed her chin. "I don't think I ever got hers. But the man signed in. I'd have it back in the office. It was something a little bit unusual—the man's, I mean. A normal name, but not the usual way to spell it, I think. Like a Gary with two 'e's, or some such nonsense."

"Was it *Grigory*? Like Gregory, but with an 'i'?"

Ms. Hernandez's jaw fell open. "Yes, that's it. How did you know?"

Fenway turned to McVie. "Grigory Potemkin was Catherine the Great's lover. Well—one of her lovers. Rumored to be her favorite. Epic love story, supposedly."

"How do you know that?" asked McVie.

Fenway shrugged. "Russian Lit when I was an undergrad." A dark shadow crossed her thoughts.

"Aha," said McVie. "So you think this was an illicit affair."

"I do. Probably something they both thought was clever."

"So we should be looking for women named Catherine?"

Fenway bent down in front of the trash can in the bathroom. "I can think of worse places to start." She fished a tissue out of the trash. It looked like it had been used to blot lipstick.

"When was the trash last emptied?" she asked Ms. Hernandez.

"Yesterday," Ms. Hernandez said. "At least, it was supposed to be."

"Supposed to be?"

Ms. Hernandez shuffled her feet. "It's the off-season. We're not busy. My daughter is on housekeeping duty."

"Which means?" asked McVie.

"Sometimes she doesn't do a, um, thorough job."

"I see."

Fenway dropped the tissue in the evidence bag.

"You're not going to leave that for Melissa?"

"I thought this should be bagged separately from the rest of the trash."

"What's special about that tissue?"

"The color is kind of unusual. I thought we might make quicker work tracking the color of the lipstick rather than waiting for weeks for the DNA."

Fenway kept examining the bathroom: opening the cabinet, examining the floor behind the toilet, looking closely at the grout on the shower.

Ms. Hernandez sighed. "I should get back. I don't think I ought to leave the front desk for this long."

"Okay," McVie said. "We'll close up when we're done and come let you know."

Ms. Hernandez scrunched up her face. "I'm not comfortable having you in here without a representative of this resort."

"You're free to stay, too," said McVie. "Nobody's stopping you."

Ms. Hernandez put her hands on her hips and sighed loudly, but Fenway studiously ignored her. She stole a quick glance at the sheriff, whose easy, quiet demeanor became even more soporific.

After another sixty seconds ticked by, Ms. Hernandez said, "Make sure you come by and see me after you're finished in here." Then she spun on her heel and walked out.

The sheriff's phone dinged. "From Melissa," he said, looking at it. "She found a gun on the beach, in the surf. It may be unrelated, or maybe the killer tried to get rid of the gun in the ocean."

"What kind of gun?"

"Let me see."

McVie texted Melissa back and turned to Fenway. "See anything else in here you want to get bagged up?"

"I want to ask Melissa or Kav about this powder on the bathroom counter."

"I take it you don't think that's baby powder."

"No," Fenway said. "I bet it will match the powder under Mr. Potemkin's nose. I think they were in the middle of a weeklong party. And I definitely want the fingerprints here."

"In a hotel room?"

Fenway shrugged. "We'll probably get three hundred different fingerprints, but maybe the daughter isn't as bad a housekeeper as her mom thinks she is."

"That will be a lot of work for the fingerprint people to go through."

"Yeah, I know," said Fenway. "Maybe I can help out in the lab in the next couple of days. Can you find out Melissa's ETA?"

McVie texted again.

"Maybe an hour, she says."

"Can she come now? We've got a window of time here and I'd prefer not to piss off the front desk lady any more than we have to."

McVie looked sideways at Fenway. "You do know *we're* the cops, right?"

Fenway smiled sweetly. "And it doesn't take a genius to know we might need something else from Ms. Hernandez and coming back in an hour because we forgot something won't keep us on her good side."

McVie chuckled as he texted. "We stopped being on her good side as soon as we asked to see the room."

Melissa arrived about forty minutes later with the fingerprint kit, grumbling. The transport van had arrived just as Melissa was leaving, and she had to help get the body moved into the van and on its way to San Miguelito. Officer Huke assisted as well, but he was getting nervous about working the crime scene rather than reporting to the sheriff's office. He had to call his supervisor, who wasn't crazy about letting him stay longer, but wasn't about to argue, as he was helping the sheriff. Officer Huke was itching to get to the station, and Melissa had left Kav to process the rest of the scene while she was at the hotel.

Melissa arrived with Ms. Hernandez, who didn't seem happy about yet another public employee traipsing through the Potemkin villa.

Melissa had brought the gun—a Ruger RCP II, a compact .380 with a short barrel—in an evidence bag. She placed it on the dresser for them to examine.

"Hmm," McVie said. "Interesting."

"What's interesting?" asked Fenway.

"For one thing, this isn't a super-expensive gun."

"You can probably get it around here for three hundred bucks or so," said Melissa.

"So—we'd be looking for—what? A middle-class owner?"

"Maybe," said McVie, rubbing his chin. "So the second thing is it's popular with women."

"Popular with women?" Fenway repeated.

"Yeah. It's a pretty serious caliber—a hell of a lot better than Rachel's .22 for protection—but it's got a light recoil. And it weighs nothing. Great to carry in a purse."

"So," Fenway said, "maybe we want to prioritize finding Catherine the Great."

"Finding *who*?" Melissa said.

"It's a whole thing," Fenway said. "I'll tell you later."

Fenway bent down to look at the gun through the clear evidence bag. She saw a distinct serial number above and to the left of the trigger—and below the etched lettering that said *Read instruction manual before using firearm.*

"How about that," Fenway said.

"I know," Melissa said. "A serial number that hasn't been filed off."

"Think this is the murder weapon?"

Melissa shrugged. "I don't know. The bullet hole might be a .380. Could be a nine-millimeter. And this gun might not have had anything to do with it." She paused. "But there are five bullets in it."

"And how many does the magazine hold?"

"Six."

Fenway nodded; the odds were good they had found the murder weapon. "Great work, Melissa. And before you start with fingerprinting, take a look at the white powder on the bathroom counter."

She went in, taking a brush and a vial out of one of her kits. She looked at the fine, off-white crystalline powder closely before sweeping it into the vial.

"Is that cocaine?" Fenway asked.

"I think so," Melissa said. "We'll have to get it back to the lab to be sure."

"Do you think it'll match the powder under our victim's nose?"

"If I remember right, it's a visual match."

After she capped the vial and sealed it in an evidence bag, Melissa started fingerprinting. While there were a large number of prints on the dresser and the handles on the drawers, the nightstands and the bases of the bedside lamps were relatively clean.

"It looks like there are twenty or thirty fingerprints on the lamp bases," Melissa said, "but on this side, I only see four or five unique fingerprints, and on the other side, about seven fingerprints, and I think two or three of them are the same as this side."

Fenway looked at McVie and smiled. He appeared nonplussed.

"Let's get those prints prioritized," said McVie, stating the obvious. He folded his arms as Melissa moved to the bathroom counter. "If you don't need my help here, I'm going to talk to Ms. Hernandez again. See if she can give us a description of this Mrs. Potemkin character. Maybe get a sketch artist. Maybe see if the car they came in is still around."

"We're fine," Fenway said. "Go do your thing."

With Fenway's help, Melissa began to collect the fingerprints from the rest of the surfaces. Some areas had the same sets of fingerprints as the bedside lamps; others had dozens and dozens of different prints.

Melissa photographed many of the out-of-place items. They collected several dozen bags of evidence as well: the clothes hanging in the closet, the hair from the drain, the abandoned suitcase, and a pair of Salvatore Ferragamo sneakers.

"No luggage tag on the suitcase," Fenway noted. "No business cards, nothing."

"This obviously wasn't a business trip," Melissa said. "Either that or Mrs. Potemkin made sure we'd have a hard time identifying who shared this room with her. And look at those shoes. Definitely more like a rich guy off his meds."

"Or a rich guy who can afford cocaine." Fenway cocked her head to the side. "Those shoes cost eight hundred dollars."

"How do you know that?"

"How do you think? My father owns two pairs."

Melissa smirked and then kept going over her patch of carpet. "So what was it like growing up with a rich father?"

Fenway scoffed. "I wouldn't know."

"What?" Melissa said. "You didn't grow up with him?"

"Nope. My mom and I were pretty much on our own since I was eight. I grew up in Seattle. I lived in her house until she passed away earlier this year."

"Oh, I'm sorry."

"Yeah, cancer's a real bitch."

They were silent for a few minutes.

Fenway's phone dinged. It was a text from McVie.

Says she sometimes saw him in a silver SUV, no make or model
Doesn't know what car they arrived in this time

Fenway repeated it to Melissa, who nodded and continued to work.

After a few more minutes, Melissa asked, "Will you be glad when the campaign is over?"

"You have no idea."

"Yeah, Dominguez County politics have always been a little more intense," Melissa said. "I think it's because there isn't anything else to do here."

"There's the beach. And the mountains. There's Coast Harbor State Park."

"That's all outdoors stuff. Lots of people here aren't big fans of nature. *They're* the ones who get all crazy during election season."

"Another reason for me to hate politics," Fenway said. "If I win, I won't have to worry about it for another four years, and if I lose, I won't have to worry about it ever again."

"You don't honestly think you're going to lose to Ivanovich, do you?"

Fenway looked up at Melissa. "I don't trust polls, especially when my father pays for them."

They worked for another half hour and then had to make several trips to the front of the hotel to carry the evidence bags to the CSI van. Melissa got a call from Kav as they were making their final trip out; he had finished up as well. McVie had made it back and he was going to give Officer Huke a ride to the sheriff's office.

"Is that the last of it?" asked Fenway.

"I think so."

"Want me to give you a ride back to your car?"

Fenway looked around. It was still chilly and she liked the cold breeze on her face—a perfect day to take the trail down to the secluded beach. But she had the teachers' union luncheon to prepare for, and sighed. "That would be great, Melissa. Thanks."

Melissa put her arm on the back door of the van to close it, and then hesitated.

"What?"

"I think we need to check their files. See if either of the Potemkins signed anything, or if Mrs. Potemkin did. Fingerprint the pages. Maybe one of them is in the system."

"Maybe both of them are."

Melissa laughed. "You're cute. I would have thought you'd have lost your optimism by now."

"Maybe the hotel even wrote down a license plate number of their car."

"Now you're just talking crazy." She picked up her kit from the back of the van then closed the door. "You want to do the honors?"

Fenway shook her head. "Mrs. Hernandez hates me."

"She's not crazy about me, either."

They both looked at each other and held their fists out.

"One, two, three," they said in unison.

"Shit," Melissa said, looking down at her hand, held out flat.

"Scissors cut paper," Fenway said. "Have fun with the world's sweetest hotel owner."

"Fine. You go do a final sweep of the villa."

Fenway started walking back along the path.

"Oh," Melissa said, "can you call McVie and tell him we'll put a rush on the prints? But tell him not to hold his breath on the DNA."

"Sure thing." As she walked, Fenway pulled her phone out and called the sheriff.

"McVie."

"Hey, it's Fenway."

"Hi, Fenway. You still at the hotel?"

"Yeah. Melissa wanted me to tell you they were putting a rush on the prints."

"Good. And we've got an ID. Officer Huke found the victim's wallet on the beach."

"Really?"

"Yep. No money in it, but there was a driver's license. Jeremy Chauncey Kapp." McVie paused.

"Is that supposed to mean something to me?" She suppressed a yawn, put her purse down on the concrete walkway next to the planter, and stretched her right arm above her head.

"He's a landscape architect. Does a lot of rich people's houses. I think they did a profile of him on one of the gardening shows last year. He's kind of a big deal."

"Oh. I don't really need a landscape architect where I live."

"No, I guess you don't," McVie said, a brief chuckle escaping. "Anyway, he lives in Birdland in Paso Querido."

"Oh, *fancy*."

"Right. Whippoorwill Terrace."

"What's he doing out in a run-down beachfront hotel?"

"I don't know." He cleared his throat. "You didn't see a Jaguar at the hotel, did you?"

"No, but I wasn't looking for one. Why?"

"He has a Jaguar roadside assistance card. Thought you might have seen something I didn't. I'm about to call the P.Q. office and talk to Gretchen," McVie said. "She can have a couple of her officers go by the house."

"Is he married?" Fenway asked.

"Yes, with a couple of kids. And he has a record. A DUI three years ago. Two calls earlier this year for domestic disturbance, one of them called in by a neighbor, one of them called in by Cricket Kapp."

"Cricket?"

"That's the wife."

"What the hell kind of name is Cricket?"

"Let's see." Fenway heard McVie tapping. "Oh, it's a nick-name, apparently."

Fenway's ears perked up. "A nickname? Is her given name Catherine, maybe?"

"No. Esmerelda."

"How did they get Cricket from Esmerelda?"

McVie ignored Fenway's question. "They've been married twenty-one years. Two kids, a daughter named Blair, age eighteen, and a son named Donovan, age sixteen."

"So Cricket isn't Catherine," said Fenway.

"Right. And it wouldn't make sense anyway. Men who have a nice house in P.Q. don't usually rent a room at a rundown beach-front hotel. Not with their wives, anyway." He kept tapping. "No passenger in the car for the DUI."

"Okay," Fenway said.

"All right, I'll see you in a bit."

"I've got a teachers' union luncheon to go to."

"Luncheon? It's only ten."

"Yeah, but I'm in my sneakers. I've got to get ready."

They said their goodbyes and Fenway hung up and stretched again, this time with both arms above her head.

As she bent down to pick up her purse, a ray of sun broke through the mist, and something near the edge of the planter glinted.

Fenway looked more closely. She took a step toward the edge of the planter and bent down. It looked like a piece of jewelry caught in one of the flowering plants—an expensive piece of jewelry, with multiple diamonds, one of them quite large. For a moment Fenway thought it might be cubic zirconia instead of diamonds. She used her phone to take pictures of where it lay.

Fenway pulled a glove out of her purse and snapped it on, getting another evidence bag as well. She reached down and pulled gently, the plant readily giving up its hold on the jewelry.

An earring.

An unusual pendant earring at that: a large hexagonal-shaped diamond, easily two carats, hung below a vertical line of five small diamonds that ended near the stem. Platinum rivets held all the diamonds in place.

It was a custom-made piece Fenway immediately recognized.

She swore under her breath.

"Dammit, Charlotte."

CHAPTER FIVE

FENWAY THOUGHT FOR A FEW MINUTES BEFORE CALLING MCVIE again. She wondered if her dislike for her young stepmother was coloring her perceptions. Was it *actually* the same earring she had seen Charlotte wearing—and bragging about—a few months before? Was it her dislike of everything Charlotte stood for that led Fenway to immediately think Charlotte was not only cheating on her father but had holed up in the beachfront hotel room with Jeremy Kapp? And did Fenway believe Charlotte could put a bullet in his forehead?

She wondered if her father even noticed if Charlotte was gone. Perhaps he was working late, or on a last-minute business trip to China or Dubai or New York. Or maybe, Fenway considered, he had his own affair he was conducting. Charlotte was turning thirty-six in a couple of weeks; maybe her father was turning her in for a younger model.

The thought both disgusted and thrilled her.

Then she called McVie back.

"McVie."

"I found something. In the planter just outside of the villa."

"What is it?"

"An earring."

McVie paused. "You think it's related? It could have been in this planter for weeks."

"I don't think so," Fenway said. "It's an *incredibly* expensive earring. Six diamonds, and one of them has got to be two carats."

"Two carats? Are you sure it's real?"

"Almost positive," Fenway said. "And *you've* seen this earring before, too."

"Me?"

"Remember when we had dinner with my father a few months ago? When we convinced him to hire that private investigator?"

"Don't remind me."

"Charlotte wore these exact earrings."

"Your stepmother? Charlotte?"

"Yes."

McVie hesitated. "That doesn't necessarily prove anything. There are lots of rich folks around here. I'm sure a lot of them have expensive diamond earrings."

"No," Fenway said, "it's from a custom designer in Santa Barbara. My father gave them to Charlotte for their anniversary in June."

McVie paused. "You're sure it's the same earring?"

"Not a hundred percent positive, I guess. But I'd be pretty shocked if it wasn't."

"Ah. That's not good at all."

"Why do you say that? She's not *your* stepmother."

"No, but this complicates everything," McVie said. "First of all, give that earring to Melissa right now."

"She's checking to see if the Potemkins—well, Jeremy Chauncey Kapp and his mistress, whoever she is—left any fingerprints on paperwork in the hotel files."

"Of course. I should have asked for that before I left." He cleared his throat. "As soon as she gets back, then. Don't move until she takes it off your hands. If the earring turns out to be Charlotte's, neither one of us can work on the case."

"Of course. Because she's my stepmother."

"And because she's married to the guy who's bankrolling my campaign for mayor," McVie said. "Oh, Barry Klein will have a field day with this if it gets out."

"Okay," Fenway said.

Fenway hung up. She waited for ten minutes before Melissa appeared on the path.

"Ten minutes—that was quick."

"She called someone when I asked to see the files. Took a while. Then she told me to get a warrant. I didn't have the strength to argue." She folded her arms. "I thought you were going to meet me at the van."

Fenway held up the evidence bag with the earring.

"What's that?"

"I think it's my stepmother's earring."

"Where did you find it? In the villa?"

"No, the planter." Fenway pointed to the dirt where she had pulled the earring loose from the stems. "Right there. And since she's my stepmother, McVie told me to give it directly to you."

Melissa rolled her eyes, taking the evidence bag from Fenway. "As if walking a hundred feet is going to make any difference."

"That's our Boy Scout."

They both searched the planters directly in front of the villa, but found nothing out of the ordinary.

It was nearly eleven o'clock when Melissa dropped Fenway off at her Accord, promising to log the earring into evidence.

Fenway, lost in thought on the drive to her apartment, struggled to explain to herself how that earring could have gotten to that particular spot without Charlotte being involved somehow in the murder.

When she pulled into her apartment complex, there was a floral delivery van with its hazards on blocking her parking space. The clock in her car read eleven-fifteen by the time she pulled into an open space next to the reserved parking, and she sprinted upstairs.

She wrapped her hair and jumped into the shower, soaping herself down quickly, and she was out in less than five minutes. She went into her bedroom, and put on the dress Millicent had selected for the luncheon. The dress was a bright electric blue, a color she never wore, fitted through the shoulders and waist with a flared knee-length skirt. She had objected that it looked too casual on her five-ten frame, but Millicent said it was perfect to fit in with the teachers: professional, but not trying too hard. She took the index cards off her bedside table.

She grabbed her purse and ran through the speech once in her head, wondering if she'd recognize any of her teachers from her younger days in Estancia.

She got to the parking lot before she noticed it.

On her silver Honda Accord, all down the driver's side, was a large word, spray-painted in capital letters in neon green.

Fenway wanted to throw up.

———————•◦•———————

The first time Fenway heard *that word*—as her father had called it—was when she was in first grade. She attended the Montessori school in North Estancia. Benjy Prescott had pushed her off the swing, and she said she was going to tell Miss Trudy. And Benjy Prescott had pointed at her and said it. Benjy had been given a time out and apologized to Fenway, but the apology was for calling her names, not for pushing her off the swing.

Her mother often picked her up from school, or sometimes her father's driver, but that day it had been her father, Nathaniel Ferris himself. Fenway hadn't seen him all week—he had been off on a business trip—but he had landed earlier in the day and hoped to take Fenway to get ice cream. Fenway told him what Benjy had said. His face had clouded over. He asked her questions about Benjy Prescott. Fenway had been mad that he pushed her off the swing and never said sorry.

Nathaniel Ferris had launched into a rambling explanation and Fenway lost the thread of it twenty seconds in. But she noticed the next day Benjy wasn't there; in fact, he never came back, and the Montessori school had brand new playground equipment installed about two weeks later. That was also when she started to notice her skin was darker than everyone else's. And Benjy Prescott's friends started avoiding her.

Fenway, back in her apartment, called Millicent Tate.

"Fenway for Coroner, Millicent Tate's office," said a familiar smooth baritone on the other end.

"Hi, Marquise," Fenway said. "Is she in?"

"She's making donor calls."

"I'll hold."

"She's got about a dozen calls left," he said.

"It's urgent. Please have her talk with me when she's through with her current call."

"Will do, boss," Marquise said. He put her on hold, and the radio commercial of *Fenway Stevenson for County Coroner* came on. It did well with the focus group, Millicent had said.

"Hey, Fenway," Millicent said. "What's up? Everything okay?"

"Nope," she said, far more cheerfully than she felt. "I need something fixed fast."

"Oh my God. What is it? Are you pregnant? Have you been arrested?"

"Someone spray-painted something on the side of my car. I need to get it off right now."

"Spray-painted something."

"A racial slur."

"A what?"

"Some asshole spray-painted *nigger* on my car."

There was silence for a few seconds.

"Millicent, are you there?"

"I'm sorry—I—I'm stunned, I guess."

"Yeah, well, I'm stunned too, but I've gotta get to the teachers' union luncheon, and I'm not going to drive anywhere with *that* on my car."

"Of course, of course," Millicent Tate said quickly. Fenway heard Millicent tap her fingers on the desk. "Where is your car now?"

"At my apartment complex."

"Okay. Hang on two seconds."

Millicent Tate put Fenway on hold and the radio commercial played again. The commercial ended and some bland instrumental pop song came on, then after about a minute faded out, and the commercial started again.

Millicent picked back up. "Okay, I'll get someone over there right now, and I mean, *right now*, to take the car and get it cleaned up. When did this happen? Last night?"

"No. About ten minutes ago. I came home to change clothes and when I came out it was on the car."

"In broad daylight?"

"Yeah, imagine that. A racist, right here in Estancia. I'm so shocked you could knock me over with a feather."

"Okay, Fenway, stop it. I'm on your side. I'm trying to fix this. Do you have any idea who did it?"

Fenway's hackles raised. Millicent Tate might be *on her side*, but Fenway was sure she had never had anything spray-painted on *her* car, or been taunted by a group of first graders for her skin color. But she paused and took a deep breath, trying to remember what her goal was in this interaction, and it wasn't trying to make Millicent Tate more sensitive. "I can't imagine anyone who'd do this. Maybe Barry Klein or Richard Ivanovich, but that seems, uh, counterproductive."

"Klein?"

"He doesn't like me. He never has. I didn't tell you what happened a few months ago."

"With the pictures in your professor's office?"

"Oh, I guess I did tell you."

"Your father told me. I wondered why he wanted to spend so much money on me, and then I found out it was personal. He doesn't care for Dr. Klein."

"That's probably the only thing my father and I have in common."

Millicent Tate laughed. "Oh, sure. Right. That's a hoot."

Fenway bristled. She and her father had *nothing* in common. He threw money at problems, never wanting to spend time and effort of his own. And as much as he loved clashing with everyone when it came to his precious oil company, he ran away from interpersonal conflict.

Millicent Tate was still talking. "Okay, listen, Rory is on his way. Meet him at your car with the key. He'll trade you for his car and you'll have your Honda back tomorrow morning. Maybe even sooner. If this is still fresh, we might be able to get it off with acetone or carnauba wax."

"You sure know a lot about getting spray paint off."

"I know a lot about a lot of things. That's why I get the big bucks."

"What does Rory drive?"

"Does it matter? You'll get to the luncheon. Personally, I wouldn't care if it's an ice cream truck. But if you don't want to drive it, what do I care? Take the damn bus. Listen, I gotta go. Anything else?"

"No. Thanks, Millicent."

"I'm glad it wasn't anything serious." And she hung up.

Fenway sighed. *It wasn't anything serious.* Millicent was nothing if not ruthlessly efficient. Insensitive, perhaps, but ruthlessly efficient.

She walked down the stairs again, pulling the Honda key off her keychain. It was almost lunchtime, but the apartment complex might as well have been deserted. Everyone was at work or school or running errands. She heard a door open and looked up. Her neighbor from the third floor was leaving his apartment. Fenway saw him walk down the two flights of stairs and turn toward his car, parked on the street. He didn't give the spray-painted Accord a glance.

A decade-old Chrysler minivan drove into the complex; Rory was behind the wheel. He stopped in front of Fenway and got out of the car, leaving it running.

"Hi, Miss Stevenson," he said.

"Good to see you again, Rory. They've got you working on your day off?"

He grinned sheepishly. "Yeah."

"How are you doing on those lawn signs?"

"Slower today. More people are at work."

"But you're still ahead, right?"

His grinned widened.

"So they decided to let everyone else catch up to you and they sent you over here?"

"I'm happy to do it, Coroner. But I'm sorry to hear about what happened to your car."

Fenway shrugged, although she felt like punching something.

"My dad owns an auto-detailing shop," Rory continued. "He gets graffiti off cars all the time. Miss Tate told me the graffiti's less than a half-hour old, so it should be real easy to remove."

She nodded. "I appreciate it. Millicent said I could borrow your car?"

Rory nodded. "It's my dad's, so be careful with it."

"No problem," Fenway said. "You'll be all right driving it?"

Rory nodded. "The sooner we get it to my dad's shop, the sooner we can get it off."

"Your dad's okay with billing me?"

Rory shook his head. "No payment needed. It's gonna take my dad thirty minutes and some acetone."

"I insist, Rory. Have him bill me."

"No, ma'am," Rory said, surprising Fenway with the force of his words. "My dad was clear you were not to pay for this."

"Okay then. Please tell him thank you." She handed Rory the key and he nodded, then walked across the lot to her car. She climbed in the minivan and drove out of the parking lot, leaving Rory and her Accord behind her, trying to get the incident out of her brain, and her speech into it.

She was aware she was breathing a little faster than usual and made an effort to calm down, inhaling deeply in through her nose and exhaling slowly through her mouth.

She got to the luncheon only ten minutes late. Millicent had called ahead and said Fenway had car trouble—*you have no idea,* Fenway thought—and the speech went smoothly enough. Fenway faltered a couple of times, but her teacher jokes got decent laughs, and her lines about supporting school funding went over well. She didn't eat, but shook a lot of hands afterward and felt sure that everyone could tell that her smile was fake, finding herself back in the minivan just after one o'clock.

She set her purse on the passenger seat and closed her eyes, trying not to think of how much she hated campaigning.

Her phone rang.

It was from the 360 area code—north of Seattle. Maybe one of her friends from undergrad. But probably not. Probably, instead, a homicide detective from Bellingham.

She had been waiting for—and dreading—this phone call for weeks.

She cleared her throat before answering.

"This is Fenway Stevenson."

CHAPTER SIX

"MISS STEVENSON, HELLO," SAID THE VOICE ON THE OTHER END. The voice was buttery smooth and quite deep. Fenway thought he could have sung bass in a choir. Or love songs, all the girls throwing themselves on stage.

"Good morning," Fenway said. "To whom am I speaking?"

"This is Detective Deshawn Ridley with the Bellingham Police Department, MCU."

"MCU?"

"Sorry, the Major Crimes Unit."

"Ah, I see."

There was a pause. "You don't sound surprised to hear from me."

Fenway hesitated. She was wondering how to respond to this. She had rehearsed what she'd say once they told her Professor Solomon Delacroix was dead. But she'd forgotten to rehearse the part up to this.

"No," she said. "I'm the county coroner, and I get calls from other cities' police departments all the time, sometimes out of state."

"I see," said Detective Ridley. He waited for her to continue, but Fenway was familiar with this technique—waiting for the interviewee to speak first. He wanted to see if she'd offer anything on her Russian Lit professor. The silence stretched out for fifteen, twenty, thirty seconds.

Fenway tapped her fingers on the steering wheel. In the end, it was Fenway who spoke first. "Did you call for a particular reason, Detective? I'm investigating a murder here, and I'm on my way to see if some evidence has been processed."

He cleared his throat. "Yes, of course. This won't take long. I don't know if you saw this, but Professor Solomon Delacroix passed away at the end of July. I believe he was one of your professors at Western."

"He was," Fenway said. "Before I transferred to the BSN program. I saw the article online a couple of months ago."

"You had a German lit class of his, didn't you?"

"I believe it was Russian," Fenway said. The minivan was getting warm inside, and she started the engine and turned on the air conditioning.

"Originally, the police thought his death was accidental. But we uncovered evidence that suggests he was murdered."

"If you're looking for some insight into the forensics of the case," Fenway said, "I'm afraid I'd have to recuse myself. A conflict of interest."

"No, that's not it," said the detective. "We've discovered he's been misbehaving with students. With many students."

"Ah," said Fenway.

"Yes." He paused again—an uncomfortably long pause. Just as Fenway was about to ask if he was still there, he cleared his throat. "And I hate to bring this up, but in the course of our investigation, we discovered *you* are one of the students he's misbehaved with in the past."

"Yes," Fenway said. "Although saying he *misbehaved* inaccurately categorizes what he did. He raped me, Detective. Once, in his office. I stuck it out in his class, I got an A, and then I changed majors."

"I apologize for my choice of words. Some people prefer more delicate terms."

"No need to apologize, Detective. I certainly understand the need for discretion in front of rape victims." She could hear him shift uncomfortably.

"Let me get to the reason for my call, Miss Stevenson."

"By all means."

"You live in California, yet your car was in the long-term lot at Seattle-Tacoma International Airport, and was driven out of the lot the day before Professor Delacroix was murdered."

Silence again. Fenway figured the detective wanted her to say something, to respond to a question that hadn't been asked. This time the silence stretched on until Fenway was sure he knew they were both playing a game.

"Are you still on the line, Detective?"

"Yes, ma'am."

Another fifteen or twenty seconds of silence.

Fenway sighed. "Detective, you said you've called me for a reason, but you haven't asked me anything. You tell me a fact, and then you're quiet for a long time. Do you need more time to organize your notes? Perhaps we can schedule some—"

"No, Miss Stevenson," Detective Ridley said. "I thought I'd give you an opportunity to explain yourself."

"Explain myself?"

"Yes. Why was your car driven out of the Sea-Tac long-term lot the day before your professor was murdered?"

"Detective, I'm sure you're quite good at your job."

"What does that—"

"Which means you've undoubtedly done your research. You have probably found out I was on a flight from Seattle to Estancia on Coastal Airways the previous Saturday. I haven't been found on any flight back to Seattle, because I haven't *been* back to Seattle. You may have found out I was in the middle of investigating the murder our town's mayor. If you found that out, you probably also discovered I was in the hospital several hours after the professor was killed. How am I doing so far?"

The detective was quiet for a beat, then said, "You're batting a thousand."

"In that case, it sounds to me like you've established facts where you can be reasonably confident I wasn't in the state when the professor was killed."

"Okay," the detective said. "But this parking thing doesn't make any sense to me. And fine, fine, I'll go ahead and ask the question. How did your car get out of the long-term lot?"

"I'll be happy to answer that, and I'll even give you a little background."

"Aren't I lucky."

Fenway ignored the snide comment; she hadn't made this easy on him. "I'd driven up to Seattle to get a few things out of storage, but I was called back by work because of the mayor's death. I had to fly back down, last minute, and I left my car in the lot. My father has a private plane, and he told me he flew one of his employees up there to drive the car back down."

"What's the employee's name?"

"I'm sorry, my father didn't tell me."

"Can you tell me where you were on Tuesday, the twenty-seventh of July?"

"If I remember right, I started quite early with the investigation that day, around five A.M.," Fenway said. "I interrogated a suspect who was being held in connection with another crime, and then, if memory serves, later that morning we found a second murder victim. It should be pretty easy to track my whereabouts all day—all week, as a matter of fact."

"That's the day your car left the long-term lot."

"If you say so. Like I said, one of my father's employees drove the car back for me."

Detective Ridley sighed. "Okay, thank you for your answers, Miss Stevenson. I'll let you get back to your own murder investigation now."

Fenway said her goodbyes and hung up, but she didn't think she had heard the last from Detective Deshawn Ridley.

She hadn't brought it up with her father yet, mostly because she was worried about what would be revealed. He had sent his private jet up to Seattle the morning after he had found out what the Russian Lit professor had done to her. At least one of his employees was on her father's plane, driving her Honda Accord out of the long-term lot and driving it back to Estancia.

But.

Fenway would like to say her father would never send one of his employees—or contractors—to kill someone. But her father was a ruthless businessman and had almost no interpersonal skills. Well, none with her, anyway. So Fenway didn't know.

And she didn't *want* to know.

She put the van in gear and drove to the station.

The air was cool, but the sun was warm. As she turned into the parking garage, Fenway wondered if she had been polite enough with Millicent Tate and then tried to banish the whole thing from her mind. She went up the ramp, and slowly drove straight into the first open space on the second floor—the minivan was much wider than her Accord.

As she walked to the office, she looked at her phone. It was a quarter after one—maybe Rachel was still in the communications office and could get lunch with her. But she hadn't been to *her* office yet. She should at least get to her email and see if any of the evidence had been processed. Although the forty-five-minute drive to the lab would have delayed it. She thought about Dos Milagros and the carnitas taco with lime and guacamole she had ordered three times in the last week already and her mouth started to water.

But the sheriff was waiting for her as soon as she walked in.

"Fenway," he said, "great, you're finally here."

"Finally?" she said. "I've been at—"

He waved his hand. "No, no, that's not what I was getting at. The Kapp family is already on their way to San Miguelito to identify the body. If you hadn't gotten here in the next five minutes, I was going to leave without you. Come on, let's get going."

"Do we have time for lunch? I'm starving."

"After," McVie said. "They'll be waiting for us as it is."

"Can't Dr. Yasuda or Kav do the identification with them?"

"I want to see the wife's reaction. And I want to ask her about drugs. We don't know yet if that was cocaine in the bathroom, but I want to know if Jeremy Kapp had a drug problem."

"That makes sense. Okay. Let's go."

"Can you drive?"

Fenway hesitated. "Um, I don't have my car right now."

"Seriously? What happened *this* time?"

"Vandalism," Fenway said simply. "It'll be fixed this evening."

"Vandalism? Somebody broke your window or something? Did they steal anything?"

"No, nothing like that," Fenway said evasively. "Let's take your car."

"Okay, remember to file a police report when you get back."

"Sure," Fenway said, although she had no intention to.

Fenway wanted to complain they weren't stopping for lunch, but didn't want to seem insensitive to the Kapps' tragedy. And she didn't much like herself for even thinking about complaining. But still, her stomach rumbled loudly in displeasure.

"Was that your stomach?" McVie said. "I heard it over the engine."

"I haven't had lunch yet."

"Maybe after the identification I can take you to that Indian place in San Mig you've told me about. The one Kav is always saying we should try."

"Oh, damn, Craig," she said. "You're ready to try something besides white-people Indian food?"

McVie laughed. "Hey, I like spicy."

Fenway chuckled. He had no idea what he was in for.

"If we go to Swaadisht for lunch today, I don't know if you're going to be fully recovered by Wednesday to take me to that steak place."

"If we go *where*?"

"Swaadisht."

"*Dished* with an E-D?"

"No, with a T. It means *sets fire to the white man's mouth* in Hindi."

"Now don't you worry about me, little lady," McVie drawled, tipping an imaginary cowboy hat as he drove. "I reckon I know a thing or two about tamin' them Indian foods."

Fenway smirked and rolled her eyes.

They arrived in San Miguelito at the medical examiner's office and pulled in next to a Jaguar SUV with a license plate that said LANDSCPE. McVie held the door to the entry open for Fenway, and in the anteroom, sitting on the brown plastic chairs, were three people, a woman who looked to be in her early thirties, with two teenagers, all Caucasian, dressed in casual but expensive-looking clothes.

The woman's long, straight hair was a light brown carefully streaked with different shades of blonde highlights. She wore a pair of Cartier sunglasses with a large trapezoidal bridge above the nose. Her olive cashmere sweater had a v-neck, revealing a chunky gold chain necklace, and her fitted skinny jeans ended two inches above her ankles. Her arms were folded and the parts of her face that weren't hidden by the sunglasses were impassive.

The two teenagers, a boy and girl, were sitting on the other side of the room from the woman, separated from each other by a single chair.

The tall, lanky boy folded into himself, making his frame appear much smaller; Fenway, knowing the secrets of tall people, recognized the defensive posture. He bit his fingernails. He had pale skin and a handsome face, but a swath of angry acne made a magenta brushstroke across his forehead.

The girl talked on her phone in a low voice. She appeared both bored and irritated, as if her father's death inconvenienced her. She didn't even seem happy to get out of school for the day. She had the same style of hair as the woman, although it was a few inches shorter. Fenway wondered if one of them had copied the other on purpose—and if so, which one it was.

They looked up when McVie entered the room. "I'm so sorry to keep you waiting, folks," he said. "I know this is a difficult time, and we'd like to make this as straightforward and simple as we can."

The woman nodded. The boy was paying close attention. The girl ended her call.

"I'm Sheriff Craig McVie," he said. "I wish we were meeting under happier circumstances. And this is our county coroner, Fenway Stevenson."

"Did you say Fenway?" the boy said. "Like the baseball stadium?"

"Ugh, stop with the Red Sox stuff already," the girl said. "I swear, every time you open your mouth you have to prove you're the biggest Boston fan in the state."

"Shut up, Blair."

"These," the woman interrupted, "are my children, Donovan and Blair. And I," she turned toward McVie and offered her hand, "am Cricket Kapp."

Fenway looked closer, and saw the woman's face revealed the telltale signs of expensive, high-quality plastic surgery, probably putting her in her late forties, not early thirties; her smooth tanned skin, her perfect nose, and her high cheekbones were almost certainly fake. Fenway looked at the girl; while pretty, she had a nose on the larger side and didn't have her mother's prominent cheekbones. The girl's skin was as tan as her mother's.

"Mrs. Kapp," McVie said. "If you'll come with me, we can get this over with and you can get back to your family and start making whatever arrangements you need to."

Cricket Kapp went through the double doors with McVie. Fenway started to follow but McVie shook his head, almost imperceptibly, and Fenway stood, somewhat stunned, in the anteroom with the two teenagers.

Did McVie expect her to make some sort of small talk with the kids? She'd thought she was going to get to read Cricket's face when she talked about her dead husband. Would she play-act, like she didn't expect the bullet in his head? Or would it be a genuine response?

One thing for sure, however: Cricket wasn't Mrs. Potemkin. The description from Lydia Hernandez wasn't like Cricket at all. But that didn't mean she wasn't the killer.

She looked around at the two teenagers. Donovan unfolded himself on the chair, like an origami bird being pulled in two directions, and then heaved his lanky frame out of the chair into a standing position. His tee shirt, emblazoned with a photo of pop star Abby Herrick holding a microphone and singing, caught her eye.

"Abby Herrick, huh?"

"I know," said Donovan. "She's such an idiot."

"What? Who?" Fenway thought Donovan was talking about his mother.

"Uh, Abby Herrick. Isn't that who you just said?"

"Right," Fenway said. "You're wearing her shirt because you hate her?"

Donovan shook his head, like Fenway was too old to get it.

"Okay," Fenway said under her breath.

She looked straight ahead, practically counting the seconds until McVie and Cricket Kapp would return. She looked at the teenagers out of the corner of her eye, and Blair was staring at her.

She turned her head.

At one point in her life, she might have smiled to try to get her to open up or to be more friendly. She wasn't thinking about being nice today.

"You're the coroner," Blair said.

"Yes."

"And you've got a dumb baseball stadium name."

Fenway hoped her annoyance didn't show. "Fenway. Yes."

Blair paused, thinking. Then she snapped her fingers. "Oh, I got it. I saw your picture at dinner the other night."

"God, shut up, Blair," Donovan said. "No one wants to hear you."

Blair shot Donovan a look and kept talking. "We all went over to dinner at Mr. Ferris's house. Dad was redoing their garden walk and they had to, I don't know, choose some sort of rocks."

"Oh yeah? I go there for dinner sometimes too."

"Why does he have pictures of you around?"

"Probably because I'm his daughter."

Blair scrunched up her nose. "Were you adopted?"

Fenway cleared her throat. "No. My mom was black."

"Oh. So Mrs. Ferris isn't your mom."

Fenway snorted. "Hell, no. She's barely older than me. My father got remarried."

Blair narrowed her eyes. "So how come *you're* not rich?"

"How do you know I'm not?"

A self-satisfied smile touched the corners of Blair's mouth. "Please. With that dress?"

Fenway set her mouth in a tight line.

Blair sat back in her seat and continued to text on her phone. Donovan, still sitting straight up, leaned back in his seat, then took out his phone too.

Fenway wondered if she had been that irritating when she was a teenager. She suspected her mom would have seen to it to modify her behavior.

They sat in silence for another few minutes.

The door opened and McVie entered the room, followed by an angry Cricket Kapp.

"This is an *outrage*," she said, melodrama dripping from her voice. "I can't believe what we've been put through. I can't believe I'm going to have to drive from this shitty little rinkydink town back to Birdland. It's insulting."

"I'm sorry for your loss," McVie said.

Cricket Kapp's lips raised into a sneer. "We moved to the coast because it was supposed to be relaxing and laid-back." She scoffed. "And Jer puts his heart and soul into that stupid landscape business and you all can't even keep him *safe*? Come on, kids, let's get moving."

"I do appreciate you driving all this way to identify the body, Mrs. Kapp. You've been very helpful."

"I *hope* you appreciate it, after the hell I've been through in the last few days. Your deputy in the Paso Querido office wouldn't even take the missing persons report!"

"Again, Mrs. Kapp, I apologize for what you've been through." He pulled his notebook out. "In fact, let me take down the information about that phone call. I'll make sure whoever took your call gets disciplined. I'm embarrassed by how we've treated you."

Cricket Kapp's eyes got bigger, as if she hadn't expected McVie to take her seriously. "Really?"

"Of course," McVie said, a soothing tone in his voice.

"Thank God someone still knows how to treat people," Cricket said, batting her eyes at McVie. "But I'm sorry to say I didn't get his name."

"That's okay. Just tell me when you made the call. There are only a couple of people on shift. I'm sure we can narrow it down."

"Um," Cricket Kapp said, "I know I was upset, but I don't want to get anyone into trouble."

"It would still be good to know. We might have been able to prevent this. When did you make the call?"

Cricket Kapp stammered. "I suppose it was last night. Probably around midnight. When Jer didn't come home—for the third night in a row."

"So you were on the phone with the police at midnight. What did you do after our deputies wouldn't take the report?"

"I went to bed."

"You were pretty upset, though, right?"

"I, uh," Cricket said nervously.

"What is it?"

She cleared her throat. "It's *possible* I may have been drinking. Just a little. I may have been a little, how should I say this, upset Jer wasn't home."

"Did you suspect anything?"

Cricket Kapp, thrown off her game, tried to recenter herself. She smiled, a thousand-watt, trophy-wife smile. "Suspect anything? Like what?"

"Oh, come on, Mom," Blair said. "They're cops. They're going to find out about Dad and all the women he whored around with. Don't play dumb."

A brief pall of indecision came over Cricket's face. "Okay, fine," she said, dropping the façade. "Jer cheated on me."

"Would you like to come back to a room where we can talk more privately?"

"What?" Cricket asked. "So you can interrogate me?"

"Mrs. Kapp, if you talked on the phone with one of our deputies at midnight, that pretty much clears you. That's the time of death. So all we have to do is get the phone records. There's no need to interrogate you. But if you know anything about his, uh, dalliances, it'll give us more leads to go on."

Cricket turned beet red. "Okay, fine, I'm sorry," she said, throwing her hands up in the air dramatically. "I didn't call in a missing persons report."

"You didn't?"

"No." And she started to cry, though Fenway noticed her eyes stayed dry. "I'm upset. I know he was sleeping around, but I loved him. I don't know what I'm going to do now."

"Stop it, Mom," Donovan snapped. "They don't care about that. They want to know if you have an alibi."

Cricket's head jerked around. "An alibi?"

"If you don't tell them, I will," Donovan said, standing up. He looked at McVie. "My mom's dealer came over to sell her some pills."

"Donovan!"

He gave his mother an exasperated look. "Mom, they're not going to arrest you for buying some Oxy when Dad just got shot."

"I've never done—"

"Sheriff, the dealer came over at about eleven-thirty. My mom answered the door, and I heard two voices in the living room, including hers, for about two hours."

"Two hours?"

"Sure. I kind of think the dealer's got a thing for her."

Cricket had turned pale, like she wanted the floor to swallow her up.

"Oh, don't be so bashful about it, Mom. Dad rubbed everyone's nose in his cheating; you could have gotten him back with that guy."

Her face red with embarrassment, Cricket firmly said, "That's enough, Donovan."

Blair looked sideways her brother. "And how do you even know? You didn't go to the midnight movie?"

Donovan shook his head. "Nope. I was home by eleven."

"I didn't hear you come in."

"You don't hear anything when you're texting with Jasper." Donovan spat the name out sardonically.

"Shut up, turd."

"All right," McVie interrupted loudly. He turned to Cricket. "Donovan's right. I'm much more concerned with finding your husband's killer than with your Oxycontin. Does your, uh, *visitor* have a name?"

"Um," Cricket said, torn. Then, in a small voice, "I just know him as Zoso."

"Zoso?"

"I know him," Fenway put in. "I can see if he remembers."

"Did Mr. Kapp own any firearms?"

"Not really," Cricket said. "He had started to collect some antique weapons. Didn't have anything yet. An old revolver like you see in Westerns. A little fencing sword. Used in some famous movie, I think."

"All right," McVie said. "Offer's still good if you want to talk to me about anything in private."

Cricket paused, then shrugged. "Okay," she said.

McVie nodded, and stepped back to the door to open it. Cricket went through first, and McVie shot Fenway a look before going through himself.

"Ugh," Blair said. She went back to her phone, head down, both thumbs moving like lightning.

Fenway leaned against the wall and looked at Donovan. He sat back down in his chair and kept playing the game on his phone. The waiting area was silent for a few minutes, and Fenway got up and began to pace. There were no magazines or plants, only a few clusters of uncomfortable chairs.

Fenway sat down, away from both of them, and cleared her throat. "Doesn't sound like you two were close to your dad."

Donovan glared at her. "Doesn't sound like you're close with *your* dad, either."

Fenway nodded. "Sure, fair enough."

"What?" Donovan said. "You think it's weird none of us are sobbing, crying, oh, Daddy's dead, poor us?"

Fenway shrugged. "A little, I guess. People usually do. But I was a nurse before this. It's not unusual. People react to death in all kinds of different ways."

"You were a nurse, huh?"

"Yep."

"You seen people die?"

Fenway thought first of her mother in the cancer ward. Then the motorcyclist. Then the woman with the aneurysm. And the murderer whom she had killed defending herself at the house in the mountains three months before. "Yeah," she said carefully, "I've seen people die."

"So they probably taught you all about the five stages of grief."

Fenway nodded. "Of course. One of the basics." Denial, anger, bargaining, depression, acceptance.

"Yeah," Donovan said, "well, *my* first stage of grief is playing video games. And Blair's is texting her boyfriend."

"Jasper's a freshman at USC," Blair offered. "Pre-law. He's brilliant."

"All right," Fenway said.

Donovan stared at her, challenging her to say anything else, for about thirty seconds. She took the bait.

"So, do either of you know anyone your dad was seeing on the side?"

Blair scoffed. "That's rude."

Donovan kept staring at Fenway. "And you should talk."

Fenway cocked her head to the side. "What do you mean?"

"Everybody knows my father liked to bang his rich clients' wives." A slow smile spread across Donovan's face. "And your dad is the richest client he's got."

CHAPTER SEVEN

———◆———

MCVIE AND FENWAY WERE HALFWAY THROUGH THEIR *BAINGAN bharta* when she brought it up.

"So, Craig," she began.

"I know, I know," McVie said. "I shouldn't have left you out there with the two kids. But I had to get the information somehow. She didn't want to talk in front of them."

"Plus," Fenway said, "I think she has a little crush on you."

McVie smiled. "I'm sure I don't know what you're talking about. And I'm sure I wouldn't use that knowledge to my advantage when trying to get information out of her." He paused, breathing through his mouth. "You sure this is medium?"

"Medium-spice."

"Medium-*spice*? Not *spicy*?"

Fenway shrugged and ate another bite, then took another piece of garlic naan, chewed and swallowed. "I don't make the rules," she said. "I just know it's *Swaadisht*."

"Okay, seriously, what does that mean? And don't tell me it means 'too hot for whitey.'"

Fenway laughed. "It means *delicious* in Hindi." She dipped the naan in mint chutney. "Did the sensitive and delicate Mrs. Kapp identify Charlotte as her husband's mistress?"

"No."

Fenway paused, waiting for him to continue. Instead, McVie took a long drink of his mango lassi.

Not wanting to wait any longer, she spoke. "Charlotte wasn't mentioned by name, or Mrs. Kapp denied it?"

McVie shook his head. "Not by name. After you told me about that earring, I thought for sure Cricket would identify her."

Fenway shook her head. "Doesn't matter. I heard her name."

"What do you mean, you heard it?"

"I mean Donovan told me his father was having an affair with Charlotte."

"What? How does he know?"

"He says he was at home one day cutting class, and his father and Charlotte showed up and thought they were alone, and had sex in their living room."

"He saw it all?"

Fenway shrugged. "He says he heard it."

"Do you believe him?"

"I don't have any reason not to," Fenway said. "But something feels weird. Maybe he didn't much care for me. Part of me thinks he was trying to get under my skin."

"That's a pretty ballsy accusation for Donovan to make if he just wanted to piss you off."

Fenway shrugged.

McVie looked up from his plate. "Maybe your gut is telling you he should be a suspect."

Fenway screwed up her face. "He was home. He saw his mother with Zoso."

"Zoso? Isn't he the painkiller pusher?"

"Yes."

"You know, just because he *said* he was home doesn't mean he was there. She was pretty out of it."

"That's true. Okay—I'll reach out to Zoso to see if he can confirm he was there with Mrs. Kapp. Maybe he saw the kids there too."

"Do any of them have an alibi?"

"They were all home. Donovan saw his mom and Zoso, and Blair says she was texting with her boyfriend all night."

"What about Blair? Do you believe her?"

"I believe she's capable of texting all night, if that's what you mean." Fenway was about to take another bite, then stopped short. "I'm afraid I'm going to have to stop working on the case. If my stepmother is involved with the victim, it's a huge conflict of interest." She put the bite in her mouth.

McVie nodded. "And I'm sure I'd have to recuse myself too. Remember that case a few years ago where the sheriff arrested his own brother-in-law? It looked like an open-and-shut case. But the defense attorney went on the offensive. Turned out the brother-in-law owed the sheriff and his wife about five thousand dollars. Made it seem like revenge right out of the gate. Hung jury."

Fenway swallowed. "I wouldn't want that to happen to us. No one would have to dig far to find out my stepmother and I don't get along."

McVie shook his head. "No, they'd find out your dad is bankrolling both of our campaigns. I think the judge would throw the case out before it even saw the light of day."

"See? I hate Charlotte so much I didn't even think of the campaign." Fenway took a drink of her mango lassi. "Who'd take over the case?"

"Dez," McVie said.

"Dez? But she reports to me."

"She wouldn't for the duration of the investigation." McVie tried to clear his throat but he coughed lightly instead. Perhaps the spices were a little too heavy for his first Indian food experience.

"Who would she report to? Not you. You've got a conflict too."

"Gretchen Donnelly."

"Oh, gotcha. And assigning her a high-profile case like this, right before the election, means your implied approval."

McVie laughed lightly. "Not that she needs it. There aren't any other serious contenders for sheriff."

"She's got big shoes to fill." Fenway paused. "Is Gretchen going to mind transferring from the P.Q. office?"

"If she gets elected, she'll certainly like the higher paycheck."

"And you're okay with everything?"

McVie paused. "I don't know. I like being sheriff. I wish I didn't have to give it up to run for mayor. But I can only run for one office at a time. I guess we'll see."

"When do we have to officially stop being on the case?" Fenway asked.

"Officially? We don't. There's no law or anything saying we can't investigate Charlotte, or your dad, or even *my* dad. But if we make an arrest, the defense will have a field day with it. I don't want to be responsible for unnecessary reasonable doubt."

Fenway murmured in agreement and took another bite of naan. She looked at McVie. He had beads of sweat on his forehead.

"We can order something else if this is too spicy," she said.

"Nonsense," McVie said.

Fenway caught the server's eye and he came over. "An order of *raita*, please," she said. "And another mango lassi."

McVie took a bit of the naan. "What's *raita*?"

"It's a yogurt sauce. Cuts the spice."

"I'm fine. You don't need to worry about me."

"The *tikka masala* is good here," Fenway said, "but the *baingan bharta* is the best I've ever had." She didn't want to start McVie slowly with a gringo dish like *tikka masala* or butter chicken. "You get used to the spice."

"We've already been gone from the office long enough," McVie said, "and besides, I'm getting full." He looked around the restaurant, with the white linen tablecloths and the shiny gold-plated and jewel-encrusted statues of Ganesh and Bodhisattva. "I thought for sure you were taking me to a buffet." He wiped his forehead with his sleeve.

Fenway smiled. "They don't do buffets here." She took her last bite, savoring it. The server came back with a large ramekin of raita. McVie looked at the raita gratefully, dipped his naan in it, and looked relieved when it hit his tongue.

Fenway insisted they order *galub jumun*; the syrup and dough relieved McVie even more than the *raita* and mango lassi had.

"Dammit, Fenway," he said as they walked out of the restaurant, "you *cannot* order medium-spice there again with me unless I've lost a bet."

Fenway laughed but felt a pang of remorse for going full-throttle.

"We can go back to the M.E.'s office before we hit the road," said McVie. "The gun had its serial number on it. That happens so rarely, I'm thinking about playing the lotto tonight."

"Yeah, I'd like to see if they've caught any prints yet. I know it's only been a couple of hours, but even if something preliminary points us in the right direction—and away from Charlotte—we might be able to get the case moved forward before we hand this off to someone else."

It was a short drive back to the M.E.'s office, and they headed down to the lab, where Kav was looking at the earring with a loupe.

"Hey, Kav," McVie said.

"Hi, Sheriff."

"We finally tried Swaadisht," said Fenway.

"Best Indian on the Central Coast. Hope you liked it."

McVie looked at Fenway out of the corner of his eye. "I don't know. I don't have Indian food often."

Kav looked a little surprised. "What did you order?"

"I don't know. I couldn't pronounce it."

Fenway shifted her weight uncomfortably. "Um, the *baingan bharta.*"

Kav looked at Fenway disapprovingly. "Oh, you're not serious. You couldn't ease him into it? You had to go with the spicy eggplant?"

"I love that dish," Fenway said defensively.

"It's like introducing someone to The Beatles and playing *Revolution Number Nine.*"

Fenway paused. "Isn't that one of their big hits?"

"No, no, you're thinking of regular old *Revolution.* The one I'm talking about is more than nine minutes of sound effects, traffic noises, and Yoko Ono screaming about getting naked."

"Oh," Fenway said. "You mean the track I always skip on *The White Album.*"

Kav nodded. "And you served *Revolution Number Nine* to the sheriff for lunch."

Fenway screwed up her mouth. "Sorry, Craig."

"It was an adventure," said McVie gruffly. "So the gun we recovered from the ocean. Have you run it through the computer yet?"

"Yes, a few minutes ago." Kav said. "First of all, the preliminary findings would suggest it's the murder weapon. One bullet spent out of the magazine. Caliber is consistent with the size of the wound, but obviously we won't know for sure until we retrieve the bullet from Mr. Kapp's, um, head."

McVie nodded.

Kav turned to his computer monitor, clicked on a few items, and read from the screen. "The gun is in the system. Registered to a Charlotte Ann Vosovic."

Fenway closed her eyes.

McVie shook his head, disappointed. "That's your stepmother's maiden name, isn't it?"

"Yes," Fenway said. "Yes, it is."

"And I guess this is where we have someone else take over the case."

The first part of the ride back to Estancia, McVie said nothing to Fenway. She searched his face, but he was lost in thought.

The last couple of months had been strange for both of them. After McVie asked her out—the day after officially filing the separation papers from Amy—the timing hadn't worked out. First, Fenway had made the excuse she needed her broken hand to heal a bit before they went on a date. Fenway had stayed home from work for a few days and binge-watched a few bad period dramas and time-travel shows. After a couple of weeks, McVie had asked her out for a Saturday night dinner and movie, then had to cancel as he had to attend his daughter's softball tournament in Fresno.

It was right about then when Barry Klein finally convinced fellow doctor and golfing buddy Richard Ivanovich to run against Fenway—and that's when Nathaniel Ferris had set his political machine in motion. He hired Millicent Tate to run Fenway's campaign, and hired an up-and-coming politico named Gene Dennett to run McVie's campaign. Overnight, their personal lives were sacrificed for phone banks, voter registration drives, precinct walking, meet-and-greets at the local restaurants—Fenway was even starting to get sick of Jack and Jill's—and dating seemed like an impossibility.

After the first week of the full-blown campaign, Millicent had told her the perils of dating in their situation. "You absolutely can't do it," she had said. "You and McVie are too high-profile, and his separation is too recent, for you two to start dating now."

"High-profile?" Fenway had protested. "This is a county with only half a million people. Literally no one cares about this coroner race except for my father—and maybe Barry Klein."

"I've seen the number of people who support you," Millicent said. "You're taking this far too lightly. The people of this county see you're not under your father's thumb like, well, the rest of the county is. They like that. Even if you *are* related to him. They see through his bullshit, and they're glad you call him on it. Dating your father's hand-picked candidate for mayor—a married man twice your age—would get everyone focusing on your relationship, not your candidacy."

Fenway wanted to say McVie *wasn't* twice her age, nor was he officially married any longer, but she knew Millicent had a point.

And the last two months on the outs with her father took its toll, even though he still bankrolled her campaign. The fight they had had—in the middle of the mayor's murder investigation, no less—had ended with Fenway saying some hurtful things to her father.

No, she corrected herself—they were *true* things. They were said in harsh way, perhaps, and the truth was difficult for her father to hear.

It probably also didn't help that the board of directors for Ferris Energy had started to call his judgment into question. Based on the two high-profile murders in the last year—and given how close Ferris was with the killers—the directors had doubts. First his director of security, then his handpicked coroner candidate.

Ferris had turned on the charm, battled through a couple of contentious board meetings—and had escaped, still CEO of the company, still president of the board. He had accepted a "censure"—but that was to appease Cynthia Schimmelhorn and a couple of the other board members who were the biggest doubters.

And Fenway strongly suspected *she* was one of the reasons Nathaniel Ferris was still atop his eponymous energy company—his support of her showed her how Ferris had a foot in the good guys' camp.

But this—his wife being a murder suspect—would be a different song and dance altogether. One murder was an anomaly; two was a coincidence.

Three was a pattern.

Fenway looked back over at McVie driving. With a start, she realized she still had to deal with her car, and Rory's minivan, and the whole unpleasant situation.

She shook her head. That's what her father would have called it—an *unpleasant situation*. She wanted to call it a *hate crime*. But she pictured Millicent Tate in her head—*I'm glad it's nothing serious*. And she closed her eyes.

When McVie finally spoke, Fenway startled awake. "You okay with me doing this?"

"What?"

"Sorry, were you asleep?"

"No. Maybe. Am I okay with you doing what?"

"Officially handing the case over to Dez," McVie said.

"Why wouldn't I be?"

McVie looked at her out of the corner of his eye. "Some people have a sense of ownership."

Fenway shrugged.

"And you know where the evidence is leading, right?"

"Well, it's Charlotte's earring, and Charlotte's gun, right? So Dez will probably need to pick up Charlotte for questioning."

"And if Charlotte doesn't have a good alibi, Dez may have to arrest her."

Fenway's eyes widened.

"What? Don't tell me you're surprised. You just mentioned the gun and the earring. We don't need any more to hand this over to the D.A. And if there's even a hint of gunshot residue on her hands or her clothing, Charlotte will be leaving in handcuffs."

"But it's all circumstantial evidence," Fenway said. "We haven't uncovered any witnesses yet."

"You uncovered Donovan Kapp saying his father and Charlotte had an affair."

Fenway looked down. She knew Charlotte was the lead suspect, yet she didn't like how the pieces fit together.

"Come on, Fenway, you know the chances are good that Charlotte was Mrs. Potemkin—*she* was the one in the hotel room."

"Villa," said Fenway automatically.

"Whatever. We should go back to Belvedere Terrace—I'm sorry, Dez should—and show Charlotte's picture to the front desk clerk."

Fenway was quiet.

"What is it?"

"Uh—it's just—look, I know I don't *like* Charlotte, but I can't believe she's a killer. She doesn't have the attention span for it."

"You don't have to believe it, Fenway." McVie leaned back in his seat. "You're not working the case anymore."

CHAPTER EIGHT

WHEN THEY ARRIVED IN ESTANCIA, FENWAY WENT BACK TO THE coroner's office. Dez hung up the phone as soon as she walked in.

"That was McVie," Dez said. "Looks like I'll be taking on the Kapp case."

Fenway nodded. "That's right. He told me you'll be reporting to Gretchen during the investigation."

Dez nodded. "Yeah, he said that too. I don't know her that well, but the officers in P.Q. seem to like her. He scheduled a conference call with her in half an hour. Said he wanted you on the handoff call too."

Fenway looked at the clock on her phone. "So I can walk you through the case—at least from my perspective. And you can talk to Melissa too. She found the gun."

Fenway walked into her office. Dez followed, holding her notebook, and Fenway shut the door behind them. Fenway took the chair on her side of the desk and Dez pulled up one of the guest chairs.

Fenway outlined everything she had discovered: the cocaine under the victim's nose, the earring in the planter, the evidence in the hotel room registered to the Potemkins.

"Potemkin?" Dez said.

"Yeah. I was thinking he was trying to be clever."

"Like Catherine the Great's lover?"

"Yes! That's exactly what I was thinking."

"So I'll keep my eyes peeled if one of his mistresses is named Catherine."

"Exactly. It's like you're reading my mind."

"You're not the only one who took nerdy lit classes in college," Dez said.

"And his wife—Cricket Kapp—she apparently knows Zoso."

"Zoso—isn't he the same guy you talked to about that designer drug a few months ago?"

"Yep."

Dez thought for a minute. "He knows Rachel's brother-in-law, right? What's his name? Peter?"

Fenway laughed. "Parker. Wrong half of Spider-Man."

"Okay. I'll see if I can get Zoso in here."

"Yeah, that's a good first step." Fenway tapped her fingers on the desk. "See if he can vouch for her alibi. Although her son was pretty clear she was there. Kind of embarrassed her. I don't think she realized her kids knew about her pills."

"So—uh, you know, you're not going to be able to tell me what I should or shouldn't do for this, right? You're off the case now. Just a handoff."

"Right. Of course. Sorry." Fenway sat back. "But, uh, Zoso doesn't trust the cops."

"He shouldn't. He's a drug dealer."

"Yeah, but he's a drug dealer who broke open a case for us," Fenway pointed out. "And he trusts me. He said he'd never come down to the station again—not if he wants to keep his distributor, which he does."

"Oh, terrific. A drug dealer with standards."

"Do you want to get good information from this guy or not?"

Dez pursed her lips. "How about I talk to him first? If it doesn't work out, we can see where we are in the investigation. Maybe we can get some sort of special dispensation to involve you."

"Yeah, if my involvement is limited to Zoso, we should be okay, right?"

Dez smiled. "I can't believe you thought you didn't want to be coroner."

Fenway tried not to return her smile, but had a hard time suppressing it. "Yeah. You were right. My *father* was right, which is even harder for me to say."

"Well, he has to be right if he agrees with me." Dez started to stand up. "Anything else?"

"Yep. The gun."

"Ah. The gun."

"Right. Melissa found it on the beach. She said it looked like it had been thrown in the ocean to try to get rid of it."

"Was the serial number still on it?"

"Yes."

"And it was your stepmother's gun."

"Right. Recently fired. One bullet out of the magazine."

"Which matches the bullet in Mr. Kapp's forehead?"

"Too soon to tell."

"Is there a connection between Charlotte and Kapp?"

Fenway nodded. "We think she might be Mrs. Potemkin."

"What makes you think that?"

"Apparently, Mr. Kapp had an affinity for sleeping with his clients' wives."

"Your father is one of his clients?"

"His biggest, apparently. At least according to his son."

Dez paused, shaking her head. "I hate to ask you this, Fenway, but what makes everyone think *Charlotte* did it, and not your father?"

Fenway's mouth dropped open. "I mean, that's crazy."

"Is it?" Dez looked at Fenway, right in the eyes.

"All of the evidence points to Charlotte."

"But if she had been sleeping with Jeremy Kapp, your father could have framed her out of revenge and planted all that evidence. He had access to her gun and her earring."

"My father can be an asshole, but he's no killer," said Fenway. But even as the words were leaving her mouth, she wasn't sure she believed it. She thought of Professor Solomon Delacroix, his dead body floating in the Squalicum Waterway in Bellingham.

"You've only been back for six months," Dez said, a gentle tone in her voice, but firm. "You don't know the man. Not really. He was gone from your life for twenty years."

Fenway turned this over in her head, thinking of the Bellingham MCU detective's conversation with her earlier.

She didn't want to think about her father's involvement in her professor's death, but if he were involved, he would have told someone else to pull the trigger. Or bash the head, or hold the face underwater, or whatever. Fenway didn't think her father, he of the pheasant entrées and the private jet and the fancy Mercedes, could be the one to pull the trigger himself.

And maybe it wasn't Nathaniel Ferris trading in Charlotte for a newer model. Maybe it was Charlotte. Fenway remembered the awkward dinner they had had a few months before, and how bored Charlotte looked. Maybe she had jumped at the chance to have an exciting affair with a landscape architect, someone with whom she could spend a few days when Ferris was out of town on business.

Fenway felt a pang of jealousy. Charlotte would never have to worry about paying off credit card debt or a hundred thousand dollars in student loans. Charlotte ate fancy food prepared by her personal chef every night. And still she was bored and unhappy.

The realization hit Fenway suddenly: perhaps Charlotte was looking for the same thing she was, namely time and attention from Nathaniel Ferris. But, she knew, Ferris was physically and mentally incapable of treating any situation as though it weren't a monetary transaction. She was angry at Charlotte for—for what, exactly? For taking her father away? He had already been gone for a decade when he married Charlotte.

Perhaps Nathaniel Ferris was as incapable of loving his wife as he was of loving his daughter.

And maybe that's why Joanne Stevenson Ferris had packed up his daughter one day while he was at work and had driven to Seattle.

"Fenway?"

She shook her head and snapped back to the present. "I'm sorry, Dez—I, uh, I went somewhere else for a minute there."

"You sure did. I didn't mean to give you an aneurysm when I suggested your daddy might have had something to do with this. I mean, if our victim *was* having an affair with your step-mother—"

"Can you not call her that?"

Dez furrowed her brow. "Uh—sure. What do you want me to call her? Charlotte?"

Fenway nodded.

"Anyway—we have to look at your father too. When there's a murder with a cheating spouse, you know we have to look at both the cheater and the cheat-ee."

"I know."

Dez looked at Fenway, a serious look on her face, but a smile at the corners of her mouth. "I know you know."

Fenway closed her eyes. She didn't get along with her father. She had never gotten along with Charlotte. Yet she didn't want them to have to go through this. She didn't picture her father pulling the trigger. Truth be told, she didn't picture Charlotte pulling the trigger, either.

Although guns were funny things. Fenway never thought

she'd have one, but she'd been put in danger several times in the last six months, and had finally given in and taken firearms training. The thought had even crossed her mind of buying a handgun.

Fenway stood up. "Let's go over to McVie's office," she said. "We can take the conference call from there."

"We've got ten minutes—and we can take the call from your desk."

"But then we wouldn't be able to stop at Java Jim's on the way."

"Oh, I see. An ulterior motive."

"Guilty as charged," Fenway said. "Come on, I'm buying."

Fenway sat in McVie's office with her half-full latte, not paying attention to Gretchen Donnelly's voice on the other end of the line. Fenway had laid everything out for Donnelly, and stared at a point on the far wall, thinking about both what McVie might wear on their first real date, and what she would order at the Argentine steak house.

Fenway's phone rang. She looked down at her purse on the floor and pulled it out. It was Millicent.

"I've got to take this," she said, meeting McVie's eyes. "Campaign."

She accepted the call, but walked out of the room, closing the door, before bringing it to her ear.

"Hey, Millicent."

"Hi, Fenway. Your car's done. Rory's driving it back to the parking garage now. Can you meet him and switch cars?"

"That was quick."

"They got to it while the paint was still fresh."

"Let me pay Rory's dad."

"I already tried. He won't take it."

"Okay, fine. I'll be in the parking garage in about five minutes."

Millicent hung up without saying goodbye; Fenway had gotten used to it.

Fenway went back into McVie's office just as Dez stood up to leave. "Hey. Got everything you need?"

Dez nodded. "I'm going to take a uniform over to talk to your—to Charlotte."

"Oh."

"Thanks for the rundown, rookie," said Dez, stepping past Fenway into the hall. "Very helpful."

"Sure." Fenway nodded and picked up her purse. "You need me for anything else, Sheriff?"

McVie looked up. "What? Oh. No, Fenway. I don't need to keep you here any longer."

Fenway stood for a moment. Something in McVie's voice didn't sit right with her.

"Except—" McVie started.

He lapsed back into thoughtful silence.

"What?" Fenway asked.

"Well—the name *Charlotte* doesn't sound anything like *Catherine*, does it?"

Fenway shifted her weight from foot to foot. "No." She looked at the floor. "But maybe that's another inside joke."

"Wasn't Catherine the Great—there were some, uh, rumors about her, right?"

"Like having sex with the horse? That's what you mean?"

McVie chuckled. "I wasn't going to come out and say it, but yes. Maybe she's got a horse or something. Maybe *that's* the inside joke with them."

"I suppose."

"Does Charlotte own a horse?"

"Of course she does. One of the first things my dad bought her when they were dating. A Camarillo White mare."

McVie screwed up his mouth. "It'd fit a little better if it was a stallion, don't you think?"

"Maybe Jeremy Kapp isn't as clever as you'd like to think."

"Right. Maybe. Maybe the joke doesn't make any sense at all."

Fenway thought for a moment. "You told me that Mrs. Kapp didn't name Charlotte as one of her husband's mistresses. Did she name anyone?"

McVie shook his head. "She knew he was cheating. She suspected a couple of women but didn't know their names. Apparently, he was discreet."

Fenway clicked her tongue. "Not around his kids."

McVie shrugged. "Kids are a lot more intuitive than grownups give them credit for."

Fenway thought about McVie's daughter, and how she knew Amy was having an affair, in spite of her attempts to cover it up—rather poor attempts, Fenway thought, but still. McVie had gotten the faraway look in his eye again, and, she suspected, was thinking about his imploding family life.

Dr. Klein hadn't yet dragged the sheriff's divorce proceedings through the public eye, which honestly surprised Fenway. Klein could have easily gotten under the sheriff's skin with a pointed remark or two. As much as Fenway liked McVie, he could react a bit irrationally, especially right at first. If Fenway were running Klein's campaign, she would have at least gotten Klein to subtly hint at family values, playing up his stable marriage. Fenway shuddered at the thought of what Millicent Tate could do with a tidbit like the sheriff's impending divorce hanging tantalizingly in front of her.

"Okay," she said, "I'll be back in a few minutes."

She walked out of the coroner's suite, this time leaving the door open, and out the front doors of the building.

The autumn sunshine was dappling the ground. Estancia was too temperate for the leaves to turn, and the Halloween decorations had efficiently disappeared in front of the City Hall building across the street. Fenway had gotten Halloween candy, but had no trick-or-treaters in her apartment complex. She'd heard of well-organized parents in complexes like hers who herded their broods around, checking for allergens and razor blades, before divvying up the candy, Solomon-like, amongst the children, from the obnoxious teens demanding more candy to the shy toddlers who could barely squeak out the request. But not in her complex.

She arrived at the parking garage before she realized it, and saw Rory idling in her car, parked in the fire zone in front of the parking garage. The paint was pristine; it looked as good as new, freshly waxed and detailed.

"Oh, you've got to be kidding me, Rory."

"What?"

"Your father did *not* have to detail the car."

"It's part of the whole thing. The wax helps get the paint off. It'd look weird otherwise."

Fenway paused. "Please tell him I appreciate it."

"I will."

Fenway fished the minivan key out of her purse and handed it to Rory. "Thanks again. I'll tell Millicent you did good work."

Rory smiled. "You're welcome, Miss Stevenson. Any time."

Fenway pointed into the garage. "The van's parked at the top of this incline, on the second floor there. See it on the right?"

Rory nodded. "Yep. I'll get it back to my dad pronto."

He took off at a run into the parking garage. Fenway watched him go, a gangly teenager getting involved in local politics and not complaining about the worst kind of crappy work, driving all around town to get the candidate's car cleaned off. She'd definitely have to tell Millicent what a good job he had done.

She turned her back on the parking garage and walked toward her car. She hit the unlock button on her key.

The world ended.

CHAPTER NINE

SHE COULD FEEL MOVEMENT, BUT SHE DIDN'T KNOW WHICH WAY was up.

It felt like an hour.

Fenway opened her eyes.

She saw the tire of her Accord in front of her. And the dark pavement underneath the car.

She lay on her side—her left side, sore from breaking her hand three months before, her arm scraped and bleeding, her dress torn at the shoulder. Her arm hurt.

A hum filled her ears, quickly replaced with a ringing sound.

She coughed. She saw a thin layer of white dust on her car.

She pulled herself up to a kneeling position. People were streaming out of both City Hall and the sheriff's office, running toward the parking garage.

The ringing was so bad she couldn't hear what was going on. Her ears felt plugged up, like she had a sinus infection.

She saw the officer from the front desk—she couldn't remember his name—run toward her, his mouth working furiously. She couldn't hear his words. She gingerly stood up.

She turned around and looked up at the mouth of the parking garage, the first-floor ramp emptying onto the second floor, where she had parked Rory's father's minivan. Several cars were damaged, their windows blown out. A car was on its side, on fire. The shell of the minivan, the windows broken and the doors blown off, was still on fire.

Rory.

All around her, chaos. A fire truck materialized and parked at the entrance of the garage, and a firefighter in head-to-toe yellow gear jumped down and turned a hose on two of the cars still burning, including the minivan.

McVie was there, talking to her, but all she could hear was the ringing in her ears. He was checking her, perhaps for broken bones, and suddenly he touched the side of her face, tenderly, looking right into her eyes, and she realized she was crying. How long had she been crying? How long had McVie seen her like this?

"I can't hear anything," Fenway tried to say, but it came out as hiccups and sobs, and she choked on her own phlegm. She couldn't even hear herself coughing.

He mouthed something, and she leaned on him, and they started to walk down the sidewalk in front of the parking garage. An ambulance, lights flashing, came around the corner quickly and braked hard, stopping at an angle to the curb. Fenway thought the sirens were probably blaring, too, though she could only hear the ringing.

An EMT jumped out of the back of the ambulance and the sheriff flagged him down, running to meet him. They were talking to each other as they walked back, and the EMT turned to Fenway and asked her a question she couldn't hear.

"I can't hear anything except ringing," Fenway managed to get out, though her voice sounded like it was underwater. "I think I'm okay otherwise. There was a boy who was driving the van. You need to see if he's hurt."

But as soon as the words were out of her mouth, she knew Rory had been killed by the explosion.

The EMT asked her a few questions, and she had to read his lips. It was Friday. She was in Estancia. She told him her address. She told him the year. He seemed satisfied.

She turned her head, and a twinge of pain made her grimace—a muscle had been aggravated or pulled—and looked McVie in the face. She recognized the look. Deep concern, yes, but more. It was the look he had when a witness was hiding something.

And Fenway hadn't been exactly forthcoming, had she? She hadn't told him about the spray paint.

She hadn't told him about her Russian Lit professor, either, but she didn't think it was any of his business. The ringing in her left ear started to subside and she started to hear, faintly, the sirens and the shouting.

"I have a lot of information you need to know," Fenway said.

McVie nodded. "After you get checked out," he said.

"I can handle it. My hearing is starting to come back. It's not that serious."

"You were in an explosion, Fenway," he said. "It *is* that serious."

"That's why I need to give you information as soon as I can," she said. "My ears will get better with time. There's nothing they can do to treat it." And even as she said it, the pressure lessened in her left ear. The right one was still ringing.

McVie folded his arms and considered for a moment. "Then you need to get to an interview room. You're a witness. I don't know if this was a terrorist attack or what."

"It was murder."

"Murder?"

Fenway nodded. "There was a teenaged boy in the minivan that blew up." She swallowed, hard, and her right ear depressurized a little; the ringing's volume cut in half. "I think they targeted *me*."

McVie looked incredulous. "What would you be doing in a minivan?"

Fenway cleared her throat. "My car was getting, uh, cleaned."

"Cleaned? You went to some sort of long-term car wash?"

"Uh—no." Fenway looked down. "There was graffiti on it."

"Your car got tagged?"

Fenway paused. "I don't want to talk about it out here. We can get to the interview room first."

McVie nodded. "Of course. We definitely shouldn't speak out in the open." He looked up at the parking garage, smoke still drifting off the second floor. He set his jaw, but there was a tired look in his eyes. "I've got to take care of some things first. I think we might get some other agencies involved here." He got on the radio. Fenway tried to hear what he was saying, but the tinnitus in her right ear made it hard to concentrate. She strained to hear him, tried to read his lips, but she couldn't make out what he was saying. And there were still sirens.

Fenway closed her eyes, but the ringing didn't go away. She put her head down and opened her eyes again and looked at the ground. The asphalt was black and rough and didn't even look windblown. Fenway didn't know what she expected to see; maybe something morbid, like Rory's shoe.

Soon Officer Celeste Sandoval appeared at McVie's side. "Fenway?"

Fenway looked up.

She offered Officer Sandoval a weak smile, but wasn't even sure if the sides of her mouth turned up at all. She was suddenly hit with a wave of exhaustion. The noise, the smoke, the commotion.

"Fenway?"

"I'm sorry, Officer Sandoval—what did you ask me?"

"I asked if you'd come with me to the station. We need to take your statement."

Fenway looked at her Accord. It had been freshly detailed not an hour before, but there was already a cloud of dust descending on the car. Not dust, Fenway thought with a shiver, but ashes from the minivan and from Rory.

"I can't keep my car here," she said.

Sandoval shook her head. "We're going to need to process it for evidence."

"I was the target, Celeste."

"Let's talk inside, Fenway." Sandoval turned to walk toward the station. Fenway walked a couple of steps behind her, slowly, deliberately, as if she were testing out all her limbs to make sure they worked, to make sure they were still there.

The footfalls on the street and then the sidewalk seemed to thump in Fenway's ears. She could feel the vibration of her foot hitting the ground all the way up to the top of her head, overpowering the sound of the sirens. Everything seemed to be going in slow motion: the steps they took around the small amphitheater, Sandoval's coughing as they approached the entrance. Then they were inside; the officers and workers shouting and trying to coordinate responses and the phones blaring their ringtones—it all seemed louder than it had been outside.

Sandoval led Fenway into the interview room. Fenway started to go to the side of the table nearest the one-way mirror, but Sandoval cleared her throat and shook her head, and Fenway went to the other side.

The side where suspects and witnesses sat.

Suspects and witnesses.

Her father and Charlotte.

Had Dez gone to pick them up yet? Had they been in the parking garage? If they had gone to see her father and Charlotte, then certainly Fenway would have heard about it—she'd have gotten a call, either panicked or angry from her father.

She pulled her phone out of her purse. Sure enough, the screen—miraculously not cracked or broken when she had been thrown against her car—showed two missed calls from Nathaniel Ferris.

She started to call her father back and then thought about the minivan blowing up in the parking lot.

Someone—maybe a group of someones—first graffitied her car. And then they blew up the car she was driving.

She looked at the phone in her hand and pulled the case off. She turned it over. There was no battery cover. She dug around in her purse for a paper clip.

Sandoval was looking at her with bemused interest.

Fenway found a metal paper clip, straightened part of it, then popped out her SIM card.

"You think someone's tracking you?" Sandoval said.

Fenway nodded. "A lot of weird stuff happened today."

"That wasn't your car that got blown up."

"But that's the car I drove today."

The color drained from Sandoval's face.

Someone must be following her. Fenway tried to remember who was in the complex's parking lot that morning. It had seemed strangely empty—but then, she was almost never in the parking lot in the middle of the day. Maybe it was always empty. She didn't know. But if someone had been watching her, they would have easily seen her get into the minivan, drive to work and into the parking garage, then leave the car and go into the building.

It raised a question in her mind: why not simply blow up the Accord when she was at her apartment? Surely that would have been the easiest way to kill her.

She looked up. Officer Sandoval was staring at her expectantly.

"I'm sorry, Celeste," Fenway said. "I'm, uh, I'm not all here."

"Blast shock," Sandoval said.

"I guess."

"Can I get you anything? Coffee? Anything from the vending machine, maybe?"

Fenway nodded. "Coffee would be good."

Sandoval looked at Fenway. "You okay in here a few minutes? I might have to make a fresh pot."

"No, don't do it if you need to make a new pot. I don't want—"

"Come on, Fenway, you've been in a, uh, traumatic situation. I don't mind."

"You don't—"

"I insist."

Fenway sat back and nodded. Truth be told, she'd rather have a latte from Java Jim's—although maybe they would have closed after the minivan exploded. Sandoval gave Fenway a thin-lipped smile and closed the door behind her.

Fenway got a look at herself in the one-way mirror. Officer Sandoval had said *blast shock,* and Fenway looked it. Her hair, usually in natural curls, was wild and frizzy, almost like a cartoon drawing of a character that gets its hand stuck in a light socket. Her face had a look she recognized as impassive pain—she had had a similar look when her mom told her she had been diagnosed with leukemia.

Fenway got a sensation like she was lifting up from her body, then looking down at herself, looking at the beige brick walls, the aluminum table, the light-skinned black woman sitting on the wrong side of the table, trying to catch her breath, trying to keep it together.

Maybe she should let that girl go. Maybe the girl at the table could cry and sob and bang and mourn for Rory. Because from up above the table, it looked manageable. It looked like she could look at the facts while the girl down there let everything out.

Fenway saw, from her virtual perch on the ceiling, the girl's shoulders start to shake. Fenway was glad she was up above the table and the girl was down there. The girl was getting overwhelmed with emotions and feelings, and she was breaking down. Good, Fenway thought. Dr. Tassajera would think it was good, too, she was sure of it. Can't push everything down, you'll snap.

So Fenway had time to think, floating there in the interview room.

Too many strange things had happened in the last forty-eight hours.

First, Lana contacting her about reopening the inquiry into her husband's death. Second, the dead landscape architect with a hole in his forehead. Third, the missing Mrs. Potemkin, almost certainly the mistress of the dead man—one of the many mistresses, if the widow could be believed. Fourth, the graffiti on her car. And fifth, the minivan blowing up, killing Rory—a kid with his whole future ahead of him.

Was it possible that all the strange things were somehow related?

Certainly Jeremy Kapp and his mysterious mistress were. Was there a common denominator in each one?

Fenway could only think of one: her father.

Lana's husband had been an employee of her father's oil company.

The dead landscape architect had been sleeping with her father's wife. And been killed by her gun.

And her father—no, there was no real connection to the graffiti or the minivan blowing up. Unless you counted Fenway as a connection too.

The door opened and Officer Sandoval came in bearing two coffees. She saw the tears running down Fenway's face and immediately set the coffees down and gave Fenway a hug.

And Fenway hugged her back, fiercely, no longer floating above herself, the grief for the dead teenager washing over her, the aches in her body turning up in volume, the sobs pulsing in her ears as the ringing subsided. It had been a long time since she had cried because she was scared.

But she *was* scared. Someone wanted to kill her.

"I'm going to drive you to the hospital," Officer Sandoval said. "I think you're in shock."

"No, I'll be okay," said Fenway, her sobs subsiding. "Just give me a minute."

"That wasn't a request," Sandoval said gently. "Let's go."

"You used to be a nurse, huh? They make the worst patients." The woman's nametag read "Geraldine Upton, R.N." She wore baby blue scrubs and bright white athletic shoes. She took Fenway's blood pressure. The nurse looked to be in her sixties, and her deep brown skin was several shades darker than Fenway's.

"I'm fine," Fenway insisted through the ringing in her ears. "I need to get back to work."

"You're proving me right. It's a little high. One-forty over eighty-five."

Fenway sighed. "Geraldine—can I call you Geraldine?"

"I go by Geri."

"Sorry. Geri. But I've treated blast victims before. And I don't have any signs of concussion. I didn't lose consciousness. I don't have any broken bones. I just have a bad ringing in my ears. And the car that blew up was the one I was supposed to be driving. I'm understandably a little wound up."

"You don't get off that easily, missy. I've treated blast victims too, you know, and the shockwave you experienced is nothing to ignore. You must know blast victims don't always know when they've been knocked out."

"But I do know the symptoms."

"So you won't mind if I ask you for your name."

Fenway sighed. "Fenway Stevenson."

"Address?"

"6448 Kenneth Avenue, apartment two-fourteen."

"Any headache?"

Fenway shook her head.

"How's your vision?"

"Clear. No issues."

"You've got a bump on your head. Does it hurt?"

"Where?"

"Right about there." Geraldine Upton ran her finger over a spot about an inch and a half above Fenway's hairline.

"Ouch. When you touch it. But not otherwise."

"Do you remember hitting your head?"

Fenway's lips twitched. "No."

The nurse sighed. "Then I strongly suggest you let us keep you for observation tonight."

"I'm in the middle of—" Fenway said. Then she realized the sheriff had taken her off the investigation.

"What are you in the middle of?"

"I was going to say an investigation. But the sheriff took me off it earlier today."

The nurse narrowed her eyes but tried to keep her tone conversational. "Did you forget?"

"No. Not exactly. I don't want to be taken off the case."

The nurse nodded and made a note on the paper on the clipboard.

"I didn't forget. I'm—uh—stubborn."

"I'm sure you are, Miss Stevenson." The nurse gave her a knowing smile.

"Oh—I am in the middle of a campaign, too."

"Stevenson for Coroner. I know. I got a lawn sign." She smiled. "Did you forget you were running for reelection?"

"No. I mean, not really." Fenway lowered her voice. "I love the job. I hate campaigning."

The nurse's smile got wider. "You're a horrible patient, Miss Stevenson, but I like you anyway."

"So you know I have work to do."

"And you know we need to keep you overnight."

Fenway knew she could refuse treatment and walk out—but then she remembered, two years before, back in Seattle, a man she had seen in the emergency room after a car accident. He had refused treatment. He had gone home and collapsed from internal bleeding. He had been rushed back to the hospital in an ambulance but died on the operating table.

And she was sure she forgot because she was just being stubborn.

But she didn't remember hitting her head.

So she nodded and thanked the nurse, and waited for the doctor to see her.

PART III

SATURDAY

CHAPTER TEN

Fenway itched to get out of the hospital, and the interminable waiting—for the doctor, for the first batch of questions, for the brain scan, for the second nurse with the blood draw, for the second doctor who tested her reflexes and looked at her bruises, especially her recently healed left hand—was excruciating. The doctors did a lot of grunting and tut-tutting.

She reluctantly agreed to overnight observation—the hospital lab was backed up, and brain scan results wouldn't be back until the early morning—and got situated in her shared room. She didn't realize how exhausted she was until she lay down, and even with the beeping of the machinery and the nurses coming in and out, she fell asleep quickly.

The nurses woke her up several times during the night. Each time, Fenway felt like she had just fallen asleep.

When morning finally arrived, Fenway's joints and muscles complained; she'd known, picking herself up after the explosion, that she was going to feel it later, and she did.

The first nurse who came in told her that the results from the brain scan were back, and after a half-hour wait that felt much longer, the doctor came in to discuss them. As expected—although Fenway had a moment of panic before the doctor read the results—everything came back normal.

"No concussion, no sign of any brain trauma," the doctor said, a little too jovially. "So we can get you out of here as soon as the paperwork clears. Should only take an hour or two."

After the doctor left and the nurses checked on her for what Fenway hoped was the last time, she dressed, taking care not to make the rip in the shoulder of her dress worse. She didn't dare put her SIM card back in or turn on her phone, so she sat on the hospital bed. She turned on the television—nothing worth watching on Saturday morning, so Fenway stared dead-eyed at the screen, thinking about who might be behind the bombing and coming up blank. Fenway started to wonder how crazy Millicent would be without a candidate for all the scheduled campaign events.

The door opened, and Fenway started to get up, but it wasn't a nurse with her release paperwork. Instead, Officer Sandoval entered, followed by Sheriff McVie, who was holding a cardboard tray with three Java Jim's coffee cups.

"Hey, Fenway," McVie said. Concern had set deeply in the lines of his face, and he looked like he hadn't slept well. "How are you feeling?"

"I'm sore," she said. "Feeling it today. But no concussion, so I can get out of here."

"That's great news." Sandoval sat on the chair next to the bed. "The getting-out-of-here part, not the pain part."

"I hope one of those coffees is for me," Fenway said, eyeing the cups.

"Sure is." McVie held out one of the cups. "Large latte."

"You remembered," Fenway said.

Fenway took the latte from McVie and sipped. Java Jim's tasted a hundred times better than the hospital coffee. It felt good going down and it calmed her a little.

"I can't stay long," said McVie. "I'm meeting with the FBI in about twenty minutes."

"The FBI?" asked Fenway.

"They've mentioned the T-word."

"T-word? Oh—terrorism."

"Right."

"And Officer Sandoval has some additional questions," McVie said awkwardly. "And I heard that she, uh, wasn't showing up with coffee, so, uh, I decided to tag along." He eyed the room; there was nowhere else to sit but on the bed itself. McVie remained standing.

Fenway felt self-conscious of the way she looked, in torn day-old clothes and no makeup, but she was touched that McVie obviously couldn't hide his concern for her. "I'm glad you came."

A long pause between them made Fenway feel anxious, and after taking a long drink of his coffee, McVie begged out of the room, repeating the information about the FBI meeting, and closing the door behind him.

"Do you want to talk about what happened?" Sandoval asked, after taking a drink of her own coffee.

"I guess."

There was silence between them for a minute.

"So, uh, Fenway," Sandoval began, nervously. "You said out there you thought you were the target."

Fenway nodded, started to speak, then hesitated.

"What is it?"

"I don't know if it's going to sound paranoid. Or crazy."

"I know you're not paranoid or crazy," Sandoval said. "So try me."

"Yesterday morning, about mid-morning, I went home to change. When I came back out to my car, some asshole had spray-painted *nigger* on it."

"Oh," Sandoval said, her eyes widening.

Fenway nodded.

"Did you report it to the police?"

Fenway scoffed. "No. Why bother?"

"Why bother? Because it's vandalism against a peace officer. And a hate crime."

Fenway shrugged. "Listen, I know *technically* I'm a peace officer, but I certainly don't do what you do."

"We still have your back. And you have ours."

"Sure," Fenway said. "But it's not like I'm out on the streets, patrolling, or knocking doors down or anything." She remembered seeing Dez swinging the battering ram, knocking the door down in the warehouse district two months before.

"So you didn't call the police."

"Honestly, I thought it was someone from Klein's campaign, or Ivanovich's office, trying to throw me off my game."

"But still."

"If I had reported it, I'm sure they would have found a way to make it about *them*. I'm bringing race into it, I'm accusing their campaign of thinking a black woman can't be coroner, and then I give a voice to everyone who *doesn't* think a black woman can be coroner. It's a lose-lose situation for me."

Celeste startled slightly. "Wait—you said your car was spray-painted yesterday morning? But I saw it before they towed it to the evidence yard. It's immaculate."

"Yeah. I called my campaign manager, and one of the volunteers—Rory, the kid who was killed—" and Fenway felt her voice start to break, but pushed the feelings aside "—had a father who owns an auto body shop. Rory had my car back to me by five o'clock."

"But it wasn't your car that blew up." Sandoval pulled out her notebook.

"But I borrowed Rory's dad's minivan that morning. Rory drove the minivan to my apartment and switched cars with me.

He drove my car to his dad's auto shop, and I drove the minivan to a campaign luncheon, and then to the parking garage."

"Did anyone see you drive it?"

"I don't know. I was only in my apartment for twenty minutes, tops. Whoever spray-painted my car could have still been there. Might have wanted to see my reaction, or admire their handiwork." Fenway thought for a moment. "Maybe someone at the teachers' luncheon, but I got there late. I don't remember anyone seeing me. And it was still going on when I left."

Sandoval nodded, scribbling in her notebook. "McVie ordered a protective detail for you."

"What? I don't want—" Fenway stopped. "No—I do want protection. It's possible—maybe even likely—they saw me get in Rory's minivan. I got to work a little after one o'clock, and I didn't go back to the minivan. I would have gotten in it to drive it home, but Rory was there with my Accord. We swapped keys, and then Rory went to get the minivan."

"Did you see Rory get in the car?"

Fenway shook her head. "So I guess I don't know if Rory was killed."

Sandoval sighed. "I'm afraid he was. It was his body we pulled out of the car. Dental records matched." She paused for a moment. "I asked you because I thought you might know if it happened when he unlocked the door, or when he started the car, or what."

Fenway frowned sadly. "No. I didn't see it."

"Is there a possibility someone blew the minivan up with a remote? Maybe you *weren't* the target."

Fenway pursed her lips. "That would be a big coincidence."

Sandoval nodded. "But it's a possibility."

"I suppose." Fenway tapped her fingers on the bed. "But the most likely scenario by far is that I'm the target, don't you think? They might have seen me survive. They might be at my apartment right now."

Sandoval nodded. "I'm sure that's why McVie ordered the protective detail. You were even checked into the hospital under an alias."

"An alias?"

"Yes."

"No wonder Millicent didn't visit."

"Millicent?"

"My campaign manager. Millicent Tate. Three days before the election and here I sit, out of commission in the hospital. She'd tell me to get out there in front of the cameras, assassination attempts be damned."

"We had an officer outside your door all night. She couldn't have visited even if she had known where you were."

"Oh."

Sandoval leaned forward in her chair. "We don't want you to go back to your apartment. You can go in once the officers have cleared it, and pick up a few things, but we don't want you staying there."

"You think this is necessary?"

"You think someone blowing up the car you were supposed to drive isn't serious?"

Fenway was quiet.

"If you get out of the hospital today, do you have anyone to stay with tonight?"

Fenway thought.

Her father and Charlotte? Dez might have interviewed them about Jeremy Kapp's murder. She couldn't ask him. Besides, she and her father were still on the outs.

She thought about McVie. If things had gone according to plan, they'd have gone on their first date a couple of months ago, and she'd leave the hospital and go over to his new apartment, and he'd take her in his strong arms, kiss the side of her face, stroke her hair, and tell her nothing would hurt her as long as she was in his apartment, in his arms, in his bed.

But politics had undone their dating before it had even started. And there was no way she could stay with him.

She could call Rachel, though.

As soon as she thought of Rachel's name, she felt a sense of relief. Rachel would need to know a lot of what went on anyway. She was sure Rachel was on the site of the explosion—as the county's public information officer, she'd have to be involved on the front lines. But Fenway was sure Rachel would say yes to having her stay over. There was even a guest room.

"Yes, I think so," she said.

"Your dad lives close, right? And he's got private security if he doesn't want the sheriff's department around."

Fenway laughed. "No, I can't call him. I mean, they have plenty of bedrooms, but they have their own problems right now." Fenway thought of telling Officer Sandoval about Charlotte's gun, but couldn't bring herself to do it. Perhaps Sandoval already knew.

"Okay, well, whoever you decide to stay with, we'll take you in a patrol car and check out your apartment before you go in to get your things."

Fenway sighed. "Millicent will *freak* out."

Sandoval smiled. "Man, am I glad I'm not running for anything."

"You could have thrown your hat in for sheriff since McVie's running for mayor."

"No, thank you," Sandoval said. "Gretchen Donnelly will be great as our next sheriff. She's been in charge of the field office in P.Q. for years now. I'm glad she's running. I'm not cut out for it. I'll let you crazy people deal with the political stuff." She cleared her throat. "Okay, now, I'm not comfortable asking this, but can you tell me exactly what happened, and in what order?"

"Starting when?"

"When you decided to go out to the parking garage, I think."

"Right," Fenway said, and took a deep breath. She told Sandoval the whole story: the phone call she got from Rory; the exchange of keys; telling Rory she would tell Millicent Tate he did a good job; turning toward her car and unlocking the door; having the world explode around her.

When Fenway was done, Sandoval thanked her and nodded.

"You have any other questions?"

"Not right now."

"Will I have to tell anyone else? The sheriff? Maybe Donnelly? Do they want to know anything?"

Sandoval shook her head. "Not right now, anyway. We've heard from a lot of witnesses. Of course, if the FBI decides to get involved, everything could change."

"So I can leave? I mean, as soon as the hospital releases me?"

Sandoval smiled. "Sure."

They made a little small talk before Sandoval said goodbye and left.

Fenway sighed and stared out the window. She hated to bother Rachel, but knew she'd need to make this call. She looked at her watch. It was almost eleven. Fenway sat and picked up the hospital room's landline phone. She called Rachel's mobile number from memory.

Rachel picked up on the third ring. "Rachel Richards."

"Hi Rachel, it's Fenway."

"Fenway! Are you okay? I heard you were hurt in the explosion!"

"No, I'm fine. My ears were ringing. My new dress got torn. I'm sore." She paused. "Are you at work?"

"Yes. I had to stay downtown until late. I thought I'd have to pull an all-nighter. All the media outlets wanted statements every twenty seconds. Some TV reporter came all the way down from San Francisco."

"Impressive, Miss Richards. You'll have your White House press secretary job in no time."

Rachel laughed. "Fortunately, I was able to get out of there about two-thirty, but I was back here at nine. Lovely way to spend a Saturday."

"I bet."

"Where are you now?"

"St. Vincent's."

"You're in the hospital? Are you sure you're okay?"

"They wanted to keep me for observation. But my scans all came back fine. I'm bruised and I've got a bump on my head, but otherwise unscathed. Considering how bad it could have been, I got off easy."

"Oh, I'm so glad." Rachel paused. "Listen, I don't mean to rush you, but I'm on deadline for a press release. Did you need something?"

"Um... I need someplace to stay."

"Tonight?"

"Yes."

"Did something happen at your apartment?"

"Early yesterday, yes. And the sheriff thinks there's a good enough chance it's related to the explosion, so I'll need to find somewhere else to stay besides my apartment."

"And you chose my tiny little two-bedroom over your dad's monster mansion?"

"I did," Fenway said. "And it's not so tiny."

"It's no problem," Rachel said, "but I'm not going to be home for a while. And I haven't gotten the place ready for guests."

"I can bring my own sheets," Fenway said.

Rachel laughed. "No, no one's been in the guest bed since the last time it was changed. I mean there are dishes in the sink, my crap is all over the bathroom counter—"

"Come on, Rachel, you know I don't care about that stuff."

"Well, it's a good thing, because I'm not cleaning it up before you get there. You still have the spare key?"

"I do, as a matter of fact."

"Great. Maybe I'll see you before midnight."

They said their goodbyes, Rachel telling Fenway about a new show she had recording on the DVR, and they hung up.

Fenway closed her eyes and thought for a minute. Although she was staying with Rachel, she knew she should call her father. She opened her eyes, took a deep breath, and dialed his mobile number.

The voice on the other end was gruff. "Ferris."

"Hi Dad, it's Fenway."

"Fenway! I've been trying to get you all night! Where have you been?"

"It's a long story, Dad."

"Well, I wish I could have gotten ahold of you. They took Charlotte away in handcuffs last night."

"They *arrested* her?"

"Yes. Second-degree murder. How come you're not investigating this case like you should be?"

"First of all, there's a conflict of interest, Dad," Fenway said. "As soon as Charlotte emerged as a suspect, I got kicked off the case."

"I don't care if you were kicked off the case or not," Ferris said. "You know Charlotte didn't do this."

"Dad, *I'm* the one who found the earring." The words were out of her mouth before she could stop them. Fenway bit her lip.

"The earring?"

"Ugh, I shouldn't have said anything."

"You found one of Charlotte's earrings at the murder scene?" His voice took on an annoying note of desperation.

"I shouldn't be discussing the case, Dad."

Ferris didn't say anything in response, and Fenway didn't want to elaborate. Finally, after about thirty seconds, she said, "Dad, are you still there?"

"You listen to me," Ferris said, and his voice was low, even, but threatening—a tone Fenway hadn't heard before. "Charlotte didn't do this. *I* didn't have anything to do with this. And I didn't put you in the coroner position so you could fiddle while Rome burns."

Fenway started to seethe. *How dare he talk to me this way*, she thought. But, in spite of her anger, she got a chill up her spine too. She knew she had proved herself, true, but she also knew it *was* her father who had put her in the job—and he was the one to suggest it to Sheriff McVie in the first place.

But her father, for all his intelligence and all of his ruthlessness, didn't seem to understand how the most basic police procedures worked.

"Dad, didn't you hear me? I'm off the case. I was put off the case because there's a conflict of interest *because* I'm your daughter."

"That's bullshit, Fenway. You've never liked Charlotte, and you don't want to have to find evidence of her innocence."

"Dammit, Dad, I know you're upset about Charlotte getting arrested, but there's nothing I can do."

His voice was still low. "We'll see what the sheriff has to say about that."

Fenway scoffed. "Good luck, Dad. McVie's been pulled off the case too."

"McVie's been pulled off the case?"

"Yes. You're paying for his campaign, so he can't investigate your wife. It's a conflict of interest, just like mine."

Ferris was silent on the other end of the line. Fenway didn't speak either.

"Fenway," Ferris said, his voice dramatically changing, now sounding hurt and confused, "the police came and took her away. They accused her of having an affair with Jeremy Kapp. I knew Jeremy—he worked for me for years. His family was over for dinner the other night. An *affair!*"

Fenway didn't say anything.

"Is it true? That they were having an affair?"

"We've got a witness who says our victim was having an affair with a lot of his clients' wives," Fenway said carefully, "and yes, he specifically named Charlotte as one of them."

Ferris was quiet for a moment, then the pain in his voice deepened. "I know I did a lot of stuff your mother didn't like," he said. "I don't know if she told you."

"No," Fenway said. "Mom never said a bad word about you."

"That's probably a lot more than I deserve," Ferris said. "But with Charlotte, it was different. I cut back on my hours. I know I worked late a lot of nights, but I took vacations with her. Romantic vacations, not work trips where she tagged along and went shopping while I worked all day. I never used to take vacations before—not real vacations, anyway. I *tried* with her. I haven't slept with anyone else since we got married. I didn't do any of the bad things I used to do when I was married to your mother. Because I didn't want to come home and find Charlotte gone with all of her stuff. I thought I learned my lesson."

Fenway shook her head. The amount of work he thought he needed to do to keep their marriage happy was incredibly low— if he was holding up his fidelity as a point he was proud of, it showed how out of touch he was.

Or perhaps Charlotte had equally low expectations. Ferris had been almost twice her age when they had gotten married, after all. And it wasn't a stretch, now that he was pushing sixty, to think he couldn't hold the interest of his much-younger wife, or she would find someone with whom to stray.

"I don't know what to tell you, Dad. The guy was a dog, sure, but it looks to me like most of the women knew what they were getting into."

Ferris was silent. All Fenway heard was the ringing in her right ear.

"All right—I've got to get going, Dad."

"I'm sorry, Fenway."

She sighed. "Anyway, I called to tell you I'm not going to be home for a few days, and I don't have my phone on me."

"You're what?"

"I'm not going to be at home."

"You're picking this time, of all times, to go on vacation? What, going up to Seattle to get more of your mother's stuff?"

"No, I'm not going on vacation, Dad. Someone's trying to kill me. I'm getting police protection and I'm not staying at my house."

"Wait—someone's trying to kill you?"

"Yes."

"I don't—I just—"

"Sorry, Dad. It's a lot to spring on you after you've been through this thing with Charlotte. But it's true. Someone spray-painted my Accord yesterday morning—"

"Spray-painted your car?"

"They sprayed the, uh, n-word on it, Dad."

"They *what*?"

"And then they blew up the car I was borrowing."

Fenway heard her father gasp. "They blew up your car?"

"Yes. It's all over the news. You haven't seen anything?"

"I've been trying to figure out how to get your—how to get Charlotte out of jail. I've been trying to reach my lawyers. You'd think that for the price I pay them, they'd return my calls on a Saturday. Where are you now?"

"I just got out of the hospital."

"You were in the hospital and you didn't tell me?"

"They had me there for observation. They thought I might have a concussion."

Ferris paused. "But you're okay?"

"Yes, Dad, I'm okay."

"Oh." There was silence for a few seconds. "Was anyone else hurt?"

Fenway took a deep breath. "Yes. The kid who lent me his father's minivan was killed. His dad took the graffiti off my car."

"What—not the guy who owns Central Auto Body?"

Fenway clicked her tongue. "Yeah. The owner's kid. Nice boy. I was—" Fenway stopped, a hitch in her throat preventing her from going on.

"Oh, no," Ferris said, his voice dropping even lower. "I've known Domingo for years. We get our car fleet repaired there if they've been in an accident." He paused. "Which kid was it?"

"Rory."

"Oh no. He was a nice kid. Smart."

"Maybe you want to call Domingo up and pay your respects," Fenway said. "Come to think of it, I should too."

They were both silent for a moment, thinking about Domingo Velásquez and his fallen son.

"Listen," Ferris said, "I know you and I aren't getting along right now, and maybe I didn't come across the right way. But you're intelligent. And I notice you're pretty tenacious at getting the truth."

Fenway shifted uncomfortably. "Thanks."

"So even if you're off this case officially," Ferris continued, "you can still nose around the edges, right? Follow up on a lead or two no one else is looking at? Maybe the D.A. is so convinced Charlotte is guilty, they're not looking for things anymore."

"Even if I find something, Dad, I'm not going to be able to bring it forward."

Ferris sighed, exasperated. "I'm not as smart as you are, Fenway, but even I know there are ways around it. I know you can give it to someone else on your team, or give them an anonymous tip. It's not brain surgery." He paused. "And even if it *were* brain surgery, you could get it done."

"Oh, you've resorted to flattery."

"Well—yes. I guess I have. Look, Charlotte was here with me on Thursday night. That's when the murder happened, right? We had dinner in, and then we watched a movie, and we went to bed a little after midnight. There's no way she could have left in time."

"Don't you have cameras all around? Can't you give them the footage showing Charlotte arriving, and then, like, what ten hours of footage of her not leaving?"

"The sheriff's office has the footage now," Ferris said.

"If the video footage exonerates Charlotte, they'll let her go, Dad."

"I don't know," Ferris said. "My name doesn't mean what it used to. There are some people in the department who are out to get me."

Fenway rolled her eyes. "Come on, Dad. Do you know how paranoid that sounds?"

"You say that now, Fenway, but you should take a look at some of the things that are happening. They've put me on notice."

"I'll keep that in mind, Dad. All right—I'm going to be heading out."

"Where are you staying?"

Fenway paused. "You know, Dad, I don't trust this line. I'll let you know later."

"Oh—who sounds paranoid now?"

Fenway snapped. "I was almost blown up yesterday afternoon, Dad. A teenager lost his life over it. I'm not being paranoid, I'm being careful. If you have one of your cars blown up when you're about to get in it, then I'll gladly support your paranoia. Until then, shut the hell up."

Ferris was quiet.

"Now, if you'll excuse me, Daddy Dearest, I've got some important details to attend to." And she hung up before he had a chance to say goodbye.

She watched television for another hour and a half, not paying attention to it, letting her mind wander, going over the evidence she had found, and trying to remember details of the parking garage. Had she seen anything out of the corner of her eye? Were there any cars parked on the street with a driver who was simply waiting?

Fenway started to get a headache and cursed under her breath. She didn't want the hospital to keep her another day. Her stomach rumbled. She needed lunch, but not here.

Finally, at about twelve-thirty, the nurse came in with her release paperwork, and she was wheeled out of the hospital a few minutes before one o'clock. There was a cruiser at the curb. Officer Sandoval was in the driver's seat. She saw Fenway and got out.

"You've been released?" Sandoval asked.

"Yeah. I guess I don't have a car."

"You need a police detail anyway," Sandoval said. "We're getting one put together. You'll have a few officers assigned to you in about an hour." Sandoval looked closely at Fenway's face. "You okay?"

Fenway closed her eyes. "Do you get along with your father?"

The officer shrugged. "Most of the time, I guess."

"You ever want to pound his face in?"

Sandoval put her hand on Fenway's shoulder. "The police detail isn't going to be ready to take you for another hour or so. Why don't we go get some coffee or something?"

"Let's go for the 'or something,'" Fenway said. "Something like tequila."

CHAPTER ELEVEN

AS SANDOVAL TURNED THE IGNITION, HOWEVER, FENWAY HEARD the voice of her opponent in the coroner's race, Dr. Richard Ivanovich, on the radio. Fenway turned the volume up.

"It doesn't behoove Miss Stevenson right now to pull the race card like this," Ivanovich said. "Honestly, I question her judgement if she wants to make this about race. The racial slur on her car isn't something representative of our town or this county, and I wonder if one of Miss Stevenson's black friends spray-painted it on there in order to make her white opponent look bad."

Fenway's jaw dropped.

"There isn't anything about this explosion that isn't tragic," Ivanovich continued, "but blaming race relations for this tragedy is simply irresponsible. Of course, I don't like that my opponent was injured, but if she decides this race is too intense for her, or if her fear will prevent her from fulfilling the duties of coroner, I think *that's* the real tragedy."

A reporter said something in the background Fenway couldn't hear.

"No, no, I certainly do care about this young man's death," Ivanovich said. "Indeed, if I were coroner, it would be the first priority for me to solve his murder. But, of course, if I were coroner, these racially motivated incidents against the city's leadership would be much less likely to happen."

Fenway felt her blood boil.

"Who knew about the, uh, n-word on your car?" Sandoval asked Fenway quietly, turning the radio down.

"Anyone who was driving by the ten or twenty minutes I was there would have been able to see my car," Fenway responded. "Of course, I wouldn't be surprised if Ivanovich—or someone sent by Barry Klein, for that matter—was following me around. That's one reason—" And Fenway stopped herself; she was about to say that was why Fenway and McVie had decided not to go out on a date, but she caught herself.

"One reason what?"

"Nothing," Fenway said, shaking her head. "But holding a press conference and saying I'm playing the race card—when I haven't said anything about it—is a low blow."

"He can't think this will help him get votes."

"I don't know. There are plenty of—"

Sandoval looked over at Fenway.

"Plenty of what?"

"Never mind. I think I'm just being a pessimist. Maybe."

"I think you're underestimating this county's voters."

"I sure hope you're right." Fenway sighed. "Okay, slight change of plans. Let me go to my office and call my campaign manager and see if she wants me to do anything."

"If you're being followed by Barry Klein, you probably shouldn't go slam tequila, either."

"Let me talk to Millicent first."

They drove out of the parking lot of St. Vincent's and drove downtown.

The street was eerily quiet, the parking structure closed down, the faint smell of ash still wafting down the main street. Fenway tried not to think about what had happened.

Officer Sandoval parked across the street from the building that housed the coroner's office. They got out and walked briskly toward the building. Fenway caught Sandoval stealing glances at her out of the corner of her eye, and tried to appear as confident and as calm as possible, although she felt anything but.

Entering the building, they went into Suite 150, where Migs was at his desk, and Piper handed him a stack of papers in a folder. Piper and Migs turned to look at Fenway as she walked in through the door.

"Fenway!" Migs said. "I heard what happened. Are you okay?"

"Your dress is torn," said Piper.

Fenway shrugged. "I just came from the hospital. Haven't had a chance to change yet. Ringing in my ears. A little bruising where I was thrown into the car. Nothing too serious."

Piper's mouth was screwed up in concern and a bit of emotion. "Jeez, you could have been—"

Migs nudged her with his knee.

"Anyway," Fenway said, "I only stopped in here to make a phone call. Celeste and I are going to lunch at Dos Milagros. It's been a long couple of days."

"Uh," Migs said, "I think there are some things about the investigation you're going to need to look at first."

"They're not bringing the FBI in, are they?"

"No," Migs said. "They've made the determination it's likely not a terrorist attack. No claims of responsibility, and the M.O. doesn't match any known groups either."

"I'm pretty sure this is an attempted murder, not a terrorist attack," Fenway said. "Whoever did this targeted me."

Migs and Piper both looked at each other with worry in their eyes.

Officer Sandoval cleared her throat. "That's the way the sheriff wants to proceed, anyway," she said gently. "And of course, that's one of the more likely scenarios."

"But I've found out some information as I've done some digging," Piper said. "I was going to hand these files off to Migs, but now that you're here, I'll tell you." She pulled the folders out of Migs's hands.

Fenway sighed and looked at Sandoval. "I guess I shouldn't leave without my official police detail anyway," she said. "Maybe take a rain check on Dos Milagros?"

"Sure," Sandoval said. "You know my number if you need anything."

Sandoval put a hand on Fenway's shoulder and gave it a gentle squeeze. "You'll get through this."

"I know," Fenway said. "The psycho who did this to me won't, though."

"That's the spirit," Officer Sandoval said drily. She left the outer office, leaving Fenway with Migs, Piper, and the big stack of folders.

Fenway stared at the stack of papers. "I guess we better get started. Do you want me to go over to your desk?"

"And waste all these printouts?"

"Can't have those trees die in vain," Fenway said.

She walked into her private office. Piper followed her, and Fenway shut the door behind her.

"So," Fenway said, opening her desk drawer and putting her phone and SIM card in it, "I'm not sure what you have for me. You know I was kicked off the Jeremy Kapp case, right?"

Piper nodded. "But this is about the Carl Cassidy case you asked about the day before yesterday."

"Oh," Fenway said, "right. I didn't think you were prioritizing it."

"Well, honestly, I wasn't," Piper said, "but I was waiting for a report to come back, and I started digging, and it was—interesting."

"Interesting?"

"Yeah," Piper said. "So, you remember you told me about your conversation with Lana—how Carl had gotten suspicious of the two holding tanks that were supposedly taken offline for maintenance, but he saw activity around it?"

"Yes."

"I figured, if there's activity around holding tanks, it means there's oil coming in, right?"

"The tanks were taken offline for maintenance, right? So the activity was probably a maintenance crew."

Piper shook her head. "Carl Cassidy would know if it had been a maintenance crew. But he was suspicious. I think it was because there was a shipment—either going out or coming in. Or maybe both."

"Really?"

"I don't think it could have been anything else." Piper held up a folder. "Ferris Energy is a public company, and I dug through all of their shipments. Crude in, refined oil and petroleum products out. Gasoline, diesel, all kinds of stuff."

"Did you find anything unusual?"

Piper rifled through the papers and pulled one out; it was a spreadsheet with five sets of two-line highlights.

"There's a ship out of Liberia," Piper said, "the *Jules Verne*. It's a class L tanker. Look, I found a picture of it online." She pulled out another paper, this one with a printed picture of an oil tanker, black with red markings, and *Jules Verne* clearly painted on the side.

"So," Piper continued, "according to the manifest, this ship arrived empty in the Estancia port six times over the last year. I haven't gone further back—but I can, if you need it."

"Okay," Fenway said. "Is that weird?"

"Not in and of itself," Piper conceded. "Then it leaves the port full of gasoline—in November, March, and May; or diesel—in

January, July, and about six weeks ago, near the end of September. That's not weird either."

"Okay."

"So then it travels to Singapore to unload. But, here's the thing. The trip takes two days longer than it should."

"That's unusual?"

"Maybe not once—they run into bad weather, or a crew member gets sick and they have to make an unscheduled stop. But two days *every* time?"

Fenway nodded. "Did they consistently underestimate the time? Maybe the engine is listed wrong or something?"

"No, I don't think that's it. The estimated times are accurate on some of the *Jules Verne's* other trips."

"So—what then?"

"I think it's making an unscheduled stop. I think it's going somewhere between California and Singapore, unloading its cargo, and then going on."

Fenway paused. "They're crossing the international date line."

Piper shook her head. "No, I accounted for that. Something else caught my eye." She pulled out a different spreadsheet. "Look, the records in Singapore say they're unloading gasoline on the November trip, then diesel in January, then gasoline in March, then diesel in May, then gasoline in July—"

"Wait."

Piper looked up, an eager glint in her eye. "You see it too, right?"

"Yes. The manifests' cargo doesn't match. The Estancia manifest has gasoline in May and diesel in July."

"Right. It's like someone was expecting a pattern, and didn't know an exception had been made."

Fenway nodded. "So, what does that mean? The manifests don't match. An empty ship comes to Estancia and leaves with cargo arriving two days after it should."

"I have an idea," Piper said.

"Yeah?"

"You listen to NPR?"

"Sometimes."

"I do too. And I remembered a couple of stories I heard on their world report."

Fenway nodded, although she didn't listen to the world report.

"They had a pretty extensive article on the rebels in Indonesia a few weeks ago. And maybe six months ago, they had one on the president of La Mitad dissolving parliament."

"You're saying those two stories are related to our oil tankers?"

Piper pulled out a news article dated in June from the *Los Angeles Times*. "Read the seventh paragraph," she said, pointing to an article titled "No End in Sight for East Timor Conflict."

> *Puzzling to international experts is where the fuel is coming from to power the rebels' vehicles, tanks, and generators. "There is an international ban on supplying the rebels with gasoline, diesel, propane, and other fuels," said United Nations official Margerite L'Overture. "We don't seem to be getting shipments out of Sudan or Iran—all the usual suspects in a conflict like this."*
>
> *Energy officials in the area are looking for rogue organizations from other countries. While there is talk from the Indonesian government of setting up a blockade, the ruling party in Jakarta has no official timetable.*

"The rebels in East Timor," Fenway said.

"Yes."

"That's an armed conflict against one of our allies."

Piper nodded. "And one of the more stable governments in the area. The ruling party is pretty pro-American right now."

"We don't sell fuel to the rebels."

"We're not *supposed* to. But that's exactly what I think Ferris Energy is doing."

Fenway paused. "That's crazy. Where did they get the crude oil from? That's not something you can just hide, is it?"

Piper pulled out yet another ship manifest and yet another set of photos. "*This* is a photograph taken by a Salvadoran couple on vacation in La Mitad. Do you see the background, in the ocean behind them?"

"The oil tanker."

"Yes."

Fenway looked at the ship manifest. It was a Dutch oil tanker named *Julius Werner.*

"Easy name to fake, if you've already got a *Jules Verne*," said Piper.

Fenway looked back at the photograph. The flag of the Netherlands was waving clearly.

"And La Mitad has been under sanction for what? Two years?"

"Closer to five."

Fenway sat back in her chair and closed her eyes. "This is huge, Piper. An American oil company breaking sanctions with two different countries. It must be worth it."

"I calculated that, too," Piper said.

"You did?"

"Yes. The *Jules Verne* is a supertanker—the manifests say it can hold more than two million barrels."

Fenway gaped. "*Million?*"

"Right. Of course, they're not going to get gas-station prices from the rebels in East Timor, but wow, the market advantages of going direct to the buyer—they're bypassing all the middlemen, plus I bet they're not going through the same rigor in the refining process. It's not like it has to pass government tests before it winds up in Humvees in East Timor."

"Rigor in the refining process? How do you know that?"

"My dad's a chemical engineer at Ferris Energy."

"Oh." Fenway paused. "What do you think they're getting?"

"I haven't done a lot of research—not much is available—but based on the articles I've read on the rebels and their funding, it's gotta be at least a hundred million dollars per tanker."

"They have that kind of funding?"

Piper nodded. "A lot of different groups are providing money and resources."

"But—that's over a billion dollars a year!"

"Yep. And most of it is pure profit." Piper shuffled her papers. "War made someone at Ferris Energy a lot of money."

Fenway shook her head. "Look, this is a nice theory, Piper. A *crazy* theory, but a nice one. But we can't make a case based on a couple of news articles, a picture of a tanker we found on the internet, and some wild conjecture." She screwed up her face. "Plus, there's no way to use that much money without drawing interest from the Feds. A billion dollars can't appear on the books out of nowhere."

"No," Piper said. "They've got to be laundering it."

Fenway scoffed. "Right. And no one can launder a billion dollars."

"No," Piper said, "but what if I told you a hundred people could launder ten million each?"

"You found a hundred people who are laundering ten million dollars each?"

"Well, not people, exactly. Businesses."

"Businesses?"

"I'm looking at a bunch of local businesses," said Piper. "I'm comparing their financial records to the amount of people on the payroll, the amount of business it looks like they're transacting, and a few of them merit a closer look."

"Any interesting ones pop so far?"

Piper pulled a stack of about ten pages out of a folder. The financial statements from September.

Kapp Landscape Architects.

"You've got to be kidding me," Fenway said.

"Nope," Piper said. "There were some hidden accounts, and there was a second management payroll account too. If you can believe it, the company created invoices for landscape consulting services—averaging about twenty consulting invoices a week, some as low as five hundred dollars, and some as high as eight thousand dollars. All with names not in the official directories, and all with no addresses or addresses that don't exist. Piper pulled out a spreadsheet. "Like this one. 378 Estancia Canyon Boulevard."

"The Coffee Bean near my apartment is on Estancia Canyon."

"Right. The address for that is 350. It's on the corner. The next block starts with 400."

"So that address doesn't exist."

"And none of these other ones do, either. Someone got lazy or creative. There's one in here for Abby Herrick."

"Isn't that the name of a pop star?"

"Yep. And one for Romeo Montague."

Fenway sighed. "The classics never get old."

"There's enough in here to put Jeremy Kapp away for a long time. But that's not the most interesting thing."

"I would imagine the bullet in Jeremy Kapp's forehead is the most interesting thing."

"Not even close," Piper said. "On the twenty-fifth of every other month, there's a large payment that goes from Kapp Landscape Architects to a company called Global Advantage Executive Consulting."

"That sounds like a shell company if I've ever heard one."

"Right. Three guesses as to where the company is located, and the first two don't count."

"The Caymans," Fenway guessed.

"Yep, those pesky Cayman Islands again," Piper confirmed. "Now, I've got to do a *ton* more research, but I bet I can uncover at least a few more organizations doing the same thing. I know what to look for now."

"Who's behind Global Advantage?"

"I don't know yet," Piper said. "But there's one other strange thing."

"Which is?"

"Global Advantage paid *Kapp* on Tuesday night. Ninety-five hundred dollars."

Fenway thought for a moment. "Maybe an overpayment?"

"Maybe." Piper pressed her lips together.

"What?"

"I don't think it's an overpayment. First of all, it's a neat and tidy sum. Second of all, this is the first time Global Advantage has paid Kapp, not vice versa."

"What, then?"

"I don't know yet. Maybe he was getting paid to do some sort of special job. Maybe it's why he was at the beachside hotel. Or maybe it's what got him killed."

Fenway drummed her fingers on the table. "Do you think he maybe saw something that got him killed?"

Piper shrugged. "I certainly think Carl Cassidy saw something he shouldn't have. And I think Lewis Fairweather did too."

"But we can't prove it."

"No."

Fenway screwed up her face. "My father—how much did he know?"

"About the oil from La Mitad? Or about the sale to East Timor?"

"Both."

Piper shook her head. "That depends on what I find when I follow the money," she said. "I'll let you know."

Fenway exhaled loudly. "Even if he didn't know anything about it," she said, "this happened on his watch. He's the CEO.

He's liable—not just from a civil perspective, but criminally. He could spend the next ten years in jail."

"But doesn't this help get—oh, sorry, I can't remember the name of your, uh..."

"Charlotte," Fenway said.

"Right," Piper said. "Doesn't this help get her off the hook?"

"Maybe," Fenway said. "Especially if she can establish she never left the house on Thursday night. My father is her alibi. And, I suppose, she's his." She crossed her arms. "Still, if someone who's laundering money from rebels from East Timor winds up getting killed—we probably should look at *more* than the supposed mistress." Fenway picked up the phone. "I'm going to get Dez down here. I guess you better tell her everything you told me."

CHAPTER TWELVE

IT TOOK A COUPLE OF HOURS ON THE PHONE EXPLAINING IT AND going over the financial evidence, but Fenway was able to convince Gretchen Donnelly to call Piper for the update. Fenway also had to shoo Piper out, because she kept asking questions about the attack.

It was past three now, and Fenway stared at the phone. She didn't want to call Millicent Tate—it would be a long call.

But the radio message she had heard earlier had the potential to open up all kinds of trouble for Fenway. Ivanovich's accusation that she had brought race into the campaign got under her skin, and she needed Millicent to give her a sanity check so she didn't explode with anger and frustration.

She picked up the phone and dialed.

"Fenway?" Millicent's voice said. "Did I see the number in my phone right? This is you? Actually calling me?"

"Yeah," Fenway said. "I've been in the hospital."

"I know. I saw it on the news. It would have been nice to get a call. I've had to make a lot of excuses to cancel your campaign events."

"The police were trying to keep my location secure," Fenway fibbed. "I couldn't call until I was released."

Millicent exhaled loudly, and perhaps somewhat passive-aggressively. "You're okay now?"

"Yes. My scans came back normal this morning."

"All right. I can still get you into a couple of events today."

And I'm so relieved you're okay, Fenway thought.

"You're in the office?"

"I am," Fenway said. "And my cell phone is out of commission right now."

"Did it break in the explosion?"

"No," Fenway said. "I don't know if you heard, but someone is trying to kill me. I took the SIM card out and turned my phone off."

"You think someone is tracking you through your phone? That's crazy!"

"I don't know," Fenway said, "but I sure as hell am *not* going to bet my life on it."

"We can get you another phone. A burner, as the cop shows say. We'll run it over to your apartment."

"I won't be there."

"You're not staying at your place? It's going to look like you're scared of this guy who's after you."

"Yeah, well, it'll have to look like that," Fenway said. "The guy's spray-painted my car, so he knows where I live, and he blew up the car I was borrowing, so I know he wants me dead. And he doesn't care about collateral damage, obviously."

Why didn't he blow up my Honda instead of spray-painting it? Fenway tried to shake the thought out of her head, but it stuck there. If the guy—or whoever it was—wanted her dead, blowing up the Accord made sense. Spray-painting it didn't. He obviously knew where she lived, knew the car she drove, and saw the mini-van she got into.

Millicent paused—possibly a longer pause than Fenway had ever experienced in a conversation with her—and then spoke carefully. "A few hours ago, Ivanovich held a press conference."

"I listened to part of it on the radio."

"What part?"

"The race card part," Fenway said. "I'm pretty pissed off about it."

"I can believe it. Ordinarily, I'd say it was an immensely stupid move. It's offensive to a huge number of people."

"But?"

Millicent clicked her tongue for a moment. "It's a dog whistle. And I'm frankly not sure it won't work. We're talking strategy and possible responses to it right now."

"Can we ignore it?"

Millicent paused. "It depends."

"On what?"

"On whether or not reporters are going to ask you about it. And regardless, we're going to have to have a response—I think it's pretty likely."

Fenway sighed. She had felt the same way as Millicent; she wanted to take the high road and stay out of the fray, but Ivanovich was taking the low road and running her over.

"So," Millicent continued, "how likely do you think it is that he took a picture of your car when it had the, uh, racial slur on it?"

"I was out there for fifteen minutes, at least. Anyone could have driven by and seen it. And it sounds like someone is following me—someone who doesn't want me around. Maybe it's Ivanovich. Maybe it's Barry Klein. Maybe it's someone else. But if someone *is* following me, they're probably taking pictures, and giving them to Ivanovich. There's probably a picture of me with the spray-painted car, waiting for Rory." Her voice broke on the teen's name.

Millicent was quiet for a moment. "I liked that kid," she said. "Whoever did this..." But she trailed off, unable to finish the thought.

"I'm going to have a police detail for the foreseeable future," Fenway said.

"That's less than ideal. It'll make the last few days of the campaign rough. You won't be able to do as much, will you?"

"I don't think it's negotiable with the department. And besides, I think this is a real threat."

"But you could come to a campaign event now, right?"

"The police detail isn't ready," Fenway said. "They'll be here soon—at least I think so—but I can't leave the office right now without them."

"Well, you can't disappear," Millicent mused. "Ivanovich has the last word right now. You can't let the voters think he's right."

"What should I do?"

"Let me think for a minute." Millicent sighed, and after a moment, she spoke. "You've been in the hospital, which is coming out in the press. Give me a couple hours—it's not ideal, but keep laying low. You were the victim of an attempted murder. Let me see how this is playing."

"How?"

"A poll, I think," Millicent said. "We need to know where we stand. Maybe we can talk to some reporters to take the temperature of the electorate. But we're going to stick around here until we come up with a decent strategy." Millicent laughed. "You know, I thought the George Nidever dinner was going to a boring evening. Now with all of this going on, Sunday's dinner should be fun."

—————◆●———————

About an hour later, when the early November twilight was shooting purple and pink across the sky, Fenway walked out with three officers she didn't know. She rode in the passenger seat of one of the two cruisers to her apartment, driven by the tallest of the three, a lanky black man whose nametag said *Young*.

"We're heading to your apartment to get the things you need for the next few days," Officer Young said.

"I don't know what I'm going to pack," Fenway said, mostly to herself, but to have something to say to Officer Young on the drive. "My campaign manager says I pretty much have to go to the George Nidever dinner. You heard of it before?"

"Yeah," Officer Young said. His voice was boyish, and his manner was easygoing, although his posture was alert. "That's the dinner the Sunday night before all the local elections, right?"

"Right."

"That's been going on for years, hasn't it? George Nidever—he was one of those guys who traded with the Chumash, right?"

"Well, *traded with* is a generous phrase. *Stole from* might be more accurate."

"It's a county tradition, anyway. Goes back a long time."

"Stealing from the Chumash?"

"No—the Nidever Dinner. They host it at the university, right?"

"Right. Since I've been off the campaign trail the last day or two, I'm going to need to make a pretty big appearance there."

Officer Young shook his head. "I don't think so. My orders are pretty strict. You need to lay low until the police figure out who's after you."

"I've already been laying about as low as I can, Officer Young. I can't miss this dinner."

"It's dangerous, Fenway," he said.

She looked sideways at him; she hadn't said he could use the more familiar first name with her. "Other politicians get threatened all the time."

"But not all politicians go through what you went through yesterday."

The slight ringing in her right ear and the rip in the shoulder of her dress served to remind her that it hadn't been a normal couple of days. She rolled down the window and looked out, the wind blowing in her face, making her curls swirl in the chilly night air. She didn't want to think about Rory.

Officer Young looked over at Fenway and pressed his lips together. "I'm sorry. I didn't mean to upset you. We don't want to see you hurt."

"I appreciate it," Fenway said, a little brusquely, turning back toward the officer. "I guess we'll figure this out."

"Sure," he said. "I get it." He cleared his throat. "So, the two officers are going to enter your apartment first. Make sure it's clear."

Fenway closed her eyes and remembered six months previously—getting attacked before she had even entered her apartment. Having to fight for her life.

"Right," Fenway said. "I'm glad you're going to do that."

They turned off Estancia Canyon at the Coffee Bean, drove another block, and turned into the driveway of the apartment complex. A florist van was parked in her parking spot.

"What's the florist doing here?" she mused, with a sense of déjà vu.

She glanced up at her apartment, on the second story, through the darkness. "Look." Fenway pointed to the second floor. "The hallway lights are out in front of my apartment." She strained to peer through the shadows.

Fenway thought she saw movement in the second-floor hallway.

"Shit!" she barked.

Officer Young jumped in his seat. "What is it?"

"I think someone is in front of my door."

"What?" Officer Young braked to a stop.

Fenway heard the sound of breaking glass. "Did you hear that?"

Officer Young nodded.

"That sounded like it came from my apartment!"

Officer Young opened the door of the cruiser. "Stay here, Fenway!" he shouted at her, and sprinted out of his car.

As she watched him run toward the stairs, she grabbed the radio and pushed the button on the transmitter. "Be advised, possible four-five-nine in progress at 6448 Kenneth Avenue, apartment two-one-four. Repeat, possible four-five-nine in progress. Officer on scene. Request backup."

The other cruiser turned in behind Fenway and screeched to a stop. Two officers got out; one followed Officer Young up the stairs; the other went to the other side of the building and around the corner.

Fenway looked up. The hallway in front of her apartment was dark, and while she thought she could see movement, it was hard to tell what was going on.

She looked in front of the cruiser at the florist van. Then it clicked.

The same florist van that had blocked her space when her Accord was vandalized.

Oh no, Fenway thought, *I'm a sitting duck here.* A police cruiser, in the middle of the brightly lit driveway. If someone wanted her dead, they'd simply have to shoot through the windshield— or the open window.

She opened the door and rolled out. She ducked low and got around the back of the cruiser.

She peeked above the trunk, and saw a man at the bottom of the far stairs.

He had a black ski mask pulled over his face, a black jacket, and dark blue jeans with black running shoes. And he was making good use of the running shoes—sprinting at full speed out toward the driveway right toward where Fenway was crouched.

Fenway didn't think—she launched herself at him as he sprinted by her and caught him from the front around the torso.

He was knocked to the side as Fenway twisted her body, as she landed on top of him on the asphalt of the parking lot.

He ended up halfway on his left side, his hand stretched awkwardly in front of him to attempt to break his fall. But it absorbed most of his weight, and Fenway heard a sickening crunch and a scream of pain. She was glad for the ringing in her right ear so she didn't have to hear as much of it.

"You bitch!" he wailed, then screamed in pain, holding his left hand, the fingers jutting at a nauseating angle.

Officer Young, panting, ran up to them. "Fenway! Are you okay?"

"Fine," Fenway said through gritted teeth. Her side ached from where she had been thrown against the car earlier. "This guy broke his hand trying to get away."

Officer Young turned the man over and handcuffed him. "What's your name?" he said.

"Fuck you!" the man screamed. "Get your dirty hands off me!"

"Think this is the guy who spray-painted my car?" Fenway asked the officer.

"I know he's the guy who just threw a brick through your front window," Officer Young said. He patted down the man, who was still screaming and trying to flail although he was prone. He pulled out a wallet from the man's back pocket.

"Put that back!" the man screeched.

Officer Young pulled out a driver's license. "Well, well," he said. He held out the driver's license for Fenway to see.

Terrance Victor Ivanovich.

The photo was of a man of about twenty-five, with the same complexion and jawline of the ear, nose, and throat doctor running for coroner.

"Ivanovich," Fenway said. "You're Richard Ivanovich's son."

"You can't take my wallet," Terrance Ivanovich spat.

"Terrance Ivanovich, you are under arrest for vandalism, destruction of property, and resisting arrest," Officer Young said.

"And you better hope you don't get connected to the car bomb, or you'll be charged with murder, too."

"Car bomb?" Terrance shrieked. "I didn't do nothin' with a car bomb. You're trying to set me up!"

Officer Young looked at Fenway and narrowed his eyes.

"Sure, you might have put a brick through my window, but you expect us to believe you're *not* the one who blew up the car I was driving?"

"I don't know what you're talking about," Terrance said, and his voice changed. "You're serious? Someone tried to blow up your car?"

"Killed a seventeen-year-old boy instead," Fenway said. "And the police are definitely champing at the bit to find the killer."

"It's not me!" Terrance exclaimed. "I did the spray paint. And the brick, sure, but I'm not a murderer."

"Did your father put you up to it?" Officer Young asked.

"I did all the spray paint and the brick on my own. But I didn't have anything to do with no car bomb. That's messed up. I wanted you to drop out so my dad wouldn't be so pissed off about losing by sixty points to a n—"

"Careful," Officer Young said, applying more pressure to Terrance's arms.

"Ow! Ow! Stop it! I just meant I didn't want to *kill* you."

"That was pretty stupid," Fenway said. She nudged Officer Young. "Miranda?"

"Right," Officer Young said under his breath. "Terrance Ivanovich, you have the right to remain silent. Anything you say can and will be used against you..."

Fenway stood up. She had thought the spray-painting vandal and the bomb-builder were one and the same. But with Terrance Ivanovich's surprising and unprompted confession, and with the fact that Terrance had spray-painted and not blown up her Accord, Fenway had to admit she now harbored serious doubt they had caught the person who tried to kill her.

So she probably wouldn't be sleeping in her own apartment tonight. Maybe even not until after the election.

———— ◆◆ ————

Another police cruiser came to take Terrance Ivanovich away, as Officer Young and the others had to stay on scene, supposedly to secure Fenway's safety.

Fenway called the building manager, who grumpily agreed to get two maintenance workers to board over the window. And even though it was well after five o'clock, the workers appeared with boards and tools about fifteen minutes after the call. Fenway suspected if she were anyone else, the manager wouldn't have called the maintenance crew until the next day—or even Monday morning. But the daughter of the apartment complex's owner was a little different. As much as Fenway didn't feel comfortable with the special treatment, she wasn't going to argue about it, either.

She started to walk out of the complex to go get a latte. Fenway was tired and needed the caffeine to deal with the situation; she figured she'd have to give Officer Young—or one of the other officers—a statement. She still had to pack, she still had to get over to Rachel's house, and she didn't see an end in sight.

"Where do you think you're going?" Officer Young said.

"Uh—to get some coffee?"

"You're not going anywhere without an escort. Do you know how much trouble I'd get in if anything happened to you on my watch?"

"But they caught the guy," Fenway said.

"You don't know it's the same guy. You don't know if he has an accomplice or a whole host of accomplices. Did you see the guy's tattoo?"

"Tattoo?"

"Yeah, the 88 on his forearm."

Fenway paused. "No, I guess I didn't."

"Yeah, well, I'm sure the tattoo is impressive on his online dating profile," Officer Young said, "and I'll bet he's involved with Dominguez White Storm."

"Involved with *what*?"

"The local white supremacists," he said. "You haven't heard of them?"

Fenway paused. "How in the world could Dr. Ivanovich even *think* of running for public office when his son is a member of a white supremacist group?"

Officer Young shrugged. "Takes all kinds. I mean, he's buddies with Dr. Klein, and obviously that's okay with him."

"Why wouldn't it be okay? Isn't he white?"

Officer Young narrows his eyes, a skeptical look on his face. "Yeah, but not the *right* kind of white—not for people like the White Storm."

Suddenly it hit her, and she felt ignorant for not seeing it before. "Oh. Jewish."

Officer Young put his finger to the tip of his nose. "All right," he said. "You want coffee, let's go get some coffee."

The two of them started down the driveway toward the sidewalk.

"You've had a rough couple of days, haven't you?" Officer Young said.

Fenway nodded. She looked at her feet, putting one in front of the other, and watched the shadows of their figures from the streetlights elongate and shrink as she and Officer Young walked down the street. She looked up to the sky; for once, the fog hadn't started to roll in yet, and she could see the stars above her. The night was moonless and dark. She couldn't see the Milky Way—the city lights were too strong—but looking up at Orion's Belt, at

Polaris, at Cassiopeia, she felt a wave of peace wash over her for the first time all day.

Had it been yesterday when Jeremy Kapp was found with a bullet in his forehead?

Had it been yesterday when she found cocaine in his hotel room?

Had it been yesterday when Charlotte's gun washed up on the beach?

Charlotte.

Fenway wondered if her father's team of high-priced lawyers had been able to get Charlotte arraigned and out on bail in time for her to be home that evening. If anyone could do it, Nathaniel Ferris could. She wondered if he would be able to wheel and deal as much with Dez and Gretchen Donnelly as he could with McVie.

They reached The Coffee Bean. It was empty of customers, and the clock on the wall read five minutes to eight—just before closing.

"Is there still time to get a latte?"

The barista behind the counter registered distress on her face but it immediately changed to a smile. "Sure, no problem," she said brightly. "Just a regular latte?"

"Yep."

"Name?"

I'm literally the only one in here. "Joanne." She turned to Officer Young. "You want anything, Officer? My treat."

"Thanks, Fen—uh, *Joanne*. Large coffee. Black."

Fenway paid.

They stepped away from the counter and she put her wallet back in her purse. Then she dug around for her phone to call her father before she realized it was in her desk drawer at work with the SIM card removed. She sighed.

"What's wrong?" Officer Young said, taking the black coffee from the barista, who moved in front of the espresso machine.

"I forgot I, uh, took the SIM card out of my phone."

"You took the SIM card out?"

"Yeah."

"Why did you do that?"

"Because I wasn't sure if the people who were trying to kill me were tracking me through my phone."

Officer Young looked at Fenway with concern.

"I know," Fenway said quickly. "Paranoid."

"Someone's trying to kill you, Fenway. That's not paranoid. It's not like you're wearing a tinfoil hat and saying aliens are talking to you through your fillings or anything."

"Well, no."

Officer Young paused and lowered his voice, although the barista was busy foaming milk and the steamer drowned out every noise in the coffee shop. "So you're staying with Rachel Richards tonight, is that correct?"

Fenway nodded.

He paused. "It's a real shame what happened to her husband."

"Yeah." She watched the barista work the espresso machine. "You work the night shift a lot? Were you working that night?"

"Um," Officer Young stammered. "Yes."

"Oh. Did you see what happened?"

"I heard about it," he said. "I wasn't assigned to the jail that night." He cleared his throat. "Does Ms. Richards know we're going to be at her place all night?"

Fenway shrugged. "She's expecting me to show up for sure, but I'm not sure she knows an officer will be with me. I told her earlier today I couldn't stay at my place. So I assume she's heard by now I have a police detail. If she doesn't know the police will be stationed outside her door, she probably won't be surprised to find out."

"She's pretty smart."

"You don't get to be the youngest public information officer in the state for nothing."

Officer Young smiled. "No. I don't suppose you do." He furrowed his brow. "Listen, the sheriff was supposed to talk to you about this. Beatherd and Sanchez will be outside, but I'm supposed to be inside. I'm not supposed to let you out of my sight."

Fenway paused. "Is that what the sheriff said?"

"Well—not in those words. I mean, I'm not coming into the bathroom with you or anything."

"Or the bedroom," Fenway said, a little more sharply than she intended to.

"Or the bedroom, right," Officer Young said. "I'm going to be stationed in the living room. But I'll be making rounds upstairs too, making sure no one is trying to break in."

Fenway folded her arms as she watched the barista pour the steamed milk into her cup. "I don't know if *that's* going to be okay with Rachel."

"I understand." Officer Young sipped his coffee. "If it's a problem, we can always put you up in a hotel."

Fenway scoffed. "I'm not going to one of the sheriff office's preferred hotels. I've seen them. They make the Belvedere Terrace look like the Ritz-Carlton."

"The what?"

"The Belvedere Terrace Hotel. It's kind of like a resort, only rundown. It's on the north side of town near the refinery."

"Oh, yeah, I remember. It was nice a few years ago."

"I was there yesterday. It's not nice now."

The barista put a lid on the cup and made eye contact with Fenway.

Fenway took a couple of steps toward the counter. The barista turned the cup so *Joann*, spelled without the E, was turned toward her.

"Thanks," Fenway said, taking the cup off the counter.

The barista smiled broadly. "Have a good night, folks." Her attitude belied the *Get the hell out so I can close up and go home* that was right behind it.

Fenway took a sip. The latte wasn't strong, and the milk hadn't heated up enough. *Serves me right for ordering it just before closing time*, she thought, as Officer Young opened the door for her.

She took a good look at the officer for the first time. His jaw was strong, and she noticed he had good posture, but also had an ease about him that suggested he was comfortable with himself. She wondered how old he was—he could have been a mature twenty-four or a young-looking thirty-five. But Fenway thought he was likely pretty close to her age. She also noticed no rings adorning his fingers. She walked past him out into the parking lot, and he followed. They started walking back to the apartment.

"So—Joanne?" Officer Young asked.

"What?" Fenway said, taken aback a bit.

"The name you gave to the barista," he said.

"Oh. That's my mom's name."

"Why do you use your mom's name?"

"Ah," Fenway said. "Spoken like someone with an easy first name."

"What are you talking about?" Officer Young said. "Fenway's easy. Easy to spell, easy to write."

Fenway shook her head. "It's unusual. Everyone thinks they've heard it wrong. I either end up with something weird like *Arwen* or *Phyllis*, or I have to go into a big long story about how my father is the world's biggest Red Sox fan."

"Ah."

"So, Officer, what's your regular, easy-to-spell first name?"

He smiled. "Todd."

"Todd," she said. "Todd Young. Nice. Short, to the point."

He shrugged. "Thanks, I guess. I like Fenway, too. The name, I mean. And I'm not even a Red Sox fan."

Fenway didn't say anything.

They arrived back at the apartment complex and Fenway saw the building manager walk down the steps from the second-floor hallway and stride purposefully toward Fenway and Officer Young. He held a manila envelope in his hand and met them halfway across the parking lot.

"Miss Stevenson?"

"Hi," Fenway said. She didn't remember the building manager's name and was a little embarrassed.

"This was under the doormat," he said.

Fenway looked at Officer Young. "Was this there when you caught Terrance Ivanovich?"

Officer Young looked puzzled. "Well, I guess I can't say for sure. He had broken all the light bulbs in front of your apartment, so it was dark. And we were a little more concerned about the brick through your window than looking underneath your doormat."

"Think it was left by the same guy who threw the brick?" the building manager said.

"I'm not sure." Fenway took the envelope from him. The name *Fenway Stevenson* was neatly printed in thick black marker, centered on a single line in the middle of the envelope. "I don't think so. It's certainly neat writing. Can you see Terrance Ivanovich printing this neatly?"

"No." Officer Young said.

"I guess it's possible, though."

"Don't open it."

Fenway looked at him.

"Someone's trying to kill you," he said. "Don't tell me you take apart your phone but you're going to open an envelope without taking any precautions. It could be anthrax or something."

"Let's go under one of the lights," suggested Fenway. "We can't see anything out here in the middle of the parking lot."

"The workers are almost through, Miss Stevenson," the building manager said. "You should be able to come through in a few minutes."

"Thanks." Again Fenway wished she remembered his name.

Fenway and Officer Young walked over to the side of the parking lot, where a bright fluorescent, so blue it made Fenway's eyes hurt, shone down on the walkway.

Fenway turned the envelope over. "It's not sealed," she pointed out. The metal clasp was the only thing keeping it closed. "So probably no anthrax."

Officer Young took it from her and made a brief show of examining it. Fenway wondered if he was amping up his machismo to impress her. "Okay," he said after a moment. "I guess it's okay to open. But let me do it."

She looked at him sideways.

"Seriously," he said, and pinched the clasp and opened the envelope. He looked inside. "Looks like it's papers," he said.

Fenway held her hand out. He reluctantly handed over the envelope, and she shook the papers out into her hand.

"These aren't just any papers," she said, looking through them. "These are love letters between our murder victim and Charlotte."

CHAPTER THIRTEEN

ABOUT TWO DOZEN PAPERS HAD BEEN PRINTED OUT. THE PAPER was cheap; probably twenty-pound bond, either generic copier paper, or perhaps low-quality printer paper. The ink adhered to the paper, shiny and not well soaked-in.

"Get me a pair of gloves," she said.

"I don't think I have any in my cruiser."

"I've got a pair in my purse. Blue."

He was back inside of a minute with a pair of blue nitrile gloves. He held out a glove for her; she hesitated, then slipped her hand in. He did the same with the other. Fenway felt it oddly intimate.

She cleared her throat. "This is from a laser printer, not an inkjet," Fenway said.

"How can you tell?" Officer Young asked.

Fenway turned the paper so the light shone off the ink. "See the way the ink is adhering to the paper, sort of like it's sitting right on top?"

Officer Young nodded.

"Laser printers do that. Inkjet printers have their ink soak into the paper more—it's not as shiny, especially on cheap copier paper like this.

"How do you know?"

"It was in one of my forensic analysis classes," she said, a little dismissively.

"So what does that mean?"

"Most people have inkjet printers at home," Fenway said. "Laser printers are usually found at offices. So maybe someone printed this out at work."

"What about libraries or schools?"

"Yeah, there might be laser printers there too."

Officer Young leafed through the papers. "These are emails."

Across the top of the first page, in a bold sans serif font, was:

Ferris, Charlotte

There were pages and pages of love missives between Jeremy Kapp and Charlotte Ferris. The emails from "Jer" were a bit overwrought, but had a poet's touch for some of the phrasing. It wouldn't have impressed Fenway, and Fenway didn't think Charlotte would like it either. But Fenway remembered the bored look on Charlotte's face the last time she had dinner at their house. She remembered thinking there was trouble in their marriage; maybe Charlotte had been taken with someone, and found his passion made up for a lack of eloquence.

The love letters spanned part of September and all of October. Fenway scanned the emails. There was a lot of typical hot-and-heavy stuff; some references to Charlotte's beautiful breasts or the size of Jeremy's penis; some references to hotel stays, especially at the Belvedere. The emails started with a lot of sexual innuendo, but as the weeks progressed, Jeremy's communications got more personal and emotional. Charlotte's remained relatively unchanged from the broad brushstrokes of lust and excitement. Yet something didn't sit right with Fenway; she couldn't put her finger on it.

She read the pages until there were only two emails left, one from Charlotte and one from Jer. The content of the penultimate email from Charlotte:

Jer,

I can't wait until I see you tonight. I can't wait until my arms are wrapped around you tight and I can feel your manly body next to mine.

You are so sexy. I know it's not right for me to cheat on Nathaniel but it feels so good when I'm with you.

Love,
Charlotte

"Not the most articulate of love notes, is it?" Officer Young said.

Fenway shook her head, and realized what the problem was. "This isn't right."

"What's not right?"

"Charlotte majored in English literature. She'd never use such simplistic language as this—not just on this one, but throughout all these emails."

"Maybe she didn't want to intimidate her lover with her massive vocabulary."

"Maybe," Fenway admitted. "But that's not the only thing." She pointed to the closing. "The woman who was at the Belvedere Terrace? She and Kapp had pet names for each other—*Potemkin* and *Catherine.*"

"From some old English novel or something?"

"From actual history," Fenway said. "Catherine the Great, and her lover, Grigory Potemkin. *Potemkin* was the name Jeremy Kapp signed in under at the Belvedere Terrace."

Officer Young screwed up his face. "Isn't she the one who—" And then he stopped talking, an embarrassed look on his face.

Fenway smiled. "There was a rumor with her and a horse, yes. But that's not the point. The point is, Charlotte would call Kapp 'Potemkin' or 'my dearest Grigory,' and she'd sign it with 'your beloved Catherine' or something equally saccharine."

"So you think these emails are fake?"

She nodded. "I can't imagine these are real."

She turned the page.

Kapp, Jeremy L.

My beautiful Charlotte,

Nothing in this world can compare to you, my dear. When I saw you in the Japanese garden a few nights ago, you were a vision. Your husband doesn't appreciate you. He doesn't recognize what a treasure you are.

I'd hike through a Russian winter for the opportunity to see the perfect face of Charlotte the Great, my darling. I know you're in an impossible position, and as the queen of this county your discretion is going to be the most important thing to you and your family, but the passion we share is something I've never felt before.

I count the hours until we're together again. I've told Cricket I'm traveling to a conference. We can spend a few days at the Belvedere, pretending we're a new political dynasty. You know the name the room will be under.

—Your Grigory

"Oh, I see. 'Your Grigory.' That's what you're talking about?"

"This doesn't make any sense," Fenway mused quietly.

"What?"

"It doesn't make sense," she repeated. "Why does *he* use it, but she doesn't? Charlotte would be all over this overwrought role-playing crap."

"But he doesn't call her 'Catherine,'" Officer Young said. "That's kind of strange."

"Right," Fenway said. "I still think Charlotte's emails are fake."

"Just Charlotte's? Do you think Jeremy Kapp's emails are fake too?" Officer Young asked.

"No—I think Jeremy Kapp's are real. Look at this last email. I bet this is the *actual* email that Jeremy Kapp wrote, just with the names switched out." She paused and turned the pages over, but they were only printed on one side.

"What makes you think it's real?"

"Okay, first, let's assume that someone completely fabricated Charlotte's side of the correspondence, not knowing that *Grigory* and *Catherine* were pet names, so they use *Jer* and *Charlotte*."

"Right."

"But in *Kapp's* email, look at this name right here."

"Oh," Officer Young said, nodding. "It says 'Charlotte the Great,' not 'Catherine the Great.'"

"If Kapp sent the emails to a woman named Laurie or Donna, whoever sent them to me would have swapped out 'Laurie' or 'Donna' for 'Charlotte,' right?"

"Sure."

"And if Kapp made a joke about 'Catherine the Great,' they would have left it, right? Just like they left 'Grigory' in them."

"Oh, I get what you're saying. So the emails must have been addressed to 'Catherine,' and they swapped out all the 'Catherines' with 'Charlottes.' Even when Kapp wrote 'Catherine the Great.'"

"Exactly. I mean, it's not irrefutable proof, but I bet the real name of Kapp's mistress is 'Catherine.'"

Officer Young nodded. "We could get a warrant for the actual emails, right? This would be enough."

Fenway nodded. "Probably. But I need to turn these over to Dez and Donnelly. I'm off the case."

"Right." Officer Young paused. "Why would someone send these emails to you?"

Fenway shrugged. "I don't know—I guess I've gotten a reputation."

"A reputation?"

"Someone who isn't afraid to go after people close to my father."

Officer Young looked thoughtful. "And there's no one closer to your dad than his wife."

Fenway suppressed a laugh. "She's almost twenty-five years younger than he is," she said. "She's only a few years older than *I* am. I can't imagine what they have in common."

The building manager appeared by Fenway's side again. "Okay, Miss Stevenson," he said. "We've boarded up the window and cleaned up the broken glass. Doesn't seem to be any other damage. You can get into your apartment now."

"Thanks. I appreciate you coming here on such short notice."

"No problem. Tell your dad 'hi' from me."

"Sure."

Fenway turned and looked at Officer Young. "Okay," she said. "I've gotta go pack. You can't let me out of your sight, right?" She noticed the coquettish tone to her voice and wondered where it came from.

Officer Young followed her up the stairs and through the dark shadows in front of Apartment 214, where the light bulbs had all been broken. Fenway went in and got a suitcase from her closet, filling it with work outfits and a couple of her more formal ensembles. She looked at her dress with the torn shoulder, and thought about changing, and then thought of her shower, warm and inviting, where she could scrub off the soot and smoke and the memory of Rory.

"Officer Young, I'm going to be a few more minutes."

"What's the holdup? We're supposed get in and out."

"I—uh—" Fenway hesitated. "Look, I almost got blown up yesterday. I'm still wearing the same dress, and it's torn. My car has been vandalized, I saw a teenager get blown up, and I smell like the hospital. So I need to take a shower. I need to stand in there for five or ten minutes."

"You can't do that over at Rachel's?"

"It's not *my* shower there. Plus, Terrance Ivanovich already screwed up your schedule, right? Fifteen more minutes is going to make a difference?"

Officer Young shifted his weight. "I guess it's not a problem. But fifteen minutes, okay? Don't say that and then stay in there for an hour."

"Gotcha."

She grabbed a change of clothes—a pair of gray sweatpants, a black ribbed tank top, and a zip-up burgundy hooded sweatshirt—and went into the bathroom, closed the door, and turned the water on.

She thought about wrapping her hair before she got in, but her hair was dusty, and even though she'd have to spend the better part of an hour on it so it wouldn't frizz, she had to wash it out. She hesitated a moment, and then locked the bathroom door.

When she got in, the hot water felt good, and she could feel the light layer of dust come off like wet chalk, at first making a light paste on her skin but then getting overwhelmed by the hot water and sloughing off. She cried for Rory, too, putting her face under the hot spray, and then her whole head. Her crying was mostly silent, and she was sure her catches of breath and light sobs wouldn't be heard by Officer Young. She felt an emptiness in the pit of her stomach for him, and especially for his family.

She wondered if it was like what her father felt when he came home from work that day twenty years before, and discovered his wife and daughter gone—with all their clothes and much of their furniture. She wondered how it affected her father, and how it might be different than what Rory's father was going through right now. With Fenway's disappearance, the possibility of reuniting one day was always out there—in fact, it was exactly what had happened, although Fenway had been a grown woman when she came back into town six months ago. But with Rory, there was no hope for him coming back, no hope for escape, no hope for anything but a long silence that would stretch forever forward.

She cried herself out after a few minutes and washed and treated her hair. She soaped up, rinsed, then turned the water off. She listened to ghostly spaces of silence between the water running down the drain and the final drops from the shower head. The echo chamber of the shower created sonic bounces and settling air currents.

She pulled open the shower curtain and grabbed her towel and stepped onto the bathmat. She dried herself off slowly and deliberately, taking a hairwrap and some avocado oil and shea butter and doing a quick hair treatment. Officer Young had said fifteen minutes, but surely he must know the time a hair treatment would take—he must have had sisters, or at least a mother, who took the time for treatments. *Stop worrying about it,* she chided herself.

She wrapped her hair, got dressed, and opened the door, letting out the steam from the bathroom. Officer Young was sitting on the sofa, leafing through one of Fenway's coffee table books—the book about the history of the Space Needle. She looked at his face; he appeared to be a little miffed, probably because she had promised fifteen minutes and she took forty-five.

"You ready?" he said. It was obvious he was eager to leave and go to Rachel's apartment, but she could see him trying not to let it show and failing.

"I'll be a few more minutes," she said, as apologetically as she could. "I just have to grab my shoes and toiletries. I'll finish my hair over at Rachel's."

"Take your time," Officer Young said, although Fenway knew he didn't mean it.

———◆———

Fenway didn't feel like talking as Officer Young drove her to Rachel's apartment, with the second cruiser following closely behind. He stared straight ahead, and Fenway closed her eyes. She flashed on a picture in her head of her with Officer Young, with him alert and watchful, and Fenway curled up in his arms like a kitten.

When they arrived at Rachel's, Fenway let herself in with the key. It was almost nine o'clock, but Rachel still wasn't home. The warm, stuffy apartment felt sterile. Fenway, her stomach growling, unzipped her hoodie and wondered if she had a message on her cellphone.

"Does Rachel know *I'm* spending the night in her apartment?" Officer Young asked.

Fenway shook her head. "Remember, I don't have my phone with me. I didn't have any way to tell her."

Officer Young nodded. "I hope the sheriff—or someone from the office—let her know. I'd hate to have her walk in and find a strange black guy on her couch."

Fenway smiled, but a little sadly. "Do you have a phone? I can call her."

Officer Young pulled his phone out. Fenway took it and dialed. She had to hold it to her left ear because her right ear was still ringing.

"This is Rachel Richards."

"Hi, Rachel, it's Fenway."

"Oh! I didn't recognize the number."

"I'm using Officer Young's phone," she said, taking the sweatshirt off and draping it over the back of a kitchen chair.

"He's with you?"

"Yes." Fenway paused. "Um—I don't know if I told you or not, but I'm under police protection tonight. For the foreseeable future, in fact."

"That's what you told me when you called. But I didn't know if it was still on—I thought they caught the guy."

"They caught *a* guy," Fenway said carefully. "But it was the guy who vandalized my car. I don't think he was the same one who blew up the minivan."

"Oh no."

"Right. So there are going to be two officers outside tonight, making sure the complex is safe, and then Officer Young is going to be inside tonight. I guess he'll sleep on the couch or something."

"I'm not going to be sleeping," he said.

"Oh. Right, I guess I didn't think of that."

"Wait," Rachel said, "*inside* the apartment?"

"Yes. Is that going to be a problem?"

Rachel paused for a moment. "I guess not," she finally said. "Weird—he'll be the first guy to spend the night in my apartment since Dylan... died."

Fenway winced. "If this is too weird for you, they can put me up in a hotel."

Rachel scoffed. "No way. I've seen the hotel they use. I might not be the world's best housekeeper, but my guest room is a lot better than anything you'll get out of the sheriff's office."

Fenway nodded, even though Rachel couldn't see her. "Right. Thanks. I'm afraid I'm imposing a whole lot on you."

"After everything you've done for me?" Rachel said. "No way, sister. You're staying over until they catch whoever did this. And that's final."

"Thanks, Rachel." Fenway cleared her throat. "You coming home any time soon?"

"I'm going to have to." Rachel clicked her tongue. "There's a lot to do here, still, but I'm running on fumes. I'm not going to make it much past ten. I've got a couple of reporters working on stories, I've given quotes to the L.A. *Times* and the *Courier*, and I've gotten a press release written and started implementing the communication plan."

"I'm sorry," Fenway said.

"Oh, for goodness' sake, Fenway, it's not your fault someone tried to blow you up yesterday afternoon."

"No, I guess not."

"Listen—I've got to wrap up a few more things here. Will you be awake when I get home?"

"Uh..."

"Never mind. I'm sure you didn't sleep well in the hospital last night. We'll talk tomorrow. Maybe I'll take you to breakfast. Help yourself to anything in the fridge. I have some bourbon on the top shelf of the pantry, too. I've been meaning to have you get it for me when you come over anyway."

"Get it for you?"

"Yes, Miss Five-Ten, get it for me. Some of us barely clear five feet."

"You don't have a stool or a stepladder or anything?"

"Do you want the bourbon or not?"

Fenway smirked. "Yes. After today, definitely yes."

They said their goodbyes and Fenway gave the phone back to Officer Young.

"She coming back soon?"

"Yes. About an hour. Of course, knowing her, that means two."

Fenway walked into the kitchen and opened the pantry. There, on the top shelf, was a bottle of Maker's Mark.

"Not bad," Fenway muttered to herself. She reached up to get it and had to stand on her tiptoes, but got her hand around it and pulled it down.

She found a highball glass in one of the cabinets, got four ice cubes out of one of the trays in the freezer, and poured two fingers of bourbon into the glass.

"You want one? Oh—never mind, you're on duty." Fenway opened the refrigerator. "Rachel's got Dr. Pepper and some banana-orange juice thing."

Officer Young smiled. "Been a while since I had any soda," he said. "I guess a can won't hurt." He reached around Fenway to get a can and brushed against her bare arm. Fenway felt a jolt of electricity with his touch, and suddenly realized the tank top she was going to wear to bed wasn't exactly modest. Although maybe she was overthinking it; the sweatpants didn't flatter her figure, and she didn't have any makeup on.

And here I am drinking a bourbon with a man I just met, she thought, *on a day where I feel vulnerable. What could possibly go wrong?*

He straightened up and opened the soda.

Fenway held up her glass. "Here's to making it out alive," she said.

"I'll drink to that," Officer Young said, a sad smile crossing his face.

The cold bourbon felt good hitting the back of Fenway's throat, and she intended to sip it but swallowed half of what she poured. Her insides burned a little as the whiskey went down, but it opened up her sinuses and for a moment she felt more clearheaded than she had since the explosion.

"Well," she said. "These last two days have certainly been horrible." And intending to finish the glass, this time, she swallowed the rest of the bourbon in one gulp, and set the glass down on the countertop. "I'm going to get ready for bed. Tell Rachel 'hi' for me when she gets home."

"Will do," Officer Young said.

She turned to go.

"Oh—" he said. "I know it wasn't under great circumstances, but I'm glad to finally meet you."

"Likewise," Fenway said awkwardly. "I mean, it's nice to have met you too."

She grabbed her suitcase and walked up the stairs to the guest room. She got the hair dryer and her toiletries out, went into the upstairs bathroom and finished treating her hair. It was quarter past ten when she came out of the bathroom, but Rachel still wasn't home. She tiptoed to the top of the staircase and looked down. Officer Young was standing by the window, watching outside, although for what, Fenway wasn't quite sure.

She went into Rachel's guest bedroom, took her sweatpants off, and got under the covers in her underwear and tank top. She wondered briefly if she'd be able to relax with everything going on in her head, and then she was fast asleep.

PART IV

SUNDAY

CHAPTER FOURTEEN

FENWAY GOT INTO HER ACCORD IN FRONT OF HER APARTMENT complex. She looked in the rearview mirror, and adjusted it so she could see out the back window. She put her hands on the steering wheel before it hit her—why did she have to adjust the rearview mirror? No one drove her Accord but her—did they?

Then Fenway felt the hands around her throat. *"Back off,"* a low voice hissed in her ear. *"Back off or it won't be the kid that gets it next time."*

Fenway sat bolt upright in bed, screaming.

"Holy shit," a man's voice said. "You're okay—you're okay."

The overhead light came on. Fenway saw nothing but a flash of bright white, and then her eyes started to adjust.

Where was she?

Officer Young was standing at the foot of the bed, his gloved hands out in front of him. Rachel was in the doorway, the hallway light streaming behind her figure in shapeless flannel pajamas, her brow creased with worry. It came back to Fenway; she was in Rachel's apartment.

"You're okay, Fenway," Officer Young said. "You had a bad dream."

Fenway was in a cold sweat and felt embarrassed—she didn't want Officer Young seeing her freaked out.

"Sorry," Fenway mumbled, kicking her sweaty legs underneath the covers to attempt to get some airflow. She was still exhausted, and her throat hurt. She coughed, a dry, somewhat painful cough.

"What happened?" Rachel asked.

"Like Officer Young said," Fenway replied weakly. "Bad dream. I dreamed someone was choking me."

"Your hands were around your own throat when I came in," said Officer Young.

"I must have been trying to pull the hands off me," Fenway said. She felt groggy and the muscles in her arms and shoulders hurt.

Fenway shook her head back and forth; her mind was muddy and her eyes were having trouble focusing. "I'm sorry, guys," she said. "I didn't mean to wake you up."

"It's okay," Rachel said, sitting down on the bed and pulling Fenway into a hug.

"Someone's trying to kill me, Rachel," Fenway whispered. "I'm scared." As soon as the words were out of her mouth, she knew it was true: she was terrified. And her body ached, even worse than it had the morning before. Had she been fully awake, she might have wanted to take the words back. But she wanted to go back to bed.

"I know," Rachel said, patting her head. "Listen, why don't you come into my room? You'll sleep better in there."

"In your bed?"

Rachel raised her head to look at Officer Young. "Don't get that gross look on your face, officer. She's been through a lot. She needs to sleep, and someone should be there to calm her down if anything happens again. We can't have you running in there just because she has a bad dream."

"I didn't have a gross look on my face," Officer Young said.

"Okay, fine," Rachel said.

"I don't think that's a good idea."

Rachel rolled her eyes. "Oh, please. She'll sleep better if she's not by herself. What do you think, Fenway?"

"I want to go to sleep," Fenway said, slurring her words with fatigue.

"Okay. You can come into my room."

"What if they come into the apartment to get me?"

"I've got my gun," Rachel said. "No one's going to hurt you."

"I think she needs to stay in her own room," Officer Young said.

"Why, in case *I'm* the one who's trying to kill her?" Rachel scoffed. "You can go back downstairs. I'll yell if anything's wrong."

Fenway exhaled through her mouth loudly, eyelids drooping.

"Come on," Rachel said, "let's go."

"I'm in my underwear," Fenway said.

"Oh for crying out loud, Fenway," Rachel said under her breath. "I'll get you some sweats for you to sleep in."

"Officer Young will see my butt."

"You can go back downstairs, Officer," Rachel said.

The officer padded back downstairs.

Rachel got Fenway out of the guest bed and across the hall to her room. She pulled the covers down from the side of the bed nearest the door. Two pillows were vertically arranged, top-to-bottom, as if it were a person in the bed. Rachel pulled the pillows out.

"Okay," she said. "You can sleep."

Fenway dragged herself over to the bed and flopped down. Rachel pulled the covers up over her and Fenway turned her back to the door.

But instead of getting into bed herself, Rachel started making noise. The sound of a chair scraping across the carpet made Fenway sit up. She rubbed her eyes.

"What are you doing?"

"Don't worry about it," Rachel said, pulling a straight-backed chair over to the door. "You get to sleep. You need it." She tipped the chair back under the doorknob.

"Are you that afraid of people breaking in?"

Rachel's face looked confused for a moment, then relaxed. "Better safe than sorry," she said.

Fenway looked at the two pillows on the floor Rachel had pulled out of bed, formerly occupying the same space she now did.

"Are *you* okay, Rachel?"

"I'm fine," she said, nodding. "Just wanted to be extra safe."

Fenway started to open her mouth, then didn't know what she would say.

Rachel walked around the other side of the bed and got in. She looked at Fenway, who was still in a half-seated position, propped up on elbows. "You good? You ready to go back to sleep?"

"Yeah."

"Okay." Rachel turned off the bedside lamp and the room sank into darkness.

Fenway lay back. She was asleep within seconds.

In the morning, Fenway woke to the smell of coffee. Her whole body ached. She turned her head toward Rachel's side of the bed; there was no one there.

She swung her legs out and rubbed her eyes. She didn't remember at first how she'd come to be in Rachel's bed, but the memory came back, as groggy as she was and as bad as she felt. The memory wasn't entirely clear; she seemed to remember Rachel pulling one of the straight-backed chairs in the room in front of the door. It seemed odd, with Officer Young there to protect them.

Cautiously, she opened the door to the hallway, and heard both Rachel and a male voice downstairs. Padding over to the guest room, Fenway found her sweats and put them on. She went into the bathroom and looked at herself in the mirror; she was decent, at least for first thing in the morning.

Walking downstairs, Fenway smelled sourdough toast added to the mix of aromas. She saw Rachel in the kitchen, opening a jar of jam, and Officer Callahan at the kitchen table.

"Hey, Callahan," Fenway said.

"Hey, Fenway."

"Officer Young not here?"

Callahan shook his head. "His shift ended a couple hours ago."

Fenway walked over to the kitchen table and sat across from Officer Callahan. "Your shift start, then?"

"Yep."

Fenway shook her head. "I hate to do this to you guys. With the election on Tuesday and everything, the last thing you need to worry about is focusing on me."

"You want some breakfast, Fenway?" Rachel said.

Fenway looked up at the clock. It was eight-fifteen.

"Oh, man," Fenway said. "I slept late. I think I was supposed to be at a campaign breakfast this morning."

"I talked to Millicent a little while ago," Rachel said. "She cancelled the breakfast, but she said she'd call back. I think she wants to talk with you. The arrest of Ivanovich's son is going to hit the news sometime this morning, and she wants to brief you. She doesn't want you getting caught by a reporter."

"I can always deny knowledge."

"Oh, come on, Fenway, I saw the police report before I left last night. *You're* the one who tackled him. And you don't know if a reporter has that on video or if they've seen the police report. You get caught lying, then *you're* going to be the story. Wouldn't you rather have the story be Dr. Ivanovich's white supremacist son who threw a brick through your window?"

Fenway began to protest. "Sure, but—"

"I know it's not fair to ask you to lay low," Rachel interrupted, "but I don't control what conclusions people jump to."

Fenway was quiet for a minute.

"You get toast and yogurt and coffee," Rachel said, putting a slice of sourdough on a plate and filling up a UCLA Bruins mug.

"Can I help with anything?"

"Yogurt's in the fridge."

Fenway got up and opened the refrigerator, grabbed a strawberry-banana yogurt, and took the plate and the coffee from Rachel. She was walking to the kitchen table when Rachel's mobile phone rang.

Rachel picked up. "Rachel Richards." A pause as she sipped her coffee. Fenway took a bite of the toast.

"No, no, she's here. Well, I know, but with everything that happened—" Rachel paused again. "Listen, I know, but it's not like we're talking about a senate race or the governorship."

Another pause.

"Sure." She held the phone for Fenway to take.

Fenway reached out. "Millicent?"

Rachel nodded, placing the phone in her hand.

"Hi, Millicent."

"Hi, Fenway. You're a hard woman to track down."

"Sorry, but that's kind of the point. Someone is trying to kill me."

"I thought they caught the guy. I thought *you* caught the guy, in fact."

"It's complicated. They don't think it's the same guy."

Millicent paused. "This is a tricky situation," she said. "You're running for office. You can't look like you're scared of this guy.

You can't disappear from public view. People will lose faith in you."

"What's their other voting option?" Fenway said. "Vote for the man whose son got arrested for threatening me?"

"I don't know how Ivanovich is going to play it," Millicent said. "He might blame you for it. I heard you broke his son's arm when you made the arrest."

"No," Fenway said. "Officer Young made the arrest."

"So *you* didn't break his arm?"

"Well, uh, he tried to get away and I tackled him," Fenway said. "And it wasn't his arm, it was his hand. Or at least I think it was his hand."

"Still," Millicent said, clicking her tongue, "it would have been better if you hadn't been involved in the arrest at all."

Fenway muted the phone and swore loudly and creatively at Millicent. Callahan looked up from the table; he hadn't heard Fenway curse like that before.

She took the phone off mute. "Listen, Millicent, I realize this could cause a problem, but I can't pick and choose who gets the law applied to them. I tackled the guy when I thought he was some random white supremacist, someone who had vandalized my car and my apartment, and who, at the time, I thought was trying to kill me. I didn't know he was my opponent's son."

Millicent sighed. "I know," she said thoughtfully. "Before the last couple of election cycles, I would have said Ivanovich was dead in the water. But I've seen some weird stuff lately. Some voters might, as crazy as it may seem, react positively to this."

Fenway took a deep breath and let it out slowly. "You're the campaign manager. Whatever you think is best—as long as it doesn't get me killed."

Millicent laughed. "Well, *I* think you should make the speech at the senior center today."

Fenway paused. "I don't know about public appearances, Millicent. That's an invitation for trouble, isn't it?"

"I don't know. You have police protection, right?"

"Yeah, but as great as Officer Young and Officer Callahan are, there's only one person on me. They can't be guarding me against everything someone could do."

Officer Callahan shook his head. "Three," he mouthed, holding up three fingers.

"Hang on, Millicent."

"Three officers," Callahan said. "We've got three people on you. One, like me, will be close at all times. And two other officers will be staking out the area, like the apartment complex, your office, even if you have a dentist appointment or something."

"Aw, crap," Fenway said. "I forgot I have an appointment with the family therapist at eleven today."

"That's Dr. Tassajera, right?" Rachel asked. "How's that going?"

"Good enough that he agreed to meet us on a Sunday."

"Really?"

"It's a make-up session. I think my father suggested Sunday on purpose so the doctor wouldn't schedule it. So now we get to have a session on a Sunday, as if I don't have enough campaign events going on."

Rachel smiled back, but a little sadly.

"Fenway?" Millicent said.

"All right," Fenway said. "Callahan says there are three officers on me. Two of them are, uh, assessing the environmental danger, I guess. That makes me feel a little better."

"So you can make one P.M. at the senior center today after your session?"

"Sure," Fenway conceded, though she sounded anything but. "I'll be done by noon."

"Great," Millicent said. "I've got your speech all prepared. I'll meet you there at a quarter to one."

"All right."

Millicent hung up.

Fenway sighed. "I'd feel a whole lot better if there was something else I could do to feel a little more safe. I hate not having my phone, I hate not having my car, and I hate hiding out. I feel like I'm missing out on my life."

Callahan nodded. "Yeah." Then he smacked the table. "Hey, I know something. Vice has bug detectors. They've got GPS tracker detectors and other devices too. I mean, some of the newer equipment can fool 'em, but it works on a *lot* of different things. It's not foolproof, but I bet it would give you much better peace of mind than *not* having it."

Fenway nodded. "Yeah, I remember wanting to get those bug detectors when I was investigating the mayor's murder."

"So you know where they are?"

"Uh, no," Fenway said, "I didn't end up getting them. But that's a great idea. If there's a tracking device or a bug anywhere near me, I definitely want to know. And I'm not going to be able to get through my speech at the senior center if I'm looking over my shoulder every couple of minutes."

"No," Rachel said, "I suppose not."

"We can get them while you're getting ready," Callahan said.

"Great," Fenway said. "Then I can keep my appointment with the therapist. Wouldn't want to disappoint my father."

Callahan radioed into the station as Fenway walked upstairs. She selected a dark burgundy pantsuit she had purchased specifically for the campaign trail and paired it with a cream-colored blouse. The outfit was still a little wrinkled from the suitcase, but she decided to hang it up while she showered. Hopefully the folks at the senior center wouldn't even notice.

When Fenway had showered and dressed, there were two small, black devices sitting on the coffee table in front of Rachel's sofa.

"Those the bug detectors?"

Callahan nodded. "The bigger one is the bug tracker. Picks up wireless cameras and microphones. I already ran a screen in here. The other one is specifically made to detect GPS trackers on your car. I used it on Rachel's BMW and our cruisers."

"You think someone would put a GPS tracker on a police car?"

"I'd sure look like a fool if someone *did* and I didn't check, right?"

Fenway nodded.

"All right," Callahan said. "Next stop, the therapist's office, right?"

"Right," Fenway said. "Listen—do you have to go in with me?"

"Not into the inner office," Callahan said, "but as far as I can. Does he have a waiting room?"

"Yes," she said. "The chairs are even comfortable. And your presence will probably piss off my father, who will want to talk about his feelings about his trophy wife spending the night in jail."

"Wonderful," Callahan deadpanned. "I can't wait."

Fenway grabbed her purse as Callahan took the two tracking detection devices and radioed to the other officers to move. Fenway gave Callahan the address of the therapist, said goodbye to Rachel—who perhaps tried not to look too relieved to have the police detail out of her house.

Fenway rode in Callahan's car, the other cruiser following. Callahan was quiet, and Fenway gazed tautly out her side window. She didn't know how long this would go on, her having to look over her shoulder constantly, in fear of every shadow and sudden movement. She could already feel the tension in her shoulders, and she sighed.

They pulled into the half-full parking lot of the therapist's office.

"Weird," Callahan said. "A lot of cars here for a Sunday."

"There's a call center in the building in the back," Fenway said. "They run twenty-four seven." She got out of the cruiser and reached into her purse to check her phone. She dug around for a few seconds before she realized it was still in her office without a SIM card.

"You got the time, Callahan?"

"Twenty minutes to eleven."

She was quite early, but she didn't know how much time it would take them to check the room for bugs and hidden cameras. She wondered if the therapist had hidden cameras in his office—either for protection, in case a patient got confrontational or violent—or for more nefarious purposes, like her Russian Lit professor had ten years previous. She blinked hard, trying to get the memory out of her mind, and then recalled Detective Deshawn Ridley and the phone call she had received two days before. She wondered if she'd be hearing from him again.

"Suite 34B, right?" Callahan said, striding purposefully across the lot. The other officers were walking the perimeter of the buildings, their eyes constantly scanning.

"Right."

Fenway briefly wondered if Dr. Jacob Tassajera was even in this early on a Sunday, since he had made special arrangements to accommodate his richest and most demanding patient. But, she reasoned, maybe another client had a special situation; if he was going to come in for one patient, he might as well schedule two or three more.

Callahan grabbed the door handle and it swung inside easily. He pulled the bug detector off his belt and switched it on.

And immediately it emitted a loud, pulsing whine, the lights flashing red.

Callahan's eyes grew wide. "There's a bug in here. A hidden microphone, something."

"Maybe—" Fenway started, and then clamped her mouth shut. She had scenarios in her head, but she didn't know the first thing about hidden microphones and bug detectors. She let Callahan do his job.

The whining got louder as he stepped into the waiting room. The flashing red lights got stronger and closer together as he approached the small table between the chairs.

Callahan's finger pointed at the small succulent in the cute little ceramic pot.

CHAPTER FIFTEEN

THE DOOR TO THE OFFICE OPENED AND DR. JACOB TASSAJERA stuck his angry face out. "You need to stop making so much noise. I'm with a client!" Then, seeing Callahan's uniform, softened. "Uh—is there a problem, officer?"

Callahan nodded, beckoning Tassajera to come out. The doctor stepped into the waiting room, somewhat reluctantly, and shut the door behind him.

"Dr. Tassajera," he said, "are you aware you have active recording devices in here?"

Tassajera swallowed hard, the color draining from his face. "I don't record my clients. That's a breach of confidentiality."

"Not even for your protection, doctor?" Fenway said. "Maybe one of your clients isn't always stable, or you're afraid they're going to get violent and you'll have to defend yourself?"

"No," Dr. Tassajera said adamantly. "Even if *I* thought it was okay, the state board would have something to say. I could lose my license."

"So," Callahan said, turning the volume down on the device, "maybe you can explain what this recording device is doing here in the waiting room."

"There's another one like it in his office," Fenway said quietly to Callahan.

"What, those little cactus things?" he said. "They were a gift from building management. My two-year anniversary in this office. They put them in here without letting me know, which annoyed me a little, but I kept them."

Fenway nodded. "They did appear recently, Officer. My father and I had our first appointment and those succulents weren't here. The next time we came, though, they were." Fenway's mind clicked on the coincidence. "I wonder."

"You wonder what?" Callahan asked.

"I don't know..." Fenway started, then shrugged and blurted the rest out. "I don't know if it's a coincidence that the recording devices appeared so soon after my father and I started seeing you. I mean," she said, seeing the startled look on Dr. Tassajera's face, "I know my father and I aren't the only clients you have. Maybe another client's spouse is afraid they're cheating, so they decided to bug your office."

"That's highly unusual," said Dr. Tassajera.

"I know," Fenway said. "It's a lot more likely the bug is there to record someone who's running for office and someone who's bankrolling the campaign."

"Like you," Callahan said.

"Right."

"What did you say last time you were here?" Callahan said. "Did you talk about anything someone would have wanted you dead over?"

Fenway motioned with her head for them to talk outside.

"I don't—" Dr. Tassajera began, but Fenway silenced him with a look. He followed Fenway and Callahan outside.

"We didn't even have our session," Fenway said. "We rescheduled it for today. We just sat in the waiting room. We even had a fight."

Oh.

Fenway swallowed hard. "I told my father I'm reopening the case where two of his workers were killed in the refinery accident," Fenway said.

"I thought that was your dad's head of security," Callahan said. "Isn't that part of what he was arrested for?"

Fenway shook her head. "We think he did it, but we didn't have enough evidence to charge him," she said. "Besides, with the two other murders we *could* prove, I guess I didn't think we had to."

"But maybe it wasn't him."

"No," Fenway said, "I'm convinced it *was* him, but maybe he was taking orders from someone else."

"Like your father?" Callahan said.

"If someone's intending to record the therapy sessions between my father and me, maybe the head of security *wasn't* taking orders from my father," Fenway said. "Maybe it was someone else at Ferris Energy. Or maybe it wasn't someone from Ferris Energy at all."

Callahan was thoughtful, then snapped back to the present.

"Dr. Tassajera," he said, "Fenway says there's another plant like this in your office."

Dr. Tassajera nodded.

"I'd suggest you get it and bring it out here," he said, "before any more of your client's private conversation is recorded."

"Callahan," Fenway hissed, elbowing him.

"What?"

"We've got to bag it up! Fingerprints."

"Oh—right," he said. He cleared his throat. "Wait—we need to bag it up. It's evidence. We'll need to come in there and get it."

Dr. Tassajera set his jaw. "I'm not going to compromise the privacy of my patient—"

"The patient's privacy is already compromised," Fenway pointed out.

"Maybe by whoever planted the recording device," said Dr. Tassajera, "but I see no reason the police need to know who's in my office getting counseling. I'm sorry, but you can either come back after my patient leaves, or you can get a subpoena."

Which will take longer than waiting for the patient to leave, Fenway thought.

"Okay," Callahan said. "I understand. Go wrap it up with whoever it is. We need to get the microphone when you're finished."

"Walking them past you will be as bad as you going in there," Dr. Tassajera pointed out. "The point is, they have the right to privacy—you shouldn't know they're seeing a therapist."

"Surely your patients walk past each other all the time."

"It's a little different, don't you think, when the police are in the waiting room?"

Callahan started to object but Fenway pulled his arm. "Okay, Doc," she said. "I get it. I wouldn't want the cops bursting in on me either. We'll give you—what do you say, Callahan? Five minutes?"

"Fenway, we can't let the evidence—"

"Callahan, we'll bag up the microphone in the waiting room now." Fenway opened the door, walked into the waiting room, and took a pair of blue nitrile gloves and an evidence bag out of her purse. Callahan and Dr. Tassajera were right behind her. "A citizen's privacy outweighs the state's right to gather evidence unless there's a compelling need. And no judge would call this compelling." Fenway dropped the succulent and pot into the evidence bag and sealed it.

"But—"

"No, Callahan. We're going." Fenway turned to Dr. Tassajera. "We'll go around the corner of the building to the left. Have your client leave. Don't touch anything in the office unless you have to. And *definitely* don't touch that succulent plant." She paused and took a breath. "We'll be back in exactly five minutes. If the client's still here, we're coming in anyway." Fenway elbowed Callahan. "And tell the guys out there to swing around the side of the building to watch me, and not the front door."

Callahan nodded and got on his radio.

Dr. Tassajera set his mouth into a line, but nodded solemnly. "Thank you, Miss Stevenson," he said. "I appreciate you respecting my patient's confidentiality."

"You're welcome," she said, "and don't make me regret this. You know I can get another therapist if I have trust issues with you." She turned, leading Callahan by the elbow out of the office.

"I'm uncomfortable leaving the evidence in there," Callahan said quietly, closing the door behind them. "He knows it's important to us now, and he could tamper with it."

"Yep," Fenway said, "but it's still better than ending up as the defendant in a privacy suit or worse, being sued yourself."

"Being sued myself?"

"There's precedent," Fenway said, turning around the corner, and they no longer kept the front door in view. "A couple of deputies from P.Q. went over to one of those walk-in clinics—they'd gotten some reports of falsified prescriptions. Did you hear about this?"

"I heard they made a couple arrests."

"Yeah, but they broke in on a doctor who was in the middle of an exam."

"An exam?"

"An exam of an underage patient who just happened to be the neighbor of one of the deputies."

"Oh."

"Yeah. The parents sued. They settled out of court."

Callahan hesitated. "Did you hear how much?"

"Let's just say I know why the coroner's office won't be getting new computers next year."

"Ah. Man, I almost opened us up to a bad situation."

"You didn't know. This doesn't happen often." Fenway reached for her phone out of habit and then sighed. "How long has it been, Callahan?"

"Enough time that I feel like we're wasting it," Callahan said, "and too little time to get anything else accomplished."

"Yeah," Fenway said. "We can't even get a coffee."

"True."

Fenway had run out of things to talk about with Callahan. The two of them didn't have much in common besides their ages. And she realized she didn't know much about him at all.

"So, Callahan," Fenway said, "You and I have been working together for almost six months now, and I hardly know anything about you."

Callahan grinned. "I can't say the same. I feel like I know a *lot* about you."

"You do?"

"Sure. You're a popular topic around the sheriff's office. Especially after you made those two big arrests. Those cases had the potential to make the office look pretty incompetent. But you solved them fast. We were all relieved, frankly."

"Well," Fenway said, feeling color rising to her cheeks, "I was happy to have helped." She absentmindedly snapped the wrists of her blue nitrile gloves. "But maybe you could tell me a little about yourself."

"What do you want to know?"

"Uh—how about your first name, for a start?"

"You've worked with me for six months and you don't even know my name is Brian?"

Fenway winced. "Uh—I guess I didn't. Sometimes I can be, I don't know, a little wrapped up in my own head."

"What else do you want to know?"

"Married? Kids?"

"No to both," Callahan replied. "Broke up with my girlfriend a few months ago."

Fenway nodded. "Okay, not to spoil our chat, but it's definitely been five minutes."

Callahan looked at his watch. "Yep. Seven minutes, in fact. Let's go."

They walked back around the corner and down the sidewalk. "Hmm," Fenway said, "Dr. Tassajera left the door open."

"On purpose?"

"Maybe." Fenway pushed the door all the way open and took a step into the waiting room. "Doctor?" she called. "We're back."

The door to his office was closed. "You think he's still in there with the client?" Callahan asked.

"I hope not," Fenway said. "It'll piss me off if he is. It took me long enough to find a therapist my father could tolerate. I'm not looking to go shrink shopping again."

She knocked on the door to his office, her nitrile glove deadening the sound a little. "Doctor!" she called. "We're back! Can you open the door?"

No answer.

Fenway looked at Callahan's face; his brow was furrowed in confusion.

"I don't like this, Callahan."

She tried the knob, her hands still gloved. It was locked.

"It's *locked*?" Callahan asked in disbelief.

Fenway nodded.

"Stand back." Callahan steadied himself as Fenway took a couple of steps back from the office door.

Callahan took a deep breath and kicked the door squarely next to the handle. The cheap lock broke and the door exploded back, bouncing against the wall and almost slamming shut again. Callahan caught the ruined door with his foot, then gently pushed it open.

He took a few steps in and looked to the right. Fenway couldn't see around him to what was on the floor, but Callahan gasped.

Fenway stepped in and craned her neck to look around him.

Dr. Tassajera lay on the ground, face down. Blood pooled around his head.

CHAPTER SIXTEEN

FENWAY PUSHED CALLAHAN TO THE SIDE AND KNELT DOWN next to Dr. Tassajera. She held up his hand and felt for a pulse. Nothing.

One of doctor's golf clubs lay by his left arm, its head bathed in blood and a bit of white matter that Fenway assumed was brain tissue.

"Dammit," she said under her breath.

"What happened?" Callahan said. He turned to Fenway; his eyes were wide open, the confusion even more pronounced on his face.

"We left for five minutes and I assume his client killed him while we were gone," Fenway said. She felt the anger creep into her voice.

"What—how—"

"Secure the room, Callahan. Make sure whoever did this isn't still here."

Fenway got up and backed against the wall while Callahan checked under the desk and in the small coat closet.

"Clear," he said.

Fenway shook her head and walked back to the body. "Can you call this in, Callahan?" she said. "And tell them I'm already on the scene."

Callahan nodded and got on the radio while stepping into the waiting room. Fenway thought she heard him say "CSI" and hoped they'd be able to find some evidence. She heard the radio click off and Callahan poked his head in the office again.

"Okay, we've got a lot more to work with than most murder scenes," Fenway said. "First of all, at least we have a seven-minute window when the attack happened." Then she knelt close to the dead doctor's head. "Blunt force trauma," she said, pointing to the golf club. "This would have done it." She paused. "You got a camera on you, Callahan?"

"Just my camera phone," he said, pulling it out of his pocket, unlocking it, and holding it out.

Fenway took it and pulled up the camera app. "That'll do." It took a second to focus, but once it did, she started snapping away.

Callahan talked with them in the outer office while Fenway took more pictures and examined the body. They stepped outside to secure the scene.

"Any cars leave the parking lot?" she said.

One of the other officers shook his head. "We didn't see anything. We were waiting on the other side of the building."

"Crap," Fenway said. "Maybe we can get security footage from building management or something."

"I'm not sure they have cameras at this office complex," Callahan said. "If Dr. Tassajera here was adamant about client privacy, he'd have picked a building without cameras, right?"

"That makes sense, but who knows?" Fenway mused. "Anything is possible. Maybe the building people installed them after the fact and he didn't want to move his practice. Worth checking, at any rate."

"Maybe."

Fenway stood up and scanned the room. She walked over to the desk. She pointed at a power cable and a monitor cable that weren't plugged into anything.

"Where's the laptop?"

Callahan shook his head. "I don't know. Do you remember seeing it in here earlier?"

"No," Fenway said. "But most people bring their laptops with them to work, right?"

Callahan nodded. "They do—but not always on the weekend. If he was seeing a couple of clients today—you and your dad, and the guy who killed him—he might not have bothered. Maybe he thought he'd take the laptop in on Monday and type up all his notes on the sessions later."

Fenway nodded thoughtfully. "That's a good point," she mused. "Even though I don't go anywhere without my laptop. Not usually, anyway."

Callahan looked around the room. "Anything else missing?"

Fenway pointed to the table next to the chair. "The succulent in here is gone."

"That was a hidden microphone too, right?"

"Yes," she said. "At least, I assume so. It looked exactly like the other one. Same ceramic pot and everything."

Callahan looked around, lost. "We were gone for seven minutes."

"Sometimes it doesn't even take that long."

Callahan sighed. "The sheriff is going to be so mad at me."

Fenway looked Callahan in the face. "No, he won't. You were following protocol, you were following case law and my guidance. We had no way of knowing there was any danger."

"I still don't like it," he said. "This happened on my watch. And it shouldn't have."

"You can't think like that," Fenway said. "And blaming yourself won't help us find the killer."

"Do you think this is connected to you?" Callahan said. "Do you think the other patient waited for you? That if you had shown up here by yourself you would have been the one attacked?"

"I don't know," Fenway said. "It'd be an awfully big coincidence otherwise. But if so, why weren't they lying in wait for me?"

"Maybe it's not you."

"I don't know," she said. "The attacks on me don't make a lot of sense. Can you think of any reason why someone besides me would be the target?"

"The therapist was seeing your dad, too, wasn't he?"

"Yeah..."

"Your dad's a pretty powerful guy. And he doesn't always play by the rules. Maybe the microphone was intended to catch him saying something he thought was protected."

"Great," Fenway said. "Another theory to stroke his ego."

Callahan looked sideways at her.

"If you're surprised, Callahan, you're the only one in the whole office who didn't know I don't get along with him."

"Yeah, but you fake it, right? I mean, you must want to be in the will."

Fenway laughed, a barking guffaw that made an uncomfortable grimace emerge on Callahan's face.

"Oh, man, I'm sorry. That was—uh, like, the worst thing to say."

"No, it's okay," Fenway said. "Brian. It's really okay. It's refreshing to hear what people think."

"Sorry."

Fenway shrugged. She looked at the top of the desk and noticed a light film of dust around the edges.

"Callahan, take a look at this."

"What?"

Fenway pointed. "Notice there's a fine layer of dust here?"

"Yes."

She took another picture with Callahan's phone. "But not here. There's no dust—look, it's in a large rectangular area right in front of the chair."

"Our killer took the laptop *and* the desk blotter."

"I think the doctor had a calendar on it the last time I was in here. Probably with the name of whoever had the ten o'clock appointment."

Callahan rubbed his face. "You know, Fenway, you're probably going to have to stay to give your statement. I am too, of course—we both found the body—but you're going to miss your senior center thing."

Fenway shook her head. "I wish there were a way to do this job *without* running for office."

Callahan nodded. "But I wouldn't worry about it. Ivanovich has to talk about his son getting arrested. I'm not sure he can spin that."

"Hah," Fenway snorted. "I think if he played his cards right, he could turn this into a positive for himself. Throw a few dog-whistle words to the white supremacists, suddenly they have a reason to come out and vote, and if he makes it about race, people will start doubting me."

"You are such a pessimist."

She handed the phone back to Callahan. "You don't have to look far to find examples."

"He's going to have to explain what his son did eventually. He hasn't given a statement yet, which means he's probably panicking and he's not sure what to do."

"I guess. Millicent is still going to have a fit."

"Can't be helped, though." He put the phone in his pocket. "I'll email the pictures to you the first chance I get."

"To everyone in the office." Fenway thought for a moment. "And Dr. Yasuda's office too, if you don't mind."

"No problem."

There was a commotion outside, and Fenway heard yelling. Two of the voices were the policemen who had gone back outside to secure the scene. The other was Nathaniel Ferris.

"Ugh," Fenway said. "My father's here."

She went out through the waiting room and opened the front door. "Hi, Dad," she said, stepping out onto the walkway.

Her father looked a little rumpled, as if he hadn't slept, and his brow furrowed. "Fenway—what's going on? Didn't we have an appointment at eleven?"

"Yes, we did," she answered. "But the crime scene tape should give you a clue that it's not going to happen today."

Ferris screwed up his face. "You can't use anything I said to Dr. Tassajera against Charlotte. There's such a thing as doctor-patient confidentiality—I don't care if you were in the session too, we *both* have to—"

"Dad!" Fenway interrupted. "We don't use crime scene tape for interviews. You know better than that."

Ferris took a step back and blinked rapidly. "I—uh, no, Fenway, of course you're right." He looked out at the parking lot and his eyes widened when he took in all the police cars, as if noticing them for the first time. "How did—um," Ferris stammered, then cleared his throat. "Is everyone okay?"

Fenway shook her head.

"Oh." His face fell and all the color drained out of it.

"Are *you* okay?" Fenway asked.

"I don't know," he said in a low voice. "First, the police arrested Charlotte, and I'm already going out of my mind. Then I go to talk to Domingo Velásquez. But I get to his house and his wife tells me he left on Friday right after work and didn't come back. And now, my therapist's office—" He took two more steps back and stared at the office door.

"Wait, Dad—did you say Domingo Velásquez is missing?"

"I don't know if I'd say *missing*," he said.

"Do you know him?"

"Yes—remember? His company does the body work on our fleet?"

"Oh—that's right."

"I went there yesterday to tell him how sorry I was about Rory."

"You went to see him?" Fenway was shocked that her father had thought about someone other than himself. She hoped the surprise hadn't registered on her face.

"I had to get out of the house. Charlotte's still in jail, you know. Rattling around that big house without her—I don't know. I had to do something."

"And what happened?"

"Nothing happened. He wasn't home. His wife said he didn't come home on Friday. And she didn't know where he was."

"The day his minivan exploded. The day his son was killed."

Ferris nodded. "I guess so."

It seemed strange that Rory's father would leave and not come back after his son's death. Fenway had seen the different ways people dealt with grief, but Fenway suspected his disappearance might be something other than grief.

"Did you pull up just now?"

"Of course I did."

"Roderick drive you?"

"No, he gets Sundays off, remember? I drove myself."

"So you weren't the person Dr. Tassajera had in his office five minutes ago, right?"

"No, of course not. I came right from home. I didn't even know he was seeing someone before us."

"I have to ask. And you don't know who had the appointment before us?"

"No idea," Ferris said. "I didn't even know he *had* an appointment before us. I show up and do what he says."

"You never heard Dr. Tassajera mention anyone he wasn't getting along with, did you? Any patients who were violent? Any spouses of his clients who were angry with him?"

"You were with me every time I saw him, Fenway. I don't remember anything like that." He paused. "Someone hurt the doctor?"

Fenway nodded.

"And he—he's not going to be okay?"

"No," Fenway said softly.

Ferris closed his eyes and nodded. "All right. Uh—you need to ask me any more questions?"

"No—not for right now, anyway." Fenway paused. "Sorry about Charlotte."

"Me too."

"Take care of yourself, okay? Have you eaten today?"

Ferris shook his head. "I figured I'd eat after our session."

"Maybe you should go get something now."

"Yes, that's a good idea," Ferris said absently. "I hope you get whoever did this." He turned and trudged through the parking lot toward the black Mercedes S500 parked in the last row.

Callahan appeared by her side. "Okay, I think we've got everything secured in the office. It should be good until CSI gets here."

"Did you hear who they were sending?"

"Both Kav and Melissa. It's not often a murder is this fresh."

"I know." And even though the murder had taken place far too close to Fenway for comfort, especially since there was a possibility *she* was the target, she felt excitement. This murder was not only fresh, but the killer didn't have a lot of time. No time to clean up, no time to wipe prints off anything, no time to make sure stray hairs were picked up or no skin was left under fingernails. "I hope I'm not jinxing it, by saying this, Brian, but there *have* to be clues here."

Callahan nodded. "I'm blaming you for jinxing it if CSI doesn't find anything."

Fenway crossed her arms. "I guess I can deal with that."

Another sheriff's office cruiser pulled into the lot. Fenway saw Dez behind the wheel, a determined look on her face. And next to her in the passenger seat wearing sunglasses, and his mouth turned down in a look of concern, Sheriff McVie.

"Oh no," Fenway groaned. "Are they going to tell me I can't work *this* case either?"

Callahan looked sideways at her. "He *was* your therapist, right? Isn't that, like, the definition of a conflict of—"

"Okay, Brian, fine, when you put it like that, sure." Fenway sighed. "I've got way too many conflicts of interests the last couple of days. It's putting a cramp in my style."

Dez walked up to her. "Hey, rookie," she said.

"Hey, Dez."

"How you holding up?"

"Fine."

Dez caught Fenway's eye with a look that said they both knew better. "Hm. You stayed at Rachel's last night?"

"Yep."

"McVie was telling me he put police protection on you." Dez said it like a question.

"Yes. They sent Officer Young for the night shift. Callahan this morning."

"You're still alive, I see. They're not completely incompetent."

"Nope." Fenway gave Dez a tired smile. "Is McVie staying in the car?"

Dez shrugged. "I don't know. He insisted on coming." She looked over her shoulder at him. "Now he says he needs a minute."

"He needs a minute?"

Dez gave Fenway a look halfway between incredulity and disapproval. "Look, I don't think it's a good idea for the two of you to do whatever it is you're doing—"

"We're not doing anything, Dez. We haven't for a long time."

"Well, whatever it is you're *not* doing, it's affecting McVie. He, uh, he had a hard time yesterday. After the explosion."

Fenway was a little shocked, but cleared her throat and looked stern. "We haven't even been on a single date yet."

"And his divorce isn't final either," Dez said. "But you two aren't exactly on a pre-first-date basis."

Fenway looked at Dez's face, nonplussed. "I know you and McVie didn't drive all the way out here just so you could tell me you don't approve of who I'm dating."

"I thought you said you hadn't gone—"

"Dez!" Fenway said sharply.

Dez cackled. "Fine, fine, fine. I won't bring it up again." Then her face grew serious. "There's one thing I wanted to talk with you about," Dez said, in a low voice only Fenway could hear. She turned her back to the police cruiser, and positioned her body between the car and Fenway. Fenway could no longer see McVie. "Officer Young."

"Young? What about him?"

Dez crossed her arms. "Rachel doesn't trust him. She called me last night."

"Doesn't trust him? That's—" Fenway was going to say *ridiculous*. But she remembered how Rachel insisted Fenway stay in her room, and how she put the chair under the doorknob.

"That's what?"

"Maybe that makes sense. But I don't know *why* she doesn't trust him."

Dez shrugged. "I don't know either. I like the kid. He and Quincy are pretty tight. I can't see it, but, hey, we all know that Rachel can be three steps ahead of the rest of us."

"Right. Did Rachel say anything?"

"I didn't have time to talk to her about it," Dez said. "He's assigned to you again tonight. I assumed if he had intended to do something, he would have done it last night."

Fenway paused. She remembered waking up from her night-mare. Was Officer Young already in the room? Was he trying to hurt her? It was an odd turn of events. Rachel probably saw something that didn't sit right with her. And Rachel had also made a mention of the gun in her bedroom. Had Rachel mentioned it specifically so that Young would hear it? And had she insisted on keeping Fenway in her room so she could keep her safe? "Did you tell McVie?"

"No," Dez said. "He's been on edge with the election, and then the car bomb right downtown. I'm not sure I should worry him about one of our officers when it's just a hunch."

But he still thinks there's a mole in the department, Fenway thought. Dez might not be aware of that. Maybe Fenway would talk to McVie about it.

The sound of a car door opening made Dez turn around. McVie got out and walked toward them.

"Hi, Fenway," he said. "Are you okay?"

Fenway shrugged.

"First the car you were driving, and now your therapist," said McVie. "This seems personal."

"I don't know, Craig," Fenway said. "I was just in the next room. If they wanted to hurt me, wouldn't they have tried something?"

McVie drew his mouth into a tight line.

Fenway looked to her left. Callahan had walked down to the sidewalk and was taking down the license plate numbers of all the cars parked on the street. "Now, you see that, McVie?" she said quietly. "I think Callahan might have the makings of a detective. He's getting all the license plate numbers from the cars on the street and in the parking lot. If the killer had come out and if he had to walk past us to get to their car, he might have ducked around the back, gone to the street, and gotten a taxi or an Uber or something."

"Or walked home," Dez said.

"Right. Leaving his car here."

"It's a long shot," McVie said, shrugging.

"I don't know how much of a long shot it is," said Fenway. "The most likely place was the parking lot, for sure, but I bet we could see maybe a quarter of the cars here. And the killer wouldn't have known how far around the corner we were. He might not have wanted to chance it, no matter *where* his car was in the parking lot." She paused. "Someone might want to suggest he study for the detective exam. He'd probably have to work with computers less if he made detective."

Dez looked down at her feet and shuffled them. She looked at McVie. He cleared his throat.

"You're here to kick me off this case," Fenway said.

"We are," McVie said. "Since he was your therapist."

Dez pulled a small notebook out of her pocket. "You also happen to be a material witness to his murder. So it's even more of a sticky situation."

Fenway nodded.

Dez smirked. "It's kind of sick and twisted that you want to get out of your campaign events so bad you're hoping a murder will come along so you'll have an excuse."

Fenway smiled sadly. "Yeah, I guess it is. I don't think I'm cut out for politics."

Dez nodded. "You're awful at the politics."

"All right," Fenway conceded, sighing. "Callahan took pictures on his phone of what we found. I had gloves on. I felt for the pulse."

Dez nodded. "Yeah, Callahan emailed them to me and Donnelly."

"I've seen them too," McVie said.

Fenway nodded. "Anything jump out at you?"

"From the angle of the wound, I think the killer is right-handed," Dez said. "But that doesn't tell us much. Did you see anything under his fingernails?"

Fenway shook her head. "But I didn't look closely."

"Okay," McVie said. "What else did you notice?"

"I think the doctor's laptop was stolen," Fenway said. "I assume it was to hide whoever had the ten o'clock appointment."

"That makes sense."

"I also think a desk blotter was stolen. Last time I was here, he had one of those big desk calendars on his blotter. That could have been why they took it."

"A laptop I could see," Dez said. "If they had to leave in a hurry, or if they decided to get a cab or an Uber, a blotter would be kind of unwieldy, don't you think?"

"Yes. So maybe they didn't take a cab. Maybe they drove off."

"Yeah."

"What else do you need to ask me?"

Dez looked at McVie. "I'm going to have to ask her some questions about her therapist."

"Fine by me," McVie said.

"No, I mean, I can't have you listening to this conversation. You should go back into the car or go out of earshot or something."

"Oh." McVie cleared his throat. "Fenway, you're doing okay?"

"Yeah."

McVie nodded. He looked awkward for a moment, but straightened up, turned, and went back to the car.

Dez tapped her pen on the notebook. "How long had you been seeing Dr. Tassajera?"

"This would have been our third session."

"He was the one doing family therapy for you and your father?"

"Yes."

"You had an appointment this morning? On a Sunday?"

"Yes, at eleven." And Fenway told Dez about the bug detectors, the succulents in the ceramic pot hiding the microphones.

"You have the hidden microphone?" Dez said.

"Sure. It's bagged up." She pulled it out of her purse and handed it to Dez. "I was planning to give it to Kav or Melissa when they got here."

Dez nodded. "Okay, Fenway, I think we have everything we need."

"Also—" Fenway lowered her voice again. "I'm starting to think whoever blew up the minivan and whoever killed Dr. Tassajera aren't trying to kill *me*."

"Who else would they have targeted with the minivan?"

Fenway shook her head. "My father said Domingo Velásquez left town. He was the owner of that minivan. Maybe whoever put the bomb in there meant to kill *him*, not me."

Dez put her hands on her hips. "Why would they kill *him*?"

"I haven't figured that out yet, Dez. But, hypothetically speaking, someone who's investigating this might look at someone besides me as the potential target, right?"

Dez pursed her lips. "I'm not sure Donnelly's going to like this."

"She likes where the evidence takes you, though, right?"

"It was taking us to Charlotte. Donnelly wants to close this and move on."

Fenway paused. "How has it been working with her?"

"Fine," Dez said evenly. "She's intelligent. She makes good connections. She's asking all the right questions. And because she's been running the P.Q. office, she doesn't have preconceived notions of Barry Klein or—well, to be blunt, your father."

Fenway crossed her arms. "I sense a *but* coming."

Dez screwed up her mouth. "The gun belonging to Charlotte and the emails between them—she's hung up on them. She wants to give the D.A. an ironclad case with Charlotte."

Fenway nodded. "My father is *very* upset about Charlotte spending the night in jail."

Dez shrugged. "She's probably going to spend more than one night in jail. She owns the gun that killed him. And she's a flight risk—with your father's money and access to a private plane, bail's out of the question."

"The ballistics matched?"

Dez nodded. "We got the results from San Miguelito this morning. Charlotte's gun shot the bullet that killed Jeremy Kapp."

"Have you looked at the security footage? My father said it'll show Charlotte coming home on Friday and never leaving."

"We have the footage," Dez said. "Our techs are going over it right now. The problem is—at least according to Donnelly— it's your *father's* security footage. She thinks it might have been tampered with. And Charlotte is denying she and Jeremy Kapp were having an affair," Dez said. "Even when confronted with the emails this morning."

"You got those email printouts from Officer Young?"

"Of course we did."

"You believe the emails are real?"

"Piper's looking into it."

"Good. If those emails were faked, she'll find out."

"I'll tell you something else," Dez said thoughtfully. "Charlotte didn't know anything about the name *Potemkin*. Now, I know sometimes people are good actors and everything, but your stepmother is definitely not a good actor. I don't think she has any idea who Potemkin is. She said she had heard of Catherine the Great—she said she was the queen who had sex with a horse."

Fenway nodded. "That *would* be all Charlotte would think about Catherine the Great. She probably doesn't even know she's Russian."

"I have my doubts about Charlotte's involvement in this," Dez said, "and ordinarily, I'd look at the husband too, but the way your father reacted when I arrested Charlotte—well, I don't think he knew anything about it. And he was so upset about Charlotte getting taken away, and I think it was genuine."

"Yeah," Fenway said, "I guess despite everything I hate about Charlotte, my father is pretty hung up on her."

"I might even use the 'L' word," said Dez drily.

"Lesbian?" Fenway asked, smirking.

Dez shook her head and rolled her eyes. "It's a good thing I like you, or I'd kick your ass," she said.

"So—you won't be closing the case any time soon?"

"Nope, we're not there yet," Dez said. "The D.A. doesn't think we have enough to go to trial and win. Not with Charlotte's ability to pay for expensive lawyers."

"The D.A. is probably right."

"Agreed. So we're looking into lots of things. Finances, especially. If they were having an affair, there's gotta be some secret credit card Charlotte used for hotels or gifts or sex toys."

Fenway closed her eyes. "Come on, Dez, I did *not* need that visual."

Dez cackled, then her face became serious. "Okay, Fenway, I've done my official duty and told you to stop working this case."

"I *haven't* been working on Charlotte's case."

"I mean Dr. Tassajera's death," Dez said.

"Really? I don't think you explicitly said anything."

"You got my intent, I'm sure of it." Dez lowered her voice. "Now, if I were you, and I were the type to take everything literally, I might think the literal words I've said would still allow me to go back to the office and get Piper to look into some financial records. I might start with the dead doctor."

Then a thoughtful look crossed Dez's face.

"What is it?"

Dez squinted at nothing in particular. "So—we've been working with the theory that the person who blew up the minivan was trying to kill you, right?"

"So far, yes."

"Suppose you're right and the father was the target instead."

"Domingo Velásquez."

"Right. And look: Jeremy Kapp was your father's contractor."

"Domingo Velásquez was my father's car fleet mechanic."

Dez nodded. "And Jacob Tassajera was your father's shrink. The three of them are connected through your father. Maybe someone tried to kill all three of them, and Velásquez is the only one who got away."

"That's an interesting theory." Fenway thought for a moment. "Maybe I should look into the auto shop's financial records too."

Dez nodded. "We've already seen that Jeremy Kapp did some shady things with money and that shell company. If either of the others did too, that could establish a pattern."

"I should be able to get to Dr. Tassajera's financials—he's dead. But good luck finding a judge who'd sign off on a warrant for the auto shop."

"Maybe you'll get lucky."

Fenway smiled. "Thanks, Dez."

"Now go talk to McVie. He's worried about you."

"Yeah, okay."

Fenway walked over to the passenger side of the cruiser, and McVie lowered his window.

"Hey, Craig."

"Hey, Fenway."

"Everything okay?"

McVie smiled. "Everything's fine with *me*. I thought you, uh, might need someone to talk to." He cleared his throat. "You, uh, have been through a lot the last few days."

"I'm doing okay. Work is obviously keeping me busy." She smiled and hoped it was convincing.

McVie craned his neck around Fenway; all the officers were around Tassajera's office, paying no attention to the two of them.

He turned back to her and lowered his voice. "I wish—I wish I could put my arms around you."

Fenway closed her eyes. "Yeah, I wish that too." She put her hand on the door, where the window had rolled all the way down, and McVie put his hand on top of hers.

"I hate this campaign."

"I hate it too."

"Gene was worried about how it would look, me being down here with you."

Fenway opened her eyes. "How it would look?"

"Gene knows I'm, uh, getting a divorce, and he knows that you and I are, uh, you know."

A frown touched the corners of Fenway's mouth.

"Obviously, it hasn't become a topic of conversation on the campaign trail," McVie said quickly, "but in case it does, Gene thinks the more I know about what's, uh, going on with you, the better. That way I don't come across as dim-witted."

"Dim-witted?" Fenway pulled her hand back.

"Look, I could be asked if you and I are seeing each other, or if we had an affair before the separation. I kind of expected that. But I didn't expect to be asked if I knew you were seeing a therapist, and if it had anything to do with our affair."

Fenway didn't expect that either, and although she and Millicent had discussed the therapist situation, she didn't think McVie should know. She didn't *want* McVie to know. "I don't—" she began. What else had Gene uncovered about Fenway—and told McVie? Did he know about Professor Solomon Delacroix? She took a deep breath. "We didn't have an affair."

"Whatever it is we've done so far," McVie said. "You know that won't come across that well."

"If it comes out."

"Anyway," McVie said lamely, "that's how I know about your therapist. So when I heard this come in, I was, I don't know, a little worried."

"I'm fine," Fenway said, too quickly. She felt a little anger—and a little humiliation—at not being able to tell McVie this on her own terms.

McVie gave Fenway a long look. "Listen," he said, "if you need to talk, I'm here. This isn't a date thing, or a Wednesday thing."

"I'm fine," Fenway said again. She looked over at Dez and nodded, and Dez began walking over.

"Okay," McVie said. "Take care of yourself."

Fenway nodded as Dez handed the keys to McVie through the window. "I'm staying," Dez said. "I'll catch a ride back with the uniforms. You can head back to the station."

"Thanks, Dez," said McVie.

Dez turned to Fenway. "We all good?"

"Peachy," Fenway said.

"All right. I'm going to check out the crime scene. See you later, rookie."

McVie stepped out of the passenger door with the keys. "If you need to talk, you know how to reach me."

Then Fenway heard the voice of Officer Brian Callahan behind her. "There you are! I wondered where you'd gone."

She turned. "Sorry, sorry."

Callahan nodded at McVie. "Sheriff."

"Everything under control here, Callahan?"

"We had a one-eighty-seven, Sheriff. The coroner and I found the body."

McVie nodded. "I heard the call come through." He cleared his throat. "All right. I'm heading back to the office. Sorry to saddle you with paperwork, Callahan, but I'll need the report on this before you go home."

"Understood."

McVie got in the car. "Thanks for taking care of this. And make sure Dez has a ride back to the station."

He backed out of the space, and drove out of the parking lot. Fenway watched the cruiser until it disappeared around the corner, and she stood alone with Callahan in the parking lot.

She wanted to tell him all her theories and crazy ideas. His mind worked similarly to hers, she suspected: running over the pieces of the puzzle that didn't fit until another solution presented itself. She thought he might make some connection—besides her father—that she couldn't see.

But she didn't trust Callahan with her crazy ideas. He was a rule-follower, after all, and he might place more value on Fenway staying away from the case due to her conflict of interest than he would catching the person who was behind it all.

"Are you sticking around?" Callahan said.

Fenway turned and started walking toward Callahan's cruiser. "Nope. Let's follow McVie back to the office. Let's see if there are any judges around on a Sunday."

CHAPTER SEVENTEEN

FENWAY WISHED SHE HAD A PHONE SHE COULD USE. BEING without one made her feel out of touch and exposed. She laughed to herself—Millicent was probably going crazy right now. Fenway had promised to call after the appointment, but the murder of Dr. Jacob Tassajera threw a monkey wrench into her plans.

"Are you sure you don't want to at least put in an appearance at the senior center?" Callahan said.

"I'll call Millicent when I get to the office. A murder's more important than a campaign stop." Fenway looked over at Callahan. His eyes were focused on the road, but perhaps his mind was elsewhere. "You seriously worried about my chances in the election?"

"You never know what can happen," Callahan said. "You don't want to assume you've got it all locked up, especially not three days before." He tapped the steering wheel, perhaps debating how to phrase the next thing he wanted to say. "And, look, I don't want to stir anything up, but I don't want Ivanovich anywhere near this position. He's bad news. He might be scrambling to distance himself from what his son did last night, but the reality is, the apple didn't fall far from the tree."

"Really?" Fenway asked. "You mean he's just as racist as his son? How do you know?"

"I went to school with the older brother," Callahan said. "The guy was always the one complaining in February about how we didn't celebrate White History Month."

Fenway shrugged. "You have no idea how often I hear shit like that," she said. "But none of those people ever painted the n-word on my car."

"No, it wasn't just that," Callahan continued. "It was the stickers he had on his binders, the band names he wrote in Sharpie on his backpack."

Fenway waved her hand. "Ivanovich comes from rich folks," she said. "I bet all of that stuff was primarily to get on his parents' nerves."

"You seem awfully—I don't know—dismissive," said Callahan.

"Don't get me wrong, there are less racist ways to get your parents' attention, but if I thought every kid who called me names growing up had parents who wanted to put a brick through my window, I'd never sleep at night."

"Maybe not with the kids you grew up with," Callahan admitted, "and maybe not with most of the kids who went to P.Q. High, but definitely with Ivanovich. He was the one at the school board meetings complaining loudly about 'reverse racism,' about whites being persecuted. He might have money, but there's not a lot separating him from the, uh, separatists."

Fenway looked at Callahan's face. His jaw was clenched and he was still nervously tapping the steering wheel. This hadn't been an easy conversation for him to bring up. It wasn't easy for her to hear it, either—she was reminded again of Benjy on the swings in elementary school. She decided to switch gears slightly and move into the actual elements of the crime she was trying to solve.

"So you think Ivanovich is behind the bomb in the minivan? Maybe he's behind the killing of Dr. Tassajera?"

"No, no." Callahan shook his head. "I mean—I guess I haven't talked to you about this yet, but it doesn't make any sense that a, um, racial slur on your car would escalate into a car bomb, and then would go back down into a brick through your window. Two of those seem like kid stuff, meant to intimidate, show you there are, uh, I don't know how to say this—white people who don't like you. The car bomb is serious. It's not meant to send a message. It's meant to kill someone."

Fenway was silent for a minute.

"And," Callahan continued, "I overheard some of what your dad said."

Fenway cocked her head. "Like what?"

"I heard that Domingo Valásquez went missing. And I don't think the bomb was intended for you anymore. I think it was intended for him."

Fenway paused. "That's funny. Dez and I said pretty much the same thing."

"Really?" He lowered his voice, even though it was only the two of them in the car. "I'm not quite sure why he ran. If it was after work, he must have heard the minivan had blown up. That's his car, right? That's not the car Rory usually drove, and it's sure as hell not your car."

Fenway nodded. "That's true."

Callahan had built up a head of steam. "Why else would he run? He should be angry, not scared. He should be beside himself with grief." Callahan looked over his shoulder to change lanes; they were almost at Broadway. "I would expect a grieving father to be giving you hell, Fenway. Saying stuff like, 'How could you let this happen to my son? He was campaigning for you, he trusted you, and you let this happen to him?'"

The words from Callahan's mouth pierced Fenway's heart like an arrow; she felt the pain in the words as if the father had spoken directly to her. She turned her face so Callahan wouldn't see her fighting back tears. He didn't seem to notice. And they turned down Broadway, and Fenway saw the police tape, the *road closed* signs. The parking garage wouldn't be the same for months, and Fenway would be seeing the reminder of the explosion—and of her failure to protect Rory—for a long time.

"But he didn't react like that at all," Callahan continued. "He packed a bag and took off." Callahan turned down Fourth Street and went in behind the sheriff's office, into the area reserved for police cruisers.

"No," Fenway said, keeping her voice even and firm. "You're right. I've seen a lot of different reactions to the death of a loved one. I've seen denial and I've seen avoidance. But packing a bag and leaving—I've never seen that kind of reaction."

They settled into the parking space and got out of the car.

"You know," Fenway said, "I saw the way you were getting the lay of the land after we found Dr. Tassajera's body."

"I know," Callahan said. "I was paralyzed. I was shocked. I know it was unprofessional."

"That's not even close to what I was going to say," said Fenway. "I was going to say I was impressed with some of the things you did. Taking down all the license plate numbers, the make and model of all the vehicles on the street and in the parking lot. That doesn't just show initiative, it shows a real mind for detective work."

"Oh," Callahan said, surprised. "Uh—thanks, I guess."

They started to walk into the sheriff's office. "I don't often see people who aren't working cases thinking through things like that. And the same thing when you overheard my father. You started to piece things together."

Fenway looked at Callahan. His ears were getting red.

"Listen," Fenway said, "have you ever thought about taking the detective's exam?"

"Uh," Callahan said, "I have. I went down to Santa Barbara about six months ago and took the detective exam down there."

"They had an opening?"

"Yes."

"Did you pass?"

"Yes."

"So why aren't you down there?"

"They promoted from within."

"Just like we should do here," said Fenway. "You know, Mark's going to be retiring next year."

"Really?"

"Yep. Full pension." Fenway paused. "You should think about applying."

"Wouldn't you be my boss?"

"Assuming I win this election, which, as you've pointed out, is no given."

"Wow."

"Unless you've got a problem reporting to a woman."

"No!" Callahan said quickly. "It's just—I never thought I'd get the chance here. I thought maybe over in San Miguelito County. I've heard they're expanding their robbery and homicide staff."

"You know, I think we're going to have an opening for a detective working identity theft cases."

"Oh—I, uh..."

"Say no more," Fenway said. "Computer work. I get it."

This time, Callahan's ears turned all the way red.

They continued walking through the office. Callahan stopped at his desk and bent down to open a file drawer.

"What are you looking for?"

"I've got a bunch of judges' home and cell numbers in one of these files." He leafed through the folders.

"We can look that up on the computer, you know."

"I trust paper more. Aha—here it is."

"Great. I can make the calls from my office."

Fenway and Callahan exited the sheriff's office building and walked across the empty street, into the building that held the coroner's office.

Fenway walked past the door to Suite 150.

"Where are you going? I thought we were going to do the paperwork for the warrants—and you were going to call those judges."

"In a minute," Fenway said. "I've got to go talk to Piper."

"It's Sunday. You think Piper's in?"

"If I know her, she is. Before I give her any more names for financials, I need to see where she is on the work she's already done."

Callahan nodded, then put his serious face back on.

They went through to the information technology suite. There, behind her desk, was the willowy, redheaded Piper.

"No Migs today trying to distract you?" Fenway said.

"No," Piper said brusquely. "But with everything going on, I encouraged him to come. He's got more important things to do, apparently."

Fenway looked at Piper's face, which was still focused on the screen. Her words had betrayed some anger towards Migs, but her face remained impassive.

Piper pulled a folder up from her desk and handed it to Fenway. "After seeing all the payment information from Global Advantage Executive Consulting, I started doing some reverse lookups. You'll be surprised—there are some names of small businesses in there—and the owners are often people we've had an interest in lately."

Fenway opened the folder. Several sets of papers, separated by binder clips, were in the folder. The name on the first set was Jeremy Kapp.

"Landscape architecture isn't exactly the kind of business I think of when I think of money laundering," Fenway said.

Piper nodded. "You'd wouldn't think so, but a lot of the maintenance work they do is cash only. They've got a dozen crews working ten residences a day. And, oddly enough, over half of them pay in cash."

"Ten residences are a lot for one crew."

"Not for a crew their size," Piper said, "but some of the people who work on the crews—I'm not sure they exist."

Callahan let out a low whistle.

Piper glared at him.

"Callahan's on Fenway protection duty," Fenway explained. "He goes where I go."

"Oh," Piper said.

"So," Fenway said, "you think they've got cash coming in, they're laundering it, and they're paying it out to people who don't exist as a way of paying—uh, who are they paying?"

"They make some payments directly to Global Advantage Executive Consulting. These fake names—I've been able to trace some of the bank accounts back to Global Advantage too, and in fact, I think it's *all* going back there."

"Why would they do that?"

"Probably so they don't look so suspicious. You can pay a consulting firm, but only so much before it starts raising red flags." Piper cleared her throat. "I've found records of over a million dollars so far coming in, and at least a half million going out."

"Almost like a legitimate business," Fenway mused.

"Go to the next set of documents," Piper said. "This is the one I told you about in my voicemail."

"I don't have my phone," Fenway said. "I was afraid someone wanted to kill me and they were tracking my movements."

"Ah," Piper said. "That would be why you never returned my call."

"And yet here I am," Fenway deadpanned.

"Indeed."

Fenway turned the page. Her mouth dropped open when she saw the name at the top.

Dr. Jacob Tassajera.

"That's our latest murder victim."

"I know," Piper said. "I heard the police scanner."

"How'd you get the warrants signed so fast?"

Piper shrugged. "I was on a comp volleyball team with Judge Chen's daughter in high school."

Fenway smiled. "Look at you with your initiative."

Piper tapped the folder again. "And look at the next set."

Fenway pulled the top two sets off the stack and saw the next name.

Domingo Velásquez.

"Wait—Velásquez? *I* was just going to apply for a warrant for his financials."

Piper shrugged. "His name came up on a couple of investment accounts in Jeremy Kapp's portfolio. I recognized the last name of the kid from—you know—and I did a search. Figured I'd pull that in, too."

Callahan cleared his throat. "I think that would tend to support my, um, earlier assertion."

"What earlier assertion?" asked Piper.

"That Fenway wasn't the target of the car bomb."

Piper cocked her head to the side. "Hmmm."

"You know Domingo Velásquez is missing?" asked Fenway.

Piper shook her head. "No—I hadn't heard that. Did someone file a missing persons report?"

"No," said Fenway. "My father told me. He went by their house, and his wife said he never came home after work on Friday."

"Have you noticed everyone I've uncovered who's been paid by Global Advantage Executive Consulting has either been murdered or is missing?"

"I *did* notice that." Fenway tapped her forehead in thought. "Almost like a pattern. The pattern doesn't include Charlotte."

"It might if she or your father are the ones responsible," Piper said. "I mean, a lot of this has to do with your father's company. It *might* be something your stepmother is involved in."

"Like what? I can't see her getting involved in a scheme to get oil from one embargoed country and send it to another embargoed country. The politics would have to be staggering. She loses it when she breaks a nail."

"Maybe she's a good actor," Callahan broke in.

Fenway guffawed, thinking of her earlier conversation with Dez.

"I don't know, Fenway," Piper said. "I hate to say this, but if your father was behind this, he'd need at least one other person to assist—even if it's only with bookkeeping. It'd have to be someone he trusted with the money."

Fenway shook her head. "Charlotte spends like crazy. He doesn't even trust her with an American Express card, never mind millions of dollars in laundered money."

Piper narrowed her eyes. "Did she major in accounting or finance in college?"

"Literature," Fenway said. "She thought *Madame Bovary* wasn't so much a cautionary tale as a how-to manual."

Neither Piper nor Callahan laughed. Maybe they hadn't read it.

"Listen, Fenway," Piper said, "if Charlotte is innocent, this is pretty serious. I know you don't like her, but—"

"I don't dislike her enough for her to go to jail for a crime she didn't commit," said Fenway.

"Okay, then," Piper said, "we need to figure out who's behind all of this. Because if we find out who's behind the car bomb, and who's behind the killing of Dr. Tassajera, we'll probably find out the same person is the one responsible for the death of Jeremy Kapp."

Fenway nodded. "That makes sense."

"Something must have happened," Piper mused.

Callahan looked at her. "What do you mean?"

Piper looked thoughtful. "I mean—look, all of this money moving around, this oil going from Latin America to East Timor, people are making a lot of money, and it's going smoothly. *Something* must have happened to start getting all these people killed."

"And you're thinking," Fenway said, "if we can figure out the catalyst for the murders, maybe we find the murderer?"

"Or at least the motive," Callahan replied.

"Right." Piper nodded. "Either someone got greedy, or a shipment came in short, or someone ratted someone else out. It had to be something like that."

"Perhaps," said Fenway. "There's no honor among thieves."

"Okay," said Callahan, "I think you're right, Piper. *Something* must have predicated this. I've seen this before—not on such a grand scale, but maybe the little guys who shoot each other over money aren't that different from the big guys."

"What are you thinking?" asked Fenway.

"I've seen payment terms change, and someone doesn't like it. I've seen something happen in the supply chain—out of everyone's control—but no one's making as much money as they used to, and someone decides they want a bigger slice of the pie. Or someone gets scared that there's a weak link in the chain. A series of murders like this doesn't spontaneously appear."

Fenway nodded. "Oil prices have gone down lately, but not a lot. Maybe five percent—but I don't think that would be enough to trigger anything." She crossed her arms. "What if we tracked traffic from the ports? That might give us a clue—some ship moving that breaks a pattern or something."

Piper shook her head. "If there's a rogue ship, it's not the *Jules Verne*. I'm tracking that tanker, and it's pretty much on the other side of the world right now. Or at least it should be." She pulled out another folder and put it in front of Fenway. "See? The *Jules Verne* should be a couple of days out from Singapore."

"Maybe there's another ship we don't know about yet." Fenway paused. "Piper, did you ever look into the finances of Carl Cassidy and Lewis Fairweather?"

"I did some preliminary work—Bradley Watermeier took care of the initial inquiry when he was here."

"Bradley Watermeier." Fenway tapped her temple. "I know that name."

"He was the firewall admin when you started here."

"Oh," Fenway chuckled. "Before he was arrested, you mean."

Piper paused. "I guess I should go back and double-check his work."

Fenway nodded. "And you've uncovered all the payments from that consulting firm with the boring name?"

"Global Advantage Executive Consulting."

"Right. But Bradley probably wasn't looking for those sorts of payments."

"No, he probably wasn't. Unless he was on the take from them too."

Fenway shrugged. "He sure doesn't fit the profile of the other people on the take. He didn't own his own business, for one."

"And he's still alive," Piper said drily. "I can still look into it."

"Sure. But I don't think Bradley had any knowledge of the existence of Global Advantage. Not unless he found something in Carl Cassidy's finances. And even if he found it, he might not have known what it was."

Piper nodded.

Fenway started scanning the three sets of financial papers. "Very similar payment schedules with all three of these companies," she muttered. "And all of them are claiming a ton of cash transactions."

"Auto repair for Domingo Velásquez, and something called 'independent counseling' for Dr. Tassajera." Piper shook her head. "You ever heard of people paying for family counseling in cash?"

"Of course I have. People pay out of pocket all the time—especially if their cheap-ass health insurance won't cover it."

"People who pay out of pocket usually pay with checks or credit cards, don't they? I'm actually talking *cash*."

Fenway shrugged. "I'm sure some people do it." She raised herself up on her toes and stretched. Her body was still sore from the explosion, but stretching felt good.

Piper shook her head. "Not as much cash as Dr. Tassajera was taking in. I think this is a red flag."

Fenway closed her eyes and breathed in. She felt alive in the middle of a murder investigation. Stressed out, perhaps, and in need of some coffee. And since Piper and Callahan had suggested she wasn't the target after all, she felt lighter, she felt like she could be a real person again and go back to her apartment and her car and her phone and her life.

When she opened her eyes, Piper was staring at her, looking worried.

"What is it, Piper?"

"Fenway," she said haltingly, "I—uh, I think this goes pretty deep."

"Yeah, I think it does."

Piper nodded. "It looks like a huge operation. Phantom oil tankers going in and out of the Ferris Energy port. A massive amount of money being laundered. And it's not in traditional money laundering businesses like car washes or dry cleaners—it's a landscape architecture firm, an auto mechanic, and a therapist. And that's only what we know about."

"Everybody has a price."

"I know."

"And those types of businesses can launder more money than a laser tag center or a car wash. They've got more high-value services. They can launder, what, twenty grand a day? Maybe more? A car wash would be lucky to do half that."

Piper nodded. "Right—but that's why money launderers stick to traditional businesses. Because the types of companies we've uncovered are ones where people usually pay by credit card or check or something. Paying by cash can get red-flagged in other businesses. But they haven't been flagged by anyone."

"How do you know they haven't?"

"I checked the IMOLIN database."

"The what?"

"It's an international database. Has a whole list of suspected money-laundering operations and links to terrorist networks."

"So what are you saying?"

"I'm saying that whoever should be red-flagging these financial transactions isn't doing their job."

"You think someone in financial crimes is in on it? Maybe even the D.A.?"

"Maybe it goes even higher," whispered Piper.

"I'm not sure I believe that," Fenway said. "Remember what Ben Franklin said about secrets."

"Which was?"

"He said, 'three can keep a secret if two are dead.'"

Piper set her jaw and held up the financial statements from Jeremy Kapp and Dr. Jacob Tassajera. "Well, Fenway, here are the two who are dead."

CHAPTER EIGHTEEN

FENWAY AND CALLAHAN WENT BACK TO THE CORONER'S OFFICE suite. Her head was awash in the ramifications of what Piper just said, and how deep the conspiracy might go. The office was locked; it was, after all, a Sunday, Dez was in the field on the job, and Piper said Migs hadn't come into the office with her. Fenway thought they might be having a fight.

Getting her keys from her purse, she unlocked the door.

A manila envelope lay on the floor; it looked like it had been pushed through the crack under the door. *Fenway Stevenson* was printed neatly on the front of the envelope. It was the same type of envelope and the same handwriting as the envelope left at Fenway's apartment the night before.

"Another envelope," said Fenway.

"Don't touch it," said Callahan. "It could be something dangerous."

"The last one wasn't," Fenway said. "And I'm more concerned with getting the fingerprints off this one than anything." She carefully stepped around the envelope and picked out a pair of gloves and a large evidence bag.

"The last one?"

"Didn't Officer Young tell you about the other envelope at my apartment?"

"When was this?"

"The envelope was left there when the brick was thrown through my window."

Callahan shook his head. "You mean the night you tackled the white supremacist we thought was going to kill you? The day after the car bomb went off?"

"Uh..."

"Yeah, I can't imagine why *an envelope left for you* would have slipped Todd's mind."

"I guess that probably wasn't the most important thing that happened yesterday."

"What was in the envelope?"

"Emails," Fenway said. "Printouts of email communications between Jeremy Kapp and Charlotte."

"Oh."

"Supposedly proving they were having an affair."

"Who would have access?"

"To the real emails? I'm not sure. I suppose his family, maybe his co-workers, maybe someone who works at the service provider or for the networking company. But I think those emails were faked."

"You do?"

"Yep. Kapp and his mistress had pet names for each other, and whoever faked the emails messed them up."

"Oh." Callahan stopped. "So did that envelope get fingerprinted?"

"We sent it to the lab," Fenway said, "but with all the commotion at my apartment, people stepped all over the envelope, and maybe three or four people handled it before giving it to me. I don't think we'll find anything useful. Besides, I think CSI is pretty busy."

"Do you have any idea who's sending them?"

"Not specifically, but whoever sent it wants me to think that Charlotte murdered Jeremy Kapp."

"Do you think that person had anything to do with the murder?"

Fenway shrugged. "I don't know. Faking the emails so poorly is pretty amateurish, but the murders over the last few days—first Jeremy Kapp, then Rory, then Dr. Tassajera—it seems, well, perhaps not exactly professional, but certainly *serious*. The stakes seem much higher than someone faking emails."

Fenway stepped into her office, picked up the phone, and dialed.

"Who are you calling?" Callahan asked.

"Melissa."

"Who's Melissa?"

"You know Melissa de la Garza. One of the CSI techs—you helped her comb the beach the other day."

"Oh, *that* Melissa. The one with the metal detector."

Fenway smirked. "Yeah, her. She's over at Dr. Tassajera's—or she should be, anyway; I can't imagine her being finished yet. I'm hoping she can pick up this envelope on the way back to San Miguelito. Otherwise we'll have to courier it over."

Melissa answered the phone on the third ring.

"De la Garza."

"Hi Melissa, it's Fenway."

"Oh, hi. I didn't recognize the number."

"I'm calling from my office."

"Gotcha. What do you need?"

"Are you still at Dr. Tassajera's?"

"Yes," Melissa said. "We'll be here at least another hour. Lots of hair, particles, fingerprints."

"It was a busy office."

"I know. And I'm sure I'm going to be read the riot act on doctor-patient privilege after we process all of this."

Fenway tapped her foot; the last thing she needed was *her* patient privilege violated. "We'll cross that bridge when we come to it. Listen, did you get the envelope that I received last night? The one with all the email printouts in it?"

"Yes, but we haven't processed it yet. We're totally backed up with everything from the, uh, crime scene in the parking garage."

"Understood. But listen, I got another one."

Melissa gasped. "Another car bomb?"

"Another *envelope*. This one was pushed under the door to my office."

"Oh. You've bagged it up?"

"Yes. No one touched it. Unlike the other one. Maybe you can run this one first."

Melissa clicked her tongue. "We've got a ton from Dr. Tassajera's to go through."

"Yeah—but I think whoever is sending me these envelopes is trying to frame Charlotte."

"Why would someone need to frame her? Isn't she in jail already for killing Jeremy Kapp?"

"I don't think she's been formally charged," Fenway said. "The D.A. wants more compelling information—and I think whoever sent these envelopes is trying to *present* more compelling information."

"What did they send this time?"

"I didn't open it, Melissa."

"You have fingerprint stuff in your office, don't you?"

"I shouldn't be the one to fingerprint it, should I? I've got a conflict of interest."

"How do you know you've got a conflict of interest?" Melissa asked. "There's no return address or sender name on it, is there? How are you supposed to *know* what case it pertains to?"

"That's dicey, Melissa. I knew what it was the moment I saw it."

"It's not dicey to a jury. I had to testify in court to something like this last year. Are there any identifying marks on it?"

"No."

"Great. Print it, and then open the envelope with your gloves on. For all you know they might have signed their name."

Fenway sighed. Maybe she was off her game; this might have been obvious to her on a normal day. "Okay. Hold on."

"Call me back. I'm in the middle of something here."

Fenway hung up. Callahan looked at her questioningly.

"I have a fingerprint kit," Fenway said. "I can't believe I didn't think about taking the prints myself."

She went into the supply cabinet and got out the fingerprint powder and a metallic brush. She pulled two blue nitrile gloves out of the drawer to the left of the cabinet and snapped them on.

Callahan watched her. "Need any help?"

"I think I got it," Fenway replied. She carefully picked up the envelope from the floor and set it on the counter.

"I'm just going to sit here like an idiot?"

Fenway sighed. "Okay then, can you get some of that fingerprint tape out of the cabinet?"

He started to move back around the counter.

"And while you're at it," Fenway said, "put on some gloves. I might need an extra pair of hands."

Callahan nodded.

It took about fifteen minutes, and Fenway had to deal with a lot of smudges, but she lifted about twelve usable prints off the envelope. "Looks like a lot of these prints are the same," she said. "Let's hope they're in the system."

"You going to open it now?"

"Yep," Fenway said.

"It's sealed shut, right?"

"Nope," Fenway said. "Only closed with the metal clasp. That's one way I know there's no anthrax in this. No one licked the seal, so no DNA."

"Lucky we got the fingerprints, then."

"It's only lucky if they're in the system."

Callahan paused. "Do you think we should get Dez in on this?"

"Probably."

"What do you think it is?"

"Something to implicate Charlotte in Jeremy Kapp's murder."

"And you'll give it to Dez?"

"I have to." She opened the envelope and shook two sheets of paper out: two photographs, printed on cheap computer paper, like the emails had been, although it was a slightly heavier weight. The photos were about four inches by six inches and were centered on each page.

The photos were of Charlotte and Jeremy Kapp. They were naked in both. In the first, they stood next to a bed with an ivory comforter and brown and cream-colored pillow shams; Charlotte had her back to the camera and was kissing Jeremy Kapp's face. In the second, the two figures were entwined on the bed.

"Oh, man," Callahan said. "I wasn't expecting naked pictures."

Fenway shook her head. "These photos are doctored."

"Doctored?"

She held the photo of one of the pages up to the light. "See? The shadow on Charlotte's face is coming from a different light source than the one in the room. It's clearly been superimposed on this woman's body."

"Or was Charlotte's whole body superimposed in the photo?"

"I don't think so," Fenway said. "The light looks right on her shoulder blades, and her, uh, buttocks too." She squinted. "And I think Jeremy Kapp was about five-nine, right? That would make the woman in this photo about five-five, maybe five-six. Charlotte's five-eight, easy."

"How do you know all of this?"

"An evidence class in my forensics program. Oh, and look at the ink."

"What?" asked Callahan.

"The other envelope I got contained emails. But they were on a different kind of paper, and those were printed on a laser printer. These were printed on an inkjet."

"Two different printers?"

"Right. The laser printer is something you'd find in an office or a school. Some people have them at home, but mostly they have these cheap inkjet printers."

"So you're thinking they printed out the emails at work, but had to go home to print the naked pictures."

"That certainly is one possibility. Seems to me to be the most likely."

Callahan pointed at the pictures. "You going to fingerprint those too?"

"Yeah, I better."

Callahan pulled the envelope out of the way while Fenway placed the two inkjet-printed photographs on the counter. She repeated the fingerprinting process with the powder and the tape.

When she was finished, she had Callahan clean up the powder—there was a magic eraser in the cabinet—and she went into her office and shut the door. She picked up the phone and called Dez.

"Hey, Fenway," Dez answered. "No rest for the weary, I see."

"Not today." Fenway's stomach rumbled. She looked at the clock on the wall. It was already four o'clock and she hadn't eaten anything since leaving Rachel's that morning. She heard the siren call of the *taquería* on Third Street but ignored it for now.

"You want me to put you on speaker? Deputy Sheriff Donnelly is here."

Fenway caught the unspoken warning from Dez not to reveal that she had done research on her own. "Oh, good. I'd like to speak with both of you. There was something interesting in my office when I came to work this afternoon."

"Oh." Dez couldn't keep the surprise out of her voice. "Okay." The audio changed as Dez put the phone on speaker.

"Coroner," said Donnelly.

"Good afternoon, everyone. I received an envelope today. It was under the office door when I got to work."

"Which door was it under?" asked Dez. "Was it the building door, or the door to the coroner's suite, or was it the door to your personal office?"

"The coroner's suite."

"Okay," Dez said. "That means it must have been put there after the building opened this morning."

"It might have been last night," said Donnelly.

"I don't think so," Dez said. "The cleaning staff would have picked it up and put in on the counter or something."

"Unless the cleaning staff let in whoever did it."

Dez paused for a moment. "I suppose that's possible."

"Coroner, do you get a lot of envelopes delivered under the door?" asked Donnelly.

"No," Fenway said. "It's never happened before. Not since I've been here anyway. You are aware there was a similar envelope left under the doormat at my apartment yesterday."

"Yes," Donnelly said. She paused. "Do you find it curious they left that evidence for *you* when you're no longer on the case?"

"I usually investigate any suspicious deaths in the county," Fenway responded. "Unless whoever it was became aware I had been taken off the case, I think it's fair to assume they thought they were giving evidence to the investigating party."

"It seems to me that most people would assume you wouldn't investigate your own family," said Donnelly.

Fenway paused. "I hadn't thought of that." She thought for a moment. "Of course, not everyone is well-versed on police procedure."

"What did you do with the new envelope?" asked Dez, a little impatiently.

"I called CSI," Fenway said, "but as the envelope was *in* the coroner's office, I got my fingerprint kit and took prints of both the envelope and the two papers inside. Quite a few usable prints. Nine separate ones, at least to my naked eye. Hopefully they're on record."

"CSI let you fingerprint them yourself when they knew you'd been kicked off this case?" said Donnelly.

"Yes," Fenway said. "After all, there's no way to have known what the envelope contained until I opened it. I followed protocol to the letter."

"Surely you thought there was a pretty good chance it would be about our prime suspect," Donnelly said.

"I don't think you'll have any chain of custody issues," Fenway said, deflecting. "Officer Callahan was with me the whole time. He'll be able to tell you I treated the evidence according to the rules and guidelines."

The line was quiet for a moment. "Sometimes we can get in trouble if we get too creative," Donnelly said carefully.

"We all want to see justice done," Dez said.

"Exactly," said Fenway. "Melissa de la Garza from CSI over in San Miguelito is going to pick up the evidence on her way back from Dr. Tassajera's, but I thought the two of you would want to see it first."

"You said there were papers inside," said Donnelly. "Is it financial data? Bank account statements?"

"No," said Fenway. "They're doctored pictures of Charlotte Ferris and Jeremy Kapp being intimate."

"Intimate?" said Donnelly.

"Having sex," Fenway said.

"Yes, yes," Donnelly said distractedly. "What makes you think they've been doctored?"

"The light's all wrong on Charlotte's face," said Fenway. "It's been done by someone with decent Photoshop skills, but nowhere near good enough to pass a forensic analysis."

"Have you had training in this area?"

"Yes," Fenway said. "I've got a master's in forensic nursing. I've taken classes on how to recognize doctored photographs."

"Oh, good," said Donnelly. "That helps us out if we have to defend our probable cause."

"So, Gretchen," Dez said, "shall we head over to the coroner's office to pick up this new evidence?"

"Yes, I think we'd better."

"Okay. Fenway, you going to be there another half hour or so?"

Fenway's stomach growled. "Yep. Half an hour should be fine. If Melissa gets here first, I'll have her wait. Hopefully she can."

They said their goodbyes and hung up.

Fenway went to the outer office where Callahan was putting the bottles back in the supply cabinet. "Come on," Fenway said. "We have barely enough time before they get back."

"They?"

"Dez and Donnelly," Fenway said. She grabbed the evidence bags off the counter. "Let's go. I've got to go see a family member who's being held in jail."

CHAPTER NINETEEN

DURING THE WALK ACROSS THE STREET TO THE COUNTY JAIL next to the sheriff's office, Fenway was hoping for a friendly face at the guard station, someone who could get Charlotte quickly and get Fenway and Callahan in and out before Dez and Deputy Sheriff Gretchen Donnelly got there. It only took a few minutes to walk over, although Callahan almost ran to keep up with Fenway's long strides. They walked through the gate of the county jail and, much to Fenway's relief, she recognized the guard.

"Fenway!" Quincy said, smiling. "Hey, Callahan."

"Hi, Quincy," Fenway said. "It's been a while."

"Yep. Aunt Dez talks about you at dinner, though. You're doing great on the campaign trail, I hear."

"Thanks," Dez said. "I have a favor to ask. Visiting hours end at five on Sundays, right?"

Quincy shrugged. "Yes, but not for investigators. You want to see someone, you just ask."

"No, no," Fenway said. "I'm here as a family member during business hours. This is officially *not* police business."

Callahan looked sideways at Fenway. If Callahan planned to blow the whistle on her, he didn't let on.

"Gotcha," Quincy said. "Come on through, you know the drill. No keys or cell phones through the metal detectors. Officer, what do you want to do with your firearm?"

"Maybe you should stay out here," Fenway said. What she didn't say was, *So you don't have to report anything you see.* She tried to telepathically send that message to Callahan, and the light in his eyes indicated he got it.

"Yes, that's probably for the best," Callahan agreed. "Besides, there are a lot of officers in there. You're surrounded by a lot of people who are going to protect you."

"In fact," Fenway said, pulling her wallet out of her purse, "I am dying for a latte. Think you could get one for me? A large? And one of whatever you want."

"Java Jim's?" He took the twenty-dollar bill from Fenway.

"Yes. They're the best."

"They sure are," Callahan said. "I love their jumbo drinks with extra espresso shots. The more expensive the better."

Fenway smirked. "You knock yourself out, Brian. My treat."

Callahan left.

"What was that about?" Quincy said.

"Callahan's been assigned to protect me. I guess he doesn't like being a gofer."

"You could have said please."

"I'll make sure to say thank you."

Quincy cleared his throat. "If you're here to see family, that must mean Charlotte Ferris."

"You got it. And I need to hurry." Fenway looked at her watch. She wanted to be back with at least five minutes to spare.

"No problem." Quincy got on the radio and walked through the rear door.

Fenway looked around at the guard station. With a metal detector, eggshell walls, a long table, and metal chairs, it reminded Fenway of a mental hospital she had visited when she was a nurse in Seattle.

Quincy stuck his head back in. "They're bringing her out now. You can go on back. Go through to the women's visitor section. Table number three."

Fenway went through the visitors' door in the rear. The corridor turned to the left and emptied out into a large room with picnic-style tables made not of wood but of hard green resin in the middle of the room.

"Lovely," Fenway muttered. She found the table with a "3" on a white plastic sign.

There was a short white woman with thick glasses on at table two. Another woman, tall with stringy hair, wearing an orange jumpsuit, sat with her, speaking in hushed tones, but with a sense of urgency in her voice. The short woman wasn't making eye contact.

About thirty seconds later, a door in the back of the room opened and Charlotte appeared, followed by a prison guard.

Even in the orange jumpsuit, Charlotte exhibited a certain confidence. She stood straight and tall. Fenway was a couple of inches taller, but Charlotte, even from the wrong side of the fence, had the air of an aristocrat, too good for the room, too good for the building.

"I never thought *you* would be the first person besides Nathaniel to visit me in jail," Charlotte said when she sat down. "The guard said you were here as a family member, too. Not as an investigator or whatever."

"Right." Fenway leaned forward and lowered her voice. "I got kicked off your case because of our family relationship. But people keep sending me things," she said. "I need you to take a look at this and see if you recognize anything. If something jogs your memory."

Charlotte sat back. "Of course. I knew your visit couldn't be because you're concerned for my well-being."

"You know I'm great at getting to the truth," Fenway said, "and the truth is, you didn't do this. And your well-being will improve if you get out of here. So shut up and look at this." She pulled the evidence bags out of her purse. "Now listen, I'm not supposed to talk to you about this case, so if you want my help, don't tell anyone about what I'm about to show you. Deal?"

Charlotte set her lips in a tight line and cocked her head to the side, but after a second, she nodded.

Fenway put the two clear evidence bags on the table, with the pictures of Charlotte and Kapp face up.

Charlotte recoiled. "What the hell is that?"

"They're two doctored photos of you and the man you were supposed to have shot," Fenway said.

"I didn't ever have sex with him! I wasn't there!"

"I know," Fenway said, as patiently as she could. "I *said* the photos were doctored. I can tell it's not you."

"How?"

"Because of the way the shadow falls on your face. It was obviously Photoshopped. Plus, you're taller."

"Oh." Charlotte leaned over and pointed to the woman's lower back. "And whoever this is, she doesn't have the tattoo I have on my back," Charlotte said.

"Ah," Fenway said. "Even more compelling." She paused. "So I have to ask you, Charlotte, who do you know who might do something like this to you?"

Charlotte looked puzzled. "Do this to me?"

"Yes," Fenway said. "Someone's trying to set you up. I think someone used your gun to kill Jeremy Kapp. Someone planted your earring there. And now someone is going through a lot of trouble to make it look like you're guilty. Who did you piss off?"

"Who did *I* piss off? Fenway, I think you know by now *I'm* not the one who pisses people off. That title belongs to my husband."

Fenway laughed uneasily. "Sure. But then they wouldn't come after you, would they? They'd come after him."

"Who knows? I sure don't know how this works."

"You said you were at home when Jeremy Kapp was murdered."

Charlotte nodded. "The police have all the footage—your sergeant and that awful woman she was with. They made sure to take it all with them when they arrested me."

"And how did your gun end up on the beach?"

"I'm sure I don't know. I didn't even know it was missing."

"You don't keep it locked in a safe?"

"No. It's in my bedside table. For when Nathaniel is on business trips, which is more often than I'd like. Our house is a big target. I feel a lot safer with a gun in easy reach."

"Did anyone have access to your room?"

Charlotte shrugged. "Sandrita. But it's not like I keep my room closed. Anyone who came through the front door, I suppose, could have gone up and gotten it."

"What about your earring?"

"I don't know how it got on the beach either," Charlotte said. "I don't think I've ever even *been* to that beach—and even if I had, I'd certainly never wear those earrings. They'd get lost in the sand—I'm frankly amazed anyone found it."

Fenway made a mental note: Charlotte didn't realize her earring was found *away* from the beach, in the planter in front of the villa at the Belvedere Terrace. It underscored Fenway's belief that Charlotte hadn't been there when Jeremy Kapp was killed. "And you don't have any enemies?"

"Darlin'," Charlotte drawled, "I live a boring life. The most interesting thing that happened to me lately is one of our dinner guests tried to sneak a peek at me when I was getting out of the shower."

Fenway fought the urge to guffaw. It would be just like Charlotte to "forget" what time the guests were showing up, to "forget" to close the door when she got in the shower, to "forget" a towel. She wouldn't put it past her.

"Oh, gosh, you must have hated that," Fenway said coldly.

Charlotte looked into Fenway's face and steeled her gaze, as if she had read Fenway's mind. "It was an accident, Fenway. I'm *sure* I closed the door to the bedroom. The little pervert was definitely looking at me."

"What about your housekeeper and your cook?" Fenway asked. "Or the driver? Did they ever come in to the house, somewhere that they could have taken your gun and your earring?"

"Of course," Charlotte said. "They all have keys to the house. Listen, Sandrita has been with us for eight years. Roderick has been driving your dad since before I met him. If they ever wanted to steal anything from us, they would have done so long before now."

"What about money?" Fenway said. "Everyone has a price, don't they?"

"I suppose they do," Charlotte said, "but we pay them well. They should have no need to accept bribes."

"Maybe it was something else," Fenway said. "Maybe Sandrita's boyfriend is in trouble or needs a job or something. Or Roderick maybe has a gambling problem and owes money to the wrong people."

"I haven't heard anything like that," Charlotte said. "They've been with us so long because their drama is at a minimum. They do their jobs, they're quiet, and we trust them."

"Okay," Fenway said. She would look into them, but something told her it wouldn't be fruitful. In any case, Dez had probably looked into them already—and hopefully at the financial records for all of the Ferris's household employees, not only their personal finances. But Fenway thought a personal vendetta against Charlotte herself was a long shot.

"It's possible," Fenway said, "there is a big issue with some, uh, illegal trading using Ferris Energy for a cover."

"Illegal trading? Of what?"

Fenway shook her head. "I can't tell you just yet. But my theory—as far as I have one—is someone is trying to frame you and my father."

"Frame us? Why?"

"It's only a theory." Fenway looked up at Charlotte. "Maybe you noticed something during one of the business dinners my father hosted at the house, or maybe you went with him to dinner with one of his investors or board members, and you noticed something amiss."

"I do know that Cynthia Schimmelhorn seems to have it out for your dad," Charlotte said. "She doesn't much care for me, either. But, then, there are a lot of women who don't particularly care for me." She looked Fenway squarely in the eyes.

Fenway ignored Charlotte's stare. "Did you have dinner with Ms. Schimmelhorn recently?"

"I got dragged to a dinner with the board and all the wives and husbands," Charlotte said. "She was challenging Nathaniel quite a bit. What with the whole kerfuffle with Robert, and then Nathaniel picking a candidate who wasn't exactly aboveboard."

Charlotte did have a gift for understatement—Robert Stotsky, Ferris Energy's head of security, murdered two people, and she could call it a *kerfuffle*.

"She wants my father to—what?" asked Fenway. "Resign as CEO?"

Charlotte nodded. "She made that pretty clear."

"Did anything come of it? Any threats?"

"No threats. At least—nothing verbal. When Nathaniel made it clear it was his company and his decision to resign—'it's my name on the front door, and I'll decide when I go'—she sat back down and was quiet. But she was fuming, and I noticed she didn't touch the rest of her dinner. She left first, before anyone else."

"Hmm," Fenway said. "I wonder what she was doing on Friday night." Fenway looked at her watch. "Oh, crap. I've gotta get back. Thanks for your time, Charlotte."

"And you're working on getting me out of here?"

"I am."

Charlotte paused. "I know we've had our differences, Fenway, but I have to say, I'm glad you're on my side."

"Remember," Fenway said, standing up, "not a word that we talked about the case. If anyone asks, I called you a golddigger and got angry at you for ruining my father's life."

Charlotte gave her a sardonic smile. "Got to keep it believable, after all."

Fenway met Callahan in the entrance hall to the jail. He handed her the large latte, keeping a jumbo cup in his hand.

"Thanks. You get something appropriately expensive to get back at me for ditching you at the jail?"

Callahan chuckled. "I was going to, but I don't like all that sweet foam whipped cream flavored soy milk crap." He lifted his cup. "I take mine black."

"I'm glad I bought you something you like."

"Good, because you bought me a large piece of coffee cake too. That was almost five bucks. I didn't save you any, either."

Fenway smiled as they walked out of the jail building.

"Charlotte tell you what you needed to know?"

"I was there strictly as family. To give her my support."

Callahan laughed, then his look grew thoughtful. "You know," he said, "at some point, you're going to have to get to a campaign event. You must have had a bunch of stuff scheduled for today."

"I did," Fenway said. "Millicent is going to be mad at me. If I had a phone, she'd be blowing it up right now."

Callahan looked sideways at Fenway. The thought of Rory flashed in Fenway's mind.

"Sorry," she said. "Poor choice of words."

"You think maybe you should reassemble your phone and get back to the real world?"

Fenway sighed. "I guess."

"Unless you don't want to have a job on January first."

"No, I don't want to be out of a job. I guess I don't want to campaign for it. Of course, my car is still in evidence. That makes getting to these campaign events a little difficult."

"That's not even a good excuse. I'm sure your campaign manager will make sure you have a ride."

"Yeah."

Callahan started to turn toward the sheriff's office, but Fenway stepped into the crosswalk.

"Did you forget something in your office?" he asked.

"I need to talk to Piper again before we go." Fenway paused. "And I guess you're right. I should get my phone from the office and reassemble it."

They crossed the street in silence. Callahan stepped ahead and opened the door to the building for Fenway.

"How long is your shift?"

"On Fenway protection duty? From six until six. Then Officer Young comes on."

Fenway remembered Rachel was skittish around Officer Young, and she didn't know why. She wondered what Rachel was concerned about.

"Hey, Brian?"

"Yeah?"

"I think Rachel is weird about Officer Young. I don't think she feels comfortable around him."

"Why?"

"I don't know. I haven't had a chance to talk with her today. But I know one of you is assigned protection to me, and two of you are supposed to secure the area, right?"

"Right."

"Well, maybe you can talk to whoever is in charge of the detail. Have them switch it around."

Callahan nodded, opening the door into the IT office. "Let me think about it for a minute."

Piper looked up from her desk. "Hey—didn't expect you back. Thought you'd be off campaigning."

"When I could be getting admonished for investigating murders I'm not supposed to be party to anymore? And miss all the fun?"

Piper looked confused.

"We found an envelope under the coroner's office door," Callahan explained. "The deputy sheriff didn't want her touching the envelope or anything, even though there was no sign it was—uh," he finished, catching Fenway's look, "well, I guess it's not important."

"I thought I'd see if you got anywhere with any of the other financial data since I've been gone."

"Financials? Not really. I mean, I've gotten additional information about earlier payments, enough to establish a pattern. But strangely enough, the pattern of payments doesn't start to change at all until two days ago."

"Two days ago? The day Jeremy Kapp's body was found?"

"Or the day of the explosion, if you prefer. That day there was a flurry of activity, and even though yesterday was a Saturday, there were quite a few transfer requests."

"What do you suppose that's about?"

Piper shook her head. "It's impossible to tell without getting access to the correspondence on this."

Fenway thought for a minute. "We could get a warrant for Jeremy Kapp's computer and email. And maybe Domingo Velásquez's as well."

Piper nodded. "That would be great."

"I can give a call to the sheriff, if you want," Callahan said. "Start drawing up the paperwork."

"And use your secret judge list to get it signed," said Fenway. "Thanks, Brian."

Callahan stepped out into the hall to talk on his radio.

"I don't think the sheriff will be in. I think he's off campaigning," Piper said. "I believe there was a dinner to-night."

Fenway closed her eyes. "Oh *no*," she groaned. "There *is* a din-ner tonight. The George Nidever County Dinner. It's tradition— all the local candidates the Sunday before election day. And all the business leaders too. I *have* to be there."

Piper raised her eyebrows. "You think Ivanovich will show his face after what happened with his son?"

"For all I know, this whole thing has emboldened all the white supremacists in the county who usually don't vote because there aren't enough racists on the ballot."

"What time does it start?"

"Six," Fenway said. "That's in less than an hour."

"Just over an hour," Piper said. "And you just got a latte. You can do this."

Fenway shook her head. "My father will probably be there too. I'm not looking forward to it."

"Are you taking someone to the dinner?"

"This isn't a date thing, Piper."

She shrugged. "I thought it was a fancy black-tie thing. Barry Klein is taking his wife."

"That's different. They're married. I'm not even seeing any-one." She sighed. "And I don't even have time to get my hair decent. Crap. That was supposed to be my afternoon—directly from the senior center to the salon."

"Well," Piper said, "maybe after the election."

"I can get my hair done after the election?"

"No, no," Piper said, frustration on her face. "You can date someone after the election."

Fenway thought of everything that happened two months before: McVie asking her out on a date, then putting that on hold until after the election—but seeing the look on his face after the car bomb, and after Dr. Tassajera's murder, gave her butterflies.

She looked at Piper, who was looking back at her; it seemed Piper knew *exactly* who Fenway wanted to be with. Fenway could feel the color rise to her cheeks. She cleared her throat. "All right. I guess I'm going to go to this stupid candidate dinner. And it's going to be up at Nidever University too. What a pain."

"Don't do anything I wouldn't do," said Piper as Fenway turned and walked out.

Callahan was in the hallway, clicking off the radio. "Okay— the sheriff is at some candidate dinner tonight, so I couldn't okay it with him, but I got ahold of Dez and they're going to draw up the warrant for the computers and emails."

"That's good news. Hopefully we'll find a clue there. Thanks, Callahan." She walked into the coroner's office, again using the key, and went into her private office. She pulled open the drawer where she had stashed her phone, and took it and the SIM card out.

"Okay," she said. "Let's get to the cruiser. I've got forty-five minutes to make myself red-carpet ready."

"Oh," Callahan looked stricken. "You have to go to the election dinner too, don't you? I didn't talk to anyone about taking Officer Young off your protection detail tonight."

"Don't worry about it," Fenway said. "Can you call him and ask if he owns a tux?"

———◆◆———

Fenway put the SIM card in her phone as soon as she got into the passenger seat of the cruiser. She powered the phone on and braced herself. Sure enough, the phone started to buzz crazily, lighting up, and giving her several overlapping alert sounds.

"Ugh," she said under her breath. "I'm sure these are all from Millicent Tate. Either from her or my father."

Callahan drove quickly to her apartment, and he stood outside the door while she went in, wrapped her hair and took a quick shower. She went to her closet to find the dress she had purchased for formal dinners like this, and briefly touched the dress she used to wear to clubs in Seattle. For a moment, she wanted to go out dancing instead of going to this stuffy political dinner, where she'd have to talk to a bunch of people she didn't want to talk to, including both her father and Barry Klein.

Although, she thought as she hastily pulled the dress on, maybe her father wouldn't come. Maybe he was so distraught over Charlotte's arrest he wouldn't make it at all.

Of course, maybe he *would* come, and he'd drink too much and cause a scene. Maybe get into a fistfight with Klein. Maybe get into a fistfight with Ivanovich. Fenway smiled at the thought of her father standing up for her, even if it would be because he was drunk.

She hadn't heard, either, if Dr. Ivanovich had publicly reacted to the news of his son in police custody. Would he stay above the fray, perhaps even disavow his son's actions? Would he try to turn this on Fenway, saying she somehow brought this on herself? That would be a bold move, for sure, and it might backfire. But if that message were delivered with enough power and force and confidence, it could change the conversation. Maybe it already had.

She didn't have time to listen to all of the messages Millicent Tate had left for her. She figured Millicent would be at the dinner and could give her the highlights then—and she would have something to do besides yell at Fenway for missing all the campaign events.

She put on her black heels, the ones she had worn six months before that had saved her life. She thought they might get her through this difficult night, like they had before.

She looked at herself in the mirror. The black dress went down mid-calf; it would have been ankle-length on a shorter woman. The sweetheart neckline had an inch-wide strap going from the front of her right shoulder around the back of her neck to attach behind her left shoulder. She turned around; the back of the dress hit her on the bottom of her shoulder blades. It was classy and elegant, but still had an air of sexiness about it. For the first time, however, she realized it might be one of the more revealing dresses in the room, and perhaps it wasn't a great choice for a political event.

When she came out of the bedroom, Officer Todd Young was sitting on the sofa. In a tuxedo.

"Oh," she said. "You *do* own a tux."

"I sure do," he said. "Wow, you look great."

"You have a story to go with that outfit?"

"It's boring," he said. "When I lived in L.A. a few years ago, I was a seat filler at the Oscars. I was going to rent a tux, but I saw one on sale, and I tried it on, and I looked damn good in it, so I bought it."

Rachel might have been uneasy around Officer Young, but he was right: he looked good in the tuxedo. He stood up; the coat was single-breasted and three-button.

"And that's a real bow tie," Fenway said. "Not one of those fake clip-ons like my prom date had."

"My father taught me well," Officer Young said. "Shall we head out?" He offered her his arm.

"Only fitting," Fenway said, "that we show up for a black-and-white ball in a black-and-white."

Officer Young laughed at Fenway's attempt at levity. This evening might be salvageable after all.

CHAPTER TWENTY

Although the George Nidever Dinner officially started at seven o'clock, all the invitees were talking and milling around the large lobby in front of the ballroom at the university hotel. Nidever was a private university, and as Fenway looked at the chandeliers in the lobby, she realized Nidever students had a much different perspective on the world than a woman who had to get student loans to attend a public university like Western Washington.

"For crying out loud, Fenway," Millicent Tate said, "you know even if you don't have your phone *on* you, you can still call to get your voicemail."

"Officer Young," Fenway said, "would you mind getting us both a glass of champagne while I have a chat with my campaign manager?"

"Certainly," he said, and turned and headed in the direction of the bar.

Millicent watched him go. "New boyfriend?"

"The cop assigned to protect me."

"He cleans up nice," Millicent said. "I hope you keep it under wraps if you have some *Bodyguard*-style hot romance."

"You don't have to worry."

Millicent kept watching Officer Young walk toward the bar. "We've definitely lost some momentum today," she said. "I didn't know you weren't going to make the senior center today. They were disappointed."

"I'm sorry," Fenway said, not sorry at all. "The family therapist my father and I see was murdered this morning. I found his body. I had to take care of a bunch of things."

"Ugh," Millicent Tate said, rolling her eyes. "I wish you were just a candidate, and not the sitting coroner. It would make things a lot easier."

"I'll make sure his family gets your heartfelt condolences," Fenway said.

Millicent turned toward Fenway and folded her arms. "Your father is paying me to run this campaign, Fenway. He's not paying me to feel bad about murder victims, or to hold your hand and nod sympathetically. He's paying me to win." She sighed. "You know, I get that your dedication to the job makes you the right candidate for it, but it's hard with you *not* campaigning."

"It must be a little easier when my opponent's son spray-paints shit on my car."

Millicent slapped Fenway on her bare shoulder. "If you're going to play the family card, remember *you're* the one whose stepmother was arrested for murder."

Fenway winced.

"Yeah, you didn't think of that, did you? You thought because you and she almost never spoke, none of the voters would associate you with her?"

"Uh—no, I guess I didn't."

"Did you see the ads that Ivanovich's been running on Channel 12 today?"

Fenway gasped. "Oh no—he mentions Charlotte?"

"No, he talks about his stance on tax shelters."

"Really?"

"No, you idiot, of course it's all about Charlotte! They've got a picture of her, and it's not a picture of her feeding orphans either. It's one where she's got a nasty look on her face, boobs hanging halfway out, a tequila shot in one hand, and a damn *tiara* on top of her head. A tiara!"

"Oh." Fenway said. She had seen the picture before.

"What, do you know the picture I'm talking about?"

"It was her bachelorette party," Fenway said. "Lots of women wear tiaras at their bachelorette parties."

"Well," Millicent said sardonically, "once we explain it's merely a bachelorette party to the voters, it should all be great. They should get right on board with us."

Fenway ignored her tone. "Have we run anything? Any counter ads?"

Millicent looked around and lowered her voice. "We're divided on what to do. You were supposed to be the deciding vote."

"What were you going to run?"

"We have a picture of your car with the spray paint on it. We have a picture of your window after the brick was thrown through it. We have a voiceover talking about how Dr. Ivanovich thinks he can use white supremacist intimidation tactics to scare you out of the race. How you weren't scared to take on your father's head of security, you weren't scared to take on the head of the most powerful pharmaceutical company in California. We were *hoping* to get you in the studio, maybe even in your dress blues, saying, 'I've taken on the most powerful men in the state. I'm not scared of anybody calling me names.'"

"Oh," Fenway said. "That would have been good."

"Yeah, you think?" Millicent's voice was thick with sarcasm. "Maybe that's why your dad pays me the big bucks."

"I mean, part of me doesn't want anyone to see the N-word spray-painted on my car. You show that to white people and they freak out. Even people who say they're allies get all uncomfortable. But I like the tough stance on stuff. Makes people realize I'm my own person. I don't answer to my father for anything."

"Or your stepmother."

"Right."

"Plus, it helps to have a different, uh, last name."

Fenway shifted her weight from foot to foot. "And skin color, you were going to say."

Millicent hesitated, but nodded. "Yes. Because you don't look anything like Charlotte. You don't have the same name, you don't have the same skin color or hair color. People will see you, taking a tough stance, and they'll think, 'Oh, yeah, another old rich white guy who dumped his wife for a hot girl half his age. Like his daughter is going to let *that* bitch get away with murder.'"

"You know I think she's innocent, right?"

"Fenway, listen to me. For the next seventy-two hours, I literally don't give a damn if she committed murder or if she tried to poison the water supply. I care about getting you *elected*." She laughed. "Your dad is paying me so much I don't care if *you* committed murder. It doesn't matter what the truth is."

Fenway's eyes widened.

Millicent Tate smirked. "That's right, Little Miss Idealism, it doesn't matter what the truth is. Not for the next seventy-two hours, it doesn't. It only matters what the voters *think*."

It only matters what the voters think.

And with a shock, Fenway realized she had been looking in all the wrong places for the killer of Jeremy Kapp.

The money laundering, the phantom oil supertanker—Fenway realized none of that was why Jeremy Kapp was killed. Uncovering those crimes had completely distracted her from looking at personal motives. But the fake emails, the doctored photos, the clumsy setup of Charlotte—those weren't the work of a professional.

Jeremy Kapp's murderer wasn't the ruthlessly efficient killer who blew up Rory or bludgeoned Dr. Tassajera—or ordered the death of Carl Cassidy, for that matter. Jeremy Kapp's death was from an amateur hand. His death exposed a lot of people in the money laundering scheme, for sure, and might have been the root cause for the latest murders—but, if Fenway was right, she needed to look at the people closest to Kapp.

She had to talk to Dez.

"Fenway?" Millicent snapped her fingers. "Where did you go?"

Fenway's eyes came back into focus. "Sorry, sorry. I just had a thought about the case."

"Pay attention, Fenway!" Millicent barked. "Keep your mind on the campaign for more than thirty seconds! Are you onboard with the ad or not?"

"I'm onboard with the ad," Fenway said.

"Great. We can get in the studio tonight after the dinner."

"Are you okay if I just step out for a second to make a call?"

Millicent's eyes went wide. "Oh, there's the camera from Channel 12. Turn around and smile. Pretend you haven't been receiving death threats."

Fenway turned, saw the camera, and smiled.

"You'll obviously have to change," Millicent continued. "A pantsuit or something. I mean, we can shoot you from the waist up, so maybe someone can run by your apartment and pick up a blazer." She took a step back and examined Fenway with a critical eye and frowned. "This dress makes you look beautiful."

"Thank you."

"That wasn't a compliment. People don't want to vote for an ingénue, they want to vote for someone reliable and competent. Maybe we can get your blazer sooner rather than later."

"This is a black-tie dinner," Fenway pointed out.

"And I have three dresses back at the campaign office picked out that are much more appropriate for a politician," Millicent said. "But at least you're not showing too much cleavage, and at least you didn't do anything fancy with your hair."

"At least," Fenway said. "Listen, I'll make one quick call and I'll be right—"

"Hang on," Millicent said, staring over Fenway's shoulder at an older white, blonde woman standing about twenty feet away. "That's Cynthia Schimmelhorn. I wonder what she's doing here."

"Cynthia Schimmelhorn?" Fenway asked, surprised. "Isn't she on the board of directors of Ferris Energy?"

"Yes," Millicent said, lowering her voice. "She has an agenda—and she sure doesn't like your dad."

"My father said she called for a vote of no confidence for him in the last board meeting."

"And if your father hadn't been so charming, he'd be out of a job right now."

"Yeah, I heard that too."

"So is she some big hotshot at the university?" Millicent said, mostly to herself, as she pulled her smartphone out and started tapping on the screen. "Oh, look, she's one of the star alumni."

"Wait—from Nidever University?" asked Fenway.

"She sure is," Millicent says. "Hey, did you know Abby Herrick graduated from here two years ago?"

"Who?"

"Abby Herrick," Millicent replied. "You know, the pop singer."

Fenway briefly remembered the tee shirt Donovan Kapp wore the first time she saw him. "Oh, right, I know who she is."

Millicent kept scrolling on her phone.

"What are you doing?"

Millicent tipped a little more champagne into her mouth. "Research," she said, winking at Fenway. "You might as well get to know her a little more since she's practically standing behind you."

"Abby Herrick's behind me?" Fenway started to turn around.

"Don't look!" Millicent hissed. "And no, you idiot, Cynthia Schimmelhorn."

Fenway stopped.

Millicent lowered her voice. "Where did you get your undergrad? Wasn't it Western Washington?"

Fenway nodded. "Go Vikings."

"Well, so did Cynthia Schimmelhorn's daughter." Millicent scrolled a little more and her eyes went wide. "Who names their daughter Nerissa?"

Fenway paused, trying to search her brain for where she had heard the name. "Oh—that's from Shakespeare."

"I don't care if it was spelled out in rose petals on the ground at the moment of conception—it's an awful name. Like 'narcissism.'" She stopped scrolling and looked up. "Okay, so that short guy who was talking to her walked away. Now's your chance."

Fenway grabbed Millicent's arm. "You're coming with me, aren't you?"

Millicent rolled her eyes. "Fine, I guess so. Wouldn't hurt to have someone else in my contact list who could singlehandedly bankroll a congressional candidate."

"Gee, thanks," Fenway said.

"What?" Millicent said. "A girl's gotta eat." She strode purposefully over to Cynthia Schimmelhorn, who was putting her empty champagne glass on a passing waiter's tray. "Ms. Schimmelhorn?" she asked, in a voice far more polite than anything Fenway had heard come out of Millicent's mouth.

Cynthia Schimmelhorn looked up. "Yes?" She looked like a well-preserved fifty, although Fenway wouldn't have been surprised if she was much older. Her skin was smooth and untouched by signs of aging; her blonde hair brushed the tops of her shoulders—and yes, she was wearing a sleeveless evening gown, with a graceful v-shaped neckline that managed to be both sexy and demure. Fenway felt envious; she hoped she looked that good at whatever age Schimmelhorn was.

"It's good to meet you," Millicent continued. "I'm Millicent Tate."

"Ah," Schimmelhorn said. "Of course. You're the magician behind some of the crazy electoral upsets in our great state."

"That's me," Millicent said. "And the architect of Fenway Stevenson's win, if I know my stuff."

"And I'm sure you do," Schimmelhorn said, turning to Fenway. "Miss Stevenson, it's a pleasure to meet you."

"Likewise," Fenway said, feeling underdressed and awkward.

"I'm sure you've heard of my little dust-up with your father," Schimmelhorn said. "I'd apologize for it, as it seems the polite thing to do, but the truth is, I'm not at all sorry. And you, of all people, should know his personal judgment has been, shall we say, subpar the last several months."

"I think he's starting to regret pulling the strings to get me appointed coroner, for sure," Fenway agreed.

Cynthia Schimmelhorn smiled. "I do so enjoy seeing young women stretch themselves beyond the orbits of the men who have taken them under their wing," she said, chewing on her words as if they were fine chocolates. "Sometimes those wings can be less a shelter than a holding cell."

Fenway could only gape at her.

"I must say, you're doing an exemplary job," Schimmelhorn said, placing her hand on Fenway's arm and giving it a maternal squeeze. "I always appreciate when the truth wins out over familial loyalty. Blood ties are so often confused for the gospel truth."

Fenway cleared her throat. "I, uh, I appreciate that, ma'am," she stuttered.

"Oh, please. Call me Cynthia. There's too much work we have to do to overcome the poor social and business positions we often find ourselves in to bother with formality."

"Sure," Fenway said. "Cynthia."

"And for what it's worth," said Schimmelhorn, "I'm appalled by the ugly business with your opponent's son."

Fenway cocked her head to the side. "With his son—how did you—"

"Oh, my dear," Schimmelhorn said, "those secrets don't keep as well as you'd like, I'm afraid. You must know by now I'm well-connected. Let's just say I'm sorry about it. Maintaining one's composure in a political campaign is difficult enough without having to deal with these, shall we say, *extraneous* issues."

Fenway was unable to mask her discomfort, but Millicent broke in and changed the subject.

"I understand your daughter and Fenway both went to Western Washington, Cynthia. Fenway thought it was a great nursing school."

A shadow fell over Schimmelhorn's face. "Ah, yes. You'll have to excuse me, I see—"

Just then, several of the staff began chiming their tiny xylophones, announcing that the dinner was about to begin. Schimmelhorn turned and glided away.

"That was weird," Millicent said.

"Maybe they're estranged," Fenway said. "Like me and my father."

"Or maybe she was disappointed Nerissa didn't pick an Ivy League school."

"Western Washington *is* rather pedestrian for a rich family." Fenway laughed. "Anyway, thank you for saving me from having to talk about Terrance Ivanovich."

"You know I've got your back."

"So," Fenway said, "we didn't really have time to brief on this dinner."

"You'll just be introduced. No big speeches at this one. It's more of a rub-elbows thing, and the press shows it off as a who's-who in Estancia."

"Cameras?"

"You can see them out here," said Millicent, "like this is some sort of red-carpet event before the Oscars. But they usually don't let cameras in there. I've been requesting they make an exception for weeks now. Flattery, freedom of information requests, offering to pay to record the university president's speech—they haven't even returned my calls. I'm not surprised—most of the candidates don't want to be filmed in a poorly-lit ballroom with a mouthful of dry chicken. I'll do what I can, but I think they want the cameras to stay in the foyer."

They both started to walk toward the double doors to enter the banquet hall. "Did Ivanovich ever make some sort of statement about what happened with his son?" Fenway said in a low voice. "Maybe that's why Cynthia brought it up."

Millicent shook her head. "I haven't heard a peep from Ivanovich, unless you count seeing his ridiculous ad a few times today."

"Think he's going to say anything about it tonight?"

"Not if he's smart," Millicent said. "I heard a rumor he was going to blame it all on *you*, saying you somehow framed his son, you're bringing race into it, blah blah blah. But we had the son's prison record ready for release, and we even found Dr. Ivanovich's name on a donation list to the local chapter of White Storm."

"Ugh."

"Now—it's *possible* he simply thought his kid was having a fundraiser and didn't know what it was for. But I think he heard we had more ammunition than he could deal with."

"How come you didn't hit him with the son's prison record and the White Storm stuff when you saw his ad?"

"Because," Millicent said, "the ad we just talked about will be far more effective. It uses his momentum against him. It doesn't allow him to change the subject, and the point he makes will become a point for you."

Officer Young in his dashing tuxedo appeared by Fenway's side. "Sorry," he said. "The line was long at the bar. They started calling for everyone to sit down before I could get you champagne."

The lights started to dim and Millicent stepped away. "Okay, now go in there and sit."

"You're not sitting with me?"

"You'll be fine."

Fenway realized she wouldn't have a lot of choice where to sit because she waited so long to go in, but she hoped it would work in her favor: she didn't want to sit anywhere near Dr. Richard Ivanovich or her father, and perhaps the seats at their tables would all be taken. But even in the fading light she could see the larger tables at the front of the banquet room were empty, with name cards on them. Her heart sank.

She approached the tables, and spied her name on one of the cards. A placard simply stating *Guest* was above the next placesetting.

"That must be me," Officer Young said. He pulled Fenway's chair out for her, and she sat. Officer Young took the guest seat to her right.

She looked at the small menu card on the table; dinner was a spinach salad, then pheasant in mushroom and wine sauce, then a chocolate mousse for dessert. Better than the barely edible food she was used to at most of the campaign events.

She looked to her right; her father's placard was next to Officer Young. She didn't see him. She looked to her left; the placard read *Imelda Ivanovich*. Ah, she thought, the missus. She wondered what had happened at home to make the son turn into a white supremacist. She looked behind her, toward the entrance.

She saw Dr. Ivanovich and a thin, raven-haired woman in a cream dress with a gauzy burgundy wrap coming toward the table.

"Not a word about Terrance," she breathed to Officer Young. "We're trying to keep the conversation somewhat decent before the election."

"I saw those commercials he ran today," Officer Young said. "I don't call that decent."

"Still," Fenway said, "it looks better for me if *I* keep things decent."

"I don't work for your campaign," Officer Young said. "Maybe I should arrest Ivanovich as an accessory."

"Please, Todd." Fenway looked in his eyes, pleading.

He sighed. "I'll keep my mouth shut," he said, "but only because I need to stick with you tonight. As soon as I'm off Fenway Protection Duty, I'm going to give that guy both barrels." He coughed. "Not literally, of course."

"Thank you," Fenway mouthed, squeezing his hand gently as the Ivanoviches sat down. Fenway put her hand in her lap. She looked at Imelda Ivanovich and smiled. Imelda shot daggers at Fenway with her eyes.

Maybe she believes her husband's press, Fenway thought.

Fenway turned back to the front of the room.

A white man with a salt-and-pepper van dyke, in a beige suit inappropriate for autumn, got up to the lectern in front of the hall. He cleared his throat and his thin, reedy voice sliced through the silence of the room.

"Good evening, ladies and gentlemen," he said. "For those of you who don't know me, I'm Dr. Alfred Pruitt, the president of Nidever University, and I'm proud to host our forty-seventh biannual George Nidever Dinner. When this tradition began, the school was in its infancy, and Dominguez County wasn't the international crossroads it is today."

Fenway looked closely at Dr. Pruitt, but found no trace of joking or irony in his face.

International crossroads. As if Estancia, whose international airport had two weekly flights to Guadalajara, could reasonably be called an *international crossroads.*

Although as she looked around the room, there were a lot more people of color in the room than she expected. She wasn't the only person of color running for office; there was a black candidate for associate judge, and two Filipinos, a man and a woman, running for the state assembly seat and the board of education, respectively.

"Back then, after World War I had ended, California was nowhere near the populous state it is today. This area was full of orchards, and a fur trapper and explorer named George Nidever inspired a group of academics from the east coast to journey west to found this great university."

Fenway looked around the room and caught Catherine Klein yawning. Mrs. Klein was in a bright red evening gown, more red-carpet formal than Fenway's dress, but as the potential first lady of the town, Catherine could get away with wearing a cocktail dress, where a candidate couldn't.

Fenway looked around the room, hoping a camera had been let in by some miracle, and might be aiming right at the yawning Catherine Klein. But no such luck.

Barry Klein was on his wife's right, with Sheriff McVie on her left, with an empty seat on the sheriff's other side. He obviously didn't have a guest to bring, going through the divorce from Amy.

Dr. Pruitt continued to drone on about the storied history of George Nidever, and put a glossy sheen on the story of Nidever and the Lone Woman of San Nicolas Island, and embellished the legend of Nidever staring down a grizzly bear, and bragged of Nidever's influence on Ralph Waldo Emerson...

Fenway allowed her mind to drift. She wondered if she could surreptitiously sneak her phone out and text Dez. And then start cleaning up some of the voicemails in her inbox. Millicent herself probably was responsible for ninety percent of them.

She quietly pulled the phone out of her purse and texted Dez.

We're on the wrong track with the Kapp murder

While she waited for Dez to respond, she brought up her voicemail. She dug around in her purse until she found one of her wireless earbuds. She put it in her ear—one would do—and heard the tone as the phone connected. She put the phone underneath the tabletop and angled it so only she could see it. She looked around; everyone seemed to be pretending to pay attention, and if she could focus mostly on Dr. Pruitt and only occasionally look down at the screen, she could get away with cleaning up her voicemails during his coma-inducing introduction.

Sure enough, the first five voicemails were from Millicent Tate on Friday night, each one asking where she was, why she wasn't checking in, and asking for a phone call as soon as possible. The number of swear words in each message seemed to increase logarithmically.

The next voicemail was from her father, hurried and frantic, not the calm demeanor he usually possessed. Fenway looked at the screen; he must have left it right after Charlotte had been led away in handcuffs.

Another four voicemails from Millicent Tate from Saturday, and then another two this morning. A reminder about the eleven o'clock therapist appointment with dear old Dad. Then another with the screaming and swearing, again with the not knowing where Fenway was, missing the senior center event.

A text came in. Fenway glanced down, hoping Dez had responded. But it was from Millicent.

Put your phone away or so help me I will come over there and shove it up your ass in front of all these people

Fenway clicked her phone off, pulled the earbud out of her ear, and as stealthily as she could, put them back in her purse.

She looked to her right: the Channel 12 camera was coming back up the side of the room toward her table.

As maddening as Millicent could be sometimes, she was often right.

Just as she put her purse down on the floor again, she caught her father out of the corner of her eye. He was clumsily moving between the seats, bumping the backs of chairs in his effort to get past the people and up to the front of the room.

Fenway turned around so he could see her better, but his focus was down on the ground, looking where he was stepping, trying to avoid toes and the bottoms of long dresses.

She had never seen him so disheveled; he wore a rumpled black suit with a dark tie, although Fenway couldn't tell in the low light if the tie was navy or black. He owned a tuxedo; in fact, Fenway thought he might have owned more than one. Why wasn't he in a tux?

His hair was jutting up in the back, as if he didn't put any of his normal styling mousse into it, and his shoes were scuffed around the sides.

His face, though, worried Fenway.

Though Nathaniel Ferris was nearly sixty, he often had the confidence and bravado of a much younger man. But the lines on his face and the weariness in his eyes told Fenway there was something wrong.

Of course there was; Charlotte was in jail.

Fenway wouldn't have believed it—Nathaniel Ferris *loved* Charlotte, the twenty-five-year-old girl he had married a decade earlier, so much that he would go to pieces in front of Fenway's eyes when Charlotte wasn't around.

Charlotte had always seemed vapid, vacant, unfeeling; obviously Fenway hadn't seen the things in Charlotte her father had.

Ferris finally got to the table and sat down heavily next to Officer Young. He leaned over and caught Fenway's eye.

"Sorry I'm late," he mouthed.

Fenway nodded and shrugged, hoping her father would understand the shrug meant *no worries, you didn't miss much.* She looked to the back of the room and saw Millicent sneak out into the foyer.

Then she was surprised by sudden applause. She looked up; the two candidates for assembly stood up and waved, a spotlight focused on them. Fenway adjusted the skirt of her dress and pushed the chair back a bit so she could easily get up when the two coroner candidates were asked to stand.

A few offices were introduced before the coroner candidates, but when Dr. Pruitt finished talking about how Dominguez County separated their coroner and sheriff positions over a decade previous—nothing Fenway hadn't heard or even explained herself a dozen times in the last six months—he finally said, "And for county coroner, two candidates: Dr. Richard Ivanovich and Acting Coroner Fenway Stevenson!"

Applause broke out around the room. Fenway thought it sounded much more enthusiastic than for the other offices, and she looked around. A lot of people seemed to be casting admiring looks her way.

Dr. Richard Ivanovich stood up, and Imelda, right next to him, stood a split second afterward. Fenway caught McVie's eye across the table and he gave her a warm smile. She pushed her chair back slightly and stood, looking around at everyone in the room with her warmest, friendliest smile, feeling fake, the spotlight blinding her.

Then the spotlight moved off them, and Imelda Ivanovich was staring at her, a sneer on her face.

She spit at Fenway, and it landed on her left cheek.

Fenway heard a few gasps.

Then an arm shunted her out of the way. She was pushed back against the chair and almost lost her balance, but she caught herself on the table just in time.

Officer Young stepped in front of her—he must have pushed her to the side. He had a pair of handcuffs out, and Imelda Ivanovich's sneer changed to a look of terror. Dr. Ivanovich turned his head to see his wife taken to the floor by Officer Young and rolled on her stomach.

Richard Ivanovich raised a fist to hit Officer Young,

"Stop!" Fenway shouted, and grabbed his arm.

"Get off me, bitch," he snarled.

McVie jumped into the middle of it and pulled Ivanovich away from Fenway and Officer Young. "Richard! You don't want to do that!"

And Imelda was screaming a stream of racial slurs.

"Imelda Ivanovich," Officer Young said, trying to catch his breath, "you're under arrest for assault and battery of a peace officer under California Penal Code 240."

Fenway looked up. Most of the other attendees had looks of shock on their faces.

And she saw Millicent Tate, in the back the room near the double doors, next to a man holding the Channel 12 camera, aimed directly onto the action, the red light brightly lit. Fenway reached up to discreetly wipe the spit off, then realized being discreet would waste an opportunity. She turned to face the camera, picked up a napkin off the table, and dabbed her face. McVie had pushed his way through and was standing next to her.

"Are you okay?" said McVie.

"I'm fine. It's just spit," Fenway said, a little louder than she normally would have if the camera hadn't been on her. "It's not like she threw a brick through my window."

"My son's a good boy," Imelda Ivanovich yelled from her prone position on the floor, hands cuffed behind her. "You broke his hand! And for what? You're ruining his life!"

The camera had picked up *that*, for sure.

Fenway wondered how this was going to play out. Had enough people in the room seen Imelda Ivanovich spit on Fenway? Had the Channel 12 camera entered the room in time to capture it? Would the events unfold in the media showing Fenway in a positive light, a victim standing strong in the face of adversity, or as a bully, using the politics of color to intimidate her opponents into submission?

From her position next to the cameraman, Millicent Tate grinned widely and gave Fenway a thumbs-up.

"I guess that answers that," Fenway muttered.

CHAPTER TWENTY-ONE

⬥

BY THE TIME THE CROWD HAD SETTLED DOWN, IT WAS CLEAR the coroner candidates were no longer going to be part of the forty-seventh biannual George Nidever Dinner. A man in a tuxedo with an earpiece shunted Fenway into one of the classrooms off the main hall. Her stomach growled, loudly this time.

She sat in one of the student chairs, remembering her last on-campus class, barely seven months before, at Seattle University. It had been a half-lecture, half-lab class, and she fondly remembered her professor and the lab work they had done. At one point they had done work identifying insects on rotting pig meat—the closest analog for human flesh without using actual cadavers. Her lab partner, a tall white man, about twenty-three, with sixteen-inch biceps, couldn't make it through any class that week without throwing up. "I don't know how you do it," he said, turning green again on the last day, when she was taking South American dung beetle larvae out of a pit in the pig flesh. He bolted for the door.

She smiled fondly at the memory, and the door opened to reveal Dez.

"Why Miss Stevenson, fancy meeting you here," Dez said. "I've come to take your statement on what happened before the, uh, mêlée."

"They introduced the coroner candidates," Fenway said, "and Imelda Ivanovich turned around and spit on me."

"Uh huh."

"That's it."

"Seems pretty straightforward."

"Channel 12 caught it on camera, right? I don't think my memory is any different than what the camera caught."

"I saw the footage," Dez said.

"And it's the same, right?"

"Well," Dez said, "technically I'm not supposed to tell you if your statement matches the footage."

"I know, Dez," Fenway said, "but there's a roomful of witnesses."

"I heard the names she was calling you, too."

"Yep," Fenway said. "I think I've been called names more times in the last three days than the last ten years."

Dez shook her head. "Sometimes I think we've come so far," she murmured, "and other times I realize we're a few hundred votes away from going back a hundred fifty years."

Fenway nodded. "Hey—I wanted to talk to you."

"Yeah, I got your text. You think we're on the wrong track?"

"I do." Fenway paused. "You have some time now?"

Dez shook her head. "Are you kidding? With the shitstorm going on outside?"

"But we're talking about a murder."

"And I'm talking about a riot. Sorry, Fenway, I know it's important, but I've got to prioritize. Maybe after I'm done here. Besides, there's a gentleman outside who's insisting on speaking with you."

"A *gentleman*?"

"A detective. Came all the way from up north."

"Oh," Fenway said. "From the Bellingham Major Crimes unit."

"That's it. Says he talked with you the day before yesterday."

"Just on the phone," Fenway said.

"Something happen?"

Fenway nodded. "The professor. The one who—uh, those pictures Barry Klein had, you remember them?"

Dez's mouth turned into an angry line. "I remember."

"The professor drowned in the Squalicum Waterway a couple of days after Dr. Klein showed me those pictures."

Dez's eyebrows shot up. "Drowned?"

"That's what the article said. But now I guess they think it was foul play."

"But you live here now. Why are they talking to you?"

"Because," Fenway said, "I think they found all those videos on the dark web, the same as Barry Klein's private investigator found, and I was in Seattle a couple of days before."

"Oh—when you went up to get your mother's painting."

"Right."

"So, what, he thinks you killed him?"

"I'm not sure what he thinks." Fenway paused. "No—that's not quite true. I think he looks at my car being at the Sea-Tac airport, he looks at me visiting Seattle, and he looks at the dead professor, and he says to himself how he doesn't like coincidences."

Dez nodded. "I get it. I don't like coincidences either."

"Maybe he's down here trying to confirm my alibi for those days."

"You still could have hired someone."

"Yeah, but he could figure all the financial stuff out online, or with a forensic accountant. He wouldn't need to come down."

Dez tapped her foot. "It *is* a pretty big coincidence."

"I agree."

"So what do you think happened?"

"Honestly, Dez, I think someone who Professor Delacroix raped either killed him, or a boyfriend or father or someone did."

Dez cocked her head to the side. "Father?"

"I know." Fenway nodded. "He found out about a day and a half before the professor died. Don't think I haven't considered the possibility."

"Do you think he did it?"

"I think he could have. I mean—he wouldn't do it himself, he'd get one of his security specialists to fly up there in his private plane and do it. He wouldn't get his hands dirty."

"Think it's likely it was him?"

"I don't know. I haven't asked him. And I don't want to."

"You said boyfriend too."

"I did."

Dez looked knowingly at Fenway.

"McVie was with me most of the time," Fenway said, "plus, he wouldn't have had money to hire anyone, plus, he's not my boyfriend."

"No," Dez said, "but you know how he feels about you."

"I don't know."

Dez looked at Fenway with a smirk. "You *do* know."

Fenway felt herself blush.

"All right," Dez said. "You want me to give Bellingham the brush off?"

"No." Fenway sighed. "Tell him I'll talk to him. I'll give him a whole forty-five minutes." Fenway felt her stomach tighten up again. "But he has to take me to dinner. Somewhere good."

———————◆———————

Detective Deshawn Ridley sat across from Fenway at a high-top table at Dos Milagros *taquería*. A couple of the other patrons glanced at her, as she still had the fancy dress on. She was by far the most dressed-up person in the restaurant. One little girl with a big mop of curly black hair and huge dark eyes kept staring at her. Her mother kept telling her in Spanish to turn around, it was impolite to stare, but the little girl couldn't look away.

Fenway had ordered two chicken tacos, and then, because the detective was paying, a *lengua* taco as well.

He was playing with the paper straw for his Coke. Fenway had wanted a Pacifico, but, because she knew she'd be grilled by the detective, ordered *horchata* instead.

"Did I hear right? You ordered a *lengua* taco?"

"Yep," Fenway said.

"You don't strike me as the type to be that adventurous with your food."

"Maybe not," Fenway said. "Maybe I ordered it because I've always been fascinated to try it and finally ordered it since someone else was paying."

"That's kind of rude," Ridley said.

Fenway shrugged.

Ridley wasn't at all what Fenway had expected. With his deep, sonorous voice, Ridley should have been about six-foot-ten and built like a linebacker. Fenway had pictured a huge hulk of a man, skin the color of obsidian, barely fitting into sport coats, his muscles bulging with every step. Instead, he was small and wiry, and his skin was almost as light as Fenway's. His temples had flecks of salt and pepper, but he didn't look old enough to be going gray yet. Fenway was dying to ask how old he was, but knew how impolite it would be.

"While we're waiting for our food, Miss Stevenson," he said, "I'd like you to tell me again what your relationship with Professor Solomon Delacroix was."

"I'm sure you've seen the video by now, Detective," Fenway said. "He was my professor. He did *that* to me. Then I worked my ass off in his class, got an A, and then I transferred from literature to nursing. After I took the final in his class, I literally never saw him again."

"Never? Not even crossing campus, across the dining hall or student union, bumping into him in town on a Saturday night?"

"Not once."

The detective nodded.

"So, Detective, you've talked to me twice in the last three days."

"True."

"I must have somehow emerged as a person of interest. But I've explained what I was doing in Seattle, you know I was on a flight back home before he died, and you know I was in Estancia the entire time in question."

"True."

"Did you just want to take me to dinner? Because there are less creepy ways—"

"No, Miss Stevenson," Ridley said, holding up his hand. "Are you familiar with a man named Akeel Montgomery?"

Fenway cocked her head to the side. "Sure. I dated him about two years ago. The summer I was doing my graduate work."

"You visited Mr. Montgomery, if I'm not mistaken, at 112 NE 38th Street, in Seattle? Three days before the professor was found?"

Fenway shifted uncomfortably on her stool. "True."

"What was the reason for your visit?"

Fenway screwed up her mouth, weighing her options. Then she decided to come clean. "I was hung up on a guy here in Estancia. And I wanted to get Mom's painting out of the storage unit in Seattle, and Akeel lives pretty close to the storage unit. And he and I used to date, and I still thought he was hot, and I thought if I spent some time with him, I could get the other guy out of my head."

Ridley nodded. "I see. There was no other reason you stayed with him?"

The woman behind the counter called "Joanne" and Fenway popped off her stool to get their orders before she had to answer.

She took her time getting the food, and getting her bearings. The line of questioning about Akeel obviously showed Ridley thought something sinister went on.

She asked for extra sour cream in Spanish. The exchange with the cook took a minute as Fenway thought about how to respond.

They had discussed her father—or at least, her father's employees—on the phone call the other day. But nothing about her father had come up so far in this particular conversation. Fenway moved onto the salsa bar, pulling a metal tray onto the counter and putting the tacos on it—Ridley had ordered three *carne asada*—and then she slowly and methodically scooped all three types of salsa into containers. Was Ridley waiting to pull out his suspicions of her father when Fenway was already on her heels about Akeel?

Fenway knew what Ridley was implying: Fenway had traded sex with Akeel in exchange for him killing the professor. But she wasn't going to let Ridley leave it in the air; he was going to have to accuse her directly. He'd have to accuse her of being a whore, in front of customers, in front of the servers, in front of a drink she could pour on his head. Fenway was going to play innocent—and play nice.

The sex-for-murder angle might have been what Fenway would think if she were the detective in a similar situation, but that didn't make it any less appalling.

She brought the tray with the tacos back to the high-top table and set it down, taking the two taco baskets and putting them in front of both of them.

She sat down on the stool across from Detective Ridley, and smiled a warm, personable smile. "Seriously the best tacos in Estancia," Fenway said. "Way better than anything in Bellingham."

"I like Rio Bravo," Detective Ridley said, then took a large bite of one of his tacos.

"The one in downtown? Doesn't even hold a candle to this place." Fenway picked up the *lengua* taco in her left hand and with her right poured a generous amount of salsa verde over the top. She briefly flashed back to a few weeks before, when she had been in line at Dos Milagros, and two teenaged girls were in front of her. Fenway was trying to psych herself up to order the *lengua* taco, but the teenagers pointed it out on the menu and were making their icky faces at it. "Eww, gross," one of them said. "I don't want to taste anything that can taste me back." Fenway had ordered the chicken.

The *lengua* taco looked like a regular taco; the meat was buried underneath the cheese and lettuce and cilantro. She closed her eyes and took a bite. It was pretty good. Tasted like beef.

She looked up. Detective Ridley was staring at her. She nodded and smiled, keeping her mouth closed and chewing. "Pretty good, right?"

"Sure," he said. "I don't know if it's better than Rio Bravo, though."

"Oh, come on," Fenway said, "you know it's better than Rio Bravo." She swallowed, thinking of the tongue tasting her all the way down her esophagus and almost laughing out loud at the mental picture. If she could handle insect larvae in rotting pig meat, she could eat a *lengua* taco.

She looked back up at Detective Ridley. His whole face was expressionless—except his questioning eyes.

Oh, he's doing his thing where he's waiting for me to volunteer information. On the phone, she had been silent until the pauses were uncomfortable. But Fenway was at her favorite restaurant, in a social situation, with someone who wanted to get something out of her and was playing games to do it. So instead of volunteering information, she made small talk.

"Did you know this place has only been here about five years? You probably saw in your records—I only moved down here from Seattle at the end of April. Last week, in fact, was my official six-month anniversary on the job." She paused, and when Detective Ridley didn't say anything, Fenway plowed on. "So I came here literally the second day I was in town. And I fell in love with this place. Dos Milagros—'two miracles'? I've gotten to know the owners, Carlos and María, they're super nice. The two miracles are their kids—the doctors told them they couldn't have babies, and boom! About a year later, María was pregnant with twins. A boy and a girl." Fenway leaned forward, and Detective Ridley looked increasingly irritated that his preferred interrogation method wasn't working. "Now, I've got to tell you, Detective Ridley, I suspect there was some, uh, help from a third party, if you know what I mean."

"I do," said Ridley, "which is why—"

"But I've never asked them about it." She took a look over behind the counter. "I wouldn't talk about this at their restaurant, but they're not here tonight. I'm not surprised. It's a Sunday—they like to be with their family. Although the kids are teenagers now. When their kids were ten, Carlos and María took a loan out and got this restaurant. It was a Greek restaurant before this. One of those restaurant locations that change hands a bunch of times, where nothing seems to stay in business very long."

Ridley attempted to interrupt, but she plowed on.

"I grew up in Estancia, you know. When I first lived here—before I was about eight years old—I seem to remember this place being a pizza parlor. But it was the bad pizza place—the good pizza place was down the street. They moved out after the owner retired, and I guess maybe ten years—"

"Miss Stevenson," Detective Ridley finally said, "I'd like to get back to the matter at hand."

Fenway cocked her head to the side. "I'm sorry. Did you ask me something?"

"I asked if you knew Akeel Montgomery."

"And I told you yes. You asked why I was visiting him, and I gave you a long answer that translated more or less into a booty call."

"And what did you talk about while you were with him?"

Fenway laughed. "I was literally at his apartment for about half an hour. I had brought a suitcase and I was ready to stay for a few days. But I got a call about the mayor's death almost as soon as I got there, and had to go back to the airport." She paused. "I'm sure I told you all this." Of course she had—but perhaps he wanted to see Fenway's face when she said it.

"A lot can happen in a half an hour," Detective Ridley said.

Fenway nodded. "Not as much as I wanted to happen, but sure."

"What did the two of you talk about?" he repeated.

Fenway chuckled. "Mostly how hot we were for each other."

"What else?"

"When the phone rang, Akeel asked if I had a boyfriend back home."

"What did you say?"

"I told him I didn't."

"Was that the truth?"

"It was."

Detective Ridley paused the conversation yet again, and Fenway almost burst out laughing. The uncomfortable silence Ridley depended on to get his suspects to crack didn't work on her, and certainly didn't work at a restaurant, where Fenway had three tacos and a tall glass of *horchata* with which to busy her mouth.

She took another bite of her taco, then purposely talked with her mouth open. "Man," she said, "I should have tried the *lengua* a long time ago. It's delicious." She held it up halfway between them. "You want a bite? I haven't eaten from this side."

"No thanks," Ridley said, his mouth turned down in a frown. Fenway took the taco back.

She chewed, slowly and thoroughly, and swallowed. Looking at Ridley's increasingly furrowed brow, she took another large bite.

The door opened. Officer Young, still in his tuxedo, rushed in from the cold night outside. "Fenway!" he said, loudly. "What were you thinking?"

Fenway's mouth was full.

"What's going on?" Ridley said, on high alert.

Officer Young pulled out his badge. "There's been credible threats against this woman's life," he said. "I've been assigned to protect her."

"Really?" Detective Ridley said. "I didn't see you anywhere near—"

Fenway held up her hand as she swallowed with difficulty. "No, no, he's right, Detective. Officer Young was giving his statement about the other candidate's wife spitting on me. I should have waited for him. Or I should have at least told him I was going with another law enforcement officer." Fenway wiped her hands on her napkin. "Where are my manners? Detective Deshawn Ridley from the Major Crimes Unit in Bellingham, Washington, this is Officer Todd Young of the Dominguez County Sheriff's Department."

They nodded to each other but didn't shake hands.

Officer Young leaned toward Fenway's ear. "You know they're talking about letting her go?" he said softly.

"Ivanovich's wife?"

Officer Young nodded.

Fenway shrugged. "Are you surprised? Political fallout. For both me *and* Dr. Ivanovich. Accusations of election tampering, or something. It'd be bad for all parties involved." She pushed the basket closer to Officer Young. "Have a taco."

"No, I shouldn't."

"You've gotta eat, Officer." Fenway took a drink of her *horchata.* "Especially since we had to leave the dinner before dinner."

"You sure?"

Detective Ridley looked nonplussed.

"Sure I'm sure."

"Great, thanks. I'm starving."

Officer Young took a bite of the last chicken taco. "Man," he said, around the mouthful he had taken, "I forgot how good Dos Milagros is."

"Best tacos in Estancia. Better than anything in Bellingham." Fenway winked at Detective Ridley.

Ridley gave Fenway a tight smile. "Listen, Miss Stevenson, I appreciate the time so far, but I think we should talk in an area with a bit more privacy."

"Detective," Fenway said, "I've told you all I know. I was up in Seattle. I got a call. I flew home and left my car in the long-term lot at Sea-Tac. A couple days later, my father showed up with my car, saying he flew one of his people up there to get it for me and drive it back. That's all I know. I have no more information for you. I never saw Professor Delacroix after my final, I never spoke to him in person or on the phone, I never emailed him or wrote him a letter. You can stand there doing your silent treatment thing all you want, but I'm not going to say anything to help your case because I don't know anything else."

"Did your father tell you who he sent up to get your car?"

Fenway shook her head. "Nope. Whoever it was, he was probably taller than me."

"How do you know?"

"Because I had to adjust the seat forward when I got in," Fenway said. "And I had to tilt the rear-view mirror like it was a taller person sitting there."

The detective took out his notebook and started to write in it.

"Or—" Fenway started.

"What?"

Fenway laughed. "This is probably because I'm in the middle of so many murder investigations now, but just because the seat was back and the mirror was adjusted doesn't mean it was a tall guy driving. The seat might have been placed back because a short driver had instructions to make it comfortable for me, the skyscraperish girl you see before you, to get into the car."

"Or he could have done it to throw you off."

"I suppose," Fenway said. "Listen, Detective, there have got to be other victims. I can't have been the only one whose, uh, *session* he recorded."

Officer Young looked sideways at Fenway through his last bite of taco but didn't say anything.

"I'm sure you understand I'm not permitted to comment on an ongoing investigation," said Ridley.

"Ah," Fenway said. "And I'm sure I can imagine several scenarios where I'm not the only one of the professor's victims to move to California. And since I'm sure the Bellingham Police Department has limited resources, they probably wouldn't send you on a trip unless it was justified by multiple interviews."

Detective Ridley tapped his temple and finished his Coke. He pulled a business card out of his jacket pocket and put it in front of Fenway. "If you think of anything else, please give me a call," he said. He got up from the table and gave Fenway a genuine-looking smile. "I'll deny it in front of anyone from Bellingham, of course, but these tacos *are* a lot better than Rio Bravo. Have a good evening."

Fenway watched Detective Ridley leave the restaurant, pause briefly outside the *taquería*, then walk to his left. A moment later, he walked back in front of the storefront and off to the right.

"He forget where he parked?"

"I guess," Fenway said. She took another bite of taco.

"What did he want?"

Fenway swallowed. "I had a professor at Western Washington. He was found dead a few months ago. When I read the article, the police were calling it an accident. Now I guess they think he was murdered."

"Why are they asking you about him? You said you were a victim?"

Fenway shook her head. "I don't want to talk about it, Officer. Very few people in the department know the details, and I'd prefer it stay that way."

"Sorry."

Fenway shrugged. "Don't worry about it. Suffice to say I'm a person of interest. And I was in Seattle three months ago, just before the professor's body was found."

Officer Young narrowed his eyes.

"I didn't do it," Fenway said. She took another bite and chewed thoughtfully. "Although I must say I'm relieved someone did."

They finished up their meal and walked back to the sheriff's office, walking through the corridors and emerging in back where the cruisers were parked. Officer Young got on the radio and another cruiser appeared on the street, waiting for them to go. Fenway got her phone out to text Rachel that she was coming back to the apartment and saw she had missed a text from Millicent Tate.

Be at studio at 10
I brought clothes 4 u

"Oh, crap," Fenway said. "I forgot. I've got to be on camera tonight."

"Not to the apartment?"

"Not yet, I guess. You know where the Channel 12 studio is?"

Officer Young furrowed his brow.

"It's near the warehouse district, on the other side of the train tracks. Twentieth and Moreno."

"Oh. Yeah, I know the area. I guess I never noticed the studio there before."

"They don't have a lot of signage up. I guess they don't want to announce they've got thousands of dollars in equipment there." She was glad Millicent had taken care of the clothes; she didn't feel like picking out another outfit.

"You've got to be on camera tonight?"

"Shooting a campaign ad. Ivanovich ran one of his own today and we've got to respond."

They arrived at the studio at two minutes after ten o'clock, but it took another three minutes for the other officers to check the parking lot and the surrounding areas before giving Officer Young the all clear. Fenway got out of the car and wondered how tired she looked. She hoped the hair and makeup people on staff could do a decent job. Millicent had seen her at the dinner, though, and she had seen Imelda Ivanovich spit on her, so she hoped everything would be ready for Millicent to turn her face into something camera-ready.

Millicent was waiting outside for her with an angry look on her face. "For God's sake, Fenway," she said, "the election is in three days. Three days! You have got to get your head on right and figure out how to get places on time."

"I'm five minutes late, and I was being interviewed by a detective," Fenway said.

Millicent opened the door and Fenway went inside. "Don't give me that. I can smell the salsa on your breath." Officer Young followed both of them in.

"It was kind of an informal interview."

"Okay, never mind," Millicent said. "We've got hair and makeup and wardrobe to do." She looked at Fenway. "You don't look too bad for someone who got spit on."

"Thanks, you look radiant tonight too."

"Okay, follow me." Millicent began walking quickly through the corridors of the studio, and Fenway, in her formal dress and heels, had a little trouble keeping up. "I had someone go over to your apartment and get a few blouses and blazers."

"Fine by me."

They arrived at a door and Millicent opened it. The artificial lights around three sets of mirrors illuminated the room in an otherworldly brightness, casting strange shadows on the walls.

"Okay," Millicent said. "In that chair, there." She pointed in front of one of the mirrors. "I'm going to tell Bethany you're here." Millicent left, leaving Fenway alone with Officer Young, who had an uncomfortable look on his face.

"You okay?" Fenway asked him.

"I guess," he said. "This feels like a creepy clown room in a haunted house."

Fenway laughed. "Halloween was last week."

Fenway's phone rang in her purse. She dug it out. "I'm going to have to turn the ringer off or Millicent's going to kill me," she muttered. She looked at the screen and didn't recognize the number.

"Fenway Stevenson here," she answered.

"Oh—Miss Stevenson," a woman's voice on the other end said.

"Yes, hi, who's this?"

"I'm sorry—it's Lydia Hernandez."

"Lydia..." Fenway had a questioning tone in her voice; she couldn't place the name.

"From the Belvedere Terrace Resort."

"Oh, yes," she said. "I hope we didn't inconvenience you too much."

"Well," she said, "you did, but that's not why I'm calling. You gave me your card when you were here and asked me a lot about the woman who checked into the villa."

"Yes," Fenway said. "You have more information about her?"

"I do. I was watching the ten o'clock news, and I saw you get spit on tonight."

"Ah. Well. Politics does crazy things to people."

"I have to tell you, after you and the sheriff asked so many questions yesterday, I was about ready to spit on you myself." She laughed, but perhaps there was a note of apology in it.

"Did you say you had information about the woman who checked in?"

"Oh, right. Yes, yes, I do. I saw the lady on the television when they were showing what happened tonight."

"The woman who checked into the hotel with Jeremy Kapp was at the dinner tonight?"

"Yes."

"Was it the woman who spit on me?"

Lydia Hernandez laughed. "That would have been good, huh? No, it wasn't. It was the lady sitting next to the sheriff."

"Next to the sheriff?"

"White lady. Real pretty. Dark hair. She had on a bright red dress."

Fenway gasped. And then wondered why she hadn't put two and two together before.

Catherine Klein.

PART V

MONDAY

CHAPTER TWENTY-TWO

FENWAY HAD TO HOLD UP THE WARDROBE AND MAKEUP PEOPLE as she left a message with Dez and texted McVie that Catherine Klein was Mrs. Potemkin. She hoped it was enough to get the first domino tipped to get Charlotte out of jail.

It took nearly two hours, but they finally got Fenway's wardrobe, makeup, and hair finished at midnight, and they all walked into the studio, where a tired-looking cameraman was waiting, the green plastic curtain and the lights in place. Officer Young was looking bright-eyed still, as he sat in on the session, stoically, not speaking or making any noise. Fenway sat, getting the lighting adjusted on her face, while Millicent discussed the different intonations Fenway should make, the different words she should emphasize.

They started the session. At first, Fenway was having trouble concentrating; she thought more about Catherine Klein and wondered if Dez and McVie had gotten the messages. After Millicent clapped at her to wake up so they could finish and go home, Fenway snapped to the present and read the script through in a few takes. Millicent had a couple of corrections.

At one point, right around twelve-thirty, one of the other people on the campaign had come into the room and handed her another sheet. Millicent broke into a wide smile. "Here," she said, "read this instead."

It was a different script altogether, with a reference to the spitting incident.

"Throughout this election cycle, I've done my job, I've faced down some tough opponents, and I've done it in the face of adversity," Fenway read.

"And that," Millicent said, "is when we'll superimpose the image of you being spit on by Imelda Ivanovich."

Fenway shook her head. "Listen, Millicent, I trust you on a lot of things, but believe me when I tell you for as much outrage as you think the community's going to feel, there's going to be a growing group of people who see that and think it's about time somebody put the 'uppity black bitch' in her place."

Millicent winced. So did all of the white people in the room. The black woman who was holding the overhead boom mic remained stoic, although Fenway thought there was a trace of her rolling her eyes.

"Do you have to—" Millicent began.

"I'm not going to sugar-coat this for you," Fenway interrupted. "Your original message was great. It elicited outrage. I don't think it undermined anything. But the voters in this county are more white than black or Latino or Asian, they're a lot more rural than city slickers, and it's a midterm year—you're not going to get young people to the polls nearly as much as you'd like."

Millicent looked sideways at Fenway. "You don't think I know all that?"

"Good, I'm glad you do. So you understand I'm not going to say the words in this script. I don't want the spitting video used. It's a dog whistle, and not one in my favor."

Millicent pressed her lips together. "We can talk about it later."

By the time they had finished with the session, it was one-thirty in the morning. The crew started turning off the lights and Fenway pulled Millicent to the side. "Millicent, listen, I found out that Jeremy Kapp, the murder victim Charlotte's in jail on suspicion of killing, wasn't having an affair with Charlotte. He was having an affair with Barry Klein's wife. She was the one with him at the Belvedere Terrace Resort the night he was killed."

"Why are you telling me?"

"Because," Fenway said, "I think it will help McVie win his race, and I thought you could coordinate the release of that information with Gene Dennett."

"Fenway," Millicent Tate said, her tone admonishing, "I wish you would concentrate on your *own* race. The polls we did last week don't mean anything now, and we don't have time to gear up for anything meaningful before Tuesday. As far as I'm concerned, it's a toss-up between you and Dr. Ivanovich. I don't get paid for mishandling these things, and the only times I ever lose is when the candidate doesn't take the campaign seriously enough." She held out a finger, pointing at Fenway's chest. "And you, my dear, aren't taking your campaign seriously enough."

"I also thought if it came out that Catherine Klein was the one having the affair with Jeremy Kapp, Charlotte would be let go. I've already told Sergeant Roubideaux and McVie."

Millicent bobbed her head from side to side in thought. "I don't know. The media's been pretty loud about Charlotte's arrest. I doubt they'll be nearly as loud if she's let go."

"Better than her still being in jail on Election Day, though, right?"

Millicent thought for a moment, then nodded. "Yes. Absolutely. All right, I'll get on it."

Officer Young drove Fenway back to Rachel's, followed by the second cruiser. It was late, and when they walked into Rachel's townhouse, an exhausted Rachel was still on the couch, watching a movie.

"Rachel, what are you still doing up?" Fenway said. "It's almost two in the morning."

"I'm worried about you," Rachel said simply. "I'm glad you're back safe."

Fenway clicked her tongue. "You don't need to do that. You know the police are starting to think I wasn't the target of the car bomb."

Rachel nodded. "Yeah. I heard from Dez. But I don't want to take any chances."

Fenway and Rachel left Officer Young in the living room and Fenway got ready for bed. The exhaustion hit her like a truck as she was brushing her teeth, and she stumbled out of the bathroom.

Rachel was standing in the hallway outside her bedroom. "I think you should sleep in my room again," she said simply.

"What?"

Rachel lowered her voice. "I don't trust Officer Young. I got a weird feeling yesterday when he was here, and then when you woke up screaming—I don't know. It was strange when I came out of my room and he was already in front of your bed."

"He was awake downstairs. You were asleep. It probably took you a lot more time to wake up and get out of bed than it did for him to run upstairs."

Rachel looked through a suspicious gaze at Fenway. "Yeah, I know," she said, "but I'm telling you, something's not right."

"You going to put a chair up against the door like you did last night?"

"Are you making fun of me?"

Fenway stared at her.

"Come in here," Rachel hissed, and Fenway followed her into her bedroom and Rachel closed the door behind her.

"Listen," Rachel said, solemnly, "I know McVie thinks there's a mole in the department. A mole who let my father into Dylan's cell to kill him. I know they haven't found that mole yet. I know the mole, whoever he might be, is tied to your dad's company. I don't think he's tied to your dad himself, but someone at Ferris Energy has someone at the sheriff's office who is giving him access."

Fenway nodded. "Yeah. McVie thinks so too."

"So—Officer Young might be handsome and intelligent and might be giving you all those good vibes, but I don't trust him," Rachel said. "And honestly, I don't care if I sound paranoid. I don't care if he starts suspecting I'm onto him, or if he thinks we're lesbians, or what. I care about keeping you safe, and if he's after you, I'm not safe either." She set her jaw. "You'll be a lot safer in this room with me, when he has to take on two people, not just one, especially if one of us has a gun."

Fenway paused, thinking, then she nodded.

"Good," Rachel said. "I'm exhausted. And I hope you don't snore like you did last night."

Fenway woke up to the smell of coffee. She turned over; Rachel was already out of bed.

Fenway sat up and stretched. The clock on Rachel's bedside table said 7:17—she felt fairly rested for only five hours of sleep, and knew she'd have a full day, between the investigation and all the campaign events Millicent Tate had scheduled for her. She reached for her phone; Dez had texted her. *Let's talk about the Kapp case. Call me after 8.*

She stretched her arms above her head, went to the bathroom, and, not quite awake, started to go downstairs to get some coffee.

Then she heard Callahan's voice, Rachel laughing along with him, and went into the bedroom to dig a bra out of her suitcase and put it on before going down.

Rachel and Callahan were seated at the kitchen table. After everything Callahan had said yesterday about Fenway not being in danger, she was surprised the sheriff's department was still placing a resource to protect her. She remembered the look of concern on McVie's face, first after the car bomb, then after the therapist's killing. Maybe McVie was being overprotective.

Rachel and Callahan didn't look up from their conversation; Rachel had her back to Fenway, but Callahan paid a lot of attention to what Rachel was saying. She was talking with her hands, something about a concert she had attended, and Callahan's face looked—well, smitten. Perhaps Rachel was the reason he had chosen, or maybe volunteered for, this particular duty.

Fenway was walking by the front door when Callahan's radio crackled to life.

"Callahan, there's a visitor approaching the door. We frisked him. No weapons. Wants to talk to Eagle."

"Roger that," said Callahan.

"Eagle?" Fenway said.

Callahan looked up suddenly. "Oh—Fenway, you're up. Good."

Fenway looked down at her flannel pajamas. "Not sure I'm in any state to receive company."

Callahan's radio crackled again. "Male, early to mid-twenties. Said his name was Zoso."

"Zoso?"

"Oh," Fenway said, "I know him."

Callahan narrowed his eyes. "I know him too. He's a dealer."

Fenway shrugged. "He broke the mayor's murder case wide open a couple of months ago. I'll see him."

Fenway turned to open the front door, but Callahan yelled to stop her, and rushed over to open the door himself.

Zoso had a five-day growth of beard. His eyes were heavily lidded, but darted from Callahan to Fenway.

"Nice jammies," he said.

"Hi, Zoso," Fenway said.

"What is this?" he said. "How come I'm getting the third degree?"

"It's possible someone's trying to kill me," Fenway said. "Police protection."

"Thought it was 'cause you were running for office. Some sort of Secret Service detail or something."

Fenway shrugged. "You want to come in?"

"Yeah, I guess so." Zoso stepped inside, saw Rachel at the kitchen table. "Hey, Rach."

"Hey, Zoso. You doing okay?"

Zoso shrugged. "Can't complain."

"So," Fenway said, shooting a look at Callahan and motioning Zoso to the sofa in the living room, "what brings you here? I would have thought the cops outside would scare you away."

Zoso laughed, a little uneasily. "Yeah, well, they would have if I had noticed them. Once they started talking to me, I figured I'd better go through with talking to you. Otherwise it'd be more suspicious."

Fenway nodded and took a seat on the sofa.

"Anyway," Zoso said, sitting down on the sofa a couple of feet away from Fenway, "did you sic that sheriff chick on me? She's been up my ass the last couple days. I never saw her around before. She new?"

"Sheriff chick?" Fenway asked, confused, then remembered Gretchen Donnelly. *Dez must have her doing some work on this too.* Fenway paused. "Did you come here to tell me something?"

"Oh, right." Zoso cleared his throat. "Uh—so, anyway, this sheriff chick starts talking to me about Thursday night. Like, where I was, who I was with. And I don't want to say anything, because I don't know what they have on me, or what they think they have on me. I said they could see me with a lawyer next time they wanted to talk to me. I've got a rep to protect."

"Sure." Fenway paused. "But your customers aren't here. Your connections aren't here. Your friends aren't here. It's just us. So where were you?"

Zoso screwed up his mouth. "I went to a customer's house. And, uh, well, it was the wife of the dead guy. The one they found in the pedestrian underpass."

"You went to see Cricket Kapp."

"Yeah."

"How long did you stay?"

"Not long. She was already on something when I got there. Oxy, probably, since that's what I—uh..."

Fenway shook her head. "I'm interested in the murder, not your Oxy business, Zoso."

Zoso glanced up at Callahan, who was still sitting at the table with Rachel.

"Hey, Rachel," Fenway said, "can you and Callahan go over to The Coffee Bean for me?"

Rachel cottoned on. "Sure. Come on, Brian."

"I'm not supposed to—"

Fenway interrupted. "I can't have you listening into a conversation with an informant, Callahan."

"If you're worried, I can go get the coffee." Rachel said. "You can stand outside the door."

"I'll even open the blinds," Fenway offered. "You can look right in. I just can't have you hearing our conversation."

Callahan looked torn.

"They already frisked him," Fenway said, "and look at him. I can take him."

Zoso frowned.

Callahan sighed. "Fine," he said. He leaned over the sofa to the front window and opened the blinds. Then he followed Rachel out the front door. Zoso watched the door close firmly behind them, and Callahan's head appeared outside the front window.

"We good now?" Fenway asked.

"Yeah." Zoso cleared his throat. "Thanks."

"Okay, so you went to see Cricket Kapp. Now when you say you weren't there for long, what do you mean? A couple of hours?"

"What? No way. I was there maybe ten minutes. Probably not even that."

"What time did you leave? Before midnight?"

"Uh..."

"Come on, Zoso."

"What time did she *say* I left?"

Fenway narrowed her eyes at Zoso. "You and Miz Cricket have a thing going?"

Zoso's eyes went wide. "A thing? Like, a sex thing?"

"Well, yeah. Why not?"

Zoso had a look of horror on his face. "For real? She's like, forty."

"Sure, but she looks great. Big boobs, nice firm butt—"

He shook his head adamantly. "No, no, unh-uh. I don't go for the cougars."

"I don't know, Zoso. Her kids seemed to think you had it bad for her."

"No way."

"All right," Fenway said. "So after you were there for ten minutes, what did you do?"

"I left. I got in and started up my car after, uh, seeing Mrs. Kapp, and I remember the clock said eleven thirty-six."

"Eleven thirty-six? That's pretty specific."

"Yeah, well, I remember it."

"You didn't stay there for two hours."

"No way."

"You didn't sell Mrs. Kapp some Oxy and then have her give you a little physical payment? Maybe a five-finger discount of another kind?"

"Ugh, Fenway, gross. She's almost twice my age."

"Okay." Fenway paused, briefly thinking about the wedding of her nearly-fifty-year-old father and his twenty-five-year-old bride. "Did you see anyone else there? Was Blair home?"

"Yeah," Zoso said. "Blair was home. So was Donovan. At least, I think so. Their doors were closed to their rooms. But Mrs. Kapp wanted me to keep it down so we wouldn't bug them."

"Keep it down?"

Zoso rolled his eyes. "Our voices. Jeez, give it a rest. She didn't want her kids to know she bought Oxy."

"The kids were there?"

"Yeah."

"How do you know?"

Zoso shook his head. "I just told you, she said they were home."

"Yeah, Zoso, but she could have been lying. Or just plain wrong. Did you see either of them? Or maybe the kids' cars were in the driveway?"

Zoso shrugged. "They're rich. They've got garages for all their kids' cars. Mrs. Kapp said not to wake up the kids, so I kept my voice down. I didn't have some sort of magic kid tracker."

Fenway nodded. "When did you get back home?"

"It was before midnight."

"Prime dealing hours, right?"

"Sometimes. I'll go to clubs and dive bars. But not Thursday."

"Thursdays are a busy night, though, right? Still at that one club?"

Zoso shook his head. "Some nights, yeah, but Thursday is two-dollar shot night there. Their Thursday clientele is always too cheap to buy kickers. They figure, why spend money on some Oxy when they can get drunk for ten bucks?"

"Fair point."

He scoffed. "You obviously haven't tried Oxy, if you think it ain't any better than a buzz off cheap liquor."

Fenway smiled. "It's a real shame I'm not a candidate for your wares, Zoso."

He smiled. "Oh, the hoity-toity talk. I always recognize my cue to leave." He stood up. "All right, hope I gave you what you need. Keep you guys off my ass for another few months, all right?"

"You got it, Zoso."

He opened the door and left.

Callahan watched Zoso walk all the way down to the sidewalk, then came back in the apartment and closed the door. "So did he help anything?"

Fenway shrugged. "It means Cricket Kapp no longer has an alibi for her husband's murder."

* * *

Fenway had to hurry through a single cup of coffee and a shower. When she got back downstairs, Callahan told her he had been pulled off protective duty—the threat on Fenway's life was no longer deemed serious. Fenway hadn't gotten her Accord back—it was still in evidence from the car bomb blast—but Callahan drove her to the St. Bonaventure Pancake Breakfast.

The St. Bonaventure Church, the largest in the diocese, had hosted a candidates' pancake breakfast for years at nine in the morning the day before Election Day. Sheriff McVie was there, along with Barry Klein and his wife. Fenway's opponent was a no-show.

"This couldn't have worked out better," Millicent Tate whispered to Fenway, who had eaten most of the plate of buttermilk pancakes. "I thought for sure Ivanovich would be pushing for the Catholic votes. But after Imelda spit on you at the dinner last night? I bet that did a number on them. Maybe Ivanovich doesn't want to show his face where he'll have to answer questions about trying to punch a cop."

"Oh man, I had forgotten about that," Fenway said. "Didn't they let his wife go last night?"

"They were talking about it," Millicent said, "but as far as I know, she's still in jail. I think they're trying to keep it out of the media."

"Are you going to change that?" Fenway asked with a gleam in her eye.

"We don't need to. Things are looking good for us: our commercial is running on Channel 12 all day, and our opponent didn't show up at the biggest campaign event the day before the election."

"And his wife is in jail," Fenway said.

As soon as the words left her mouth, Fenway saw Dez out of the corner of her eye. With a start, she realized she hadn't called her before she left for the church.

Dez entered the hall. She snaked her way through the tables and stopped in front of Barry and Catherine Klein.

Fenway strained to see what was happening—a few people kept walking through her field of vision, and Dez faced the other way. But she heard, clearly, Barry Klein's voice say, "Whatever she has to say to you, she can say it in front of me."

She didn't hear what Dez said next, but Klein's response rang through the hall. "We don't need to go anywhere more private, Sergeant. I don't have anything to hide."

Again, Dez's voice was too muted for Fenway to hear, but again, Klein's agitated response: "Is this out of revenge for the things I've said about Nathaniel Ferris?"

"No," Dez said, "I—"

Klein stood up. "Maybe it's because you're taking bribes from Ferris?"

Dez pulled herself up to her full height, still a few inches shorter than Klein, but more imposing. "Maybe you want to take that back before I sue you for slander."

"It's not slander if it's true," Barry Klein said.

Fenway looked at McVie's face. He was horrified.

Dez bristled. "Just because your wife was with the murder victim in a hotel room the night of his death does *not* give you the right—"

Fenway then couldn't make anything out. Barry Klein was yelling; Catherine Klein was yelling, an angry look on her face; McVie stepped up and tried to separate them, and Dez finally pulled Catherine Klein out of the scrum and tried to lead her off.

"You're not taking her anywhere!" yelled Klein. "This is a stunt by the sheriff's department because you don't want me to be mayor!"

Dez walked quickly, Catherine Klein ahead of her, and went through the double doors at the front of the hall.

Barry Klein kept yelling, and McVie kept blocking his path. "You've been getting kickbacks from Ferris for *years*—and you've got the whole department gunning for me!" he said.

"That's not true, and you know it, Barry," McVie said, loudly but calmly.

"Get out of my way, McVie, or I'm going to punch you in the face."

"Don't add assault on a police officer to your troubles today, Barry," McVie said. "I won't have any qualms about locking you up."

The two of them stared at each other for a moment, then Barry Klein took a step back, straightened his tie, and strode off through one of the side doors.

McVie had an angry look on his face. He walked slowly back to his table, then stood with his hand on the back of his chair, staring at his plate of half-eaten pancakes.

Fenway walked over to McVie.

"You okay?"

"No," McVie said, quietly. "I hate this stupid election." For a moment, he looked stricken. Fenway longed to take his hand, but didn't dare in front of all the people at the breakfast. Finally, he sighed and looked Fenway in the eyes. "I have a confession to make, Fenway."

Oh no, Fenway thought. *He's going to tell me he's taken bribes from my father.*

McVie took a deep breath. "I don't want to be mayor."

Fenway blinked. "What?"

McVie shook his head. "I don't want to be mayor. I only want Barry Klein *not* to be mayor. I don't know what I was thinking. I'm a good sheriff. I *like* being sheriff."

"You had to run for sheriff before."

"It was nothing like this," he said, "and the last couple of times, I've run unopposed."

"I hate this election too."

"Yeah," he said, "but at least you *want* to be coroner."

Fenway nodded, a little sadly. "Did you hear—are they arresting Mrs. Klein?"

McVie shook his head. "Material witness warrant. They're compelling her to give a statement. Dr. Klein didn't want her to cooperate, so they had to take her down to the station."

"Donnelly keeping you in the loop?"

McVie nodded. "And Dez." McVie looked squarely at Fenway. "I wish this election hadn't screwed up my dating life," he said. "I think you and I would really be something."

Fenway felt her heart swell. "Yeah," she said. "Me too."

He smiled, a little sadly. "We still on for dinner Wednesday night?"

Fenway nodded. "Yes. I'd like that."

She felt like putting her arms around McVie and pulling him close, but she knew she couldn't. She turned and started walking away from him and almost smacked into Millicent.

"What the hell are you doing?" Millicent hissed through a smile.

"Seeing if my friend is okay," Fenway replied.

"I thought you two were going to start making out."

"Oh, stop it." Fenway walked back toward her table. Millicent followed her.

"Yeah, well, let's hope no photographers caught the two of you making goo-goo eyes at each other. You'll have a lot to answer for if they did."

Fenway rolled her eyes and shook her head as she came to her seat. "Honestly, Millicent, you might be good at managing campaigns, but you don't know what's going on when it comes to interpersonal relationships." She took her seat.

Millicent took the seat next to her. "I know you're not Catholic," she said, smirking, "but I don't think it would be a good idea to lie during the church breakfast."

CHAPTER TWENTY-THREE

AS WAS THE CUSTOM AFTER THE PANCAKE BREAKFAST, ALL THE candidates and their staffs went to Monday morning mass. The service was thankfully drama-free—no one burst in with warrants for anybody's arrest, no one accused anyone of sleeping with anybody, no one set off a car bomb, nobody was spit on, and no one bashed anyone over the head with a blunt object. Fenway sighed. It was a pretty low bar, but one the events of the last few days hadn't managed to clear.

She turned her phone back on when she exited the church, stepping out into the cold air of the early November day. At this time of year, the Santa Ana winds would often come from the south, warming Estancia up enough for shorts and tee shirts, but today the wind blew from the northwest, off the ocean, making Millicent shiver in her light windbreaker.

"Everything went smoothly," Millicent said. "You crossed your arms when they offered the sacrament, which was good—respectful, but you look practiced doing it. Didn't look like you'd never been to church before."

"I've been to church before," Fenway said irritably.

"You know what I mean. Now, I was able to reschedule the senior center thing for one o'clock. You can stay in those clothes—they'll like the church outfit, I'm sure."

"Okay. You have a speech prepared?"

Millicent handed Fenway two sheets of paper. The speech was in large type, difficult to miss, peppered with phrases like "fight for justice" and "no matter who the criminal is, or how well they're connected." Fenway fought for a moment over the singular/plural disagreement, letting her lit major background wash over her, but knew it would sound better than switching it to "he or she" so she let it go.

"Thanks," Fenway said.

Her phone buzzed. She had missed three calls.

The first voicemail was from Dr. Michi Yasuda, the San Miguelito medical examiner. "Good morning, Miss Stevenson. I wanted to let you know we didn't get a hit on the fingerprints on either of those envelopes, or the papers inside. Whoever it is, he or she is not in the system."

Fenway felt a rush of affection for Yasuda when she heard the *he or she*.

Dr. Yasuda took a breath and continued. "We also have some results from the autopsy of Jeremy Kapp. He had a significant amount of cocaine in his system. From the analysis of his nasal tissues, it looks like it was snorted."

"At least he went out on a high," Fenway murmured.

Yasuda paused on the voicemail. "On a personal note, Miss Stevenson, I'd like to wish you luck in your election. I've enjoyed working with you so far and I'd like it to continue."

She clicked off.

The next message was from her father. "Fenway, I don't know what you did or how you did it, but they're releasing Charlotte this afternoon. They're dismissing the charges. You're a miracle worker, honey. You're probably going crazy with all your campaign events today, but let me know if you have time for lunch or even coffee today with your old man."

He, too, clicked off.

Fenway elbowed Millicent. "Charlotte's getting released this afternoon."

Millicent nodded. "Good. Excellent news."

And the third voicemail was from an unknown number. "I'm disappointed you haven't used the evidence I've given to you," a voice whispered, crackling and distorted, probably with a voice-changing box. "There's nothing innocent about Charlotte Ferris, I can tell you for sure, and she needs to be locked up."

"Huh," Fenway said.

"What?" Millicent asked.

"Listen." Fenway put the phone up to Millicent's ear. Millicent's expression didn't change. "What do you think?"

Millicent shrugged. "Doesn't seem professional."

"I know."

"And who talks like that? It sounds like someone who's watched too many cop shows."

Fenway thought for a second. "Millicent, I'm sorry, but I need to call Dez. I've been meaning to talk to her since last night."

Millicent looked at her watch. "Well, make it quick. We've only got a half hour, and you've disappointed those seniors enough for one election cycle."

———————◆◆———————

"Hey, Dez."

"Hey yourself, rookie," Dez said. "Thanks for waking me up last night with your text."

Fenway cringed. "Sorry. I thought you'd turn your phone off or set it to do not disturb."

Dez chuckled. "It's fine. Useful information. I'm sure your stepmother is happy about it. You said we're looking in the wrong place for Kapp's killer?"

Fenway took a deep breath. "After the car bomb, and Dr. Tassajera, and the money laundering, I thought everything was linked. We even thought the same person who spray-painted my car also set off the car bomb."

"Right," Dez said. "But we don't now. Terrance Ivanovich is still adamant he didn't make the car bomb, and so far, the warrant we served didn't turn up anything. No bombmaking materials, I mean. Plenty of hate speech, some Nazi memorabilia. A couple of ounces of weed, but that's not even illegal anymore. We're still holding him, sure, but there isn't anything we've found to connect him to your stepmother."

"So we can't assume any of these crimes were committed by the same person," said Fenway.

Dez clicked her tongue. "But Piper has uncovered the payments to all of those people from Global Advantage Executive Consulting—well, not Rory, but Rory's father. I can't believe *that's* not somehow related."

"It might be related, Dez, but we shouldn't assume it's the same murderer."

"Why not?"

"The other murders are professional. Plastic explosives. Narrow windows of opportunity to get away." Fenway cleared her throat. "But Kapp's murder—and the way Charlotte was framed—really amateurish."

Dez thought for a minute.

"I got hung up on the big, complex crimes," Fenway said. "I just realized that it doesn't all fit together."

"So—you're thinking a personal motive?"

"Right. Especially since Zoso stopped by Rachel's this morning."

"What did he have to say?"

"He shot a hole in Cricket Kapp's alibi. He only stayed that night for ten minutes, not two hours. He was away from the house at eleven thirty-six."

"That's an awfully specific time."

"He said he remembered it exactly when he turned on the car."

"That's plenty of time to get to the hotel and commit the murder," Dez mused.

"And that shoots a hole in the kids' alibis, too."

"Are you sure?" Dez asked. "There's a lot of money at stake here. Millions of dollars. People have killed for a lot less."

"No question—Kapp was involved with some seriously complicated crimes," said Fenway, "but I don't think that's why he was killed."

"You're thinking someone in the family."

"Or maybe Catherine the Great."

Dez hesitated. "Let's not get ahead of ourselves," she said carefully. "We've got Mrs. Klein down here on a material witness warrant, not on suspicion of murder."

"But she was there."

"Which is why she's a material witness."

"Did you get a statement from her yet?"

"She lawyered up as soon as I took her outside. She's cooling her heels in the interview room while we wait for her expensive lawyer to get here."

"For a material witness warrant?"

"Yep."

"Wow. She's got something to hide, obviously."

"Of course she's got something to hide. She was having an affair, she's a politician's wife—of course she doesn't want to talk about it. It'll be entered into the public record. Doesn't mean she committed murder."

"Maybe she'll help you if you promise to keep her out of the public record."

"Maybe. We'll see."

"If Catherine Klein killed Jeremy Kapp, it would explain a lot of things."

"It would?"

"Yeah. Well—I mean, it would fit some of the evidence we have. For instance, the financial payments don't get dispersed until *after* Jeremy Kapp gets killed. And there's no activity between Kapp and the consulting account in the two or three days before he gets killed, either."

"That doesn't necessarily mean anything. He might have gotten a big cash payout. Someone might have stolen a suitcase full of cash from that hotel room."

Fenway thought for a moment. "Even if that were the case, wouldn't it make sense for Catherine Klein to be the one to steal it? She might have needed money to get the campaign out of debt—or maybe to get herself out of debt. And maybe when the money went missing, it started a war inside the organization. People thought other people stole Kapp's money. Someone thought Domingo Velásquez stole it. Somebody else thought Jacob Tassajera stole it." Fenway's brain started working more quickly than she could keep up with it. "It didn't have to be money, either. Maybe it was drugs. Dr. Yasuda called me, and said Kapp had a lot of cocaine in his system. Maybe Kapp owed too much money to his dealer and things got out of hand."

"Sounds to me like you're trying to get the facts to fit your theory."

"Uh," Fenway said, "maybe I *am* throwing darts."

"And none of your theories account for why your stepmother was framed."

Fenway paused. "No. I guess they don't."

"Don't get me wrong, rookie, your enthusiasm can be contagious. But without a theory that fits all the evidence, we're not going to be making any arrests. We're letting your stepmother go this afternoon."

"I heard. Those fake emails were enough?"

"It was the video footage, actually. Piper looked at all the footage that your father had from the security cameras. She can't find any evidence of tampering. Not even a little. I was with her when she was going over it. She said that the type of high-definition cameras your father owns creates footage that's hard to fake. There are watermarks, and the time code is on each frame, linked to a centralized clock. If your father wanted to fake something, he'd use a different system."

Fenway chortled. "Imagine that. My father, honest about something for once."

"All right. Catherine Klein's lawyer is supposedly getting here in a couple of hours. In the meantime, I've got a ton of paperwork to fill out. Then maybe I'll go interview the Kapp family again. See if anything is out of place."

"Oh—and speaking of framing Charlotte—I just got a voice mail from the person who sent me those envelopes with the faked evidence."

"The emails between Kapp and Charlotte, and those pictures?"

"Yes. Unknown number. I can forward the voicemails to you if you want."

"Anything useful on there?"

"I'll be sorry if I don't use that evidence against Charlotte, stuff like that."

"Forward them to Piper. She'll be able to run some analysis on it."

"No problem," Fenway said. "One more thing, Dez."

"Sure."

"Am I going to get reinstated to this case since Charlotte is no longer a suspect?"

"I'll talk to Donnelly. If Charlotte's involvement was the only conflict of interest, there's no reason to keep you out of it. And I guess McVie's conflict of interest disappears too." Dez laughed. "But obviously people think you're still on the case and continue to send you evidence anyway."

"Uh—if I get reinstated, can I come to interview Cricket with you?"

"If your chaperone lets you leave." Dez cackled.

"Thanks."

Fenway heard a loud honking and looked across the parking lot at a BMW with an irritated Millicent behind the steering wheel.

The senior center event went off without a hitch. Fenway didn't flub her lines once during the speech, and the seniors laughed in all the appropriate places. Her apology—"I would have been here yesterday, but I was called away to be a coroner instead of a candidate"—was met with knowing smiles instead of frowns.

She felt herself build momentum during the speech, and she ended on such a high note, the applause she received was more than she was expecting. Millicent pulled her aside.

"That was aces," Millicent said. "Every person in here is going to vote for you instead of Ivanovich—it doesn't matter if they were going to vote for Ivanovich before. I chatted with a few of them and they all saw his wife spit on you. They thought it was disgusting and disrespectful."

"Great. I'm getting the pity party vote?"

"I'll take the votes any way I can get 'em," said Millicent. "And I said the police confirmed Charlotte's alibi and she'd be released. One of them shook her head and said, 'If Fenway were in charge of the case, she'd still be in jail.'"

"Huh," Fenway said.

"Remember," Millicent said, leading Fenway by the arm out to her BMW, "it doesn't matter what the truth is today. It only matters what the *perception* of truth is. If that translates into a vote, so be it."

"Scorched earth," Fenway said under her breath. Millicent didn't hear it, or if she did, she didn't say anything.

"We still have the softball tournament this morning?"

"Yes. It's next."

"Am I still throwing out the first pitch?"

"Yes."

"Everyone think I'll be safe enough?"

"Uh—sure."

"You didn't tell the police I was doing this?"

"You'll be fine. You practiced?"

"Yeah, a little last week. I was okay."

"You played softball in high school, though, right?"

"Look at me, Millicent."

"Oh. Basketball. You get a scholarship?"

"Hah. I was tall. I just wasn't any good."

The trip to the softball fields was uneventful, and the first pitch went smoothly as well. Fenway threw high and outside, but not enough to embarrass herself. She said a few things about loving Estancia, growing up here, law and justice, comparing the rules of evidence to the rules of softball, then encouraging every-one—"of voting age, of course"—to get out and vote.

"Two for two," Millicent said as she ushered Fenway back into the car. "Far more eloquent than our practice sessions. If I had known you were this good at campaigning, I would have got-ten you out in front of everyone *much* earlier."

Fenway looked at her out of the corner of her eye.

"I know, I know," Millicent said. "You're in this because you want to be coroner, not because you want to campaign."

"Speaking of campaigning—how's McVie's campaign going?"

Millicent sucked in a breath through her teeth. "I honestly don't know. He's a good campaigner, but it's almost like he doesn't have the stomach for all the stuff Barry Klein does. And your dad's money is great, but it only goes so far."

"What does your gut tell you?"

"It's going to be close." She sighed. "And I can tell McVie's heart's not in it, which is frustrating for Gene. He's a great campaign manager, but even Gene is having a hard time putting his best foot forward for someone who's not sure he wants to be mayor."

"I hope McVie wins," Fenway said.

"Well, of course. Barry Klein is a royal jackass. He'll be lording his mayoral power over everybody the first chance he gets." She laughed. "So I take it something happened with his wife, right?"

"Yeah."

"Want to tell me what it is?"

"Yeah, I definitely want to tell you. It's juicy." Fenway paused. "But I'm not sure I should."

"Something to help your boyfriend out?" Millicent opened the car and they both got in.

"He's not my boyfriend."

"Sure he isn't. Will it help him or not?"

"I don't know. Probably."

"Doesn't help that McVie's getting divorced. Lots of people think he's got a little something on the side." She looked at Fenway. "It's not you, is it?"

"With any luck, it will be, after the election," Fenway said. "We haven't dated yet."

"But you've done stuff."

Fenway smiled. "Sort of." She cleared her throat. "Not for a while. Not since I announced my candidacy."

"Ah." Millicent nodded knowingly and turned the car on. "So you two actually listened to me when I told you not to date?"

"Yeah."

"Well, how about that? There's a first time for everything."

"You have candidates who don't listen to you?"

Millicent laughed derisively. "Of course. Especially the men. They can't keep it in their pants. And the women aren't much better. What they hear is I can't find out about their trysts. And if they're careful enough to keep it from me, they're careful enough to keep it from the press and from their opponents."

"Really?"

"Not always. Most of the time, though."

They went to another event, this one an Elks meeting. She gave another speech, perhaps five minutes long, and left to a smattering of applause.

"Next," Millicent said.

"I didn't exactly wow them."

"Can't win 'em all."

As they got in Millicent's BMW, Fenway's phone rang.

"Fenway Stevenson."

"Hey, Fenway. It's Melissa."

"Melissa, hi. You have something for me?"

"Yeah. The succulent plant in Dr. Tassajera's waiting room?"

"Right."

"So first, yes, there was a miniature recording device in it. It recorded on solid-state equipment and transmitted over Bluetooth. So someone needed to download it, but it would have only taken a few minutes."

"Someone like a fake therapy client. Sitting in the office with a smartphone, right?"

"Yes. We got an ID number from the app it synched with. We're trying to get the registration from the company that makes the app, but they're not exactly being forthcoming. Looks like we'll need a subpoena, which probably won't come till tomorrow."

"What about the ceramic pot?"

"A lot of blurred fingerprints, for sure. I think we got a useable partial. Not sure if anything will match our database."

"Did you find out anything about who manufactures it? There can't be a whole lot of them around, can there?"

"Only one manufacturer. Desert High Tech."

"What about their records?"

"Called them this morning. It's one of these irritating companies that wants you to interact with a chatbot instead of a real person. I left a message. I'll call first thing tomorrow if I don't hear anything tonight."

"Thanks, Melissa. Anything else?"

"Nothing right now. Still working on a bunch of evidence."

They said their goodbyes and hung up.

"All right," Fenway said to Millicent. "Sorry. What's next on the schedule?"

"I tried to get a dinner thing happening tonight," Millicent said, "but Monday night on short notice is tough. I didn't think you should show up randomly at someone's house."

"Guess who's coming to dinner," Fenway said drily.

"Not like that," Millicent said. "I mean you tend not to hide who you are. And there are a bunch of people who'd love to vote for you, but you might not, uh, get along with them."

"Everybody loves me," deadpanned Fenway.

"Especially on stage and from a distance," said Millicent.

"You know how to make a girl feel special."

"I know how to make a girl get elected," Millicent pointed out. "The day I care about your feelings is the day I lose my edge."

"So maybe I can do some coroner work this evening?" Fenway asked.

"Or you could go home and chill out," Millicent said. "Now that the police have determined you're not under threat and you don't have to spend every waking moment with a uniformed officer, don't you want to go home and maybe kick your shoes off and turn on the TV?"

Fenway felt the itch to interview Cricket Kapp. "I guess. There's just this one interview—"

"Oh, for crying out loud, Fenway," Millicent Tate sighed. "Fine. Where do you want me to drop you off?"

"Well," Fenway said, her mind churning, "the sheriff's office would probably be best."

CHAPTER TWENTY-FOUR

FENWAY WALKED INTO THE SHERIFF'S OFFICE AS OFFICER CELESTE Sandoval was leaving.

"Fenway!" Officer Sandoval said. "How're you doing?"

"I'm good."

"I mean from the explosion. They let you out of the hospital day before yesterday, right?"

"Yeah," Fenway said. "Worst night of sleep I've had in a long time. They kept waking me up."

"Concussion protocol."

"I know why they did it," Fenway said, elbowing Sandoval in the ribs. "I used to be one of those nurses who drove patients crazy doing it myself."

"Oh—right."

"Hey, Celeste—did you see whether or not Catherine Klein was brought in here?"

Officer Sandoval nodded. "Yes. Maybe ten minutes ago. And she didn't look too happy about it. She's in the interview room."

"Is Dez with her?"

"Yep. She went in right after the lawyer got here."

"Has anybody gone into the viewing room? The sheriff, maybe?"

"I don't think so."

"All right."

"You better not be sneaking in. Or if you do, you better not let me see you."

"I'd do nothing of the sort, Celeste."

"And you'd never eavesdrop on a witness interview."

"Never," Fenway said, smirking.

"All right, catch you later."

Celeste walked out the door and Fenway went into the viewing room. She opened the door as quietly as she could; the room was empty.

Catherine Klein sat on the far side of the table, looking both irritated and nervous. A tired-looking white man, bald with a half-circle of short white hair stretching from his temples around the back of his head, was sitting with her. Dez and Deputy Sheriff Gretchen Donnelly were on the near side of the table.

"Listen, I don't know what I could have done," Catherine Klein was saying. "I was there for a couple of days, sure, but we were having fun."

"By *fun*, you mean doing cocaine and having sex all day?" Dez said.

The man put up his hand. "You don't have to answer that."

Catherine Klein shrugged. "There's no law against infidelity in this state," she said, "and Jer was the one with the cocaine, not me. I don't touch the stuff."

The lawyer rolled his eyes.

"So let's go over what happened Thursday night," Donnelly said. "You'd already been there a couple of days."

"Right. And Thursday was no different. We watched a movie on TV. We ordered in."

"The Belvedere Terrace has room service?" Dez asked.

"There are a few restaurants Jer knows. They deliver to him all the time."

Rich people, Fenway thought.

"What movie did you watch?" Dez asked.

"The weird spy movie that came out last year. The British one that won all the awards."

"What was it about?"

"Uh, British spies, I guess," Catherine Klein said, blushing.

"So you didn't watch a movie. What were you doing?"

"Asked and answered," the lawyer said, but Catherine was already talking.

"I mean, the movie was *on*," Catherine said. "Jer and I just weren't paying attention to it."

Fenway shook her head.

"I gotcha," Dez said. "A little extra-movicular activity. So you'll need to walk me through this. What time did the two of you finish up?"

"What?"

"You don't have to—" the lawyer began.

"I don't know," Catherine interrupted.

"I mean, did he last the whole movie? Because if so, damn, girl, you are one lucky woman."

"I didn't see the clock. I fell asleep."

"Maybe a repeat performance?"

Catherine sighed. "I mean, he was a good lover. That's why I was there."

"Did you conclude your activities before or after the movie finished?"

"Before, I guess. And when I woke up in the morning, Jer was gone."

"He didn't tell you where he was going?"

"He had trouble sleeping a lot of the time. I mean, he might still have been high, too. One of the reasons we picked the Belvedere Terrace is because we liked going down to the beach at night."

"It's on the beach?" asked Dez. "I didn't think it was close."

"There's a footpath. You have to go through a grove of trees, maybe, I don't know, a five-minute walk, maybe ten. But it's pretty. It's a little tough to keep your footing in the dark, especially if it's wet, but it's a nice little beach. Very secluded. Hardly anyone goes there. You can have some, uh, private moments."

"Sounds delightful," Dez said.

"Well, it *was*. We went down there the day before. It was nice."

"Of course it was."

"Sergeant," the lawyer said, "if you want my client to continue cooperating—"

"My apologies, counselor." Dez's voice dripped with insincerity.

"I don't know what to tell you," said Catherine. "I waited for a while for Jer to come back. I thought he might have gone to get some more drugs or some coffee or something. I left the room around six-thirty and I walked around the property."

"Maybe he drove off?"

"He didn't have his car. His wife had dropped him off at the airport and he took a cab to the hotel." She hesitated.

"What?"

"I took the footpath down to the beach, thinking Jer might be there, and I saw a police van. I didn't want to answer any questions about the drugs in the room or anything like that. So I went back, and I packed up and left."

"You just abandoned Jeremy?"

Catherine set her jaw. "If he had seen the cops before I did, he would have left me there, too."

"Lovely," Donnelly said. "Anyone else visit you?"

"That morning?"

"At all. During your whole stay."

"No. It was just him and me."

Dez leaned back in her seat. "So when did you find out about the murder?"

"What?"

"When did you hear that Jeremy Kapp had been killed? Later that day or something? I mean, you're married to a guy who's running for mayor. He must have said something to you. Or his campaign manager must have pointed it out. He mentioned his murder in his campaign speech yesterday, trying to get a dig in at the sheriff. You were standing right next to him."

Fenway was impressed Dez had managed to uncover that tidbit. Catherine Klein looked down at the table.

"Well? When did you find out Jeremy Kapp was murdered?"

"Later that day," Catherine said.

"And what? You didn't think it was important enough to come forward?" Donnelly asked.

"My husband's running for mayor," Catherine Klein said.

"What does that have to do with anything?" questioned Donnelly.

"I don't want it to get out."

"That your husband is running for mayor?" cracked Dez.

"Stop being stupid," Catherine snapped. "I didn't say anything because I didn't want anyone to know I was cheating on my husband. Especially when he was running for mayor."

Fenway thought of how her first date with the newly single McVie had been postponed for three months while the two of them dealt with the campaign, neither one of them wanting the complications of a relationship to muddy the waters of the election. And Catherine Klein—who was married to the candidate—shacked up with her also-married lover in a hotel a few miles away from City Hall.

But she had to marvel at how Dez burrowed under Catherine Klein's skin. The candidate's wife was clearly on the defensive and was saying things in anger she shouldn't.

"You're badgering my—" started the lawyer.

Dez interrupted. "Even though you knew we were looking for the woman he had shared the hotel room with."

"Imagine that," Catherine said, anger bubbling under the surface of her voice. "I chose my marriage and my children over an open police investigation where I wouldn't have been able to provide any useful information anyway."

"It's nice for you to be able to choose your marriage when it's convenient for you to avoid questioning," Dez said, "and *not* choose it when it comes to getting laid in a hotel room surrounded by a mountain of cocaine."

"One more remark like that and this interview is over," the lawyer said, glaring at Dez.

Catherine Klein shook her head and crossed her arms.

Donnelly pulled a folder out of the leather business satchel at her feet, and placed it in the middle of the table. "So, 'Catherine the Great,' do you happen to recognize these?" She pulled the emails out of the folder and put them in front of Catherine.

Catherine only gave the email printed on top a cursory glance at first, but then something caught her eye, and she did a double take. She then read the first email carefully, then went through each of the emails with narrowed eyes.

"I don't understand," Catherine finally said, after she had read the last email. "Where did you get these? And why are these addressed to Charlotte Ferris?"

"So you're saying you *do* recognize these emails," Dez said.

"I recognize the—uh—the ones from Jer," Catherine admitted. "But he sent those to *me*, not to Charlotte." She frowned. "Where did you get these?"

Dez shrugged. "These were anonymously sent to the police," she said. "Either Jer was sending the same love poems in email to both you and Charl—"

"Jer *wasn't* seeing Charlotte," Catherine said angrily. "He knew how I felt about her. He wouldn't have dared."

"Or what?" Dez asked.

Catherine screwed up her mouth in anger. "If I had found out Jer was sleeping with Charlotte, I would have killed *Charlotte*, not Jer," she seethed. "I can't stand that bitch. And I can't stand the rich pig she married, either."

Catherine's reaction shocked Fenway. Catherine talked as if she had history with Charlotte. They looked about the same age. Maybe they went to high school together, or college. Maybe, Fenway thought with a start, they had once fought over the same man.

Please don't let that man be my father, Fenway thought.

"You get why this looks bad for you, right?" Dez stood up and leaned on the table. "You don't come forward when you find out the man you shacked up with for three days in a cheap hotel was murdered. We find emails between your lover and a woman who it seems you don't like. It's not hard to find motive there. And by your own admission, you don't have an alibi for Thursday night. For all we know, you and Jer took a walk down to the beach, nothing but the night sky, the wind gently blowing in off the ocean, and the gun you stole from your frenemy Charlotte. So maybe *you're* the one who blew a hole through his forehead."

Catherine snarled.

"What is it, Catherine?" Dez taunted, leaning closer to her. "You want to say anything to me?"

The lawyer cleared his throat. "Are you charging my client with anything, Sergeant?"

Donnelly looked at the lawyer. "Catherine is a material witness. The sergeant is asking her if she knows anything about what happened, and she's so far been unhelpful."

"That's a 'no,' then."

"We don't have the evidence to arrest Catherine for murder, if that's what you're asking." Donnelly turned to address Catherine. "But there's a lot more you've done that's iffy. Withholding evidence is a misdemeanor, and that's only a fine, but I could lock you up for the night and hold a press conference about your potential role in the murder. That wouldn't look so good on your husband's résumé, would it? It wouldn't look good to the voters, either, especially the day before the election. Be a sure way to put Mayor McVie into office."

"You're crossing the line," the lawyer said sharply.

"No, I'm not," Donnelly said. "I don't have any conflict of interest. I don't have skin in the election game between McVie and your husband. You've done something illegal, Mrs. Klein, and the only question is whether I'm going to look the other way or not."

"We'll turn it into political suicide for McVie too," Catherine said.

Donnelly shrugged. "You say that as if I care," she said. "Hell, maybe they'll make a Netflix miniseries out of it if things get juicy."

"What actress do you think will play me?" Dez said. "I'm thinking Halle Berry. Maybe it'll get her an Emmy."

Catherine closed her eyes. Fenway could see the wheels turning in her head.

"Look," she said, calmly and evenly, without any malice in her voice, "I've been sleeping with Jer for about three months. He's great. He makes excuses to his wife about out-of-town conferences. I say I'm going down to see my sorority sisters in Orange County. We stay a few days at the Belvedere. We barely leave the room. I like the arrangement. Barry doesn't have any idea—he's already so obsessed with winning this stupid mayoral race anyway—and my mom loves spoiling the grandkids. I have absolutely no reason to want Jer dead. I swear to you, I was in bed from the time Jer turned the spy movie on, until I got up around six or so. I don't have anyone to give me an alibi, but I don't have any reason for doing this." She sighed. "Look, I guess you want me to apologize for not coming forward, but I can't imagine what would happen, how angry Barry would be if this got out. So I guess I'm saying I'm sorry, but you've got to understand why I kept my mouth shut."

Dez looked at the lawyer, who gave an almost imperceptible shrug. She sighed. "And you didn't see anything strange on Thursday night. No one strange walking by the windows. No one doing anything out of the ordinary in the hotel parking lot."

Catherine shook her head.

"Okay," Donnelly said. "I appreciate your candor. You're free to go."

"She's free to go?" the lawyer asked, surprise in his voice.

Catherine looked up, almost disbelieving, at their faces.

"I can still file the papers for withholding evidence," Dez said. "And even if you're married to the mayor, you're not above the law."

"Thank you," the lawyer said.

Both Catherine and the lawyer stood up. Catherine picked up her purse, and the lawyer held the door open for her. He followed her out.

Dez stood up and stretched.

"We're nowhere closer to finding out who did this," Donnelly said.

"But we know someone was trying to frame Charlotte."

"I tend to agree with you, but are we sure?"

Dez looked at Donnelly. "The fake emails and the doctored photographs. Someone obviously gained access to Jeremy Kapp's account and took the content from his emails and tried to make it look like it was an email conversation with Charlotte Ferris instead of Catherine the Great."

Donnelly tapped her fingers on the table. "I have to admit that's looking more and more likely." She chuckled. "Especially with the security camera footage."

"Right. She's got an alibi too."

The deputy sheriff sighed, thinking for a moment. "You're right. Charlotte is no longer a viable suspect. Which means Coroner Stevenson no longer has a conflict of interest."

"And neither does McVie," Dez said.

Donnelly paused and thought for a moment. "Right," she conceded. "If his, uh, benefector's wife isn't a suspect anymore, he's good to go too." She smiled and took a deep breath; Fenway saw her shoulders and neck relax. "And that means I can go back to P.Q."

"And we'll get Fenway back on the case?" Dez asked.

Fenway decided not to push her luck anymore. She opened the door quietly, slipped out, and walked out of the sheriff's building over to her own office.

Fenway had been in her office about fifteen minutes when Dez came in, followed by Donnelly.

"Ah, Fenway," Dez said. "I was hoping you'd come back here. We were going over some final checklists to hand the case back to you."

"Good thing I came back before you left, then," Fenway said, a wide smile on her face.

"Do you always look so happy when the case is this tough?" Donnelly asked, barely suppressing a grin. "Fine, you can work on it now—I don't see any conflict of interest with any of the suspects anymore." She looked sideways at Fenway. "Of course, it's still possible that the Kapp murder is tied pretty closely to the murders of Rory Velásquez and Jacob Tassajera. If I were running this department, I wouldn't let you touch those either, because of your relationship to the victims." She cleared her throat. "But it's ultimately McVie's call. Or maybe it's your call. I just know it's not my call." She walked over and shook Fenway's hand. "At least for another couple of months."

"Thank you for your assistance on this, Sheriff."

"I'm still a deputy sheriff until January first," Donnelly said. "Assuming I win, that is."

And she was out the door.

"Okay, rookie," Dez said. "Now that you're officially reinstated, let's go interview the grieving widow."

CHAPTER TWENTY-FIVE

THEY RODE IN SILENCE TO THE KAPP HOUSE. IT WAS TWENTY minutes out to Paso Querido, and off the main highway, a few miles up Querido Valley Drive, then the road crested the summit and wound down into the canyon. The Kapp house was in the "Birdland" development, surrounded by scrub brush and ironwood trees. As soon as they crossed the border into Birdland, it was lush and green, something rarely seen in this part of California after the recent years of drought. Most properties in the county kept their grounds full of plants needing little water, as well as sturdy trees, cleared back from the main buildings to provide no fuel during fire season.

But the Birdland properties were different, with vibrant shades of green. As they turned onto Whippoorwill Terrace, long grasses like verdant waterfalls cascaded down steps made of naturally occurring brown and gray stones. Dez's Impala rounded a turn and the Kapp house came into view.

The large plot of land—perhaps an acre and a half—was beautifully designed, as one might expect to find at the residence of a landscape architect. The house itself, however, was far less like Nathaniel Ferris's house than Fenway had pictured. While her father's mansion was an exercise in overstatement and opulence, the Kapp residence was less ostentatious and significantly smaller than Fenway expected.

It was still a large house—if she had to estimate, perhaps four thousand square feet. Looking to her left, there was a four-car detached garage with a covered breezeway connecting to the main house. The long driveway meandered around a large oak tree, and Dez left the Impala on the driveway, under its shade.

The front door opened, and the young, handsome face of Donovan Kapp peered out. The acne on his forehead had cleared. "Coroner?" he asked, a little taken aback.

"Hey, Donovan," Fenway said. "Can we come in?"

"Uh, sure, I guess so." He stepped back from the door and it opened wide. Fenway stepped into the entryway, followed by Dez.

"I guess you can sit down in there." Donovan motioned to the great room. The large space was separated into two areas: one with a sofa and a love seat, and behind the sofa, three glass-topped display cases; the other area had two leather recliners facing a large flat-screen television mounted on the wall.

Donovan put his hands in his pockets, and then seemed to remember his manners. "Oh, you want anything to drink? Water or something?"

"You have any coffee?" asked Fenway. She walked around the display cases. The first housed several dozen old-looking coins, all in matching settings. The second, the largest of the three, had a fencing epée and two antique revolvers.

"Uh... I don't think so. Not unless there's still some in the pot from this morning."

"These are nice," Fenway said, looking down at the weapon display. "This is a .44, right?"

Donovan screwed up his mouth and walked over next to her. "I don't know. That sounds right, I guess. My dad started collecting these when we moved here."

Fenway squinted. "Unless I'm mistaken, that's a Colt Single Action .44 Special."

"I guess."

Fenway moved on to the coin collection. "Some of these coins look expensive."

"I guess."

Fenway walked to the sofa and took a seat. "Your mom here?"

"No," Donovan said. "She went to see a friend in Santa Barbara."

"Oh. When will she be back?"

"Late tonight, I think. She's got an appointment with the funeral director tomorrow morning around ten."

"Ah," Dez said. She was still standing next to the love seat. "I guess we should have called first. Of course, it's almost never a convenient time right before a funeral."

"I saw the news tonight," Donovan said, a little carelessly. "I guess you let your stepmother go."

"Yeah," Fenway said. "Turns out she's got a pretty airtight alibi. Video footage and everything. She couldn't have done it."

"Oh," Donovan said.

"You sound disappointed. You were hoping Charlotte was guilty?"

"Uh...no, it's not that." Donovan paused and walked to the love seat. "I thought you had my dad's killer. It was, uh, a little easier to sleep at night, I guess."

"I see."

"I'm sure surprised you didn't keep her longer." Donovan sat down on the arm of the love seat.

"Hah. I wasn't even on the case," Fenway said.

Donovan cocked his head to the side. "You weren't even on the case?"

"I got kicked off as soon as my stepmother's gun was found at the crime scene. Conflict of interest."

"Oh," Donovan said. "I guess that makes sense."

"You *wanted* me on the case?"

Donovan folded his arms. "Well, yeah."

"Why's that?"

"You caught the mayor's killer a few months ago, didn't you? And he was some super-rich guy with a lot of big-time connections. And the old coroner's murder before that. I thought you make sure rich people with powerful friends don't get away with it."

"You think Charlotte got away with something?"

Donovan shrugged. "I don't know."

"Just because she's rich and powerful doesn't mean she did anything."

Donovan barked laughter. "That's a good one. Let me tell you—she did *something*, for sure."

"What do you mean?"

"Something. Rich people lie and cheat and steal as a way of life."

"Even you? *You're* rich."

Donovan smiled. "My dad was rich. It's not the same thing." He paused thoughtfully. "I guess if Charlotte has an alibi, she didn't kill my father. But she could have hired someone, right?"

Fenway looked at Dez. "We'll make sure to look into all the angles, Donovan."

Dez said, "Is your sister home?"

Donovan shook his head. "She went down to L.A. to visit Jasper."

"So soon after your father was killed?"

Donovan shrugged.

"Will she be back tomorrow too?"

Donovan shrugged again.

"So you're holding down the fort."

"I guess."

"While I have you here, then," Fenway said, "let me ask you a couple of questions."

Donovan's eyes flitted from Fenway to Dez. "Sure, I guess so."

"You said when I talked to you a couple of days ago your mom's dealer was here Thursday night."

"Yeah."

"You still say he was here for a couple of hours?"

"Yeah. I didn't look at the clock though."

"Because he has a thing for her."

Donovan shrugged. "He sure seemed like he was into her. Trying to get her alone, being all cutesy with her."

"I spoke to him. He says he was only here for ten minutes."

Donovan shifted his weight from foot to foot. "That doesn't surprise me. His girlfriend gets crazy jealous. He'd probably deny the whole thing."

"His girlfriend? How do you know her?"

Donovan smiled. "I don't. That's what the dealer says to my mom. 'We better be careful. My girlfriend gets crazy jealous.'"

"You heard the dealer say that?"

"Sure."

"Even though your door was closed?" Dez asked.

"They're loud."

"Zoso says he didn't see either you or your sister that night," Fenway said.

"He didn't even notice, he was so busy trying to get in Mom's pants."

"Your mom says she doesn't remember anything."

"Yeah, well, she was pretty out of it. She tries to hide it from us, but we know."

"Okay. A couple more things, if you don't mind."

Donovan opened his mouth to speak, and then shut it again. He shuffled his feet, and looked at Fenway. "I don't know," he said. "I'm a minor, right? My mom probably wouldn't want me talking to you without her here."

"I just have a couple of tiny things I want to clear up."

"No, Fenway," Dez interrupted. "It's true. He's a minor. We can't talk to him without his parent or guardian present." Dez handed Donovan her business card. "Have your mom give me a call as soon as she gets back."

Donovan nodded. Fenway and Dez left the house, Donovan closing the door quickly behind them, and they walked back to the Impala.

"What do we do now, Dez?" Fenway said. "I think we've got to talk to Cricket Kapp. Should we go down to Santa Barbara and try to find her?"

"No, I don't think so." Dez was quiet for a moment, unlocking the car. "Did you think Donovan acted strange?"

"Sure I did," Fenway replied, sliding into the passenger seat. "I think we need to consider him a suspect too, just like his mom."

"He's hiding something," Dez mused. "His evasiveness. He kept touching his face. He seemed to be fine when he opened the door to see us, but by the time we left, he was sweating. Not a great liar."

"He could be covering for his mom. He seemed to have an alibi all laid out for her."

"What about the daughter?" Dez asked.

"I guess he could be covering for her too. Let's see what she has to say when she gets back from L.A."

"Maybe she's not in L.A. Maybe she fled the country."

"We should check," Fenway admitted.

"Or maybe he's covering for himself," Dez said.

Fenway thought for a minute. "He's the one who said Zoso was there until two in the morning. Why would he lie if it's something so easily disproven?"

"Maybe he didn't think we'd believe a drug dealer."

"Maybe. Or maybe Zoso *is* lying and covering to keep his girlfriend from knowing where he was. He protested a little too much when I talked about being hot and bothered for Cricket."

"If Zoso was there for two hours, wouldn't Cricket say something? I read McVie's interview notes. Cricket Kapp said she had no recollection of seeing Zoso at all. So Donovan might be lying."

"Or Cricket might have been so high she doesn't remember."

Dez tapped the steering wheel. "We might have results from those emails and doctored photos in the next two or three days. It might tell us the type of laser printer or inkjet ink that was used."

"Or the type of paper."

"Don't hold your breath on that one, rookie. Ten to one that paper is generic and cheap."

"You never know. It might get us closer."

Dez turned onto the freeway, going back to Estancia. They rode in silence for a few minutes.

"Two or three days?"

"If we're lucky."

Fenway thought for a moment. "Dez, how much of the footage from my father's security cameras did you get?"

"Just from Thursday night," Dez replied.

"You know the Kapps had dinner over at my father's house the week before, right?"

"That's how Charlotte's name first came up, isn't it? That your father was one of Jeremy Kapp's clients, and he had a thing for sleeping with his rich clients' wives."

"I wonder," Fenway said.

"What do you wonder?"

"I wonder if Cricket Kapp stole Charlotte's gun while she was over at my father's house the other night."

"Or Donovan."

"Right. Or Donovan. Or Blair, for that matter."

"You think it would be on the security footage?"

Fenway shrugged. "Only one way to find out."

Dez watched the road, twitching her lips back and forth. "You think your father's going to be okay handing over those security tapes to us?"

"Ordinarily, probably not," Fenway conceded. "But since his only daughter just got his loving wife out of jail, maybe he'll consider it." She took the phone out of her purse and called her father.

"Hi, Dad," Fenway said, stepping into the mansion.

Her father, barefoot in a track suit, eyed her warily. "Hi, Fenway." Even dressed as casually as he was, Ferris looked better than he had the night before; the distracted, lost look was gone from his eyes.

"You know Sergeant Roubideux, right?"

"Call me Dez, please," she said, leaning around Fenway and shaking Nathaniel Ferris's hand. "Your dad and I have met several times before, Fenway. Good to see you again, Mr. Ferris."

"Listen," Ferris said, holding his hands out in front of him, "I've had a hell of a day. Charlotte just got home this afternoon. This isn't going to take too long, is it?"

"I don't think so," Fenway said. Dez followed her in and Ferris closed the door behind them. "I need to see the footage from the night the Kapps came over for dinner."

Ferris shook his head. "I don't know what you'd need that for," he said. "It was about a week and a half before Jer was killed." He set his jaw and looked at Fenway. "Listen, we already went over the footage proving Charlotte and I were here all night. We came in, and we didn't go out again."

"I know," Fenway said. "But you know Charlotte's gun ended up in the murderer's hands."

"I've already told the police we don't know how. We've already asked Sandrita. Roderick, too. In fact, we asked everyone who works for us. Do you want to interview them? I'll make them available. Sandrita's cleaning up from dinner."

Fenway shot a look at Dez. "Yes, that would be excellent. And we won't have to have them come down to the station house. Dez?"

Dez looked sideways at Fenway, but nodded. "Sure. I can ask them questions about Charlotte's gun."

"And I can look at the video footage."

Ferris looked between Dez and Fenway. "Okay," he said.

"Should I go into the kitchen, then?"

"Sure," Ferris said, a bit preoccupied. Dez walked through the foyer and into a butler's door to the kitchen.

"Okay," Fenway said. "The footage."

"Right," Ferris said, nodding. "The cameras record everything but it's sent via a live feed to the security company—well, the footage is stored in the cloud, but the security company has all the access privileges. I can review the footage whenever I want."

"Is there a monitor somewhere?"

"I usually view it on my phone," Ferris said. "I mean, I hardly ever have a reason to, but that's how I found the footage from Thursday night."

"So can you find the footage of when the Kapps were here?"

Ferris stroked his chin. "I'm trying to remember."

"Maybe Charlotte knows."

"She's upstairs right now. I don't want to bother her. I can find it. Here—let's go into the study."

Ferris's study was a masterpiece of set design for what one would think a rich person's library should be. Three walls were lined with books, mostly leather-bound tomes Fenway doubted Ferris ever opened. There was a freestanding dark wood stand about five feet in front of the desk, whose spherical basket contained a massive globe in grays and sepias.

The desk itself was mahogany, with thoughtfully arranged sets of items: expensive-looking pens and pencils, a leather desk blotter, and perched on the corner of the desk, a little precariously, was the latest Mac laptop, with a single wire disappearing under the lip of the desk.

"You've been in the study before, right?"

"Not for a long time," Fenway said. She hadn't been in the study on her infrequent visits to the house since she moved back, but she vaguely remembered this room from her childhood. She stepped closer to the shelves. The titles of the rows of leather-wrapped books came more fully into focus: some of the classic books, from *Don Quixote* to the collected works of Plato, but she also saw some Ralph Ellison and Toni Morrison among the Shakespeare and Swift. A smaller title, both in height and thickness, revealed itself as Aphra Behn's *Oroonoko* upon closer inspection. Fenway wondered if her father hadn't read all of these books—these titles seemed strangely curated. Perhaps some of it had been her mother's influence.

"Now, listen," Ferris said, "I don't have this available to you to go putting it into evidence. I talked to Charlotte's lawyer this afternoon, and she doesn't want us handing anything over without talking with her."

"But you'll let me see the footage."

Ferris shifted his weight from foot to foot. "I don't think her lawyer would like it, but yes. But you have to promise you won't use any footage in court."

"Without a warrant or a subpoena."

Ferris shrugged. "Fine."

"Dad, I'm on your side. If I find someone taking the gun, it'll help Charlotte out."

"I said it was okay, Fenway," Ferris said. He picked up the laptop and opened it. He balanced it with one hand and typed and clicked the trackpad with the other. Fenway went around the back of the desk and sat down in the leather armchair. It sank, satisfyingly, under her weight, but made a squeaking noise, like the leather chairs in Dr. Tassajera's office. Fenway wondered how much the sound of the leather chairs in the therapist's office reminded her father of his study—and how much that had to do with her father's decision to use him as their therapist.

"Okay," Ferris said, setting the laptop down in front of her, "it was two Saturdays ago. You can see their SUV pulling into the driveway right here—a couple of minutes after five o'clock." He pointed to the screen. "You've got all four cameras: front entry, driveway, and then long views of the front and back of the house."

"Anything by the garage?"

Ferris shook his head.

"Are all your cameras outside, or do you have anything inside?"

Ferris scoffed. "What, and risk someone selling videos of Charlotte on the dark web?"

Fenway flinched. Had her father made an insensitive reference to her Russian Lit professor? She set her jaw. "I take it someone had a visit from the Bellingham police force."

"Yeah. He was a wiry-looking black guy with a big Barry White-type voice," Ferris said absently.

Fenway sighed. "Detective Ridley."

"Oh, so he's talked to you, too?"

"Yep."

Ferris shook his head. "I don't know why he made the trip. He was here when we got back from picking Charlotte up."

"We?"

"Roderick was driving me, Fenway."

She nodded. "Sorry."

"Anyway, Ridley sat right out on my sofa, made himself comfortable, and started asking all kinds of questions about the professor. I told him it wasn't a good time, but he said he had flown all the way from Seattle. As if a two-hour flight is something to write home about. Boo hoo."

"Yeah, he talked to me too. Last night."

Ferris shrugged. "I didn't even know the professor was dead. Did you know before he talked to you?"

"Yes."

"When did you find out?"

"A couple of days after—uh... after I told you. About what he did." She swallowed. "To me."

Ferris pursed his lips. "And you didn't mention it."

"Well, no."

"Did the cops up there call you to tell you?"

"I read an article online about it."

Ferris nodded. "How come you didn't mention it to me?"

Fenway looked back at the laptop screen and shrugged.

"Because you thought I had something to do with it," Ferris said evenly.

"I don't know, Dad. I guess I thought the timing was a little weird."

"You think I'd kill somebody?"

"No, you were here when he died. I knew you weren't the one to do it."

"Then what?"

Fenway was quiet.

"Oh," Ferris said, and Fenway could almost hear the gears in his head clicking into place. "You think I *hired* someone to do it."

Fenway shrugged. "I don't think anything, Dad."

Ferris was quiet, and Fenway looked at the footage of the Kapp family arriving. There was no sound, and her father's even, deliberate breathing put her on edge.

"I guess if you saw your professor was killed right after I found out what he did to you, it would explain why you thought I might have something to do with Jeremy's death," Ferris said softly.

"I try to go where the evidence leads," Fenway replied.

On the screen, the SUV parked without incident. All the Kapps, including Blair and Donovan, got out of the vehicle. Cricket Kapp almost lost her footing on the driveway and Donovan grabbed her arm to prevent her from falling.

They all walked toward the front door, Cricket leaning heavily on Donovan.

Jeremy Kapp was in an aloha shirt, untucked, and khakis, with sandals on. Cricket and Blair were both in loose print dresses, Blair's with cap sleeves with orange flowers, and Cricket's with wide shoulder straps and no sleeves, with a blue and lime green design. They both carried white purses, Cricket's a little larger than Blair's. Donovan brought up the rear, with a dark polo shirt, a little large for him, tucked into his faded jeans, with a hole ripped artfully at the knee.

Jeremy Kapp was in front to ring the bell, and when Nathaniel Ferris answered the door, they shook hands and smiled. Fenway didn't see Charlotte, and all four Kapps entered the house, Donovan steering his mother inside.

"Where was Charlotte?" Fenway asked.

"She had just gotten in the shower."

"Seriously? So close to the time your guests were coming over?"

A rakish grin slowly spread over Ferris's face. "We might have lost track of time."

"Ugh." Fenway rolled her eyes and turned back to the screen, fast-forwarding the video. About twenty minutes later, Jeremy and Ferris exited the house through the back door, and walked down a rocky path out of view of the camera.

Something was out of place, nagging at the back of Fenway's mind. "What's back there? The pool?"

"No," Ferris said. "The pool's around the other side. Jeremy did such a good job with the fountain, I wanted him to work on the garden. We're walking to the area I wanted to have Jeremy working on next. It's overgrown right now. Charlotte wanted to put a vegetable garden in there, but I'm afraid we didn't have time to take care of it. Kind of a fire hazard."

"And Charlotte was still in the shower when you and Kapp left the house?"

Ferris nodded. "Yes."

Fenway thought for a moment. "Dad, did you know Charlotte said one of your recent dinner guests walked in on her when she got out of the shower?"

"What?"

Fenway shrugged. "That's what she told me."

"She didn't tell *me*."

"Maybe she didn't think it was a big deal." Fenway paused. "Who else have you had over for dinner lately?"

Ferris shook his head. "The Kapps are the only ones recently. In fact, they're the only ones since you and the sheriff and, uh, Everett Michaels came over a couple of months ago."

"Are you sure? I thought you two were social butterflies."

"I've been busy. A lot of late nights with the board of directors up my ass."

Then it clicked into place. "Wait—she didn't say 'walked in on me,' she said, 'sneaked a peek.'"

Ferris looked at Fenway. "What's that supposed to mean?"

"That's the turn of phrase you'd use if your friend's sixteen-year-old son walked in."

"What?"

Fenway searched her memory. "She also called him 'the little pervert.' That's a phrase you'd use on a teenager, too."

"Fenway, what are you talking about?"

"You left Cricket and the two kids in the house while Charlotte was in the shower, and you and Jeremy Kapp took a little stroll."

"Sure. Sandrita was serving drinks. Dinner was almost ready. Why not take a walk?"

"Someone took Charlotte's gun, and I want to find out who."

"And you think it was one of the Kapps?"

"Maybe it was Donovan."

"You're saying he walked in on Charlotte, and then stole her gun?"

"Or maybe he sneaked into the room to steal the gun, and got caught on the way out and had to act like he was trying to see her naked."

"I'm not sure I believe that."

Fenway shrugged. "Maybe not. Charlotte came back downstairs and no one was guarding the room, right? So it could have been Cricket, or even the daughter. You guys didn't have it in a safe or anything, right? It lived in Charlotte's bedside table?"

"It makes her feel more secure."

"You don't have to defend it to me, Dad, I'm just saying the drawer wasn't protected. Anyone with access to the room could have gotten it." Fenway paused. "When did you see it last? Before that Saturday or afterward?"

"I have no idea. It's Charlotte's gun. Probably about four weeks ago, for me. I went to put away something of Charlotte's and opened that drawer. The gun was in there then. Charlotte would have seen it much more recently."

"Okay. I'll have to ask her."

"And you think it's Sandrita. Or maybe Roderick."

"If Charlotte didn't do it, and you didn't do it, it was somebody else—someone who took the gun from the drawer. If the last time either of you saw the gun was a month ago, we've got to look closely at everyone who came to the house." She pointed at Blair walking outside the front door, talking on the phone—to her boyfriend Jasper, Fenway was sure. "That's why I'm looking at these three people."

Blair didn't have her purse with her—she must have left it inside. And she was much more interested in her conversation than anything else. Fenway looked closely, but she didn't think it was possible for Blair to have the gun. Not during her phone call anyway.

She fast-forwarded to when Jeremy and Ferris came back from the garden. Nothing strange. She fast-forwarded again; the sun went down and the Halloween decorations lit up. Her father and his wife had gone with tasteful gourds and pumpkins more appropriate for the background of a clothing catalog than for any actual Halloween purposes. No ghosts, no spiderwebs, no witches, and nothing humorous or playful.

Finally, around ten o'clock, the Kapp family departed. Jeremy came out first, followed by Blair and Donovan, with Charlotte stepping out with them. Jeremy hugged Charlotte, perhaps holding it for a little too long. Cricket came out, her purse over her shoulder, and Jeremy broke from the embrace. Cricket had a worried look on her face.

Fenway zoomed in on Cricket's purse, looking for a telltale bulge or the glint of the stock of the gun, anything to give the game away. She found nothing.

"Was Cricket drunk or high or something?" she asked.

"She seemed a little out of it," Ferris said. "She kept insisting she was fine. Honestly, Jeremy seemed a little embarrassed."

"I wonder how good an actor Cricket is."

"What do you mean?"

"I mean, she was stumbling all over herself when she gets to your house. But when she leaves, she can definitely put one foot in front of the other."

Ferris shook his head. "She had quite a bit to drink at the house. She was there for a few hours, so I guess it could have worn off, but I had to open a new bottle of vodka for her Cape Cods."

"Interesting," Fenway said, under her breath.

Next, she rewound the video and zoomed in on Blair's purse. She didn't see anything that looked like a gun, even after viewing it again.

She did the same with Donovan. He might have been carrying the gun in his waistband, but she didn't see it. The polo shirt was long and draped almost to the midway point of his hips, but he didn't walk strangely.

"Do you see anything?"

Fenway shook her head. "No. Dammit. I thought for sure there'd be something here."

Sandrita appeared at the door of the study, "I'm sorry, Mister Nathaniel," she said, "but Miss Charlotte wants to see you."

"Sorry, Fenway," he said. "I'll be back down in a minute."

"I'll finish up," Fenway said.

He left the room, followed by Sandrita, and Fenway fished the USB drive out of her purse. She looked at the laptop and realized that her father, of course, had one of the fancy Mac laptops that didn't have a regular USB port. Cursing silently, she pulled a drawer open, then another, and found the right cable when she lifted up a pair of expensive headphones.

She quickly plugged the drive in, went back to the desktop, and copied the video files over to the USB drive. It took a few minutes, through which Fenway could hear nothing but her heart pounding in her ears, but finally it finished. Fenway had the cable back in the drawer and the USB drive back in her purse as she heard her father's footfalls on the stairs.

"I asked Charlotte about the gun," Ferris said, coming into the study. "She went to the shooting range about three weeks ago and ran into Jeremy and Donovan. She invited them for dinner. She doesn't remember what day it was, but she had the gun cleaned and prepped after her target practice. So—it was definitely taken in the last three weeks."

Fenway nodded, trying to get her heart to calm down. She had only taken footage from her father, after all, not stolen money.

"Okay," Fenway said, "I'm done here."

"And Sergeant Roubideaux finished her interviews as well," he said.

Fenway stood and they walked to the foyer, where Dez was waiting for them.

"One more thing, Dad," she said.

"Yes?"

"Have you ever heard of a company called Global Advantage Executive Consulting?"

"Global Advantage? No. We use a leadership training organization, but that's not their name—unless it's some big umbrella company I don't know about."

"Maybe GAEC?"

Ferris furrowed his brow and shook his head. "Doesn't ring a bell. Why do you ask?"

"I wondered specifically if you knew anything about payments to or from that organization."

"Never heard of them, and I certainly never got a payment from them."

"You sure?"

"Of course I'm sure."

The three of them stood there in the foyer, not speaking for several awkward moments.

"Okay," Fenway finally said. "Election Day tomorrow. Millicent is going to want me to be pretty visible. You voting?"

"Mailed it in last week," Ferris said. "I figured out who I was voting for pretty early on." He winked.

"You doing okay?"

"Sure. You know." Ferris shrugged. "I'm glad Charlotte's home." He paused.

"All right," Fenway said, opening the door.

"Wait," Ferris said. "I just—thank you, Fenway. I know you got kicked off the case, and you didn't have to do anything to try to get Charlotte out. I know you and Charlotte haven't gotten along, and I know it would have been easy for you to keep her in there."

"No, Dad," Fenway said. "It wouldn't have been easy. She wasn't guilty. I knew she wasn't guilty."

"I'm trying to tell you I appreciate the extra work you did to get Charlotte home to me," he said, and his eyes were watery. "Just accept the damn thank you and I'll call you up tomorrow to congratulate you."

"Oh, Dad, don't jinx it," Fenway said. "But—uh, you're welcome."

"All right."

For a moment, Fenway turned over the thought in her mind of asking about seeing another therapist—maybe one of the doctors who had been on *her* short list—but simply nodded and turned to leave. Dez followed her out and opened the Impala for them.

"Where to now?"

"Just drop me at home, Dez."

"Yeah. It's late. And you've got a couple of final campaign appearances tomorrow, right?"

"Don't remind me. I wish I didn't have to dress up to go vote."

"Aw, rookie, you look so precious in a pantsuit." Dez cackled. "And think of how the photo will look, blown up life-size on the wall of your office for everyone to see."

"I'm not getting a life-size picture of myself."

"Oh, you might not be paying for it, but Christmas is right around the corner."

Fenway rolled her eyes. "Hey—did you find out anything from Sandrita or Roderick?"

Dez shook her head. "They don't know anything. The driver didn't know Charlotte had a gun, much less where she kept it."

"What about the housekeeper?"

"She doesn't open drawers."

"A housekeeper who doesn't open drawers?"

"I got the feeling she was put off by something she found once. I didn't want to ask a lot of, uh, probing questions."

Fenway made a face.

"My sentiments exactly," said Dez.

As soon as Fenway walked in the door, she got a call on her phone from a number she didn't recognize. She thought it might be another call about the evidence against Charlotte. She swore lightly—she hadn't downloaded a phone call recording app—but she thought if she could talk to the person, she might be able to figure out who it was.

"Fenway Stevenson."

"This is the Hanford Women's Facility calling Fenway Stevenson," a crackly voice on the other end said. "I have Lana Cassidy on the line."

Lana. "I'll take the call."

"Miss Stevenson?"

"Hi, Lana. I didn't expect to hear from you so soon."

"Oh." Her voice was heavy with disappointment. "I guess that means you haven't started looking into Carl's death."

"On the contrary," Fenway said. "It seems like it's wrapped up in a lot of complicated matters."

"With Ferris Energy?"

"Yes." Fenway coughed. "The investigation is just starting, but it seems like it might be big. I wish I could say more. I'm in the middle of another murder investigation right now, but I promise, Lana, this is one of my top priorities."

"Okay," Lana said. She hesitated. "I don't get a lot of mail. It might be nice if you could keep me up to speed. These phone calls cost me a lot of money."

"I understand. I'll do whatever I can as long as it doesn't jeopardize the investigation." Even as the words were coming out of Fenway's mouth, she doubted she'd write a single letter to Lana Cassidy.

They said quick goodbyes, and Fenway felt a burst of adrenaline from the conversation. She had trouble winding down after that, but with a few episodes of some stupid television shows and a glass of red wine with the delivery of penne arrabiata from Zorro's, she calmed down enough to go to bed. It wasn't even ten o'clock yet, but the week had taken a lot out of her, and she had a busy Election Day ahead.

She wondered if Piper would be able to assess anything on the footage she had on the USB stick, or if the lab had analyzed the paper or ink from the printers yet. She was sure it would lead to Cricket, or Donovan, or Blair. And there would be enough evidence for not only an arrest, but a conviction—even if the Kapps *could* afford a high-priced criminal lawyer.

She walked around her bedroom with her toothbrush sticking out of her mouth. Her phone buzzed on her bedside table. She glanced at it; the message was from McVie.

It's me

The doorbell rang.

Fenway looked down at herself; the night was chilly, and her light blue flannel pajamas, while comfortable, weren't exactly flattering. She went into the bathroom to spit out the toothpaste, and grabbed a long robe from her closet, before deciding it looked even worse than her pajamas.

She opened the door. McVie was there, in a white shirt, navy blue tie, and gray slacks.

"You just come from a campaign event?"

McVie nodded.

Fenway's eyes raked over McVie's body. "You clean up pretty good, Craig."

"I'm down by five points in the latest poll."

"What? That's crazy."

"And I don't care," McVie said, and he stepped inside, wrapping his arms around her.

Fenway turned into him and put her hand behind his head, running her fingers through his hair, and then pulled him into her, kissing him fiercely, melting into the emotions she had to put on pause the last three months. He put his arm around her back, pulling her closer.

Fenway's other hand started to loosen his tie.

McVie's other hand closed the apartment door solidly behind them.

They kissed, both of them feeling the weight of the last few months leaving their shoulders, their muscles, their hands as they intertwined. Fenway broke from the kiss so she could pull McVie's tie over his head. McVie's hands started unbuttoning her pajama top.

They fell together onto the sofa, and forgot about the election for a while.

PART VI

TUESDAY

CHAPTER TWENTY-SIX

AT FIVE O'CLOCK IN THE MORNING, FENWAY WOKE UP AS MCVIE tried to disentangle their arms and legs. "Five more minutes," Fenway mumbled, but McVie's stubble scratched her face as he kissed her goodbye.

"Can't have the press seeing me leave your apartment on Election Day," he said, pulling on his boxer shorts and slacks. Fenway watched his muscular torso through half-lidded eyes as he walked around the near-dark room before going out to the kitchen to locate the dress shirt he had worn the night before.

After he left, Fenway tried to get back to sleep. Twenty minutes later, she gave up. It was an unexpected way to start Election Day, but she was in a good mood. The pent-up energy between the two of them had needed release, and if the price to pay was four hours' sleep, she might as well make the most of it.

She pulled on her sweats and laced up her running shoes, looped her apartment key through her shoelaces, and dug through a drawer to get a headlamp. It still worked. She was about to grab her phone when she saw a call come in.

Millicent Tate.

Didn't that woman ever sleep? Fenway decided to ignore it—she could say she was in the shower. She'd return Millicent's call when she got back.

She was out of her apartment at five forty-five and turned left down to the end of the street, then up to the hiking trail and to the canopy of trees that served as a butterfly waystation in May and October. Her jostling headlamp lit the hiking path and showed her the fork in the trail that led down to the ocean.

Just as she stopped where the hiking trail emptied out onto the beach, the first fingers of light escaped over the horizon and lit up the black water to a brilliant indigo. Fenway closed her eyes and took a few deep breaths, hearing the waves crash over the rocks, listening to the seagulls starting to wake and cry out.

What would she do if everything Ivanovich had done had somehow resonated with most of the voters? She wasn't worried too much about the young voters, or the voters of color, but most of the county residents were older and white. She wasn't even worried about Estancia proper—or about Paso Querido. It was the rural areas, the people who lived off the county roads. The people who lived off 326 and whose pickups had confederate flag bumper stickers. Or worse.

The people who were neighbors and drinking buddies with Terrance Ivanovich. Would they realize their friend was way over the line? Or would they think Fenway was getting in the way of their friend, she was somehow to blame for the vandalism he caused?

Would it resonate with them that Ivanovich played the race card—while accusing Fenway of doing so? Would it give some of Fenway's supporters a reason to change their minds and go with someone who looked like they were in the same tribe?

She couldn't think like that.

But she could go back to a normal life. She could go back to nursing, and she and McVie could date, like a real couple, and he wouldn't be leaving her bed at five in the morning.

She stretched her legs, then started to run back. The light was brighter now, and she could see where her feet landed. She didn't need her headlamp, but it gave her comfort anyway.

She started to sprint as she saw the end of the trail in her sights.

Then she was on the ground, gasping for breath, her knee screaming in agony.

Fenway squeezed her eyes shut. The sharp, intense pain radiated from her kneecap outward, tingling and stinging. She'd been hurt before—her broken hand three months previously, for one—and the pain had been worse than this. This was still bad.

She opened her eyes. A tree stump stuck out of the ground next to her leg. She must have smacked her knee on it when she fell. As the pain dulled into a throb in her knee, she realized something was wrapped around her ankle. She rolled onto her side so she could see it.

A rope.

Someone had deliberately tripped her.

She pushed herself up into a sitting position. She looked back and to her left.

Holding the end of the rope was Donovan Kapp.

"Donovan," Fenway gasped, trying to get her breath back. "What the hell?" But she knew. As soon as she saw his face, she knew.

And she realized what she had missed watching the video. Donovan's shirt had been neatly tucked in when they arrived. Afterward, it had been untucked. Nothing in and of itself, but that's where he had hidden Charlotte's gun.

"I'm sorry, Miss Stevenson," Donovan said. "I didn't want that to be necessary, but I guess it was." He unzipped his jacket and awkwardly pulled a revolver out. Fenway recognized the Colt Single Action .44 Special from the display case at the Kapp house.

"It's not as new of a gun as Charlotte's," he said. "But it'll do the job pretty well, if it has to."

"What are you doing?" Fenway said.

"I knew you ran this trail in the mornings," Donovan said. "That white power website has all kinds of information like that. Plus your address, the make, model, and license plate of your car, all kinds of stuff. It was only a matter of time before you had your car vandalized or your apartment broken into."

"Seriously?"

"I think you of all people should have figured out you were on that site," he said.

"So what's this?" Fenway said. "Why did you trip me? Why the gun?"

"You knew, Miss Stevenson," Donovan said quietly. "When you came by the house yesterday, you knew I was the one who sent you all those letters. You knew I was the one trying to point the finger at Charlotte." He stared at the gun in his hand like he had never seen it before, but then his eyes glazed over and he set his mouth in a line again. "You said there was video footage. And I realized, of course, a rich guy like your dad is going to have video footage of everything. And I saw something light up in your eyes when you said 'video footage,' like you were going to find something. Like you knew where to go."

"I didn't have everything figured out."

He sighed. "If you didn't, you would before long."

"You think getting rid of me is going to keep you out of jail?" Fenway said. "They'll put other detectives on the case."

Donovan chuckled derisively. "I wish I had known you were off the case. The other investigators wanted Charlotte to be guilty from the get-go. I screwed up with those emails and photos, sending them to you instead of them. I should have known I couldn't fool you."

"Why *did* you send those emails and photos?" Fenway said. "I was off the case—I wouldn't have even *tried* to get Charlotte out of jail. But then I got those. And those were faked."

Donovan looked stricken. "I thought I did a pretty good job of making those look real," he said quietly.

"Okay," Fenway said. "So what's your plan here? You going to shoot me?"

Donovan shook his head. "You're going to walk to the cliff. And then you're going to jump off. Into the rocks."

Fenway shook her head. "I don't think I'm going to do that."

Donovan nodded. "You are. If you don't, I'm going to shoot your kneecap. Then I'll push you off."

"They'll find the bullet in my knee. They'll know it wasn't an accident."

Donovan shook his head. "Not after the waves and the rocks are done with your body. It'll be so mangled, no one'll know what happened."

Fenway didn't think Donovan was correct, but she saw no point in arguing. He thought he had found a way out for himself, and he wasn't going to let it go.

"Up," Donovan said, motioning with the .44.

Fenway thought of her phone on the counter in her apartment. She tested her knee out.

"What's the problem?"

"I cracked my knee when I fell, is the problem," Fenway said. She gingerly put weight on it and a bolt of pain shot down her leg. Fenway gritted her teeth. But the pain wasn't too bad—she could walk and it was still bearable.

"Sorry," Donovan said dismissively. "Now, hand me your phone. And don't try anything stupid."

"I don't have my phone."

"What?"

"I left it on the counter at home."

"I don't believe you."

"Well, it's true."

"Turn out your pockets."

360 | PAUL AUSTIN ARDOIN

"I'm wearing running pants. They don't have pockets."

Donovan was quiet for a moment. "Fine," he said.

Fenway thought about screaming, but it being so early in the morning, she didn't know if her voice would carry through the butterfly waystation. And Donovan was already nervous. He could decide to shoot her. Or, more likely, he could shoot her if she started screaming and decide it was bad idea after she was already dead.

"You're not keeping your phone somewhere else?"

"Where would I keep it?" Fenway asked, somewhat irritated.

Donovan narrowed his eyes.

"You want me to strip to prove it to you? I bet you'd like that. Just like watching Charlotte step out of the shower."

Donovan flinched. "How did you—"

"Charlotte *saw* you. What happened, Donovan? Did you go in there to get the gun and couldn't resist taking a little peek?"

"I don't—"

"How did you know about the gun, anyway?" Fenway said. "Oh—of course. You ran into Charlotte at the gun range."

"Me and my dad," Donovan said absently. "He brought me to the range for some *male bonding time*." He spat the last words out. "As if I want to shoot some Old West gun."

"Your dad try to chat her up?"

"Did he try to what?"

"Hit on her. Flirt with her. Get in her pants."

"Shut up."

"Well, did he?"

Donovan shook his head—not a denial; it was as if he were trying to get the memory out of his head. "She was loving it. Laughing at all his jokes, touching his arm, batting her eyelashes. She was eating it up. She even invited us to dinner."

"So you thought your dad was sleeping with her, too."

Donovan shrugged. "They talked about getting together for coffee. Talking about target practice. As if I wasn't even there. Just like..." He trailed off.

"Just like all the other women he picked up?"

"Okay, enough," Donovan said. "Start walking. Up toward the cliffs."

"I can't put weight on my leg," Fenway fibbed. "I don't think I can get there."

"I'm *sure* you can," Donovan said, cocking the revolver.

Fenway set her jaw. "Fine," she said. She hobbled around.

She put her left foot forward and then made a show of dragging her right foot up to it, grimacing and wincing. On the fifth step she let out a little cry.

"You better hurry up," Donovan said. "I want to get there by sunrise."

"You should have thought of that before you broke my knee," Fenway said.

"Listen," Donovan said, "I'm the one with the gun. I get to make the rules."

Fenway's mind raced. The limp was buying her time, but for what? Finding another jogger on the trail? Putting an innocent bystander in jeopardy?

How serious was Donovan? Could he pull the trigger?

What a stupid question. Of course he could. From the physical evidence, he had held the gun inches from his own father's forehead and pulled the trigger. Had he also led him outside? Maybe his father left the villa to get some ice and Donovan had marched him right to the pedestrian underpass, where he had put a bullet in his brain and then—what, changed him into the homeless clothes?

No, Fenway realized, Donovan wasn't afraid to pull the trigger. Maybe he'd have more trouble doing it to someone he didn't detest, someone who hadn't cheated on his family or someone who wasn't high on cocaine. But Fenway didn't want to take the risk. Not before she had to, anyway.

"Okay," Fenway said. "I'm going as fast as I can."

The butterfly waystation looked different in the growing light of day. The sun hadn't yet peeked above the mountains, but the light behind it was brightening the sky, gently filtering through the canopy of trees.

The morning was clear—not much fog or haze, which was fairly typical of early November. The low fog banks that bathed the coast every morning in the summer were rarely found in the autumn months, and when it wasn't raining, the days were often clear and bright.

Fenway breathed in the fresh air. If she had to die, it might as well be in this beautiful place, in the place her mother had painted all those years ago. Spending the last six months in Estancia, Fenway ran this trail a few times a week. It might be Fenway's favorite place in the world.

There were worse ways to go.

"The silence is killing me," Fenway said.

"Too bad."

They got to the fork in the trail where she had taken the path on the left down to the beach earlier, and looked at the path on the right that led up to the cliffs.

"You might as well tell me about how you murdered your father," Fenway said, "since you're going to kill me anyway."

"I don't want to talk about it. Keep going. Up toward the cliffs."

Fenway dragged her foot but took the path on the right. "My last wish, then. You going to deny a dying woman her last wish?"

Donovan shrugged. "I broke into his email account the last time he took off for a week. I knew he did some stupid Russian sexual role-playing shit in that disgusting hotel. So this time, when he was gone for two days, then three, and my mom kept popping pills, I had enough. I took Charlotte's gun and I went to the hotel, and I caught him right when he came out of the room with an ice bucket." Donovan laughed, a sardonic, wry sound. "Honestly, I thought he had Charlotte in there with him. I kept telling him I was going to kill him with his girlfriend's gun. He was totally confused."

"Even when he saw the gun?"

"I guess. He didn't put two and two together. Not real bright, my dad."

"Good with the ladies, though."

Donovan shrugged again. "Like that ever helped him out. Got my mom hooked on pills, drove my sister to get with guys just like him, drove me to—well, put a bullet in his forehead."

"And then you threw one of Charlotte's earrings into the planter in front of the villa where he was staying." Fenway paused. "Then you dragged him a quarter of a mile to the pedestrian underpass. You covered him with blankets."

"Old ones from the trunk of my car," Donovan said. "He didn't think I'd do it. He thought I was a coward. Of all the stuff he ever challenged me on, all of the times he embarrassed me in front of my friends, didn't show up for my science fairs, yelled at my teachers, he honestly didn't think I'd pull the trigger."

"Did you give him a chance?"

"Sure, I gave him a chance. I told him to tell me he was sorry. Promise you'll stop sleeping around with all these women. Either commit to Mom or tell her it's over and divorce her so we can all get on with our lives."

Fenway turned and looked at Donovan. His eyes were unfocused, staring vacantly at the side of the trail. Fenway slowed a bit to try to get closer to him, to try to maybe take him out when he wasn't paying attention. But he raised his head to look at her, and she turned back around.

"And you know what? He *laughed* at me. He's there in his ridiculous drug-binge clothes, where he looks like a homeless guy, he hasn't showered in a couple of days—I don't even know how any woman could stand being with him. His pupils are dilated, he's talking to me about 'finding my center' and 'knowing my true self,' and then the next minute he's telling me that I'll never amount to anything."

"He practically dared you to pull the trigger." Fenway slowed her steps down, but kept walking.

Donovan sniffed. "Whatever."

"Did you?"

"Did I what? Find my center? Know my true self?" He chuckled lightly. "Yeah, sure."

"I mean did you pull the trigger?"

Donovan shrugged. "Like you said, he practically dared me."

"You proud of yourself?"

Donovan's voice went from dreamlike to serious. "Shut up."

Fenway crested the hill and the grove of trees thinned out, leading to a plateau in front of the ocean. The trail narrowed into a path up a steep grade, where the cliff overlooked the rocks with the lone cypress tree. She had seen the cypress hundreds of times in her mother's painting. She knew she didn't have long.

Donovan had said he would push her off the cliff. But if she wasn't on the edge—if he had to drag her body up that steep grade, maybe he wouldn't do it. Even if he put a bullet into her knee, even if she could never walk again, surely that was better than jumping off.

"Go up to the cliff," Donovan said.

"No."

"What did you say?"

Fenway turned around. "You're going to have to shoot me," she said. "I'm not going up there, and I'm not jumping off. That's a painful, horrible way to die. And I'm not making it any easier for you. You can shoot me and kill me, but then it will be bullets from an antique Colt .44 Special in my body, laying here, fifty yards from the cliff. You're going to have a tough time dragging my body up that grade. And any detective—even the bad ones who you think can't find their ass with two hands and a map— even *they* will be able to figure out who did it. And they'll do it fast, too."

Donovan raised the gun.

"And don't think you're going to have a head start," Fenway said. "I'm already late to my first meeting. It's Election Day. My campaign manager is probably leaving a panicked voice mail for me right now. The sheriff will know something's wrong. You shoot me, and I guarantee someone will be looking for me before you get back down the trail and get to your car. Try getting three hundred miles to the Mexican border only five minutes ahead of the police."

Fenway saw the barrel of the revolver shake almost imperceptibly.

Fenway took a shuffling step forward. Her heart pounded in her ears, overpowering the roar of the sea behind her.

"You tried to save your family, Donovan. And that's heroic. Your mother, your sister—they might not like that you killed your dad, but I know they'll admire that you tried to save the family."

"Don't come any closer," Donovan said.

"But if you kill me? You kill the woman who was trying to find out who did this to you. They won't admire you. They'll hate you. They'll hate that you took the coward's way out."

The barrel of the gun shook a little more. Fenway looked at Donovan's face. A tear ran down his cheek.

"You may be a killer, Donovan, but you love your family. And you're *not* a coward."

Donovan blinked hard, and a tear ran down his other cheek.

"There's a way out of this, Donovan," Fenway said. "I can't promise you it will be easy, but there's a way out."

"There's no way out," Donovan said, quietly, his teary eyes on Fenway's.

"Yes, there is. You're a minor. Your father pushed you too far. There are circumstances the D.A. will take into account. You won't be in jail for the rest of your life. You might get out in just a few years. Maybe you won't go at all. Your family has the money for a good lawyer."

The barrel of the gun started to droop.

"No—a *great* lawyer. Someone who'll argue like hell for you. Someone who'll challenge everything I did. Everything the other detectives did. Maybe you won't even go."

"Maybe I won't even go," Donovan repeated, distantly, as if his voice were playing through a tape recorder.

"Right," Fenway said, taking another step forward. Her mouth was dry. "So just hand me the gun, Donovan. This will all be over."

"This will all be over," Donovan repeated.

And Fenway knew, a split second before it happened.

And she was powerless to stop it.

Donovan put the gun to his temple and squeezed his eyes shut.

The sun broke over the mountains into Fenway's eyes just as the Colt revolver fired, a deafening sound that rang in her ears, just like the car bomb's explosion had. All Fenway could see was sunlight.

An unkindness of ravens took flight at the sound of the gunshot, shaking one of the cypress trees on the edge of the field. They broke apart the rays of the sun as they rose into the air.

It seemed to take a long time for Donovan's body to fall, crumpling to the ground. Fenway saw her hand reach out toward him, grasping for a rip cord that wasn't there.

Fenway closed her eyes.

She heard the waves crash into the rocks and the cypress tree, heard their deafening cacophony merge with the chattering of the ravens and the gunshot echoing across the field, echoing to the cliff, echoing to the butterfly waystation, and to the grove of trees, and beyond that to the dead-end street, and beyond that to Fenway's apartment, where her mobile phone waited for her, and from which, twenty minutes later, choking back tears and trying to stop from shaking, she dialed 911.

CHAPTER TWENTY-SEVEN

MILLICENT TATE FLITTED BETWEEN INTERVIEWS AT CHANNEL 12 and the *Estancia Courier*, and had to juggle half a dozen scheduling sessions with constituents as well. She confidently said there had been a big break in the Jeremy Kapp murder case, and Fenway was unavailable—fighting for justice was more important than her campaign schedule. Millicent had no choice in the matter—Fenway was a mess. After Celeste Sandoval took Fenway's statement, Millicent spent two hours giving Fenway a pep talk and pulling her into and out of the shower, getting her makeup and clothes on.

Millicent drove Fenway to her polling place, a church about six blocks away from the apartment complex. Fenway pulled the ice pack off her knee, and got out of the car, walking purposefully, trying to minimize her limp, a serious expression on her face, making sure she looked calm and professional. She stood in line, went into the voting booth, then stood a hundred feet from the entrance and took pictures with Millicent, and then by herself, the oval "I Voted" sticker prominent on her lapel.

Back in the BMW, Millicent turned to Fenway. "Can you do any more campaign activities today?"

Fenway swallowed hard. "Absolutely. I'm ready. Lunch with the paramedics' union, right? Then do you think we can reschedule any of the events I had to miss this morning? Maybe squeeze them in?"

Millicent looked hard at her, and then sighed. "I'm not sure you need to do this to yourself, Fenway," she said softly. "This morning, when I told the reporters outside the sheriff's department there was a break in the case, and your job was more important than campaigning, you should have heard the cheer from the people on the sidewalk. I'm all about optics and getting in front of your opponent and controlling the story. Well, this is a good story. And your opponent has gone into hiding."

"You think I can win without doing any more campaign events?"

"I do," Millicent said. "I think getting back to work and closing this case out is the best thing you can do for your campaign." She leaned forward. "And if you ever repeat that, I'll work for your opponent next election."

Fenway smiled, but she knew it was a tired, sad smile. "Thank you." She closed her eyes and immediately saw Donovan in front of her, gun at his temple. "And I feel like I need to talk to Cricket. She lost her husband last week and her son this week. She's going to be a mess, and she deserves to hear the news from me."

Millicent shook her head, a smile playing at the corner of her mouth. "And that's why this county loves you, Fenway." She started the car. "I predict a landslide."

In front of her office building, Fenway struggled to get out of the BMW, then stood blinking in the sunshine. She looked to her left; the parking garage was already under repair, with a crane on one side, where the blast had been. A few steel girders were already in place. She walked into the coroner's office and immediately saw Dez.

"I heard what happened," said Dez. "You okay?"

Fenway smiled and lowered her voice. "No, I'm not okay. I've got to make it through the end of the day, and I've got to go to my victory party. I'd call in sick tomorrow, but there's too much to do."

Dez looked at Fenway's face, searching for answers to questions she hadn't asked. "Okay," she said. "What do you need to get through your day?"

"I need the door closed," Fenway said. "I need to finish up some paperwork. And then I need a ride to Paso Querido to talk to Cricket Kapp. She deserves to know what happened."

"I can shut your door," Dez said, "and I can take you to P.Q."

"Thanks, Dez."

Fenway hobbled to her office, shut the door, and sat behind the desk. Turning on her PC, she pulled out all her police identification, pulled her favorite pen out of her pencil cup, then got Incident Report Form 310B from her filing cabinet. She spent the next couple of hours printing other forms and filling them out.

At about two o'clock—she hadn't eaten and didn't want to—Dez knocked on her door and told her it was time to go to Paso Querido to see Cricket Kapp. Dez wore an "I Voted" sticker, and Fenway remembered she had the post-election party to go to. She wasn't sure she could put a smile on her face at the victory party.

She looked at the forms she'd filled out and sighed. She got up, grabbed her purse, and walked with Dez to her car.

"Where did you park?" Fenway asked.

"With the garage under construction, a couple blocks away." Dez smiled. "Leaving my Impala on the street. What's the world coming to?"

"Yeah," Fenway mumbled, her eyes on the ground. While the murder of Jeremy Kapp would be closed, it had uncovered a conspiracy that ran deep and wide, a conspiracy which might be at the center of the two other murders that Fenway needed to solve. She realized she—along with Piper, Dez, and McVie—had barely scratched the surface of the issue, and this all started with her looking into the deaths of Carl Cassidy and Lewis Fairweather in the refinery accident. It hadn't even been a week since Lana had asked her to look into her husband's death, and already it had resulted in more pain and anguish than she cared to think about.

"All right," Dez said, when they arrived at the Impala, "you can't be like this when you talk to Mrs. Kapp. She's going to pick up on your energy, and it's negative. You've got to figure out how to pull yourself out of it." She unlocked the car and they both got in.

"Her son—"

"Yes," Dez said, starting the engine and pulling out onto the street, "her son killed himself in front of you this morning. The wounds are still fresh. You have every right to be shell-shocked and stunned. But you *don't* have the right to do it in front of her. She lost half her family in the last week. You don't get to grieve in front of her. You have to receive the grief, and you're going to do it professionally."

Fenway looked at Dez, and she studied the older woman's face.

"Yeah, you're right," Fenway said.

"I know I'm right. You going to do it?"

Fenway was quiet.

"You have permission from me to fall apart as soon as you get back in the car. We've got a twenty-minute drive back to Estancia. You've just got to take her grief while you're talking to her."

"I can do that," Fenway murmured.

They pulled off Querido Valley Road onto Whippoorwill Terrace, up the long driveway, and came to a stop in front of the door.

Fenway closed her eyes, and again she saw Donovan pull the gun up to his temple.

"Are you ready?" Dez asked gently.

I'm never going to be ready, Fenway thought, but she nodded.

She opened the door and got out.

When Fenway told her Donovan was dead, Cricket Kapp fell apart. She sank to her knees, wailing, in a way she hadn't even approached when informed about her husband's death. Fenway had been professional, and had given her a shoulder to cry on, quite literally; she helped Cricket get up, then walked with her into her kitchen where Fenway made a pot of herbal tea and Cricket calmed down.

Cricket asked a lot of questions about Donovan's last moments, and Fenway answered them as clearly as possible, leaving out the speech about heroism and cowardice, and leaving out the gunshot and the gore and the ravens.

Blair was back from her visit to USC, where Jasper had broken up with her the night before. Fenway wondered what kind of parent would let her eighteen-year-old daughter skip a Monday at school in order to go shack up with her boyfriend, but she bit her tongue—Cricket had been through enough. Besides, it might have been another teacher in-service day. Blair came out from her bedroom halfway through the interview, her clothes and hair again startlingly like Cricket's. Listening to music with her headphones, she had neither heard Fenway and Dez enter nor her mother's stricken cry. But after Cricket told Blair what had happened, mother and daughter cried together.

After about half an hour, they had no more questions, and Fenway left the business card of a grief counseling service on the end table. The card didn't seem to be enough to contain the emotions of the moment. Neither Cricket nor Blair got up from the sofa, and Dez and Fenway saw themselves out.

Although she had gotten permission from Dez to break down emotionally when back in the car, Fenway shed no more tears. She looked out the window at the Birdland greenery, then the scrub brush, then the trees. She looked up at the sky, where she saw a single raven flying across the highway until it darted into a clump of ironwoods.

She thought of the party she would be going to, the smile she would have to force all night. She thought of how hard Millicent had worked, and all the campaign workers and volunteers. She thought of the old department store her father had rented for the campaign headquarters and how it would be empty the next week.

And she thought of the murders she hadn't solved yet.

She thought of Dr. Jacob Tassajera.

She thought of Rory Velásquez, a kid with a promising future, taken too soon, another innocent bystander caught in the middle.

She thought of Carl Cassidy and Lewis Fairweather, two Ferris Energy employees who saw too much and paid for it with their lives.

Fenway knew her work was just beginning.

The party was in full swing when Fenway arrived about a quarter after five. Dez had insisted she eat something, and once she had the first bite of the turkey sandwich Dez brought her, she realized how ravenous she had been. Millicent wore a flattering red dress, her hair done up, and Fenway was comfortable in a navy business suit, even if it looked a bit conservative.

Fenway saw her father across the room. Nathaniel Ferris was in a similar suit to the one he had worn to the George Nidever Dinner, but the suit was neatly pressed, his shirt was crisp, and the crestfallen look that had been on his face was replaced by a radiant smile. Next to him, and looking radiant herself, was Charlotte. Her evening dress was more subdued than what she usually wore, and her eyes looked a bit tired—although Fenway was probably the only one who would notice.

Ferris caught Fenway's eye and raised his glass—it looked like scotch. Fenway smiled and nodded in return.

Callahan appeared by her side. "Hey, Miss Stevenson," he said.

"Hey, Brian. I didn't know you'd be here."

"Rachel invited me." He pointed, a beer in his hand, at Rachel, who was animatedly talking to Millicent.

"Rachel invited you, huh?"

Callahan shrugged. "Yeah. We got to talking when I was protecting you."

"You guys dating?"

"No. Well, not yet, anyway." He took a sip of his drink. "Oh, I hear congratulations are in order."

"They haven't announced anything yet, Brian. Don't jinx it."

"I wouldn't dream of jinxing anything." Brian smirked. "I meant for closing the Jeremy Kapp case."

"Oh," Fenway said. "Thanks, I guess."

"You're not happy about it?"

"You didn't hear what happened?"

"No," Callahan said. "It's all very hush-hush. Millicent Tate has been saying there was a big break in the case, and you were busy making sure the suspect was apprehended."

"Did she say 'apprehended'?"

"Yeah. Did the suspect get away or something? Off on a technicality?"

Fenway hesitated. "He committed suicide right in front of me."

"Oh." Callahan winced. "I guess I put my foot right in it. I'm sorry. And now you have to show up all smiles at this party." He looked at her. "You okay?"

"I wasn't okay earlier. I'm doing better now."

"All right," Callahan said. "You let me know if you need anything."

"Will do."

Fenway made the rounds with her supporters and volunteers and campaign staff, shaking a lot of hands, kissing a lot of cheeks. She had to resist the urge to check her watch—the minutes seemed to crawl by. She hoped the results would be in quickly after the polls closed at eight o'clock, because she didn't think she could take another hour or two—or three or four—of not knowing. Of having to be the candidate for any longer than she had to.

She was talking to a woman who said she had made over a thousand calls for Fenway when the screen at the front of the room turned on, showing Channel 12's newsroom cutting away from the newly elected governor's victory celebration.

"And for local elections," the anchorwoman said, "with forty-five percent of the precincts reporting, we're projecting Fenway Stevenson will be the winner of the coroner's race in Dominguez County." A bar graph appeared on screen; Fenway had more than three-quarters of the vote.

She didn't think she had been stressed about it—there were certainly far more important things to worry about—but as soon as she heard the words come out of the anchorwoman's mouth, she felt lighter and stronger.

The anchorwoman reviewed other local elections too—as expected, McVie's handpicked successor, Gretchen Donnelly, won the sheriff's race handily. The mayor's race was closer, with Barry Klein and McVie within a hundred votes of each other—but Klein was in the lead.

"Congratulations!" Fenway turned and saw Millicent Tate smiling and happier than she had ever seen her. Millicent pulled her into a hug, bouncing her side to side. "You better enjoy this moment," Millicent said into her ear. "Very few people in this world ever win an election. You've done well. Your father is delighted. And he's proud of you too."

Fenway drew in her breath sharply. "Thank you, Millicent. Tell him he could say that to my face every once in a while."

"Have a drink or something," Millicent said, still embracing her. "You need to look like you're enjoying yourself, like you *want* to be coroner."

"You know I want to be coroner."

"I know it," Millicent said, "but the cameras need to see it."

"You're right," Fenway said.

"Of course I'm right." Millicent broke from the embrace and looked Fenway in the face, holding her by her upper arms. "And before you spend the next twenty minutes trying to figure out how to ask me when you can leave, you need to stay here at least another hour. Minimum."

"I have a lot of work to do tomorrow."

"Of course you do," Millicent said, smirking. "You were a refreshing candidate to work for, Fenway. Infuriating, but refreshing."

Five minutes later, Fenway was summoned to a side room to take a call from a subdued Dr. Richard Ivanovich.

"Congratulations on a well-run campaign," he said, a little robotically.

"You too," Fenway said.

"For what it's worth, I didn't—" Then he caught himself, and Fenway heard silence on the other end for a few seconds.

"Dr. Ivanovich? Are you still there?"

"Best of luck for the next four years," he said, and hung up.

Fenway felt oddly calm. She left the room and told Millicent, and Millicent got up in front of the room, told everyone Ivanovich had conceded, and a huge roar went up from the two hundred or so attendees. Millicent had a victory speech prepared, and Fenway read it with animation and effervescence, although she barely processed what she was saying. As she finished, she saw on the screen that Barry Klein had widened his lead over McVie to four percentage points, with sixty percent of the precincts reporting, and Fenway felt her heart sink.

Then it struck her how much she missed McVie, not just how much she missed the ebb and flow of their bodies together, but how much she missed his camaraderie, how much she missed working on cases with him. The election cycle had robbed her of a lot of joy the last three months.

The camera operator from Channel 12 started to pack up; Fenway supposed it was to cover other, closer races. Perhaps even the mayoral race.

She distracted herself by thanking supporter after supporter profusely, expressing her appreciation to volunteer after volunteer, and shaking hands with all the staff people who had worked under Millicent. She remembered more names than she expected to, and she was somewhat astonished they all chose to support and work for her, giving their money, time, and effort to get her elected.

When Fenway finally checked the time on her phone, she was surprised it was almost ten o'clock, and she was far from the first person to leave the party. She told everyone she had work early in the morning, there were still open investigations, and the people of this county didn't hire her to come in late after a night of celebrating. Her supporters—about sixty were left—cheered her short speech, and let her leave. Fenway walked out of the building and realized her car was still in the evidence lot. She sighed.

A beige Toyota Highlander pulled into the parking lot and Fenway felt her pulse race a little bit. It was McVie. He was in a dark gray suit with a light gray shirt and a blue-and-red striped tie. He looked good.

She started to walk over to the Highlander. The driver's side window rolled down.

"Hey, Craig."

"Hey, Fenway. Am I late to the party?"

"It's still going, but I'm leaving. I've got work in the morning, you know."

McVie smiled. "All right."

Fenway put her hand on his side mirror. "Are you okay?"

"I conceded about fifteen minutes ago."

"Oh," she said. "Oh, Craig, that sucks. I'm sorry."

McVie shrugged. "Don't be. I'm sorry Barry Klein is going to be our new mayor, but I'm not sorry I *won't* be." He cleared his throat. "Anyway, I wanted to be here. The mood was pretty subdued at McVie headquarters. I thought you guys might be celebrating. Dancing. Champagne. You know, the works."

She smiled coyly. "Too bad I'm such a party pooper. Leaving at ten. You might not get a chance to have a good time."

"Yeah."

"But I do need a ride home."

"I can give you a ride," McVie said. He unlocked the doors.

"Perhaps we can have a little private celebration."

"I'd like that." He grinned, and Fenway hardly saw a trace of the election loss in his face.

Fenway walked around to the passenger side and got in the car. In their business suits, the two of them looked like they'd just left work on Wall Street.

"You glad the election is over?" McVie said, turning out of the parking lot.

"I am," Fenway said. "I didn't realize what a weight this was on me." She looked at him out of the corner of her eye. "And—it was nice to be able to forget about all that last night."

"It was very nice," McVie said. "When the returns came in, and the little green checkmark appeared next to Barry Klein's name, I thought, 'Man, am I glad that's over.'"

"Yeah."

McVie started to laugh.

Fenway smiled, but McVie's laughter continued a little longer than she thought the irony warranted.

"What's so funny?"

McVie wiped his eyes, still chuckling. "Speaking of stuff being over—Amy had the divorce papers served to me at the campaign headquarters tonight."

"Are you serious?"

"Yeah. I wouldn't be surprised if she had to pay the process server extra just to stick it to me after the election results were in."

"And you're laughing about it?"

"Of course I am. She obviously spent a long time dreaming this up. She must have thought it would bother me."

"And it doesn't?"

"Maybe it should. But, to be honest, last night went a long way toward taking the sting out of it. Besides, these last three months, with the separation—it's made me realize this divorce is coming way too late. Our marriage has been over for years."

"Did you sign the papers?"

"I'll have my lawyer look them over. I've got thirty days."

"What are you going to do now?"

"Me?"

"Yeah."

"You mean after I give you a ride home?"

She elbowed him lightly. "I mean professionally."

"I don't know. I could apply for a detective position, maybe. But there aren't any openings right now."

"Consultant, maybe?"

McVie scoffed. "Like Mayor Klein would ever approve the expenditure."

"Ugh," Fenway shuddered. "'Mayor Klein.' Even saying it makes my stomach turn."

"I've got until the end of the year to figure it out."

"Yeah."

The ride back to the apartment complex seemed to take no time at all, and McVie parked in Fenway's spot.

Fenway put her hand on McVie's leg. "Would you like to walk me up, sir?"

"Absolutely."

There was a charge between them, an electricity in the air Fenway could feel. Neither of them wanted to say anything. Fenway got out of the car, noticing she barely felt the pain in her knee. Maybe it was the adrenaline of the win, or the anticipation of a repeat performance. She knew her emotions were raw from Donovan's suicide and the election: she was right on the verge of breaking down, but she was also on the verge of elation, of dizziness, of ecstasy. The night air made her ears cold but her heart was warm, and when she and McVie got to the top of the stairs, she took his hand and ran her fingers over his. The times they kissed flashed through her mind, and she remembered the delicious ache in her bones from the adrenaline coursing through her veins the night before.

And in the walk from the top of the stairs to the door of her apartment, as she got her key out of her purse and opened the door wide, wide into her apartment, wide into the possibilities, wide into the next four years of her being the county coroner, everything fell away.

The industrial accident.

The car bomb.

The dead therapist.

The mole in the sheriff's office.

The money laundering.

The phantom supertanker.

The boy's crumpled body in front of her on the beach.

All faded into the background, out of focus, even if just for a moment.

There was McVie, and there was Fenway, and there was the electricity between them.

Fenway's phone rang in her purse.

"Don't get it," McVie said, kissing the side of her face.

"Spoken like a civvie," Fenway teased, reaching down into her purse and pulling her phone out. "It's Charlotte. Let me get her off the phone, then I'm all yours." She answered. "Charlotte, hi, listen, it's not the best—"

"Fenway?" Charlotte said, choking back tears. "Something happened to your father."

"What? What happened to him?"

"They arrested him, Fenway. For *murder*."

"What? For *whose* murder?"

"Solomon somebody. I don't even know anyone named Solomon."

"Professor Solomon Delacroix," Fenway said evenly.

"You know who that is?"

"Yes, I do," said Fenway, "and I'm afraid we're in for quite a fight."

ACKNOWLEDGMENTS

Many thanks to my editor, Max Christian Hansen, as well as my "early reading team" who made a huge difference: the members of Wordforge Novelists, Michelle Damiani, Blair Semple, Jeff Mansour, Siobhan Ordorica, Timarie Shelton, Debbie Degutis, Devin McCrate, Christina Bellinger, Carolyn Ardoin, and Beverly Ange. The feedback, input, criticism, and corrections you gave me made this a much better book, and I sincerely appreciate it.

A bazillion thanks to the tireless efforts of Cheryl Shoults, my marketing manager, who gets the word out about Fenway Stevenson.

Thanks to Kelly and Erin Enders-Tharp, whose dogs provided me with two excellent character names.

And I couldn't do this without the support of my wife and kids, who put up with my long hours of writing and sometimes bring me snacks.

BY PAUL AUSTIN ARDOIN

FENWAY STEVENSON MYSTERIES

The Reluctant Coroner • *books2read.com/Fenway1*
The Incumbent Coroner • *books2read.com/Fenway2*
The Candidate Coroner • *books2read.com/Fenway3*
The Upstaged Coroner • *coming soon*

Bad Weather • *books2read.com/BadWeather*

I hope you enjoyed reading this book as much as I enjoyed writing it. If you did, I'd sincerely appreciate a review on your favorite book retailer's website, Goodreads, and BookBub. Reviews are crucial for any author, and even just a line or two can make a huge difference.

Please sign up on my mailing list to get
tidbits and trivia about Fenway's world,
reviews of other mysteries, free book promotions,
and notifications of new releases.
www.paulaustinardoin.com

Made in the USA
Monee, IL
26 October 2020